Praise for the Lonely Lords series

"Grace Burrowes just keeps getting better and better with her Lonely Lords series. I was blown away by how different she was able to make each male lead."

—*Romancing the Book*

"Delightfully different… Burrowes brings to life a deeply moving romance that's sure to be remembered and treasured."

—*RT Book Reviews* Top Pick, 4.5 Stars (on *Darius*)

"There were moments in this book that had me laughing and weeping and continuously turning the pages."

—*The Royal Reviews* (on *Nicholas*)

"Extraordinary… I was totally intrigued with the enigmatic hero. I couldn't put it down."

—*Night Owl Reviews* Reviewer Top Pick (on *Ethan*)

"Intriguing… a witty, sensual historical romance that will capture readers' attention from the very first page."

—*Romance Junkies* (on *Beckman*)

"Exquisite… a riveting historical tale and an amazing love story."

—*Long and Short Reviews* (on *Gabriel*)

"Absolutely lovely! This is definitely my new favorite Grace Burrowes book… a brilliant historical romance."

—*Imagine a World* (on *Gareth*)

Also by Grace Burrowes

The Windhams

The MacGregors

The Lonely Lords

DOUGLAS

GRACE BURROWES

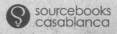

sourcebooks
casablanca

Published by Sourcebooks Casablanca, an imprint of Sourcebooks,
Inc.
P. O. Box 4410, Naperville, Illinois 60567-4410
(630) 961-3900
Fax: (630) 961-2168
www.sourcebooks.com

Printed and bound in the United States of America.
VP 10 9 8 7 6 5 4 3 2 1

To men who stay.

One

THE CHILD WAS SMALL, HELPLESS, AND IN HARM'S WAY.

As Douglas Allen drew his horse to a halt, he absorbed more, equally disturbing facts:

The grooms clustered in the barn doorway would do nothing but mill about, moving their lips in silent prayer and looking sick with dread.

A woman—the child's mother?—unnaturally pale at the foot of the huge oak in the stable yard, was also likely paralyzed with fear. The child, standing on a sturdy limb of the old tree thirty feet above the ground, was as white-faced as her mother.

"Rose," the woman said in a tight, stern voice, "you will come down this instant, do you hear me?"

"I don't want to come down!" came a retort from the heights of the oak.

Douglas was no expert on children, but the girl looked to be about five years old. Though she stood on one limb, she also anchored herself to the tree with a fierce hold on the branch above her. When she made her rude reply, she stomped her foot, which caused the branch she grasped to shake as well.

Douglas heard the danger before he saw it. A low,

insistent drone, one that would have been undetectable but for the stillness of the stable yard.

At Rose's display of stubbornness, the woman's hands closed into white-knuckled fists. "Rose," she said, her voice an agony of controlled desperation, "if you cannot climb down, then you must hold very, very still until we can get you down."

"But you *promised* I could stay up here as long as I wanted."

Another stomp, followed by another ominous, angry droning.

Douglas took in two more facts: The child was unaware of the hornets' nest hanging several yards out on the higher branch, and she was not at all unwilling to come down. She was *unable*. He recognized a desperate display of bravado when he saw one, having found himself in an adult version of the same futile posturing more than once in recent months.

He stripped off his gloves and stuffed them into the pocket of his riding jacket. Next, he shed his jacket, slung it across the horse's withers, turned back his cuffs, and rode over to the base of the tree. After taking a moment to assess the possibilities, he used the height of the horse's back to hoist himself into the lower limbs.

"Miss Rose," he called out in the steady, no-nonsense voice his governess had used on him long ago, "you will do as your mother says and be still as a garden statue until I am able to reach you, do you understand? We will have no more rudeness"—Douglas continued to climb, branch by branch, toward the child—"you will not shout"—another several feet and he would be on the same level as she—"and you most *assuredly* will not be stamping your foot in an unladylike display of pique."

The child raised her foot as if to stomp again. Douglas

watched that little foot and knew a fleeting regret that his life would end now—regret and resentment.

But no relief. That was something.

The girl lowered her foot slowly and wrinkled her nose as she peered down at Douglas. "What's peek?"

"Pique"—he secured his weight by wrapping one leg around a thick branch—"is the same thing as a taking, a pout, a ladylike version of a tantrum. Now come here, and we will get you out of this tree before your mama can devise a truly appalling punishment for your stubbornness."

The child obeyed, crouching so he could catch her about the waist with both hands—which did occasion relief, immense relief. The droning momentarily increased as the girl left her perch.

"You are going to climb around me now," Douglas instructed, "and affix yourself like a monkey to my back. You will hang on so tightly that I barely continue to breathe."

Rose clambered around, assisted by Douglas's secure grip on her person, and latched on to his back, her legs scissored around his torso.

"I wanted to come down," she confided when she was comfortably settled, "but I'd never climbed this high before, and I could not look down enough to figure my way to the ground. My stomach got butterflies, you see. Thank you for helping me get down. Mama is very, very vexed with me." She laid her cheek against Douglas's nape and huffed out a sigh as he began to descend. "I was scared."

Douglas was focused on his climbing—it had been ages since he'd been up a literal tree—but he was nearly in conversation with a small child, perhaps for the first time since he'd been a child.

Another unappealing aspect to an unappealing day.

"You might explain to your mama you were stuck," he said as they approached the base of the tree. He slipped back onto the horse, nudged it over to where the woman stood watching him, and then swung out of the saddle, Rose still clinging to his back. He reached around and repositioned her on his hip.

"Madam, I believe I have something belonging to you."

"Mama, I'm sorry. I was st-stuck." The child's courage failed her, and weeping ensued.

"Oh, Rose," her mother cried quietly, and the woman was, plague take this day, also *crying*. She held out her arms to the child, but because Rose was still wrapped around Douglas, he stepped forward, thinking to hand Rose off to her mother. Rose instead hugged her mother from her perch on Douglas's hip, bringing Douglas and the girl's mother into a startling proximity.

The woman wrapped an arm around her child, the child kept two legs and an arm around Douglas, and Douglas, to keep himself, mother, and child from toppling into an undignified heap, put an arm around the mother's shoulders. *She*, much to his shock, tucked in to his body, so he ended up holding both females as they became audibly lachrymose.

Douglas endured this strange embrace, assuring himself nobody cried forever. While he waited to extricate himself, several impressions came to him.

The first was of warmth. Douglas had forgotten a human embrace could be warm, and the crying woman was warm indeed. Her body heat radiated against his chest, bringing with it the second impression: fragrance. She smelled of soap and something spicy—lavender with rosemary, at least. The child, whose hair was tickling Douglas's chin, smelled of the same soap and of the out-of-doors and of little-girl sweetness.

Douglas hadn't known little girls had their own scent.

And the final impression, strongest of all, was a sense of pleasure his body took in being close to a warm, adult female, one well formed and unself-conscious of their proximity. Douglas didn't censure himself for this realization—bodies would be bodies, after all—but neither did he allow himself to explore it.

With a sigh and possibly a final, small lean against his shoulder, the woman stepped back, leaving Rose anchored to Douglas's chest.

"Sir, I cannot thank you enough. Will you introduce yourself?"

Now Rose was willing to hop down off his hip, but the girl disconcerted Douglas by taking his left hand and standing beside him. Mother and child wore the same expectant, teary expressions, and Douglas found himself unwilling to shake his hand loose of Rose's. She had, after all, been through an upsetting business—and she was a child.

"Douglas Allen." He bowed over the lady's hand. "Viscount Amery, at your service."

They were both bare-handed, so he dropped her fingers at the first acceptable moment, but not before he noticed even her hands were warm. Not hot, sweaty, or clammy, but warm.

"Miss Guinevere Hollister," she replied, offering him a curtsy, then swabbing her handkerchief over Rose's cheeks. "Will you come up to the house for tea, your lordship?"

"Tea would be appreciated." He slung his jacket over his shoulder, his one hand still held captive by Rose. As they turned to walk toward the house, Miss Hollister aimed a glower at the stable boys standing in the door to the barn.

"For heaven's sake, Ezra, take the viscount's horse and see about that hornets' nest when it is safe to do so."

Douglas heard her ordering the stable help around, but was preoccupied with matching his stride to a small child's.

"You could carry me," Rose said, smiling up at him as if she'd divined his thoughts. She had dark hair in a riot of curls around a gamine face, and guileless green eyes.

"Rose." Her mother's tone portended a sharp rebuke.

Douglas swung the child back up to his hip. "We will have our tea that much sooner," he pointed out. When the girl laid her head on his shoulder and sighed like a tired puppy, he wished he had not been so complicit with her schemes.

This child was the most... presuming person he'd met in recent memory. To his everlasting relief, when they gained the entry to the house, Rose was handed off to a footman with instructions that she be taken to her nurse, there to await her mother's judgment.

Rose turned halfway up the stairs and waved at Douglas with the hand not clasped by the footman. Not knowing what else to do, Douglas offered the child a slight bow in response.

This exchange was not lost on the mother—*Miss* Hollister, as she'd so boldly introduced herself—but she withheld comment on a grown man who'd bow to a grinning, waving child.

"This way, if you please." Miss Hollister led him down the hallway to a small parlor toward the back of the house. As she rang for tea, Douglas rolled down his cuffs, shrugged back into his jacket, and took in the appointments of the room.

The furnishings were more for comfort than elegance, this being in the way of a family parlor. A small blue velvet sofa was positioned under a window opposite the hearth, and two well-cushioned chairs with a low table of mellow blond oak between them sat along the inside wall. Before the hearth, but angled toward the center of the room, stood a sturdy oaken rocking chair.

Silence had fallen between Douglas and his hostess while he'd inspected the surroundings. She regarded him from her seat in one of the chairs, her expression politely curious.

"I invite you to be seated, my lord. I've taken the liberty of ordering some sustenance with our tea, it being nigh to luncheon and you having ridden out from Town, unless I mistake the matter."

Douglas took the other chair. "You do not. Mistake the matter, that is."

A small, pained smile crossed Miss Hollister's features, suggesting she would somehow rise to the challenge of exchanging pleasantries with a man who regarded small talk with as much affection as he did epidemics of influenza.

"While I know our families are connected," she began, "I am at a loss as to why you would honor me with a call, not, of course, that you are unwelcome."

She looked down at her hands. Douglas feared she was blinking back more tears, contemplating the morning's outcome had he *not* come to call.

"Miss Hollister, the child is safe, and I have no doubt one of the grooms would have been up that tree had I not happened along. You must not dwell on the miseries that could have befallen you."

Ignoring the miseries that *had* befallen one could also be useful, though Douglas kept that observation to himself. His hostess offered him a genuine smile for his assurances—false assurances though they were—then rose to accept the tea tray from a parlor maid.

While Miss Hollister fixed the tea, Douglas recovered from that smile, from the sheer, dazzling surprise of it.

His first impression of her had been one of plainness. Her features had been pinched with desperate concern; then she had been crying in relief. As he studied her over the tea service, he surmised that she sought to minimize her feminine attributes.

Her hair, a rich, glossy chestnut, was scraped back in a severe bun. She wore a mud-brown dress, one without a single bow or ruffle. Her attire did the job of decently covering her with a vengeance, the collar coming up to her neck, the sleeves covering her wrists. But she couldn't hide a pair of wide, slanting green eyes, high cheekbones, or a generous, even lush mouth.

Nor could she entirely disguise an amply endowed female figure, though from the cut of her clothing, she tried to.

"How do you take your tea, my lord?"

Her voice was as subtly lovely as the rest of her, a soothing contralto, though her hands had the slightest tremor as she maneuvered around the porcelain tea service. The teapot sported cabbage roses, all pink petals and soft greenery.

She did not strike Douglas as a silver-tea-service sort of woman, which was appealing to a man who'd sold all but one set of good silver.

"Strong, three sugars, no cream." A silence followed, one he knew he ought to fill with… words. Or something.

"Are you always such a serious fellow?"

"I have much to be serious about," he replied, taking the tea from her. Their fingers brushed, and a faint blush crept up the lady's graceful neck. How odd, that a woman in her position would blush so easily.

"You have me at a loss here," Miss Hollister replied, busying herself with her tea. "While you are former brother-in-law to my cousin's wife—do I have that right?—I am not familiar with your… specific situation. May I offer you a sandwich?"

She offered him two, heartily stacked with beef and cheddar, as if she knew the hours since breakfast for Douglas had been long and busy. He dragged his attention from the food on his plate—he even spotted a dab of mustard on the bread—and framed a reply.

"My late brother was married to Astrid Alexander, the woman who is now your cousin Andrew's—Lord Greymoor's—wife," Douglas said. "His countess, rather. I find it curious you and I have not been introduced, but I understand from Greymoor you prefer to rusticate."

With her bastard child, which hardly needed mentioning.

"My doting cousin," the lady said, sipping her tea placidly. "Greymoor probably told you I am his steward here at Enfield—or perhaps he referred to me as his chatelaine if you caught him in a gallant mood." She had watched as Douglas demolished his first sandwich, but now excused herself to murmur something to a footman outside the half-open parlor door.

Douglas waited until she was back in her seat, then got down to business.

"Miss Hollister, I do not know what your cousins have told you about me, but if I am serious, to use your word, it's because I appear here today to solicit your assistance."

She considered her tea with enviable calm. "I am in your debt, my lord. Any assistance I can render you, it will be my honor to provide."

Those words were as much invitation as he'd hear, so Douglas launched into his rehearsed speech. "Your cousin holds your abilities as a manager of this estate in highest esteem. Greymoor says you have taught both him and his brother Heathgate much about the details of profitable landholding."

This was not flattery, but rather, simply stated fact, and it had his hostess looking... bashful. Momentary shyness rendered her beauty even more alluring, lending her an illusion of innocence that made a man want to, well, *nuzzle* her. To run his nose along the line of her jaw, to inhale the fragrance of her skin and hair. To steal a march on her reserve and tease her into flirtation.

What extraordinary thoughts. Douglas cut them off with brisk self-discipline, the way one might swat a capering horse into behaving by brisk application of the riding crop to the beast's quarters.

"My cousin exaggerates," Miss Hollister replied. "Enfield prospered when our grandfather held it. I have merely kept it organized, and I have enjoyed doing so."

Douglas recalled her casual orders to the stable hands, and thought that yes, she indeed enjoyed being lady of the manor here. Lord *and* lady of the manor.

"It is my hope," he said, sitting forward to pour himself more tea, "that your cousin—"

Miss Hollister's hand closed over his on the handle of the teapot. Douglas sat back, dropping his hand.

"I beg your pardon," he said, hoping he wasn't, for the love of God, blushing. "I am a bachelor, Miss Hollister, and quite used to seeing to my own comforts. Pour for me, please?"

"You were saying?" she prompted as she added cream and three sugars to his tea, then held it out to him.

He was careful not to allow his fingers to touch hers this time, though as for the cream—cream was a luxury, but a man intent on begging was due some fortification.

"I was saying I hope your cousin did not exaggerate

regarding your skills, because I have need of a competent steward. I believe Greymoor made mention of my situation in his letter of introduction?"

"I confess, my lord, we are in the midst of the apple harvest, and my attention to correspondence has been lacking in the past few days."

Despite her demure bearing, Douglas had no doubt she'd been out in the very orchards, perhaps even on a ladder, possibly without even a hat to shield her perfect complexion—

This time, he brought a mental hatchet down on his wayward thoughts.

"Well, then, madam, with your permission, I will explain more fully—"

The footman returned, bearing a plate of cakes. Lovely, artfully decorated little confections Douglas could gobble up in about two bites each.

Miss Hollister didn't ask if she could serve him, but put four on a plate—it would hold no more—and passed it to him. "You must not be shy about satisfying a sweet tooth, my lord," she said, smiling that beguiling, alluring smile again.

"My thanks."

And how was a man supposed to think, much less hold forth articulately, when he was battling tea cakes, a perfect cup of tea, and that smile?

She served herself one cake, a small, chocolate sweet, which she held briefly under her nose—a definite nose to go with that wide mouth and those slanting eyes—inhaling the scent of the tea cake before biting off half and savoring it, only to catch Douglas staring at her.

"My lord?" she said, though Douglas could recall no particular question on the floor. Neither could he recall the last time the sight of a woman nibbling at a treat had held his interest, much less fascinated him.

"I beg your pardon." Douglas sat back. "I was explaining, Miss Hollister, I have need of a competent steward, and your cousins suggested you." Had suggested her in glowing, admiring terms, in fact.

Douglas's pronouncement provoked a thoughtful consumption of the remainder of Miss Hollister's tea cake.

"That surprises me, my lord. Andrew and Gareth—Greymoor and Heathgate—know I love it here and consider this estate not simply my place of employment but my home and Rose's too. Andrew has agreed I might have a life estate here at Enfield. He cannot transfer the property to me in fee simple, because it is entailed to the barony, which he holds. He has no need of the property, though, and is in negotiations with his solicitor regarding the possibility of a life estate here for Rose as well. Then too, women are generally not stewards of anybody's land but their own."

Though many a widow took an interest in her holdings, women were not generally stewards of even their own land, or rather, *ladies* were not.

Douglas ignored that salient fact, and tried to ignore the remaining cakes as well. "I was not aware of the legal arrangements between you and Lord Greymoor, and I do not offer you a permanent position."

His hostess arranged four more cakes on a plate and held it out to him, which rather resembled a discharge of firearms directly at his concentration.

"What sort of position do you offer?"

"I need an advisor," Douglas said, and now that the point of the meeting—visit—was again under discussion, he did not permit himself so much as a glance at the plate on his knee. "Lord Greymoor has offered to sell me his estate in Sussex at a price just above insultingly reasonable. I need an assessment of what the land is truly worth, and Greymoor recommended you in glowing terms for such a project. Your cousin Heathgate was equally complimentary, and we do share a family connection, however remote."

Elsewise, Douglas would never have considered a female as a source of advice on anything of significance—not that he'd seek advice from many men, either.

"This would mean travel to Sussex?"

He bit into a chocolate tea cake with raspberry icing, to be polite and perhaps to stall a moment. "Of course, travel at your convenience."

Her brows knit, like the wings of a butterfly closing. "I'm sorry, my lord, but I am not in a position to assist you."

A beat of silence went by, while Douglas chewed his positively scrumptious chocolate tea cake, the sweetness in his mouth at variance with the bitter notion of having to beg the woman for help.

"You will not allow me even a fair hearing?" He put the question with perfect civility, as if this project could not possibly be the last straw within reach of a drowning man.

"Explain at your leisure, my lord, but my decision will not likely change."

Explain, he would, but he'd been ingesting sustenance steadily, and his body needed to move—and to put distance between himself and the infernal plate of distraction—so he paced to the window and laced his hands behind his back.

"My finances… my family's finances, rather, are not what they should be." He remained at the mullioned window, his back to his hostess, her sandwiches, and her luscious cakes—and her smiles. "My father and my brother before me did not manage well, and the estate is heavily in debt as a result—this is a situation I am not willing to put before some factor, some man of business, whose discretion is merely professional."

His hostess said nothing. He plowed on—he was good at plowing on, though he knew precious little about plowing land. He knew far too much about grieving for an older brother who'd pissed away his inheritance, and a younger brother who'd sought to steal that inheritance for himself.

May a merciful God allow them both to rest in peace.

"Lord Greymoor has proposed that I buy from him this estate in Sussex," Douglas said, returning to the matter at hand. "He claims it is a profitable concern, and believes it could be made even more so, but I must ask myself: If the land is so profitable, why would he turn it over to me?"

With his back turned, he held up a hand to stay any comment his hostess would have made.

"You are thinking," he went on, "Lord Greymoor, being a decent sort, is simply allowing me a chance to get on my feet and pay off my remaining debts, which include debts within the family. This is perhaps the case, but I cannot afford to trust his generous nature, Miss Hollister. For that matter, I cannot afford to trust much of anything except the evidence of my own eyes and my own experience."

"Yet you are willing to trust my opinion of the land's potential?"

"No," Douglas said, turning and finding her the picture of serene propriety, sitting by her tea service. "Not entirely. I am willing to listen to your opinion and consider it along with my own assessment. I am not stupid, Miss Hollister."

Though he was uneducated about husbanding the land. He was also proud, but couldn't consider that entirely a failing if it kept him from begging this woman for her aid.

She studied her teacup as if searching the dregs for words. "Your lordship, I cannot assist you, though I am flattered at the faith my cousins place in my abilities. I am not in a position to leave Enfield for any length of time."

He thought she'd say more, but she fell silent and looked him up and down. Douglas knew what she saw: height, a few inches over six feet in fact, which had made an atrociously gangly adolescent out of him; blond hair queued back because it was less inclined to lie neatly than he'd prefer; and blue eyes, probably shadowed with fatigue, because sleep often eluded him.

He had been told he had a sensual mouth, whatever the hell that meant. The thing formed words and ingested food, which was all Douglas required of it.

Though it did a bloody poor job of convincing his hostess, apparently, and that was tiresome.

"You have been honest with me," she said at length, "and I will offer you some honesty in return: I do not want to leave Enfield, my lord. Ever. Not for a month in Sussex, not for a week in Town. I am content here."

Her words were plain enough, and yet, Douglas suspected she was a trifle reluctant to be turning him down. Perhaps a trifle reluctant to immure herself here in the countryside with her bastard child, season after season. His request was unorthodox, just as her position as manager of Greymoor's property was unorthodox.

The plain dress, the severe coiffure, the lack of even a brooch to adorn her person made her look like the matron of some institution for wayward girls.

Perhaps, despite her past—because of her past?—she was concerned about the appearances?

"If it suited you," he said slowly, "we could travel together as man and wife, using some fictitious name. I do not foresee making a lengthy stay in Sussex."

"Travel together as man and—" She set her teacup down with a clatter, all pretense of genteel hospitality gone from her expression. "What sort of backhanded insult do you offer me, Lord Amery? Do you think because I am a mother that I am not due the same courtesies as any other woman?"

She rose, and it struck Douglas that, in addition to all her other attributes, she was a tall woman. He preferred tall women, felt less of a lobcock around them—though in point of fact, he preferred tall, *calm* women.

"Do you think, my lord," she went on with quiet venom, "that my cousins would tolerate such an improper arrangement?" She whipped around in a flurry of mud-colored skirts and made for the door, but Douglas beat her by half a step. When she grabbed for the door latch, he reached past her shoulder and pushed the door shut.

He remained thus, his arm extended over her shoulder, his hand flat on the door, holding it closed. He spoke quietly, because his mouth was very near her ear, and his nose was close enough to catch a whiff of her rosemary and lavender scent. "I apologize, madam, if you think I offered you insult. That was the furthest thing from my intent. Will you hear me out?"

He stepped back, wanting to shake the infernal woman for her silly fit. Greymoor had said she was frighteningly competent at her work, but skittish, and likely the victim of ill usage by the child's father. Douglas recalled that last comment as he watched Miss Hollister resume her seat, her spine stiff, her eyes—may God have mercy upon him—suspiciously bright.

"I apologize," he said again, still standing, as she had not bid him to do otherwise. "I am in need of your services, and I thought to offer an uncomplicated means of achieving that purpose—*nothing more*. If some other arrangement is better suited to traveling together, I lack the imagination to conceive of it."

"I accept your apology," she said in arctic tones. "Please do sit, my lord. That is, if there is more you would say?"

Such manners, when Miss Hollister clearly wanted to see the last of her guest. Those manners shamed Douglas's assumptions regarding fallen women, not that he'd met many.

"There is a bit more I would convey to you," he said, sinking into the rocking chair at the opposite corner of the small room. His choice of seat put him at a small distance from the remaining tea cakes and clearly relieved his hostess.

A pragmatic appeal had failed, which left Douglas with… the unpragmatic. The undignified, the honest.

"My family situation is… troubled," Douglas said, his voice softer for all he was sitting at a greater distance. "My older brother was an unhappy, frivolous man. My younger brother was no better, and my mother is no longer inclined to go about in Society. I am the last exponent of my line still functioning, our finances are a disgrace, and I need…"

He needed to shut up. He looked off, and for an unguarded moment, fatigue, grief, and isolation swamped his reserve and no doubt showed in his eyes. He tried to reassemble his features into some bland, polite expression, but in the silence, his hostess spoke.

"You need what I have here," she finished for him. "You need sanctuary."

Relief at having been saved further explanation warred with self-consciousness.

"A place," Douglas said, unable to keep wistfulness from his tone, "a place to rebuild, to make something good and new. But I am not an experienced man of the land, and our family seat is little more than a manor with a home farm. Some factor hired at arm's length to assess the property would not do. This purchase in Sussex…"

He trailed off, and they were quiet for a few moments, a not uncomfortable silence that allowed Douglas the privacy of his thoughts.

"You saved my daughter's life, at the least." Miss Hollister spoke quietly too. "You did so when you didn't know her; when people, including her own mother, who should have seen to her safety, did not or could not. I owe you."

Douglas did not interrupt what was clearly a difficult recitation, and as his hostess had earlier, he resorted to the study of her teacup. Unlike his sturdy, rosy little cup, hers was delicate green porcelain, with a parade of white unicorns encircling the rim.

Fragile and odd, but lovely.

"Because I owe you, my lord, and because I want—I need—to be beholden to no man, I will do as you ask. I will travel to Sussex and see this land of yours. I will make recommendations and offer advice. I will do so without remuneration because we have a family connection, but there will be conditions."

He nodded. Every gain in life came with conditions.

"The terms, my lord, are these." She took a deep breath and clutched the arms of her chair as if she were in anticipation of brigands appearing in her parlor, her calm voice and steady demeanor notwithstanding. "My role will not be as steward, but as some innocuous female, your cousin, something of that nature—not your wife. *Never* as your wife. Rose will come with us, and we will travel as discreetly as possible. You will provide a chaperone, and in that capacity, I believe my aunt, Lady Heathgate, will serve." She shot him a very direct look, a challenging look. "Are we agreed?"

Though it beggared his pride, she was going to help him. For a bit of humility on his part, he would know if the hope—the stubborn, irrational, unbecoming, inconvenient hope—that had sprung up unbidden when Greymoor had made his offer was grounded in reality.

"We are agreed, Miss Hollister."

He rose to take his leave shortly thereafter, and would have bowed over her hand again, except she dipped to fuss over the tea tray and came up holding out a linen serviette to him.

"The tea cakes, my lord. I've had enough for the present, and Rose certainly won't be having any sweets for a while."

He accepted the offering of sweets and tucked the napkin into his coat pocket. When Miss Hollister had called for his horse, he expected her to leave him at the front door of her home. Instead, she accompanied him out onto the wide front porch and showed no signs of abandoning him until the horse was brought around.

"I will call on you tomorrow to discuss the details of our journey," he said as the groom named Ezra led the gelding out. "Tonight I will be a guest of your cousin, the Marquess of Heathgate. And, Miss Hollister?"

She shifted her glance from his horse—a big, shiny bay, who'd walked over to a tree full of hornets at his master's simple request—to Douglas. "Yes, your lordship?"

"Rose…" he said, frowning at the fact that the irons had already been run down the stirrup leathers, which was not exactly a best practice. "You mustn't be too hard on her. She was frightened, overfaced, and too proud to say so. In an innocent child, we cannot take very great exception to that, can we?"

He was away down the steps without giving her a chance to reply—what did he know about children or innocence?—then at the mounting block and up on his horse. "Shall we say ten of the clock, Miss Hollister?"

"If you are truly interested in learning to manage the land, my lord, make a day of it. Get here as soon after sunrise as you are able, dress as comfortably as you can, and be prepared to spend the day in the saddle."

"I have my orders, ma'am." He nodded politely, saluted with his crop, and turned Regis in a neat pirouette before cantering down the drive.

As soon as he was out of sight of the house and the woman standing on its porch, Douglas brought his mount down to the walk, withdrew the tea cakes from his pocket, and devoured them, slowly, methodically, one right after the other.

❧

Gwen watched Douglas, Lord Amery, canter off, noting with one part of her mind that he had an elegant seat, even as the other, louder part began castigating her for this morning's business.

If Rose hadn't been up that tree, Douglas Allen could never have wrested this agreement from Gwen. But Rose *had* been up the tree, and worse, she could be laid out in the parlor at this moment, *dead and disfigured* as a result of her childish misadventure. And for just an instant, the man had looked… *desolate*. He'd looked as

Gwen had felt so often, yet he hadn't the comfort of even a child to console him.

Douglas Allen had the ability to proceed calmly with the next necessary task, though, and that was a fine quality in a man who intended to find his salvation in the land. And he'd been right about something, too: Rose had been frightened out of her wits, and unable to ask for help. Gwen knew that condition intimately, and she would not judge another harshly when suffering the same state.

Two

"So why," Amery asked, "do you have calves arriving in the autumn?"

"Some calves," Gwen corrected him. "For a late heifer, or one slow to mature, the extra six months before her first calf is a blessing. Autumn grass is rich, and the cooler weather agrees with the babies more than the summer heat. We get fewer cases of scours, and we aren't competing with all of the spring market gluts, so we get better prices for them. The same is true of autumn lambs, if you can get the rams and ewes to cooperate."

They were on horseback, which made conversations about rams and ewes and other earthy, reproductive things less mortifying—for Gwen, at least.

"If it's such a good idea, why don't you have all your calves in the autumn?"

She wanted to say the bulls would go into a decline if limited to a single breeding season, but Amery would get that pained look on his face, an expression between bewilderment and disappointment.

"We have two primary calving seasons to spread the risks."

"Can you clarify that? Spread the risk how, Miss Hollister?"

Please elucidate further, Miss Hollister. Can you give me an example, Miss Hollister? Why is it done thus, Miss Hollister? His lordship was a sponge for knowledge, but if he hadn't patted his horse from time to time, Gwen would have feared she was riding out with an automaton.

"With the land, there is always risk," Gwen said, though she far preferred those risks to the ones she'd face if she ventured back into the view of Polite Society. "You risk drought in the summer and try to manage that risk with irrigation. You risk severe cold in the winter and try to manage that with good fodder and shelter. You hope for a good hay crop but manage that risk by leaving some land in pasture and planting corn in addition. You dodge what nature throws at you if you can't turn it to your advantage, and you pray constantly as you try to predict the weather."

Not that different from the challenges of parenting.

Amery went silent, though Gwen was getting used to this aspect of his companionship. His silences were mentally industrious. He sorted, tagged, cataloged, and prioritized all incoming information in those silences, and Gwen was happy to leave him to it. Wherever they went—the dairy, the home farm, the kitchen gardens, the home wood, the fields and cottages—he had questions, and she answered until he fell silent again.

"You are attached to this place," he observed as they rode into the stable yard at midday.

Such was the caliber of the viscount's conversational gambits. "Lord Amery, this is my *home.*"

He'd dismounted while Gwen remained on her gelding, answering the groom's question about a lame plow horse. When she unhooked her knee from the horn of her sidesaddle, Amery stood beside her horse, as if they'd just ridden in for the hunt breakfast.

She could shoo him off, though she sensed she'd offend him if she refused his assistance, or worse, hurt his feelings.

Assuming he had any, beyond dignity and pride.

Gwen put her hands on his shoulders and found herself effortlessly lifted from the horse and standing in the narrow space between Lord Amery and her mount. She paused there awkwardly, unable to step back and unable to meet his gaze. In close proximity he had a beguilingly pleasant, woodsy scent, and he was appreciably taller than she.

"I believe, Miss Hollister, the customary response is 'thank you, sir.'" He kept his hands on her waist, and she, foolishly, found her hands were still on his rather broad shoulders. He stepped back and dropped his hands just as Gwen murmured, "Thank you, my lord."

"You are welcome," he replied, offering her his arm. His gesture was a reflex born of bone-deep manners and habit, but still she hesitated long enough that he could not have failed to notice. He solved the issue by reaching for her hand and placing it in the crook of his elbow.

"Miss Hollister," he began in patient tones as he matched his steps to hers, "it would save us both much confusion were you to recall I am a gentleman. I might growl, but I do not bite; I do not press my attentions on reluctant young ladies; and being titled, I do not suffer a lack of females who welcome my interest."

He was strolling them up to the house while Gwen was torn between outrage at his lecturing and a real desire simply to run from him.

Except she had given this man her word that she would assist him, and it couldn't be any harder for her to leave her hand on his arm than it had been for him to climb into a tree full of angry hornets.

"I beg your lordship's pardon. I am out of the habit of enduring a man's polite company. I do not mean to give offense." She was also out of the habit of justifying her reactions, must less apologizing for them—rather like an old dowager, set in her ways and hard of hearing.

When had that happened?

"Do you think *I* mean to give offense?" Amery asked, though his question was rhetorical. "When I commit the unpardonable affronts of assisting you from your horse? Offering escort? Holding a door for you?"

"I will ring for luncheon," Gwen said, dropping his arm as they reached the house, lest answering his questions try her manners beyond tolerance. "If you would like to freshen up, you may use the first bedroom on the right at the top of the stairs. I will join you in the breakfast room shortly, my lord."

She gave a nominal curtsy, which he returned with a nominal bow, and then they went their separate ways, like pugilists retiring to neutral corners at the end of a hard fought round.

❧

The breakfast parlor was along the southern side of the house, and when Amery arrived, Gwen was standing near a window, her back toward him. She knew the instant he'd crossed the threshold to the room, but didn't turn until he scraped his boot on the floor—deliberately?

He was that attentive to his infernal manners. He stood in the doorway, unwilling even to enter the room without her permission, a punctilio that struck Gwen as more stubborn than considerate.

"My lord, shall we be seated?"

Amery held her chair for her, blast him, and waited for Gwen to serve him.

Something in her expression must have betrayed her feelings, for Amery sighed as he spread his serviette on his lap. "Madam, you cannot be bristling and cringing every time I am in the same room. If it's that difficult for you to be in my company, I will withdraw my request for your assistance."

Gwen considered him and considered his point. She had spent the entire morning mentally castigating him for a lack of warmth, but perhaps she was guilty in some regard of a lack of... hospitality.

A lack of nerve.

"Please help yourself, my lord," she said, indicating a towering plate of sandwiches. "I decided informal fare would better suit a productive luncheon conversation."

He plucked a sandwich at random from the tray. "I appreciate that I have raised an awkward topic, Miss Hollister, but you are prevaricating."

She was. *Where to begin?*

He tore into his sandwich—no prevarication there.

"I am out of the habit of allowing men into my... into proximity with me. My cousin Andrew is the only fellow who does not respect my wishes in this regard, and I must tolerate him."

Amery reached for the teapot and poured for them both. "In that case," he said, adding sugar to his tea, "you must simply add me to the appallingly short list of men you tolerate. Sugar?"

She took the sugar bowl from him. "I can fix my own tea, thank you very much."

"And you can learn to tolerate me," he said, sipping his tea.

Gwen stirred cream and sugar into her favorite cup rather vigorously. "Why can't you learn to keep your distance from me?"

He sipped his tea again, and yet Gwen had the sense all his monumental calm hid a volcano of impatience, waiting to erupt and spew masculine indignation all over her.

"I could learn to keep my distance from you, of course, Miss Hollister. My proximity to you is a function of courtesy and expedience, it being inconvenient to learn husbandry of the land from you exclusively by post, and I having been raised with the manners of a gentleman. Why can't you use me as an opportunity to reacquaint yourself with the harmless exponents of my gender?"

Gwen snorted. "Your gender has no *harmless* exponents, yourself included." She chose a sandwich from the opposite side of the tray from where he'd taken his.

His lordship put down his teacup and regarded her with an intensity that made Gwen wish she could bolt out of her chair and hide in the attics as Rose did when she'd misbehaved.

"What?" she asked, not liking his silence or his perusal.

"Whoever he was," Amery said at length, "I believe I must stand in line behind your cousins should an opportunity arise to shoot the bastard—pardon my language. Eat your sandwich," he added. "You must be famished after the morning we put in."

She was. She was also too unsettled to eat, and Amery was too perceptive.

Gwen put her sandwich on her plate and addressed herself to it. "This simply isn't going to work."

Amery, who was halfway through his second sandwich, returned that unnerving blue-eyed regard to her.

"We have to make it work, Miss Hollister. Here." He took her hand in his, lacing their fingers. Because they were at table, neither wore gloves. Gwen just had time to be shocked at his boldness—and to notice that he had a warm, steady grip—when he extricated his hand from hers. "Now what was so terrible about that? Eat your sandwich."

Gwen couldn't imagine consuming anything while this man was, was... touching her. *Bothering* her. His hands were warm, elegant, strong, and... too strong.

"It wasn't terrible," she said, though if she'd been asked, she might have admitted to fearing it could be. "A simple clasping of the hands can lead to other things, and those things can be terrible."

Amery regarded her as if she were speaking Mandarin, then his expression changed, becoming frigid rather than his standard cool.

"I will not impose myself on you, nor will I suffer any man to impose himself on you, nor to visit harm upon your person. Eat your sandwich, please."

He looked like he might say more, but his infernal decorum prevented him from whatever lectures were boiling up from his manly indignation. Abruptly, Gwen felt an absurd temptation to laugh—at herself. Amery shifted from casually demolishing her sandwich tray to offering her shocking assurances, and went about both pursuits with an intensity of focus Gwen could relate to easily.

"Do you believe me?" Amery asked, glaring at her over his plate.

She'd known him little more than twenty-four hours. He had been polite, if brusque and impatient. But his shocking assurances were something she had needed to hear, and because he was brusque and impatient, she also found she could trust him, at least a little.

Then too, Amery seemed incapable of flirtatious innuendo or deceit.

"I believe you," she said, taking a bite of her meal. "Until I have evidence to the contrary."

"That's a start, I suppose. You are the despair of your cousins, you know."

"What?" She couldn't hide her consternation at that sally, so she took another nibble of her sandwich to safely occupy her mouth.

"You are," he said, looking like he might consider yet another sandwich. Did nobody feed this man? "Heathgate, Greymoor—and I suppose we must add Fairly to the list— are quite protective of you. When you pull this sniffing and silence on them, it hurts their feelings."

"It hurts their feelings because I'm reserved in their company?"

"Of course." Amery put a second sandwich on her plate, though she wasn't done with her first. "They are chivalrous men, and you insult them when you act as if they could have less than your best interests at heart. Or perhaps"—he paused and set the mustard nearer her elbow—"you bewilder them."

"They are good men," Gwen conceded, studying the crust of her sandwich. Why had the kitchen not trimmed the crusts on the rare occasion of company at Gwen's table? "I do not mean…"

"Yes?" He'd moved on to the tray of tea cakes now, selecting the four largest pieces to add to his plate.

"I do not mean to be unwelcoming, your lordship. Reserve has become a habit." She was using that word too frequently: habit, when refuge or crutch might have been more honest.

"Habits," he replied, refilling his teacup yet again, "can be retrained. More tea?"

"Please." She reached for a tea cake, then realized his perishing, bottomless lordship had appropriated all of the chocolate ones. Seeing her scowl, Amery held his plate out to her.

"My apologies," he said gravely.

Gwen watched his eyes as she removed a chocolate cake from his plate.

"There. You see? You did it again."

She set her cake aside untasted. "Did what?"

"You watched me as if at any second I were going to drop that plate and vault over the table to ravish you."

"Nonsense. You're not the ravishing kind, my lord."

"Miss Hollister, if I am not the ravishing kind—which characterization I might find slightly offensive, by the way, did I fancy myself as a dashing swain—then why do you regard me so warily?"

She opened her mouth, prepared to put him firmly in his place, but nothing came out, so she took a bite of cake instead.

"Well?"

"I suppose, my lord," she said when his stare had ruined her first bite of chocolate cake, "that having been betrayed by my judgment egregiously in the past, I am hesitant to rely on it now. Surely you can understand this." She tried for another bite of her cake, hoping his lordship choked on the boldness of her implied admission.

"Miss Hollister," his lordship rejoined so dratted gently, "it wasn't your judgment that betrayed you, but a flesh-and-blood man who should be called to account for his sins."

This topic—her lapse from propriety and its results—usually lurked beneath a conversation, whether she spoke with her tenants, her cousins, or the Enfield staff. That Amery would face it directly—and regard her as a wronged party—was a disconcerting relief.

"Perhaps he should," she replied, "but that man is long gone, while my judgment remains on hand." She took the final bite of her cake, pleased to have had the last word, though in truth, "long gone" was a stretch when Rose's father spent much of the year in nearby London.

"Have you finished your meal, madam?"

"I apparently have."

"Then I thank you for a very filling repast and will await you in the stables." He rose, bowed, and withdrew without another word.

❧

When Douglas gained the peace and quiet of the stables, he first checked on Regis, who was swishing flies in a shady paddock. The horse had grass and water and seemed content to nap in the afternoon sun.

While Douglas beheld his somnolent steed, he tried to quell his own internal tumult.

What in the name of Jesus and the Apostles had got into him that he would challenge Miss Hollister as if she were some close associate of long standing? He had made a thinly veiled reference to the word *rape* in the presence of a woman connected to his family, and he'd done it purposely.

And she had looked so… dumbstruck, so innocent.

That exchange with her over lunch had told him things, things a man didn't ask a lady outright regardless of her shadowed past.

Her shock suggested she was sexually inexperienced, for all that she was the mother of a bastard child.

And he'd learned other things, too: Her skin, when he'd taken her hand, was *kissably* soft. As close as he'd stood to her at several points in the day, he'd learned that if he were to take her in his arms, she'd fit him. She was tall and well formed and curved generously in the right places. And he'd learned something else, something that made him oddly… happy: *he could desire her.*

This insight had come to him when he'd stood, his hand on the door, blocking her exit the previous day, and he'd known the surprising impulse to press closer to her, to breathe her in and let her feel the evidence of a man's desire right up against her feminine curves. A momentary impulse, but he was honest with himself, and it had been an honest impulse.

Within that impulse was nothing less than a revelation.

Douglas had felt the need for sex before, but always in the nonspecific sense that he'd simply wanted to spend. In the past few years, it had become the less complicated option to spend in his hand rather than into the body of a willing female stranger.

He had desired this woman, specifically: Guinevere Hollister. She was pretty enough, but Douglas was drawn to her not because of her looks but because she utterly eschewed the flirtation and simpering of many of her peers. Her lapse from propriety had, if anything, imbued her with more dignity, not less, for which he had to like—to admire—her.

That she did not acknowledge any reciprocity was immaterial, and whether he ever fornicated with the object of his attraction was equally irrelevant. He was relieved simply to experience normal adult male longing for a woman.

One of the grooms approached and interrupted Douglas's peculiar reverie. "My lord?"

Douglas shifted away from the fence. "Yes?"

"Mistress says you may use one of our mounts for the afternoon. She's up at the barn, awaiting yer pleasure."

Fascinating notion. Douglas walked back to the barn, half-curious regarding what Miss Hollister's mood might be.

"My lord." She was leading out the same rawboned chestnut she'd ridden in the morning.

"Miss Hollister." Douglas followed her into the stable yard as she gave the girth a final tug.

She looked at him askance. "Sir?"

"I will assist you to mount," Douglas informed her, reasoning that if she could tolerate his fingers laced with hers, she could tolerate his hand on the ankle of her boot, because when all a man had to offer was good manners, by God, he would offer same.

And something about their exchange at lunch had made it imperative that he offer them to Miss Hollister, will she, nil she.

"That would be most kind," she replied. "On three," she said, bending her left knee so Douglas could grasp the ankle of her boot and hoist her aboard her gelding. "Thank you, my lord."

"Most welcome," he replied—sincerely—before going to his horse, checking the girth and fit of the bridle, then swinging up. "What is our agenda for the afternoon, Miss Hollister? I confess, when you offered me the use of a guest room at luncheon, I was tempted to catch a nap."

She smiled over at him as their horses walked out of the yard, the fleeting, shy, genuine smile that hinted at the girl she'd been. Her mood, it seemed, was improved for having eaten—or for having been given a respite from his company.

"We did get an early start. We will ride up to the trout pond and inspect the ditches used for irrigation along the way. Autumn can be as dry some years as it is wet other years, and then you end up with less grass the next spring, not even realizing how much you lost from drought rather than cold."

"There is much to learn. I am feeling decidedly overwhelmed."

"Good." The dratted woman's smile turned smug. "Taking responsibility for the land and the people on the land is a serious endeavor. Agriculture has become a rapidly changing science, and if the owner of the property doesn't care to keep pace, why should his employees or tenants?"

"You make a valid point," Douglas allowed, then fell to considering her point silently. After noting numerous locations where the lads would have to clear ditches and grates before winter set in, Miss Hollister drew up at a stand of trees, in the middle of which lay a sizeable pond.

"This is one of my favorite places on the estate. Let's get down and let the horses rest a bit, shall we?"

Douglas's weary fundament found that a capital notion. Before the lady could hop down on her own, Douglas was beside her mount, reaching up to assist her from her horse. She allowed it without comment, and even remembered to murmur her thanks. She slipped off her horse's bridle and indicated Douglas should do the same.

"Your daughter is taking the air." The pond, its copse of trees, and a small white gazebo sat in a high meadow overlooking the buildings and grounds of the Enfield manor house. In the distance below, Rose skipped out on the terrace, a large pad of paper in her hand, a nurse and a shaggy brindle mastiff trailing behind.

"She likes to be outside," Miss Hollister said, "as do I."

For several minutes they watched Rose settling in at a table, the dog arranging itself at her feet, then Miss Hollister walked off toward the gazebo. "Come," she said, "we can sit in the shade, and I will explain to you about ponds."

A riveting prospect indeed, though Miss Hollister's retreating form also bore a certain charm.

What Douglas would have enjoyed most at that moment was taking off the boots he'd had on since sunrise and stretching out on a blanket in the grass, there to sleep for several hours in blissful solitude. He was not so tired, however, that he didn't notice Miss Hollister was continuing on her way without him.

A bit of teasing was permitted. Just a bit, for form's sake, surely?

"Miss Hollister?" She stopped, turned, and arched a brow at him. He winged his arm at her. She pressed her lips together and came striding to his side.

❦

Gwen let the blighted man escort her to the small, white octagonal building at the edge of the pond and gestured for him to sit beside her. She began a discourse, explaining the benefits and burdens of trying to raise trout in a pond, about the evils of pond scum, and the trials of dry years versus the trials of wet years. When she had prosed on for a good five minutes—and again noted what a pleasant scent Amery wore—Gwen realized she had yet to hear a single question from his perishingly proper lordship.

Her companion had fallen asleep, wedged against one of the supports holding up the roof. For a moment she was insulted; then she reasoned a man of his exaggerated sense of propriety would not deal her such a slight intentionally. She watched him fall more deeply asleep, his head turning against the pillar, his hand going lax against his thigh.

To see a grown man fall asleep right before her eyes was novel and more interesting than it should have been. A muscle leapt along Amery's square jaw once, his breathing evened out, and his hand slid off his leg to fall against Gwen's thigh. On a soft sigh, he was gone into the arms of Morpheus.

In sleep, Douglas Allen was appallingly, surprisingly handsome. Waking, his features were schooled to a chronic pained reserve. The relaxed version of those same features was infinitely more appealing. Slumbering, his thin, disapproving mouth was fuller, his lips more sculpted. His blond hair, usually swept back in a queue, had come loose from its ribbon and spread over his shoulders in golden disarray.

After a few more minutes studying her companion's sleeping visage, Gwen let the lazy quiet of the afternoon penetrate her senses, to the point where resting her eyes gained appeal. She wouldn't fall asleep, of course, not in the presence of a man who was nearly a stranger to her—

When she awoke, the sun wasn't much changed in its position, but *she* had changed *her* position.

"Steady," her pillow said. "Rising too quickly can leave one dizzy."

Mindful that the warning bore some merit, Gwen did not abruptly abandon her location. She was cuddled against a warm slab of male muscle, one bearing the pleasant, spicy scent of Douglas Allen. His arm rested loosely around her shoulders, and for an instant, Gwen battled an impulse to close her eyes and go back to sleep. Amery's proximity should have felt distasteful and presuming, threatening even… Except, it didn't.

"Beg pardon, my lord."

"Now, Miss Hollister," his lordship chided gently, "you weren't contemplating abandoning me here when I was having such a lovely meditation, were you?" He retrieved his arm and shot his cuffs, not a hint of self-consciousness or hurry about him. "I do feel somewhat refreshed, but I confess I missed some of your profundities regarding the care and feeding of pond trout, for which I heartily apologize. For my penance, I suppose you must harry me off on yet another lesson?"

Gwen watched him, knowing she regarded him with the look he detested, the wary, careful appraisal that anticipated mischief. His expression was more relaxed though, as if he really had needed a nap to restore his spirits. He rose and extended a hand toward her, a hint of challenge lurking in his eyes. She braced her free hand on the back of the bench and let him assist her to her feet.

"Oh, blast and perdition," Gwen muttered, glaring at the hand she'd rested on the wooden bench. A small drop of blood welled on the outside of her fourth finger. A splinter lodged there, but the angle of penetration made it hard for her to examine, much less extract with her teeth.

"Allow me," Amery said, reaching for her hand.

"No thank you." Gwen snatched her hand back. "I can tend to it when we return to the manor."

"Of course you can," Amery agreed pleasantly. "And ride all that way without gloves—because you surely don't intend to put a glove on over that—and blister your fingers for no reason other than your abundant pride."

Was he laughing at her? Gwen thrust her hand under the arrogant length of his nose.

He grasped her hand and slowly turned it to bring her finger against his mouth. With his tongue, he traced the side of her finger, finding the sliver of wood and *acquainting himself* with its angle of entry by virtue of explorations that made Gwen's insides leap.

Gwen turned her head, unable to hold his gaze while his tongue probed at her flesh. The wet, warm feel of his lips and tongue against her finger, the challenge in his eyes as he held her hand to his mouth… Hot, uncomfortable, complicated feelings spiraled up from her middle, made all the worse by her conviction that Amery found the whole business amusing.

His teeth gently scraped at Gwen's finger just as her insides nearly collapsed from an answering mortification—it had to be embarrassment causing those odd sensations—and then his mouth was gone.

"There." He held a mean little dagger of wood on the end of his finger for her to see then flicked it into the weeds. "No wonder it hurt." He withdrew a handkerchief and wrapped it around Gwen's finger, applying a snug pressure while she submitted to his assistance.

"Wouldn't you do the same for me?" he asked quietly. When Gwen mutely gazed out over the water, he sighed and answered his own question. "I see you would not, which is just as well. I relish asking for help no more than you do. Shall we be on our way?"

He offered his right arm, and Gwen accepted it, wondering at the significance of his last comment. They made the journey back to the manor house in thoughtful silence until they were walking up the driveway, their horses side by side.

"You will spend the balance of the afternoon with Rose?" he asked her as they approached the stable yard.

"She might be napping, but from when she awakens until she goes down tonight, I will be more or less with her."

Amery dismounted and came around his horse. "What is more or less?"

This had nothing to do with stewardship of the land, and yet Gwen answered him. "If I have accounting to do, she might play in the library while I work at the books. She might come with me if I need to visit the home farm or the propagation houses. I reserve tasks near the manor for the end of the day, and if it's safe, she comes with me."

He lifted her off her horse and likely would have stepped back in the next instant, but Gwen pitched a bit forward on landing, so his hands lingered on her waist a moment longer.

"Thank you, my lord."

"Most welcome," he replied, taking that step back and offering her his arm. The horses were led away, and the idiot man remained standing there, his elbow winged out until Gwen took his arm and he started a sedate progress toward the house.

"You don't have to do this, you know."

"I beg your pardon?" His tone wasn't begging anything and suggested he never would.

"You don't have to make it your personal mission to return me to the land of gentlemanly manners," she bit out. "I concede defeat, your lordship. I will acquiesce in your displays of civility, but you need not be so willing to put your hands on my person."

"Are my hands on your person, then?"

"You know to what I refer."

"I do," he allowed. "You referred to it as manners and civilities. Let me ask you a question, though, Miss Hollister."

He paused on a slight rise offering a view of the autumn gardens. Asters and pansies bloomed in colorful abundance, and the chrysanthemums were coming into their glory.

"Your question, my lord?"

"Have I at any point touched you against your will?"

"No. No, damn you, you have not."

❧

Miss Hollister dropped Douglas's arm and strode away into the house. From the set of her shoulders, she was crying again, which was understandable. She'd had much to cry about, and unless he missed his guess, she'd probably allowed herself very few tears.

They were similar in that regard, he and this fallen, knowledgeable woman who loved both her child and her land so fiercely.

He took himself back down to the stables and arranged to leave Regis in his shady paddock and ride his borrowed mount over to Willowdale. He would swap horses tomorrow, and Regis, at least, would get some rest.

This assumed, of course, Miss Hollister was willing to have him and his gentlemanly manners tagging along again the following day. Because such an assumption might well be faulty, Douglas retraced his steps to the house, using the kitchen door and finding both the cook and a scullery maid on hand.

"Your pardon, but where might I find Miss Hollister?"

The cook was elbow deep in bread dough but gave an awkward imitation of a curtsy, as did the scullery maid at the sink. "She be in the nursery, milord. Third floor, back o' the house," the cook replied.

"My thanks." He went in search of his quarry, though the maid and cook exchanged a smirk as he turned to go, of which he was quite aware. All the women in this house were in want of proper guidance—or something.

The location of the nursery was easy to ascertain, because Douglas could hear a child's voice from halfway down the corridor, singing an old folk song, something about not having wings to fly.

Rose sprang across a combination playroom and schoolroom. "Hello! Mama says you are our cousin. How do you do, Cousin?"

She hugged him around his thighs, stepped back to make a child's curtsy, then held up her arms as if to be lifted into an embrace. When Douglas blinked down at her presumption, she gave her arms a little shake, suggesting he hadn't noticed their upraised position.

Needs must. He hefted the child up onto his hip. "Hello, Miss Rose. How are you today?"

"I am all punished. Do you want to see?"

Douglas's little backside would have been thoroughly striped for a misadventure such as Rose's, but then his father had sought any excuse to discipline his sons, and his mother had never interfered. Surely Miss Hollister was of a more enlightened bent?

"I suppose you will not rest until you show me," he said, setting the child down.

"Rose, who are you…?" Rose scampered past her mother's skirts as Miss Hollister emerged from an adjoining room, probably the child's bedroom. "Lord Amery." Her greeting was a verbal cannonball fired across Douglas's quarterdeck.

"Miss Hollister." He gave her a bow worthy of the churchyard on Easter morning. "We parted before making plans for either the immediate or the near term. I am loathe to present myself on your doorstep only to find my company is an imposition."

And he did not want to part from her in anger, though anger was probably much of what sustained her.

Rose came bouncing into the room, several sheets of paper clutched in her hands. "Do you still want to see my punishment?"

"Most assuredly," Douglas said, letting himself be led to a low table surrounded by small chairs. As they passed Miss Hollister, he caught a bracing whiff of lavender and indignation. Rose popped onto one of the chairs, but

Douglas, fearing to look ridiculous while he broke one attempting the same, sat cross-legged on the floor beside the child.

"This," said Rose, "is my first one."

Her work was surprisingly expressive as she described in images one nasty possible outcome of her tree-climbing after another. She had caught with appalling accuracy the fear on her mother's face, the horror on the stableboys', and a grim determination on Douglas's own visage. The final picture was of Miss Hollister sitting next to a gravestone, over which a huge bouquet of pink and purple flowers had been placed.

"'Cause I could be dead."

"But you are not," Douglas countered softly.

"I'm not!" Rose bolted for the next room. "I'll be back!"

"She draws amazingly well," Douglas said to her mother as he got to his feet. Miss Hollister leaned against the doorjamb, arms crossed, her expression hard to read.

"She enjoys it. Do you like children?"

"I hardly know. Miss Rose is the first child with whom I've any acquaintance, unless you count her little cousins at Willowdale and Oak Hall. And they, thankfully, are still quite in the nursery."

"Mama, I'm ready!" Rose careened back into the room, a small bonnet in her hand. "Can we go now, and will Mister… Cousin Douglas walk with us?"

"He will," Douglas said, deliberately cutting off any objection Miss Hollister might have made and silently excusing the child's faulty grammar—and use of familiar address.

The girl chattered incessantly down two flights of stairs, through the house, and out onto the back terraces. She reported on what she saw, what she thought, what she felt, and what she would have felt if various contingencies—such as a wild unicorn from Mongolia galloping into the garden—were to occur. When they reached the gardens below the back terrace, Rose galloped off to see if a certain bush still had any flowers, abandoning her mother to Douglas's company.

Had Rose's mother ever been so voluble and carefree?

"Managing a few thousand acres must seem a lark after trying to manage that one child."

"Sometimes," Miss Hollister replied. "Not always. An estate can't love you back."

Douglas gave her a curious look, but she said no more on this topic, and he did not ask her to elucidate particulars, though elucidating particulars was one of her strengths. Miss Hollister had walked off a little way to sit on a stone bench with a clear view of her cavorting daughter.

"She'll come back from time to time, then go off, then come back," Miss Hollister explained. "We might as well have that discussion about our calendar, my lord."

Douglas gestured to the bench. "May I?"

She swished her skirts aside. "Of course."

"I foresee a complication, Miss Hollister," Douglas said, his gaze on the child as she systematically sniffed each rose in a blooming bed. "You have apparently instructed your daughter to refer to me as Cousin Douglas, and yet you, who would be my closer relation were I Rose's cousin, are still referring to me as my lord, and Lord Amery, and so forth."

"Children are often permitted less formal address."

He certainly hadn't been as a child. "Will it not confuse Rose if you address Heathgate and Greymoor by their Christian names, and yet I remain a title to you?"

"It's time Rose learned something of proper address. You might as well be the example."

He expected stubbornness from her on this matter—on every matter thus far and for the foreseeable future as well—and because he, too, was stubborn, he liked it about her, for the most part.

"When we travel to Sussex," Douglas said, "you have assured me you will do so only as my relation or something of that nature. You do not refer to your familial relations formally, though both of your cousins hold titles. Rose knows this much and will surely remark on your inconsistency at some point when others are in her hearing."

Children were demons about adult inconsistency. Even Douglas knew that much of their natures.

"Do as you will." Miss Hollister stalked off in the direction of her daughter.

That was not quite clear permission to address her by her Christian name, which was, of course, what he had been angling for. She *did* call Heathgate, Greymoor, and even Fairly—Astrid Alexander's brother, and thus no relation to Miss Hollister at all—by their Christian names, and she *had* insisted she and Douglas travel to Sussex as relations.

"Mama!" Rose's scream pierced the afternoon quiet, a scream conveying fear and pain. "Maaaaaaamaaaaaa!" The screaming continued as Douglas sprang off the bench and vaulted hedges and walls to get to the child.

"Rose!" Douglas bellowed. "Hold still. Stop thrashing this instant!" Then in a more civil voice, he called out, "She's all right." And she more or less was, though Douglas's heart pounded with both exertion and the mortal dread her screams had inspired.

"I am not all right!" Rose screeched. "Ouch!"

"I misspoke," Douglas conceded. "If you will hold still, I will extricate you from those bushes, and all will be well."

"All will not be well," Rose spat back. "I saw a snake and he scared me and then the rose bushes grabbed me and they are using their thorns to bite at me."

"What shameful manners," Douglas observed as he separated Rose's clothing from the offending bushes. "Tonight their mamas will make them draw pictures of what dire fates can befall rose bushes that bite innocent little girls."

"I'll have the gardeners rip them out," Rose said. "I'll put poison on their roots. I'll plant daisies here that don't have any old thorns. I'll let the bugs eat up all the roses, and leaf spot, and beetles, and all manner of awful things."

Douglas disentangled Rose from her tormentors, grabbed her elbows, and hoisted her straight up, then swung her out of the flower bed over to the grass.

"Mama! There was a snake and he scared me and the roses bit me and their mamas must punish them. Cousin Douglas said."

She hurled herself against her mother's skirts; Miss Hollister knelt and brushed dark locks back from Rose's forehead.

"Sweetheart?"

That particular tone of voice was one Douglas had not heard from the lady before—gentle, coaxing, soft, and reassuring. He *felt* her tone of voice as much as heard it.

"Yes, Mama?"

"Was there really, truly a snake?"

Rose looked away, her bashful expression reminding Douglas of her mother's similar fleeting bouts of shyness.

"There was," Rose decided indignantly. "It was an awful, mean old snake, like in the Bible."

"Perhaps you could describe this ferocious serpent?" Douglas suggested.

Rose thought for a moment, her imagination no

doubt warming to the subject. "He was huge and he had mean eyes and he waved his tongue at me." She demonstrated dramatically. "He was miles long and he hissed steam out his nose and he was green, with great ugly black spots."

And of course, this horrible monster was male.

"A terrifying prospect," said Douglas, finding it needful to study the pink roses flourishing nearby. "I believe I am familiar with the species. It particularly delights in flinging little girls into rose bushes when they feel a great falsehood coming on."

"Let's go, Mama," Rose said, tugging on her mother's hand and shooting Douglas a puzzled look. "I don't want the snake to come back. Come, Cousin Douglas, or that snake might gobble you up."

"I am atremble with trepidation," he replied, taking the hand Rose proffered. Before he'd escorted the ladies back to the terrace, Rose was off once more, chasing a butterfly.

While Miss Hollister regarded Douglas with the faintest hint of... *a smile*. "You are quite the athlete, my lord."

"I had never considered what excitement raising a child entails. It is nerve-wracking, is it not? Hornets, snakes, thorns... I've known Rose only two days, and she has enlivened my existence considerably."

Which was nothing less than the honest and surprising truth.

"And you hers," Miss Hollister said, smiling more broadly. Rose was making a complete circuit of the garden at a dead run. "She's going to fall." Sure enough, on a tight corner, Rose slid in the grass, got right up, and pelted off.

"Nerve-wracking. May I call you Guinevere?" Because every occasion when he called her *Miss* Hollister, he felt a bit uncomfortable for her.

Put like that, a simple request humbly made, and she was again looking bashful. Douglas wondered how long it had been since a man had *asked* for the privilege of familiar address with her. Such intimacy was a family member's privilege, a close friend's, or… a fiancé's. "I do not mean to be forward, Miss Hollister, it just seems that under the—"

She put a finger on his lips then, a light, fleeting touch, accompanied by a shake of her head.

"Gwen. And I shall call you Douglas."

"Just so. You shall call me Douglas."

They fell into another silence, this one different from any of the previous gaps in their conversations. For Douglas, the quiet had a sweetness, a stirring of benevolence toward his hostess and her noisy, happy, nerve-wracking child.

They walked together to the stables and agreed Douglas would borrow the gelding and return the following day.

"I'll be off then," Douglas said as they ambled down the barn aisle. "If I make another day of it with you here, then spend through Wednesday in Town, we can be on our way early Thursday. Has Rose a pony?"

"This one." Miss Hollister—Guinevere—gestured to a stall where a petite and venerable white mare lipped at some hay. "If I thought Daisy would make the journey, I'd bring her along, but it would be asking too much. And I'm sure any property Andrew owns will have decent riding horses."

Miss—Guinevere—accompanied Douglas to the stable yard where he checked his gelding's girth one last time, then swung up without benefit of a mounting block and turned the horse down the drive.

"My thanks, Guinevere, for an informative day." He touched his crop to his hat brim. "Until tomorrow."

As the gelding's hoofbeats faded, Gwen mused on the form of address her departing guest had chosen: Guinevere. Andrew teasingly called her Gwennie; Gareth and David, Lord Fairly, stuck to plain Gwen. The help and the locals called her Miss Hollister or ma'am. And now this from Lord Amery.

Rose's father had had many sweet little names for Gwen, words now stricken from her vocabulary that she hoped and prayed she'd never hear applied to her person.

But to Douglas she was simply Guinevere.

Despite herself, she liked it. From him, she did like it.

Three

THE PEACE AND QUIET, AH, THE PEACE AND QUIET.

Gwen spent the first morning of travel as wound up as Rose, gaze riveted to the scenery outside the window. Six long, long years had passed since she'd left the environs of Enfield for more than a day, and she hadn't realized how hungry for variety she had become.

Even while the whole idea of it had frightened her into near banishment.

But here she was, having the coach to herself, and allowing her daughter to go cantering off up before Amery as if he really were their cousin.

He treated her and Rose with nothing but deference and courtesy, more than her true cousins showed her. Lady Heathgate had sent word she'd be joining them in Sussex, citing the social obligations of the Little Season. Andrew and Gareth had both endorsed this trip heartily, assuring Gwen she could not have a more conscientious escort than Douglas Allen.

And Amery was "practically family." The wretches had smirked while they'd made that pronouncement, probably knowing exactly how ill-suited Gwen was to Amery's brand of company.

Gwen was half-asleep, mentally listing things to inspect at Linden, when the coach pulled into a noisy yard. She was glad, not for the first time, to have Douglas shouting orders, directing traffic, and taking charge in a way she could not. A cheerful maid showed them to the best rooms in the house, a sort of suite including a private sitting room connecting two bedrooms.

"These rooms are acceptable to you?" Amery— *Douglas*—stripped off his gloves, and Gwen had to force her gaze from the sight of his hands. Why she'd be preoccupied with such a common human appendage was unfathomable, except she'd touched one of those hands, almost held it for an instant or two.

"The rooms are lovely. Thank you for taking Rose up with you this afternoon. She'll dine out on that adventure for days."

"And where is Rose?" Am—Douglas asked, slapping his gloves against his thigh.

"She's putting away her things, reading a story to Mr. Bear, drawing a picture of the prettiest thing she saw today. She is a busy young lady." And this sketch was to be a gift for "dear Cousin Douglas."

"She comes by her industry honestly. I am having a tray sent up, the common appearing noisy and crowded. Will you be wanting a bath?" Douglas's tone was all business—as usual.

"Not for me, but Rose will need a bath, if it can be brought to our bedroom after supper."

"I did wonder," Douglas said as he reached for the door latch, "how you keep her smelling so delightfully sweet."

He was out the door, leaving Gwen to wonder at him and his curious compliment. After hours in the saddle, Douglas yet bore a particular scent, clean and a little spicy, with cedar or sage or something of the out-of-doors. His fragrance was one of a few things she liked about him.

Another was his sense of responsibility. He would see to their dinner, order Rose's bath, get them safely on their way tomorrow, and generally execute the duties of an escort without prompting or flaw. He seemed to need responsibility, much as Gwen did. For his sake, she hoped the property in Sussex was suited to his goals. With any luck, he'd be able to make a go of it on sheer determination.

"Dinner is on the way," Douglas informed her when he returned to their sitting room. "And you look like you should enjoy it then climb immediately into your bed. Your eyes are shadowed."

Such an observant fellow was Lord Amery. "I usually read for an hour prior to blowing out the candles, though I am a bit fatigued," Gwen admitted from a comfortable chair by the hearth. "Travel has the ability to be both boring and wearying."

Though at some point, she'd lost the ability to apply those descriptors to present company.

"You were bored today?"

"I have been in that coach, hour after hour, with that child, and the same books, the same games, the same incessant demands for snacks, the necessary, and so forth," Gwen pointed out. "So yes, I will admit to a certain boredom."

Douglas stretched his long legs out before him as he settled on the raised hearth—without seeking Gwen's permission. "Why didn't you ask me to take Rose for a time here and there? I impressed her into the cavalry for the past few miles only because her whining was nigh making Regis ill."

Gwen was saved from a reply by a knock on the door and a procession of servants bringing in the dinner trays.

Rose scampered out from the ladies' bedroom and began her recitation of the day's adventures. "And here," she added with a huge smile, "is my drawing of the best thing."

"What was your best thing today?" Gwen asked as she fixed her daughter a plate.

"It's me, Cousin Douglas, and Sir Regis—you are in the coach, Mama, but the coach is too far back to be in the picture. We cantered and cantered and cantered. Sir Regis is not old, like Daisy, and he likes to canter. Someday, when I'm older—"

"May I?" Douglas interrupted, reaching for the picture. "I see you caught Sir Regis's smile. He must appreciate that you knighted him today."

"He's brave, kind, and ever so handsome," Rose answered as she scrambled onto Douglas's lap. "And he likes to go charging forth."

"All necessary attributes to a knight errant," Douglas said, looking somewhat taken aback as Rose settled like a nesting partridge on his knees.

"What's a night errand?" she asked, putting her picture aside and curling up against Douglas's chest.

"A knight errant," he explained, wrapping an arm gingerly around Rose's back, "is a fellow who gallops about the kingdom, rescuing damsels in distress, vanquishing evil, and being a good sport. He must have a trusty steed like Sir Regis, who is interested in the same pursuits."

"I am going to be a knight errant when I grow up," Rose pronounced, popping a thumb into her mouth and snuggling closer to her fellow cavalryman. "Daisy can be my trusty steed, though she will have to get better at cantering."

"A sound plan," Douglas allowed.

He was sitting *carefully*. As if Rose were fragile or a half-tame cat who would leap away at the slightest provocation. But Rose looked blissfully content as she curled against Douglas, her thumb in her mouth, her eyes closed. The tableau was soothing, but also... disquieting. Douglas had risked his life for the child, but did Rose have to trust the man so easily? So completely?

"I think the fair damsel is falling asleep," Douglas said.

"I am not," Rose retorted around her thumb, her eyes flying open.

"Then get down from yonder knight," Gwen said, "so you can eat your dinner." Rose scrambled down and took her place beside Gwen, while yonder knight looked relieved.

The roasted chicken, mashed potatoes, bread, and buttered peas were good, and fortunately they appealed to Rose's somewhat finicky palate. Before the pudding had been consumed, another tap on the door heralded the arrival of the bath and bucket upon bucket of steaming water.

Rose sat up indignantly. "Mama! You didn't tell me I would have to take a bath tonight. That is *not* fair. I did not even touch the dirt today, I am not dirty..."

"Miss Rose," Douglas interrupted, "you will want to take that bath, because Sir Regis is particularly fond of little girls who smell as little girls should, of soap and sunshine rather than of tantrums and disrespect."

"Tantrums do not smell," Rose informed him with regal dignity before getting down from the table and disappearing into the bedroom.

Fifteen minutes later, Gwen dried off a clean and sweet-smelling Rose, bundled the child off to bed, and eyed the still-hot, lavender-scented water. When would Rose learn that a bath was a luxury to be savored?

Gwen heard no movement from the other side of the door, suggesting the day's travel had worn Douglas out too. The bathwater was still hot, the soap a luscious rose-scented hard-milled French bar, and the temptation to soak for even a few minutes too great to resist. Gwen disrobed and slipped into the water quietly, lest she wake Rose.

"Guinevere?" Douglas poked his head around the door just as Gwen came up from dousing her hair. "Dear God, I beg your pardon."

He yanked the door shut before Gwen had a chance to even sputter her indignation. As she hastily finished her bath and dried off, she assured herself the bedroom was dimly lit, and she had been largely submerged when Douglas had peeked around the door.

She threw her flannel nightgown over her head, belted a dressing gown over that, and slipped her feet into mules before leaving the bedroom. Her only thought was to confront his snooping lordship and deliver the blistering set-down such a maneuver deserved. She threw open the door, prepared to storm across to Douglas's room, then caught sight of him sitting in near darkness on the sofa, staring into the fire.

He rose as soon as Gwen entered the room, and in the flickering shadows, particularly without his jacket and cravat, he was too tall, too masculine, and entirely too… underdressed.

"I most humbly beg your pardon," he said, bowing formally. "I did not want to knock loudly for fear of waking the child, and it did not occur to me you might change your mind about the bath."

She studied the gravity of his expression, the absolute absence of teasing or disrespect in his eyes. Perhaps he had knocked, albeit softly, and she'd not heard him. She *had* refused a bath, and if his knocking had awoken Rose, Gwen would have resented it.

"No harm done." She did not want to withdraw, lest he know she was overcome by self-consciousness, but the thought of sitting beside him was equally untenable.

"Guinevere, my intrusion was not intentional, and as to that, the room was quite dark and your modesty well preserved, I promise you."

Dry stick that he was, Douglas seemed as embarrassed as Gwen, and that... that helped. She'd never once seen Rose's father embarrassed, but it occurred to her now that the man should have been mortified at his own misdeeds. She tucked that revelation aside to savor later and at length. "What was it you wanted to talk to me about?"

"Do you accept my apology?"

She didn't want to. She wanted to stay in high dudgeon with him over something, though the sentiment was unfair and unbecoming. "I accept your apology."

"Thank you. Are you sure you wouldn't rather leave any discussion until tomorrow?"

"Let me get my hairbrush."

She wasn't going to let her hair dry all willy-nilly, even if that meant she had to brush it out in Douglas's company. Her hair was thick and naturally curly, and it would be nothing short of a fright if she didn't see to it before going to sleep.

Douglas gestured to the sofa. "Please, make yourself comfortable." He remained standing while Gwen took up a corner of the sofa, sitting sideways so her back was against the arm and her feet were tucked up under her.

"For pity's sake, Douglas, you needn't loom over there as if I'm going to snarl and snap. I've accepted your apology, and travel will result in enforced proximity between even strangers. What is it you wanted to talk about?"

He sank down at the far end of the sofa, gaze on

Gwen's slippers peeking from beneath her hem. "There is a woman who resides in the neighborhood of Linden."

Many women resided in the neighborhood of Linden. "Go on," Gwen said, starting with the brush at the bottom of her hair and immediately hitting a snarl.

"Her name is Claudia Pettigrew, and she could create… difficulties."

What in all the wide world could Douglas mean by difficulties? "She is a former amour of *yours,* Douglas? Whatever were you doing, trolling clear down in Sussex?"

"She is not a former amour of mine, and I'll have you know I do not *troll* for the companionship of women. Stop ripping at your hair, if you please."

Gwen looked at the hank of hair she was working on, shrugged, and took the brush to it again. "What about this woman?"

"She is a former amour of Lord Greymoor's," Douglas said. "He… disported with her before he went traveling several years ago, however briefly. If she's as brazen as Greymoor intimates, she'll no doubt be calling—Would you *please* stop tearing your hair that way?"

"It's thick hair, Douglas, and it's my hair," Gwen shot back, chin coming up.

"It's lovely hair, and you jolly well won't abuse it in my presence." He got up, plopped down on her end of the sofa, and snatched the brush from her hand. "Turn around, madam."

She glared at him, sternly, meanly—a glare that would have had her cousins rushing off to see to the press of business posthaste—but he merely held her gaze.

"Please," he added, nothing of entreaty in his tone.

Then, more softly, "Guinevere, you are tired, and you are upset to be away from Enfield. Because you are upset, Rose is being a handful. You must not take it amiss if I don't know how to be of use to you, particularly when you are so stubborn you'd rather die than ask for help. Now, for the last time, please turn around. I have the patience for this task while you do not, and there's nobody to tattle about a small impropriety between nominal cousins. Allow me this, and we'll both find our beds a little sooner."

What he asked of her was closer to an outrageous presumption rather than a small impropriety—also a consideration Gwen had never been shown before. She did not yield the point verbally, but she did scoot around on the couch, giving him her back.

"Thank you," he said, using his fingers to smooth her hair over her shoulders and down her back.

"There's more to it than that," Gwen said from her position facing the fire. Long-dormant female intuition chose then to awaken and warn her she'd reached that dangerous stage where fatigue would loosen her tongue rather than send her off to her bed.

Though Douglas would respect her confidences, of that she was certain.

"More to it, how?"

"I resent you," she said, keeping her face averted, "for the way Rose adores you and the way you seem to manage her with no effort." And Claudia Petti-Whoever could go hang.

"Ah. You have had Rose all to yourself for five years, Miss Guinevere Hollister, and you are not inclined to share your treasure."

Another man had made a similar accusation six years ago, also referring to a reluctance to share her treasures, but his tone had been winsomely naughty, not half-stern and admonishing.

"I am not greedy," she corrected Douglas, his insight

vexing but not vexing enough to excuse dishonesty. "I am afraid of losing her."

"I would be afraid of losing such a child too, but you won't lose her; you will share her, or you should." He'd worked out the big snarl Gwen had been swatting at and smoothed the brush down her hair. He soon found another knot and went to work on it.

As lady's maids went, his lordship was not without ability. Gwen feared he might have potential as an unlikely confessor too. "Why should I share her?"

"If you don't show Rose you can share her, then she will not learn she can share you," Douglas pointed out. "She will grow up clinging to her mama, because her mama clings to her, and this will serve you well, provided you can arrange to die before your daughter. Your daughter, however, will be left quite alone." He drew the brush down in a long, soothing stroke again. "You have lovely hair."

He delivered the compliment as dispassionately as if he were approving of a well-sprung barrel on a yearling heifer from the Jersey Isles.

"You are saying I am selfish."

"Maybe a bit. But more likely, you are self-reliant and protective. And the truth is, nobody thus far has been willing to insist you behave in any fashion other than the one you choose."

"What's wrong with how I behave?" Gwen hated the note of genuine consternation in her voice. The question of a woman who knew herself to be an outsider of necessity and circumstance both, if not an outcast, but wasn't entirely reconciled to it.

"The way you behave is quite acceptable, if you are Miss Hollister and you like being the lord of your cousin's manor. If you are Rose Hollister, however, you might want a few more options—you might want some of the options your mama had when she was a young girl."

He was speaking gently again, reasonably and even kindly, saying things her titled cousins and their wives had likely thought but never bothered to confront her with. Gwen laid her forehead on her knees. "I hate you."

This conversation was possible due only to an abundance of fatigue and a paucity of firelight—that, and Douglas Allen's confounded, infernal, perishing, unflinching straightforwardness.

Or perhaps her own.

"Of course you hate me," Douglas replied, smoothing the brush down her hair. "You need to hate somebody, Guinevere, for taking those options away from you. I will be honored to fulfill the purpose, if needs must, but while you are hating away your life, please don't take those options away from your daughter."

"But, Douglas"—Gwen turned in exasperation—"she is a *bastard*. She will have no decent options unless her cousins settle substantial wealth on her. When I lost those options, I lost them for both of us."

And that was a sorrow and shame without end, for Gwen could easily accept the consequences of her foolish actions for herself, but Rose deserved so much better.

Douglas ran his thumb over the bristles of the brush, the way some men tested the edge of a knife. "Might you be seeing things from a slightly narrow perspective? Were she male, Rose would not inherit any entailed land or titles as a function of her illegitimacy, but I would be surprised if Heathgate, Greymoor, and Fairly have not already made provision for her. You should ask them."

"Hah," Gwen retorted, glowering at the fire. "And if I ask them, and they haven't set anything aside, then do you think I want them embarrassed into settling funds on her? Bad enough I am a poor relation, without making demands for my daughter as well."

At least she was a poor relation who took care of the property she dwelled upon.

"If Rose's relations, all of whom are indecently wealthy, have not made provision for her, then they should. I can understand that you are reluctant to raise the issue. Would you like me to raise it for you?"

He was scolding Heathgate and Greymoor in absentia, scolding them convincingly.

"What? Of course not. They are my family. I'll deal with them." Except, Douglas would charge forth on Rose's behalf, when Gwen had hung back for years, not knowing where to start such a discussion.

"They are my family too, to hear them tell it. I would casually mention it to Fairly, who is deuced canny," he went on, as if discussing a strategy for winning at pell-mell. "He will take it up with his brothers-in-law, and then you will have your answer. You really are too shy, you know."

"I am not shy," Gwen said, a yawn showing her declaration for the formality it was.

"We will consider the matter settled, then. Do you prefer one braid or two?"

Gwen allowed the change of topic with something like gratitude. "One."

"There," Douglas said after several moments of silence. "Off to bed with you."

He flipped a thick, tidy braid over her shoulder and stood, extending a hand to her with perfect courtesy. She put her hand in his and nearly lost her balance as she both turned and rose in the space between the sofa and the low table.

"You are tired," Douglas said, frowning down at her.

He kissed her forehead and stepped back. "Good night, Guinevere, pleasant dreams."

"Good night, and thank you," she said, feeling oddly subdued. "Thank you for braiding my hair," she added by way of clarification.

Pleasant dreams indeed, she thought as she climbed into bed. There really was very little to like about Douglas Allen, even if he did make an excellent lady's maid—and nursemaid.

He never smiled; he never made mistakes; he never faltered in what he perceived as the execution of his duty. He lacked anything approaching charm and went charging into conversational thickets Gwen's family never acknowledged, much less approached.

Finesse was not in his gift. Not to any degree.

Though he was unfailingly kind to Rose, patient, and in his own way, good-humored, even if he didn't smile... And most intriguing of all, Gwen could trust him to brush her hair—simply to brush her hair—when she was so tired and bewildered her eyes were nearly crossing.

Oh, she really, truly could not find much at all to like about him.

❧

Linden was a lovely manor. Purple asters clustered around a fountain in the middle of the drive, and a wide granite terrace fronted the building. The main facade sported eight stately white pillars and twenty-four windows on each of the three fieldstone stories, each accented with white trim and shutters. The whole was brought to a pleasing symmetry centered around a bright red door.

That the place could present well even in a pouring rain reassured Douglas on a level comparable to a schoolboy's first impression of a smiling new tutor.

After seeing Rose settled in the nursery, Douglas appropriated Guinevere's company for a tour of the premises. The rotund little housekeeper—Mrs. Kitts, by name—prattled along through all three floors, attics, cellars, and every space in between, putting Douglas in mind of Rose.

"Well," Mrs. Kitts said after almost two hours of touring the house, "there you have it, your lordship, ma'am. Linden's grand tour. Will there be anything else?"

"When might we expect a call from the steward?" Douglas asked. "I believe Lord Greymoor alerted him to the purpose of our visit."

Mrs. Kitts's smile faltered, the first such lapse Douglas had seen. "Mr. Tanner is away from the property, but we did get his lordship's note and passed it along to Miss Tanner. When shall we serve dinner?"

Guinevere did not appear to have heard the question. She ran her hand over a sideboard, the top of which bore an inlaid floral design that made the heavy piece look considerably more graceful. "Guinevere, what would suit?"

"You skipped luncheon," she said, a slight maternal scold in her tone. "Could we have tea in the small parlor, Mrs. Kitts, then supper for his lordship and myself about eight of the clock?"

"Why, of course, ma'am."

Douglas dismissed the woman with thanks for her time and all the information she'd imparted about the house.

"Rose is fine," he said as they returned to the small dining parlor.

To his surprise—his pleased surprise—Guinevere slipped her arm through his. "How could you tell I was fretting?"

"You left her in the care of a nursery maid you'd

never met before, it has been almost two hours, and you love that child. Hester seemed a good sort though, and as the oldest of a large brood, she'll manage Rose easily." He tucked his hand over hers as they passed the main staircase, the better to prevent a detour to the nursery. "What do you think of the house?"

"You'd be a fool not to buy it if the price is reasonable."

She enjoyed a conviction about her opinions Douglas did not share. "Because I could sell it for a profit?"

"You could do that," she said, preceding him into the parlor and taking a seat on a blue brocade sofa far more plush than the one in her own parlor at Enfield. "You told me once you were looking for a place to put down roots, to call home. This is that place, Douglas. This house is waiting for someone to love it. Please stop frowning at me and be seated."

Rather than accept her invitation—her *direction*—Douglas paced the small confines of the room. "Houses do not await love."

"This house has a lovely little Vermeer hanging in the front stairway, and nobody ever sees it. The curtains are Flemish lace, the rugs Aubusson, the wine cellar stocked with some of the most appealing vintages ever laid down. If these things convey, then this house is waiting to be loved."

"They convey." Though he hadn't noticed half of them, being instead absorbed with an absence of dry rot, mouse droppings, flaking plaster, dust, and cobwebs. "Why do you suppose Greymoor did this?" He waved a hand to encompass the house, its appointments, the effort made to fill it with grace, beauty, and comfort, right down to this elegant little jewel of a parlor, whose blue, cream, and gold appointments set off Guinevere's coloring wonderfully.

"Do you believe, Douglas Allen, you are the only man to whom life has been unkind?"

He considered her question while a substantial tea tray—a silver service, no less—was brought in.

"I've seen Greymoor's other properties," Douglas said when the maid had departed. "Neither Oak Hall nor Enfield is as well-appointed as Linden. The houses are smaller, more manors than country seats, and the grounds not as elegant. Why would he sell his most attractive property?"

Because the simplest hypothesis that answered the question was that Greymoor was taking pity on a poor relation.

Douglas reached for the teapot when Guinevere's voice stopped him. "Shall I pour?"

Damn it. "Please."

She gave him the sort of smile young people directed at their dotty elders. "Douglas, you haven't eaten since breakfast at the last inn. Don't stand on ceremony. I am not yet hungry and will have to join Rose in the nursery before dinner."

"Thank you." Douglas helped himself to a sandwich while Guinevere prepared his tea: strong, three sugars, cream—bless the woman—and piping hot.

"You won't at least join me for a cup of tea?"

"In a minute."

"You want to watch me bolt my grain?" He tore into his sandwich, manners be damned.

"I'm considering how to answer your last question, about why Andrew would sell his most attractive property. I should think it obvious."

"So enlighten me." And God above, she was right: he'd been famished.

"Linden is the only property that isn't entailed, for

one thing," Guinevere said, ticking off on her fingers. "For another, I don't think Andrew was particularly happy here. For a third, his wife has recently given birth to what is likely the first of many children, and this estate is distant to the other two. It being inconvenient to travel with children"—Douglas lifted his teacup in salute to that sentiment—"he would likely have to visit this one on his own, and Andrew is much taken with his spouse."

Much taken—a euphemism for being head over ears to a degree Douglas could only envy.

"You don't mention the one reason I might have brought up first," Douglas said, selecting a second sandwich. Guinevere did pour herself a cup of tea then, adding two sugars and—he was pleased to note—a healthy tot of cream.

"Greymoor can use the money from selling this place to finance the initial expenses of his stud farm," she said, "but one thing that branch of the Alexander family does not need is more money." She poured another cup of tea for Douglas, who perused a lovely plate of cakes while making inroads on his second sandwich. "They aren't going anywhere, Douglas."

"Who isn't?"

"The cakes. You don't have to stare them out of their impulse to leap up and leave the scene. I assure you, the cakes will be there when you finish your sandwich. How was the chicken, by the way?"

Douglas patted his lips with his serviette. "Above reproach."

"Douglas," she said gently, "you just ate two sandwiches of roasted beef."

Four

WHEN GUINEVERE ABANDONED DOUGLAS TO CHECK on Rose, he was left with some time to fill and a backlog of correspondence to address. He took himself off to the library with a final cup of hot, sweet tea, and in his pocket, a pair of smuggled tea cakes.

The big mahogany desk near the window beckoned, the windows affording light and the nearby hearth taking the chill off an otherwise gloomy day. He started with the letter from his mother, though her hand had grown so crabbed and her prose so repetitive, he wondered why he bothered to respond to her carping.

By seven of the clock, Douglas was only halfway through with his correspondence, but he gave up anyway. He was not properly attired for dinner, the tea cakes were but a happy memory, and he was feeling… both peckish and cranky.

Like Rose at the end of a long day.

"How was Miss Rose when you left her?" he asked Guinevere when he presented himself in the family parlor precisely on the hour.

"Fast asleep," Guinevere said. "She did not nap this afternoon, and so was quite worn out after her supper.

Then too, she'd had her bath and could tumble right into bed."

Douglas poured two fingers at the sideboard and held a glass out to Guinevere, images of the lady at her bath flitting through his damned fool, tired brain. "One can consider a tot medicinal, given the damp weather."

"Perhaps half that amount?"

At least she wasn't going to fuss over the consumption of a bit of spirits. "You are content with the arrangements here for Rose's care?" Douglas asked, pouring a second, smaller drink and handing her the glass—crystal, of course, at once luminous and delicate.

"Hester is very patient," Guinevere replied, taking a sip of her drink. "And yet, it's difficult…"

Douglas stood with an elbow propped on the mantel, a safe distance from a pretty, if tired, woman in a pretty, if out-of-date, green velvet dress. How did a lady of lively intellect pass the time when her only companion on a dreary afternoon was a small child?

"You don't want to leave Rose with strangers?"

"Maybe it's that, or maybe I am the one who feels homesick, and I fret over my child to deal with it." She took another sip of brandy, which Douglas took for a small concession to nerves.

Interesting.

"I should note," Douglas said, addressing the drink in his hand, "you look quite nicely put together tonight." Even he, however, knew the dress Guinevere wore, while flattering and elegant, was not in the first stare—or the second. Still, the forest-green color became her, and the style accentuated the curves she'd kept camouflaged in her drab attire heretofore.

Had she worn that dress for him? The notion was both surprising and… pleasing.

"Thank you, my lord."

He'd wanted to set her at ease with his compliment, and based on her expression, had failed. Abruptly, Douglas wished he had a fraction of the charm her wealthy cousins could exude, a fraction of their experience with the ladies.

"Shall we take ourselves in to dinner, or would you like to linger here?"

She accepted his proffered arm without protest, gods be thanked. "I am hungry. You must be as well."

He was nigh ravenous, which seemed to occur more often in her company.

"I suggest we spend tomorrow getting acquainted with the estate books," Douglas said as he seated her at the small dining table. "Greymoor ordered them readied for our inspection, and the ground will need a day or two to dry before we can safely ride across country."

In truth, Guinevere would want to stick close to the nursery for a day or two, though Douglas kept that notion to himself. Over the soup course, he instead invited her to list the aspects of the external estate she'd be most interested in assessing. Her list was exhaustive and would keep them in the saddle for days.

"You are not simply self-reliant as a function of your status as mother and land steward, are you?" Douglas asked as he refilled their wineglasses. Guinevere had been right about the cellars, and the kitchen was apparently attempting to make a good impression.

As was he, curiously enough.

The *chicken* had been excellent, as had the *ham*. The golden highlights Guinevere's hair caught from the dinner candles and firelight were also most appealing.

"I was my parents' only child, as Rose will be my only child," Guinevere reflected. "My father never enjoyed robust health, and my mother died when I was little. We were not well situated, Father having disdained to remain at Enfield and take over the reins from Grandpapa. My earliest memories are of reminding my father it was time for supper."

Did she also have memories of reminding of him of what he'd recently eaten? "Was there adequate provision for that meal?" Douglas asked, knowing he could be considered rude for doing so.

"There was—as soon as I learned to cook and to manage the stipend Grandpapa sent."

A briskness in her tone suggested the time had arrived to change the subject. "How old were you when you came to Enfield?" He ought to be offering her more wine or a bite of pear, except he wanted to take advantage of her willingness to answer questions.

"Eleven or so."

A girl of eleven might help her mother in the kitchen, or begin to prepare simple dishes with supervision. In a household with any means, she did not cook whole meals on her own or manage budgets.

"You look displeased," Guinevere remarked as she cut into a pale, succulent pear.

"I expect I frequently look displeased to you. Usually, I am merely thinking." In this case, about a young girl who'd had an aunt and grandparents, at least, in a position to take her father in hand, and who had neglected to do so.

"While you think, perhaps you can tell me how it is a second son was not educated to take over the entailed estate in case tragedy struck the heir."

Turnabout was fair play, and to be expected with a worthy opponent.

"I have wondered the same thing," Douglas admitted,

spearing a small, juicy bite of pear. "My grandfather might have had that education but neglected to pass on to his son anything other than the ability to regularly ignore the dutiful reports of an overworked steward. My dear brother Herbert lived for his hounds and horses. He never stood a chance of putting the estate to rights."

"Was he dear?"

Douglas split the remainder of his pear with one audible slice of the knife. "Why would you question my regard for my brother?" Though how highly could Douglas regard a brother who'd taken better care of his hounds than his wife or his inheritance? And poor Henry, the youngest of the three Allen brothers, had made Herbert seem a saint in comparison.

"I have no siblings," Guinevere remarked.

Douglas cut each half into quarters, and each quarter into three small bites, noting that the hue of Guinevere's décolletage was as pale as the fruit—an observation more interesting than the topic of siblings. "Go on."

"The idea of having a brother or a sister... Well, to my mind, it would be lovely. I surmise it doesn't always work out that way."

He considered a lone bite of sweet, delectable fruit. "You surmise correctly. A question for you, however. Why do you insist Rose will be an only child?"

"You listen too carefully," she muttered, to which Douglas made no reply rather than observe that she'd become too careful in *many* regards. She tilted her wine-glass, peering at the dregs. "I will not put myself in a circumstance where I could make the same mistake twice."

Miss Hollister was *certain* of this opinion too.

"And would it be a mistake to fall in love and allow some decent fellow the chance to take away your loneliness?" That Guinevere Hollister would punish herself indefinitely for a lapse committed years ago, when she'd had no mother to guide her and none to avenge the wrong done her, rankled.

Rankled exceedingly.

She set her glass down rather forcefully. "You did not ask that question in a purposeful attempt to hurt me, my lord, but you will see upon reflection it is either a stupid question or a thoughtless one. If by 'take away my loneliness,' you mean marry me, then firstly, you already know that is a sensitive topic with me, and secondly, marriage is *not* a guaranteed antidote to loneliness. Thirdly, a decent fellow would not pursue me for decent ends, and the indecent ends remaining are not, I can assure you, aimed at assuaging loneliness either."

A veritable rant from Miss Hollister—complete with a *my lord*—and what she'd admitted by omission was as troubling as the declarations her speech contained.

As troubling as the hurt she tried to keep from her eyes.

"My apologies, Miss Hollister. I meant only to inquire of the possibility, should a man with an honorable suit appear, that you might allow yourself to take the opportunity he presented." Such a fellow would be a lucky man, assuming he could win the lady's trust.

"Douglas, I will say this once: I have no interest in marriage. Nothing, *nothing* about the wedded state could appeal to me as much as having my independence and my daughter to myself. Despite the fact that I am a mere poor relation, I have no need to marry and no desire to marry, and we will not discuss this again."

Douglas set a bite of pear on her plate, feeling a sense of the lady protesting too much. He ought to desist, but her convictions bothered him—and made him sad for her. "So under no circumstances would you consider providing a step-papa for Rose or a spouse for yourself?"

"The question is moot. But what of you, your lordship? Why not assuage your loneliness within the bonds of matrimony?"

"Brilliant, Miss Hollister." Douglas nodded in congratulation, though he well deserved her riposte. "Except I do not recall admitting to any loneliness." In her company, no admission was necessary. That they shared something even as bleak as loneliness gave Douglas a peculiar sense of connection to the lady. "Now, if I promise to drop this subject, will you join me in the library for a final nip of brandy?"

While he held her chair and escorted her from the table, Douglas wondered: As eminently suited as she was to motherhood, as ferociously as she loved her daughter, as lonely as she must be, what had befallen Guinevere Hollister that she would shut herself away from the prospect of a respectable union and more children to love, even when presented as a mere theoretical possibility?

❧

Douglas Allen's mood was not hard to read; it was *impossible* to read unless the man himself wished to reveal it.

"I will join you for a small tot." Gwen let him hold her chair, let him hold the door. When he'd winged his arm at her, she had taken it. Her acquiescence had to be a measure of her fatigue, because on the strength of one shared meal and a short journey, Gwen could not be enjoying his company—could she?

"Guinevere." Douglas lowered his voice and leaned close enough that Gwen could catch his brisk, spicy scent as they paused outside the library. "Sometimes a simple 'Shut up, Douglas' will serve when my questions become bothersome. *In extremis*, 'Go to hell, Amery' will save us both some time and embarrassment."

She ducked her head lest he see her smile. Her best guess was that this was his version of teasing or apology, though one could not be certain. Not with Lord Amery. They got through their nightcap without Gwen having to resort to Douglas's suggested strategems, though she itched to make him admit that he was, indeed, lonely.

That he was lonely, too.

"You are asleep on your feet, madam, and there is nothing more we need discuss tonight. May I light you up to your room?"

"Please." Before she broached topics a well rested, more prudent woman would know better than to explore. She set her empty glass on the sideboard. "The thought of laying my head on a soft pillow is irresistible— even a lumpy pillow, for that matter."

Douglas lit a single tall candle and held the door for her. This time, she was grateful for his arm. She was that tired, also a bit disoriented from taking spirits both before and after her supper.

An earlier stray thought about being a poor relation assailed her, along with a startlingly profound bout of homesickness. Coupled with that, she was able, however dimly, to see the years not so far ahead, when Rose would be grown and gone. A twenty-five-year-old woman might spend her day roaming all over an estate, managing this and inspecting that, but what of a forty-year-old woman? A fifty-year-old woman?

When, if ever, could she allow her vigilance to lapse, her penance to end? Desolation welled up, bringing Gwen to a familiar moment of self-doubt. Her life managing Enfield while she raised her daughter worked for now, and she was grateful for it.

But Douglas was right: She needed in the years to

come to find other options for Rose, if at all possible, and then where would that leave her?

"You grow suspiciously quiet," Douglas said, pausing outside her room. He opened the door, and because her candles had not been lit, preceded her inside.

"I am merely tired." So tired, and on so many levels. Gwen suspected Douglas would understand that—if she could tell him—because he was weary too.

He lit a sconce on either side of Gwen's bed and a branch of candles on her mantel, then set his light down and came to stand before her just inside the door. He closed the door, likely to shut out the draft from the hall, and regarded Gwen with a frown—a thoughtful frown, perhaps even a concerned frown.

He should not have closed that door, because the resulting privacy tempted Gwen to wonder when Douglas had last been private with a lady in her bedroom.

"Shall I ring for a maid?"

"I'll manage well enough," Gwen said, not moving.

"Will you?"

She nodded once. Of all times to disregard propriety, his frowning lordship chose now, when Gwen wanted to indulge in a much-deserved, completely useless fit of the weeps. She was tired, far from home, and just a bit tipsy.

That business he had raised earlier, about marrying some decent man, was to blame for her misery. For the most part, she accepted that she'd made the poorest of decisions regarding marriage, but sometimes…

"Guinevere?" Douglas's faint frown had shifted toward puzzlement.

Gwen was mortified beyond endurance when a tear slipped down her cheek.

His lordship lacked the sense to flee. Instead, Douglas put a hand on each of Gwen's shoulders. Gently, he drew her one step closer and took one step closer himself. His arms came around her, and Gwen found, to her guilty pleasure, their heights matched such that she could rest her head on his shoulder.

His hands slipped around her back, and he held her against the warmth and strength of his body. On a sigh, Gwen leaned into him more heavily. The lump in her throat eased, and she closed her eyes and let herself have this moment of... comfort.

"Forgive me," Gwen murmured against his shoulder, inhaling a steadying breath before she organized herself to regain her balance.

"Hush." Douglas brought his hand up along her back and pressed her gently closer when she would have moved away. She allowed it. For long, stolen moments, she allowed him to simply hold her.

She'd known the pleasure of a man's embrace, also the folly and danger to be found there, but never had she felt this sense of sheltering and consolation. Before she began babbling or fell asleep in Douglas's arms, Gwen drew back, and this time, he let her go.

"You are tired," he said, picking up his candle before Gwen could offer some trivializing inanity. "It is late, and I will see you in the morning. I appreciate your making this journey, and I wish you good night."

Without touching her anywhere else, he kissed her cheek, lingeringly, as if asking a question or making sure she grasped the answer to one, then left her in the chilly shadows of her bedroom.

❧

Strong spirits consumed in quantity might dampen a man's ability to act on his desires, but Douglas doubted the entire Linden cellar held enough brandy to erase from his mind the feel of Guinevere Hollister, tired, pliant, and so, so female in his arms.

An hour after Douglas had bid her good night, he lay on his bed, letting her haunt his body and his imagination. She had been in want of a simple embrace, and he had been able to provide that without making advances toward her. Now, recalling her lithe curves and the floral fragrance of her hair, he wondered where his resolve had come from. She was a lush, lovely armful and clearly in want of a man's touch.

Though she was in want of respect more. To have attempted liberties with her tonight would have been… ungallant. Not only bad timing, but also bad form.

Still, a part of Douglas, a wicked, long-dormant, lusty-young-male part of him wondered if he might have seduced her—if even *he* could have persuaded her to allow him intimacies. He would have used her fatigue, her loneliness, and her long sexual deprivation to patiently lure her into his bed, and then…

She was a woman who would appreciate patience, in bed and elsewhere. The images aroused by that realization had Douglas closing his hand around his already erect cock as he lay alone amid his covers, and bringing himself to a languorous and gratifyingly intense orgasm.

Guinevere Hollister was not amenable to even discussing marriage, which preserved Douglas from all manner of interesting conundrums, though it also puzzled him. He had no interest in an emotional entanglement, and the begetting of an heir wasn't something he would take on in the near term.

But of all women, he found himself attracted to Miss Guinevere Hollister, and he suspected if he were respectful and careful and did not presume on her privacy, Guinevere Hollister might allow herself to desire him in return.

Though only for the duration of a brief, mutually satisfactory affair.

On that intriguing thought, he drifted off, only to dream more of the same lovely, arousing, intriguing thoughts.

✎

"Why is Amery writing to *you*?" Andrew Alexander, Earl of Greymoor, asked as David Worthington, Viscount Fairly, passed him a single sheet of paper.

"Read the postscript," David said, switching Greymoor's infant stepdaughter Lucy to his other shoulder.

"My, my, my…" Greymoor murmured as he read. He folded the letter and tapped the crease against his lips in time with the rhythm of the chair in which he rocked. "Our Gwennie has bestirred dear Douglas's protective instincts—at the least."

"My reaction precisely, but the woman is your cousin, while neither Gwen nor Rose is related to me by blood. I thought I had best alert you before I take my curious little self down to Sussex."

Greymoor's blue-eyed expression was thoughtful as David slowly paced the room with the sleeping baby. "Are you sure you want to interrupt them? I continue to believe Gwen can take care of herself."

"Just as you believe she can take care of Rose, Greymoor?"

"For your rubbishing information—and Amery's too," his lordship retorted, "we established a trust for Rose before I married your sister. Heathgate and I contribute to it regularly in equal amounts. You are welcome to go shares with us, but I have not found the proper circumstance to inform Gwen of its existence."

"Coward." David cuddled his niece closer and tried not to feel jealous of her step-papa, who was permitting

David the indulgence of putting the child to bed. "Get me the details, and I'll be happy to contribute. As for the rest of Douglas's Epistle to the Philistines, I thought your mother was supposed to chaperone this expedition to Sussex."

"So did I," Greymoor said on a frown. "Do you suppose that's the point of Douglas's letter, to let us know Gwen is without a chaperone?"

"That is exactly the kind of self-defeating thing he would do," David said, nuzzling the wee bundle on his shoulder. "Alerting us to the situation with Rose seems to be the more apparent agenda. What a prince old Douglas is."

Greymoor let his chair come to rest. "Douglas is an odd duck. You like him?"

"I don't know him well enough to really say. I think I would like him, were he to allow it. I can admit to respecting him." And to worrying about him. Any man who'd buried two brothers in the space of a year deserved some worry—a lot of worry.

"I can admit to respecting him as well, as can Heathgate." Greymoor's dark brows drew down on this uncomfortable admission. "We're half hoping Amery and Gwennie take a liking to each other. They're both… a bit lost. The ladies endorsed this scheme wholeheartedly."

David suspected his sisters had, in fact, come up with the idea, and deftly allowed the menfolk to think the notion their own.

He pressed a kiss to the baby's downy crown. "Amery is so damned alone, he provokes one to protectiveness. His mother is said to be enjoying a permanent if dramatic decline out in Kent, and his late brothers were a pair of useless, barely decorative ciphers. How they both managed to come to grief by virtue of misuse of firearms is a damned unfortunate mystery. I admit myself pleased that you, Heathgate, and my sisters have taken him in hand. He has no people left worth having, and I know how that feels."

Greymoor slouched lower in his chair and propped his chin on his fist. "But your sisters married brilliantly, so Heathgate and I can now keep you from the worst of your follies."

David ignored that small, familial jab, bloody true though it was. Why did babies always smell so good— except when they didn't? "This prevention of folly works in both directions, Greymoor."

"So you're off to Sussex to look after Douglas? He won't appreciate it."

More to the point, Douglas wouldn't *recognize* care-taking, though perhaps Gwen Hollister might introduce him to the concept. "I'll look after Douglas, Gwen, and Rose. I shall be an honorary relative to all and sundry. And I must say, Greymoor, my dear little niece seems to be thriving. I do think she'll keep the fair good looks she no doubt inherited from her uncle David."

David gave the child's fuzzy head one more nuzzle, put the baby back in her crib, and turned to Greymoor, who watched him silently from the rocking chair.

Which had the unusual result of provoking David to a spate of quiet babbling. "You might at least wish me safe journey, tell me my sister will miss me, or offer some familial sentiment to keep me warm as I slough through the autumn downpours."

"I might, but instead I'll warn you to keep your hands off my cousin," Greymoor said, getting to his feet. "Gwen has been unwilling or unable to journey from Enfield for years, and she doesn't need you meddling with her newfound courage. Do not tempt Douglas to reckless imbibing, and don't you dare risk your horse trying to make time on the muddy roads."

As familial sentiments went, that would have to do. David blew a kiss to the sleeping baby and preceded his host out of the nursery.

❦

"Rose seems to be settling in nicely," Douglas remarked as Gwen's daughter went shrieking past them down the banister.

Rather than reply to that helpful observation, Gwen stomped down the stairs, just as another little girl went hurtling past on the banister, landing on a giggling Rose at the bottom of the steps. Two more little girls joined the tangle of arms, legs, and laughter, leaving a horrified Hester at the top of the stairs.

"Oh, dear me," Hester muttered, bustling down the steps past his lordship. "Oh, dear goodness... ma'am, milord, I am so sorry. You girls!" Douglas stood silently by as Gwen took turns with Hester, scolding and fussing over the four little girls who had found such hilarity in disobedience.

"But, Mama," Rose protested, "you never said we couldn't slide down the banister."

Douglas sauntered down the steps, hands in his pockets, and drat the man if his expression didn't reflect curiosity as to how the ever-competent Miss Hollister—his latest sobriquet for her—would handle this situation.

"I am telling you now." She was nearly bellowing it, in fact.

"And I," Hester added, shaking a finger at her younger sisters, "have told you and told you not to slide down the banister at the rectory."

"But this isn't the rectory," one of the twins pointed out.

"Barristers, the lot of them," Douglas muttered loudly enough for Gwen to hear. He sank onto the bottom step rather than take his observant self elsewhere. "As I recall, sliding down forbidden banisters is thirsty work, though it does leave such a nice polish on the wood. Of course, once one knows a banister is not for sliding upon, one would never, *ever* again make the same mistake, would one?"

"No, Cousin Douglas," Rose said, sneaking a measuring glance at Gwen.

"Miss Hester," Douglas said, "if you take the miscreants off to the kitchen for some cider, I'm sure they'll be much better behaved in future."

And off they went, a band of small female rogues beaming smiles over their shoulders—at Douglas.

Gwen sat on the step beside him as the girls departed, drew her knees up, and dropped her forehead in defeat. "Sometimes, the hardest thing about being a parent is not laughing."

Douglas slipped an arm around her and squeezed her shoulders. "If you say so, though from what I hear, motherhood doesn't exactly start with a walk in the park."

"No. That would be fatherhood."

"Temper," Douglas remonstrated. "Having quelled the native insurrection, shall we get back to those inventories?"

Drat the blasted inventories, the natives, and the humor in Douglas's blue eyes.

Gwen nodded, but made no move to return to the library. After several days inspecting Linden on horseback, she was confident the estate had much to recommend it. The stables were nothing short of lovely, and the other outbuildings in good repair.

But problems lurked, as well. The home farm was small, the home wood, by contrast, large and overgrown. Little of the land was under cultivation, most of it having been overgrazed by the ubiquitous sheep. Fencing was an issue, as was irrigation. Both were expensive and necessary, as Gwen had gently indicated to Douglas.

Douglas huffed out a sigh and lifted his arm from Gwen's shoulders. "I am usually good at following figures through a transaction, but with the accounts we've seen, I am flummoxed, for there's no telling if this estate is profitable or not." He rose from their step and held out a hand to assist Gwen to her feet.

She did not glare at his hand, did not drop his fingers as if they were unclean, and did not sniff her grudging thanks—wasn't even tempted to, come to that. She let him haul her upright and tuck her hand over his arm.

When and how had his civilities become charming? When had they become endearing? For she would miss them when she was back at Enfield, riding acres that did not belong to her, keeping a house she would never own.

"Linden *is* profitable, Douglas," she assured him as they moved into the library. "These books do not show any large disbursements to Greymoor's accounts. The money is here somewhere, we just have to find it." And she badly wanted to find it for him.

"Perhaps. Or perhaps we have to admit the books are rotten, the land is tired, the house an expensive little jewel I do not deserve, give up, and go back to Town."

He settled beside her on the sofa, and Gwen thought, not for the first time, she was coming to be at ease with, even to like his proximity.

Not simply like his probity and mannerliness, but to like *him*.

"Guinevere?" Douglas regarded her, his expression puzzled. "Where in the world did you get off to?"

She'd drifted, caught up in the memory of Douglas grabbing her bare hand when they'd shared lunch the first day she'd met him; of him holding her, tired and weepy, in the bedroom upstairs; tucking her hand around his forearm as they went in to dinner; and gently interrogating her while deftly dodging her own queries.

Douglas had asked her something, but Gwen was distracted by an abrupt physical awareness of him, sitting so close their thighs touched. So close she could catch a whiff of sage and cedar over the scent of the wood fire in the hearth. "You were saying?"

"Nothing of any moment, apparently." He sat back and stretched his arm along the back of the sofa.

Which left Gwen with a dilemma. If she sat back too, his arm would be almost around her shoulders, but she couldn't exactly hunch away from Douglas or stand up without appearing rude.

Nor did she want to.

"You are still shy of me." Douglas was not happy about this, but Douglas-fashion, he was not angry, either.

Gwen smoothed a hand over the blue brocade of the sofa, a lighter blue than Douglas's eyes. She *was* shy of him. Also… curious. "Shy is an improvement over unnecessarily anxious."

"It is at that."

Douglas's hands settled on Gwen's shoulders, tugging her back against him. She resisted mostly for form's sake, but allowed herself to be tucked against his side, his arm coming around her. This was not so very different from a tired embrace at the end of the day, a chaste kiss to the forehead or the cheek.

"So tell me, Guinevere, what your impressions are of intimate relations between a man and a woman."

Her heart sped up, and her stomach felt as if it were taken over by a flock of hummingbirds. Even so, were she to bolt off the couch in horror, panic, or sheer surprise, Gwen knew Douglas would escort her in to dinner that night with the same manners he'd shown her for the past week. All he'd done was put an arm around her and ask her a question. A simple, direct question.

And she was not horrified. Not horrified at all— though she should be. Horrified and mindful of all the risks that had lurked as close as London since the day Rose had been born.

"In truth, I have few impressions of those relations you allude to. My experience was the minimum needed to result in… Rose." Also in years of rustication, in shame and ruin.

Douglas drew a pattern on her arm with his elegant fingers, and the quality of his touch warned Gwen his intent was not strictly to comfort or to offer mere affection. The hummingbirds flew upward, creating havoc in her lungs.

"Should I be sad for your sake," Douglas mused, "because you have paid such a high price for so little pleasure?"

"For no pleasure whatsoever." Not even the pleasure of a soft, sweet caress on her arm or a good-night kiss to her cheek. Not the pleasure of arguing over the best use of a fallow field, or the pleasure of a quiet, shared meal at the end of the day.

"No pleasure *whatsoever*? Now that is unfortunate." Douglas's voice took on an edge. "Were you at least willing?"

"At first," Gwen said, closing her eyes. He was doing it again, pulling confidences and confessions from her without her intending to part with them—and without her objection.

"But then it hurt," Douglas surmised, "and your lover would neither stop nor discipline himself to see to your comfort, much less your pleasure."

Gwen did not move, despite the havoc Douglas's quiet conclusion wreaked with her composure. In six years, not one person had raised with her the topic of that bewildering encounter, not one person had intimated that Gwen might have been ill-used. "He stopped eventually."

"And a few weeks later you realized you had lost more than your virginity and your innocence."

The edge in his voice was at odds with the gentle stroking of his hand along her back, neck, and shoulders. Gwen did not want to contaminate that welling, stealthy pleasure with more words, and certainly not with more old memories.

"I lost my ignorance." But she'd lost those other things he'd named too, and they had been precious.

"I would like to discuss a transaction with you, Guinevere, but if you find the topic distasteful, we will drop it and forget I ever mentioned it."

So beguiling were his caresses, Gwen had to concentrate to grasp the meaning of his words: he wanted to talk business.

"I'm listening." To his hand, to the warmth of him beside her, to his lovely, woodsy scent. To the soft roar of the fire and the ticking of the clock.

And to hummingbirds, soaring about inside her in anticipation of what, she dared not guess.

"You have mentioned that on occasion you will consign goods or products into the keeping of a trusted merchant. You handle wool this way and firewood. If your bailiff cannot find custom willing to pay the price you set, your goods are returned essentially undiminished, and you're free to offer them elsewhere."

"I insist on a contract when dealing on consignment," Gwen managed. She picked up a small green brocade pillow and traced its fleur-de-lis pattern, lest she yield to the desire to apply her hands to Douglas's person.

"I seek a sort of contract with you," Douglas said. "A consignment of nonperishable goods, on a temporary basis, for your inspection and possible use."

His fingers on her neck were exquisitely pleasurable, warm, sweet, and unhurried. Douglas was never in a hurry, and yet Gwen had failed to appreciate that a measured, deliberate approach to life's pleasures might have intimate appeal.

"Can't this consignment wait until our task here at Linden is done, Douglas? I'm sure Greymoor or Fairly would be happy to entertain commercial negotiations with you."

His finger traced the curve of her ear, and Gwen shivered.

"That will not do. The goods I have to offer would have no appeal to your relations. I hope they have unique appeal to you."

She should pull away. She should ring for the blasted tea tray. She should… keep her eyes open. "Douglas, *what* are you doing?"

"Indulging myself, which is part of the bargain I envisage, but by no means all. And the door is locked, Guinevere. Mrs. Kitts is off at market, and it's half day for the footmen. We will not be disturbed."

Douglas and his details. He rubbed her earlobe between his thumb and forefinger, slowly, which was not a detail when Gwen had never experienced that particular sensation before.

She rose off the sofa on shaky knees, the hummingbirds having migrated to her limbs and even her earlobes. She moved a quartet of candle holders on the mantel so they were evenly spaced. "What goods are we discussing, Douglas?"

He stood as well and prowled toward her, but she did not turn. The heat of the fire was before her, and Douglas stood immediately behind her.

"*I* am the goods in question. Myself, Guinevere. I offer myself into your temporary keeping."

Gwen had to brace herself with a hand on the mantel as Douglas's breath fanned over her neck. "You offer *yourself* on consignment?"

His lips touched that vulnerable place where her shoulder and throat met, the softest, most tender caress Gwen had endured in her entire life. When his arms slipped around her waist, she was grateful for the support.

"I offer my body for your delectation and pleasure," Douglas said. "I have something more to offer you as well, Guinevere Hollister."

Two thoughts collided in Gwen's brain, the first being that she should stop him *soon*. He was presuming, and his civilities had shifted to improper advances, and those… they led to places Gwen ought not to be so interested in. Places she had not admitted to herself she might go with this man.

With *any* man, ever again.

The second thought was pernicious and wicked—also irresistible. Douglas would be a thorough, considerate, even lavish lover. He would attend to every detail, spare no effort, his discretion would be faultless, and his hands—

"What else do you offer, Douglas, that I haven't been offered a hundred times before?"

The question she'd intended as starchy came out

woebegone. His embrace became more snug, though surely Gwen imagined its protective quality.

"Firstly, you know I would marry you, were you to conceive my child."

She did know it, but that mattered not at all, for she would never marry him. "Marriage is no inducement to me and never will be."

"Secondly…" He paused and nuzzled her hair. She hadn't known grown men suffered the urge or had the ability to nuzzle. "I would never, ever cause you discomfort or awkwardness, Guinevere. Copulation is supposed to be pleasurable for both parties, and I would do my utmost to share that pleasure with you."

Douglas Allen's *utmost* was tempting argument in itself.

"How often do you suppose a man has said words like that to me? Many men, for that matter, because they all seem to think I want to hear them."

"But this man," Douglas said, widening his stance, "is promising you pleasure and something else, Guinevere."

Douglas's promises were trustworthy. Even regarding this unexpected, dangerous, alluring topic—especially regarding this topic—his promises would be trustworthy. "What else do you offer?"

The part of her lost to caution wanted him to touch her breasts—ached for it, and yet Gwen knew Douglas would not presume that far without her permission.

"I would promise you *control*," Douglas said, his voice dropping to a purr. "When we couple, if we couple, it will be on your terms or not at all."

His promise was dazzling, the secret wish Gwen did not voice even to herself: to have an intimate companion, somebody who knew her but did not ask her to sacrifice what remained of her reputation, her freedom, her privacy. Somebody she could spend time with far from the prying eyes of family and Polite Society—somebody *safe*.

She brought his hand up to cover her breast. "And if I do not find the goods to my standards?"

"You decline their further keeping." His voice had gone from purring to growling, and against her backside, Gwen felt the unmistakable tumescence of male arousal. His fingers closed softly over her breast. "What say you, Guinevere?"

She said prayers—for her sanity, for her reason, because the feel of his hand, gentle, exquisitely knowledgeable, and warm on her breast created havoc with her every faculty.

"You will think ill of me if I embark on this… consignment with you."

His hand went still then shifted to rest over her heart. "My dear Guinevere, I think ill of the man who used you so poorly and took so much without giving anything in return. I want to take from you, too, make no mistake, but I want to *give* as well."

Between the fire before her and the man holding her, Gwen was warm, but when she gazed at the dreary autumn landscape beyond the windows, she recalled that bleak sense of looking down the years, down the decades, with nothing but more coping, more duty, and more maternal devotion to sustain her.

She had crafted an existence that avoided pain and indignity, avoided any chance of encountering those who might disrupt her peace or threaten Rose's well-being, but her life also avoided pleasure, intimacy of any variety, and even companionship.

Five years ago, when scandal had hung close at hand and heartbreak even closer, those choices had been understandable, but now, when she considered the idea of Douglas Allen *giving himself* to her, the hummingbirds went into a frenzy.

"I don't know if I am capable of enjoying intimacies the way you describe, Douglas. I was told—"

He turned her by the shoulders, which allowed her to rest her head on his shoulder and hold onto him.

"—I was emphatically assured I was not suited to intimate relations."

"And I was told I couldn't sit a horse for anything."

"You ride beautifully."

"I ride well enough to enjoy it," Douglas replied, stroking a hand over her hair, "because I practiced on the equine version of a schoolmaster until I was competent."

"And you're a schoolmaster?" Though in some regards, that term suited him perfectly.

He traced his nose along her eyebrow, the gesture affectionate, approving even, and not characteristic of any schoolmaster in Gwen's acquaintance. "By no means am I expert at bedsport, though I am proficient enough that you'll have pleasure from me. A woman is entitled to that, Guinevere. Shall I show you some pleasure?"

Five

GUINEVERE WAS IN HIS ARMS AND MORE THAN TOLER-
ating his advances, and yet, Douglas knew the battle
against her nerves, her fundamental propriety, and even
her shyness was not yet won. Five years ago, even a year
ago, he would never have importuned a decent woman
like this, but he'd learned that life could upend the best
plans, and opportunities to discreetly, respectfully share
pleasure were fleeting and few.

Which point would not be made with lectures
and homilies.

He kissed Guinevere's cheek, a warning shot, another
chance for her to step back, hustle away to the nursery,
or find some damned correspondence she needed to tend
to. She leaned into him, and he resisted the urge to lay
her down on the nearby sofa.

"I'd very much like you to kiss me, Guinevere."

My, how articulate he sounded. His voice did not
betray the riot going on behind his falls or the way his
heart thumped hard against his ribs.

"I thought the fellow did the kissing."

Argument, of course. He was coming to relish it
from her. "When the fellow has handed the lady the

reins, she decides the pace and direction taken on the outing."

Guinevere did not have to go up on her toes to kiss him, but she had to look up. Her green eyes were wary, which was wise of her, given the tenuousness of Douglas's control. Watching him, she brushed her lips to his cheek.

Douglas closed his eyes and waited, waited for that soft, delicate press of her mouth to wander to his lips, waited for the clamoring of his cock to subside enough that he could wallow in the pleasure of Guinevere kissing him.

The impact came gently, hesitantly, devastatingly, then came again, and Douglas could not prevent himself from gathering her closer. "Again, please. Kiss me again."

Please kiss me forever.

Guinevere did not kiss like a woman starved for the familiar pleasure of carnal attention. She kissed like a woman who had no experience with the way two mouths might pleasure and torment each other. She kissed hesitantly, as if… *she feared getting it wrong.*

Tenderness crested up and over Douglas's arousal, and chagrin with it, because he'd taken the situation amiss. Guinevere did not want a man who'd permit her to manage their intimate dealings, but rather, she sought a man to whom she could entrust the considerable remainder of her innocence.

"Take your time, sweetheart," Douglas whispered. "Take all the time you need."

Gradually, the kiss became a mutual endeavor, though easing it onto that footing took eternities of patience from Douglas, and very likely wagonloads of courage from Guinevere. When Douglas was nigh to spending in his breeches, she traced her tongue over his lips then paused, as if analyzing his taste.

"Do that again, love. I like it. I like it a lot."

She fused her mouth to his on a quiet moan, and such kissing ensued as Douglas had never thought to experience in the mortal realm. Guinevere shy but determined was a force of nature; Guinevere giving vent to her curiosity was equal parts trial and triumph. Douglas cupped her derriere for dear life, and she—lovely woman—pressed herself tightly into his embrace.

Until she broke away, panting, and took a step back. She bumped the mantel, her expression dazed as she angled away half a pace. "I must think."

The wrong words, the absolute wrong words. "I *cannot* think."

She looked surprised at his admission, then pleased. "You are overwrought?"

"Give me your hand."

The surprise turned a bit wary. "Why?"

"I adore your independent nature, Guinevere, but please give me your hand."

She stretched out a hand, and Douglas made a note to list for her all the things he adored about her, for there was a list—a growing list. He brought her palm to his falls, behind which something else had grown considerably too.

"I will not importune you for favors you are unwilling to grant, I will stop when you ask it of me, and I will not cause you pain." He said these words with their joined hands pressed over his arousal.

Guinevere withdrew her hand slowly. "The Romans swore oaths like this—hand over the testes, or so I once read. I wasn't sure whether to believe it." Her tone said she wasn't sure whether to believe *him*. "One becomes… overwrought."

Her mind was a wonderful place; her hand over his

erect cock was wonderful too. "I am not overwrought, my lady, I am aroused." He did not descend into cliché, but the term "on fire" came to mind. "I desire you intensely, and hope I can provoke a reciprocal interest on your part." Hoped it desperately.

She moved away from the fire, back toward the bookshelves. "So this is to be a mutual consignment, your passion traded for my own?"

"Passion, companionship, affection, all that those imply."

A gong sounded from the direction of the kitchen. Gwen stopped examining the spines of a lot of useless old books, while Douglas wondered if he had time for further exhibitions of his passions before lunch.

"I must see to Rose. She's to join us at table."

Douglas held his ground as Gwen made for the door. Her skirts brushed his breeches, so closely did she come to him, and yet, he did not importune her for favors she was reluctant to give.

Reluctant being worlds and universes away from unwilling.

❧

"What do you mean, she isn't coming?" Guinevere looked more than a little disconcerted, and when she put the question to Douglas, her tone was abrupt.

"Lady Heathgate has come down with a bout of influenza," Douglas replied, handing Guinevere the letter. "She says it's making the rounds in Town, and travel would be unwise until the epidemic has run its course."

Guinevere paced the library, the same room where yesterday afternoon they'd begun the pleasurable business of becoming lovers. Since then, the lady had avoided him. She'd absorbed herself with attending Rose at lunch, taken a tray in the nursery at supper and breakfast, and hidden in her room until Douglas had found her this morning in the library.

"Her ladyship's absence upsets you."

"Of course it upsets me," Guinevere countered, whirling on him. "Is my reputation not deserving of protection?"

Ah, treacherous waters indeed. "Your reputation is apparently less fragile than Lady Heathgate's health, at least in her opinion."

"But, Douglas…"

He leaned his hips against the front of the desk and crossed his arms over his chest. "Yes, Guinevere?"

"Don't call me that."

He made a mental note, probably irrelevant given her present mood: no post-coital naps for him, should he and *Miss Hollister* become lovers. The lady was inclined toward intense self-doubt when left to her own devices. "Do I take it you have had second thoughts about the suggestion I made to you yesterday?"

"You made a proposition, not a suggestion."

He didn't dignify that with a reply, but as she prowled around the library, Guinevere did not look… well rested. Her bun was a bit untidy, her cheeks were flushed, and lines of fatigue bracketed her mouth.

"I will not quibble with you over vocabulary, Guinevere. If you are not interested, you have only to say so. If you are troubled by something specific, I am available for discussion." And at the conclusion of said discussion, he would chop half a cord of wood, dig a mile-long irrigation ditch in the cold, hard ground, and use a dull saw to prune every tree in the orchard.

She paused, facing him several paces away. "You," she said peevishly. "You have me agitated, as you are well aware."

"So I can divine the thoughts of others now?" He

knew better than to take that tone with any woman, much less a woman he was attempting—more or less—to seduce. Even so, disappointment made him willing to give her the rousing donnybrook she was spoiling for.

"Douglas," she said, her tone moderating to include a bit of dismay, "I can't... how can I face you? How can you face me, knowing that I've touched... that you've... I can't do this."

Her shoulders slumped, and she mimicked his body language, crossing her arms.

"I have not the disposition," she said softly, "for intimate, frivolous pleasures. To indicate to you otherwise was misleading of me, and I apologize."

That pronouncement seemed to settle her down a bit, but when Douglas took two steps to close the distance between them, her eyes filled with anxiety. "What are you doing?"

"Winning an argument," Douglas replied, dipping his head and grazing his lips along the line of her jaw.

"Douglas," she began sternly, "didn't you hear what I just said? I've misled you, I'm not suited to this, and..."

She nattered on a bit more, while he settled his lips at the juncture of her neck and shoulder. She tasted lovely—clean, flowery, and feminine, an intriguing contrast to her starchy tone. He rested his hands on her hips, steadying her—and himself. His thumbs rubbed along the crests of her pelvic bones—did a man ever feel *anything* more sublime under his hands than the cradle of a woman's pelvis?—and she fell silent on a sigh.

He paused, drawing back enough to take her hands and place them around his waist before resuming his kissing. While his mouth stole closer to her lips, he slid his hands around to cup her derriere, gratified when she angled her neck to offer herself blatantly to his questing lips.

She was tall, but she still had to draw herself up to kiss him. When Douglas finally allowed his mouth to touch hers, Guinevere's hands were linked behind his neck, her fingers loosening the ribbon that held his hair in its queue.

He was patient with her—patience being the only possible course with Guinevere—waiting for her to gather her courage and kiss him back, waiting for her to sift her fingers through his hair, waiting for her to sigh her pleasure into his mouth.

When he lifted his mouth from hers, Douglas kept his arms around her and drew her against him.

"That was not fair, Douglas."

"But you would agree kissing is an intimate, frivolous pleasure, and your disposition is adequately suited to it?" To kissing *him*, in any case.

"You make my point for me," she said as she slipped from his arms. "My body may be more than adequately suited to the pleasures of your kiss, but the rest of me…"

Profound annoyance did not make a comfortable companion to arousal. "You will not permit me to offer you an honorable suit, but you will be insulted by anything less, is that it?"

Her gaze flew to his, consternation in her expression. "No! I am not insulted, Douglas, though I suppose I should be. Maybe I am beyond insult, or I do not regard these attentions as an insult from *you*. I am not insulted, I am overwhelmed, I suppose… Oh, I can't seem to make myself understood."

She was pacing again, her arms crossed over her waist, her posture hunched as if a cold wind off the Channel had found its way into the cozy library.

"Try to make yourself understood, Guinevere. Try harder."

Douglas's voice was steady enough, while his emotions were in riot. He wanted to throttle her, to ravish her, to wash his hands of her and this whole misbegotten queer start. He'd allowed himself to think something pleasing and fine could be shared between them, just for a little time, to be enjoyed and savored and treasured in memory. His spirits had lifted at the prospect of winning Guinevere's trust, sharing with her the joys and pleasures of sexual congress, and having her in his life where no other woman had been.

Fool that he was, he'd succumbed to the lure of hope.

She came to rest at the sideboard like a drifting rowboat might bump against a jetty at low tide. "I have lost my nerve. I don't know how to regain it."

Her voice, her posture, her green eyes conveyed not only hesitance but also... bewilderment, as if it wasn't simply her nerve she'd lost but something more profound and precious, something she could not fully grasp herself.

Insight hit him like a blow in the region of his heart: she *had* lost her nerve, not merely for a discreet dalliance in the wilds of Sussex, but *as a woman*. That greater loss was old, probably rooted back in her childhood, when her distracted father hadn't even acknowledged her existence much of the time. An elderly grandfather had simply leaned on her willing shoulder and made her into the son he'd lost, and then Rose's father—with pain, and shame, and abandonment—had finished the job.

Even now, by leaving Guinevere to manage Enfield, her cousins were complicit in a scheme that was well intended, but that disregarded a woman's right to her family's protection.

Every vestige of Douglas's pique vanished in the face of emotions both protective and oddly sweet. He put his question gently, prepared for any answer she might give. "Guinevere, do you *want* to regain your nerve?"

Her chin came up. "Yes."

Some distant, disgraced relative of chivalry hurt for her, that she'd been left to rebuild her feminine confidence in near isolation, when a discreet *affaire*, a shared *tendresse*, even a bit of gentle flirtation might have spared her much self-doubt.

"Some journeys cannot be undertaken alone."

"Douglas…" She stood halfway across the room, solitary and torn, and he did not approach her because she had to know the decision was hers. He might not like her choice, but he would neither question it nor fume nor pout nor brood—very much.

He wouldn't make it easy for her, though. She would have to come to him and put her trust in him for the duration. That he could be firm on this point even after a long sexual drought was a fig leaf for his dignity.

"I need time," she said. "With every change, there is loss and gain. I have to know what I'm losing and gaining."

She'd had too much time. "One can't always know those things, my dear. Every decision has unintended consequences, and you must resign yourself to living with those consequences."

That wasn't what the lady had wanted to hear—she'd been parenting an unintended consequence for at least five years—and yet, Douglas wasn't finished. "I would beg you to recall, Guinevere, should you decide you want no further personal dealings with me, that choice will bear consequences as well."

That, he saw, gave Miss Hollister pause. Douglas was not threatening her with gossip or a fit of the male sulks. He was pointing out that she probably wouldn't have another opportunity like this—and neither would he.

Out from under the watchful eyes of the community.

Away from the protective—and meddling—presence of family.

Free from the usual duties and obligations at home.

The silence lengthened while common sense, curiosity, and a rebellious determination waged war in Guinevere's eyes. The battle raging silently inside her tore at Douglas too, though, until he felt like the emotional equivalent of a plundering Visigoth.

"Guinevere, I would not distress you with this needlessly."

She held up a hand and took a step toward him. While his lungs seized and something like a lump formed in his throat, she took another step, then another. When she stood immediately before him, he continued to wait in silence, though his heart thumped so hard against his ribs, she should have heard it.

Guinevere lifted his right hand with both of hers, then laid her cheek against his palm, closing her eyes. He took the gesture as a silent form of surrender and a… a welcome.

Warmth, sweet and soft, bloomed in his chest. Affection for Guinevere Hollister blossomed along with the warmth, and for the first time in years, Douglas felt himself regarding the immediate future with a sense of gratitude. She'd accepted his offer—accepted *him*. She would become his lover, and he would become hers. For a few weeks, they would cherish a time together of pleasure, respect, and sharing.

"That's all right then," he said, drawing her to him and wrapping her in his embrace.

They stood together for long moments, Guinevere's cheek pressed to Douglas's shoulder, arms looped around each other, his hand cradling the back of her head.

Before arousal could start up in earnest, Douglas let her slip away.

He perched on the desk rather than snatch her back and ravish her senseless. "How would you like to proceed from here? If you are undecided, I would request the opportunity to better acquaint myself with your preferences." He'd like to strip her naked and acquaint his mouth with every inch of her delectable skin, for example, and he did not apply so much as a pair of mental pruning shears—much less a hatchet—to the images engendered by that wish.

"I don't have any preferences," she said, not sounding anything like a woman who had embarked on a dalliance.

"Dear lady, I insist that this undertaking be pleasurable for you. And while I could avail myself of your charms right here and right now"—several times, and in a variety of positions—"and enjoy every moment of it, that would not be respectful of, or right for, you."

Her rejoinder was preempted by a knock on the library door.

"Enter."

Douglas expected a servant, or perhaps—the Almighty being possessed of an ironic sense of humor—the vicar coming to collect his wayward daughters. He did not expect, did not in his wildest nightmares expect, to see the blond, handsome David Worthington, Viscount Fairly, sauntering into the library.

Fairly offered him an excruciatingly correct bow. "Amery. Miss Hollister." He bowed over Guinevere's hand, and his salutations were returned with all due civility. Fairly's fey eyes—one blue and one green—missed nothing. Douglas did not doubt the damned visiting viscount was sensing *undercurrents*.

"To what do we owe the pleasure of your visit, your lordship?" Guinevere asked, and she managed to sound only curious, not a hint of consternation—or dismay—in her tone.

"None of that lordshipping business among family," Fairly retorted. "I've come down from Surrey to escape the domestic atmosphere in the Alexander households, if you must know. They are knee-deep in babies, and London is rife with the flu. One finds one's diversions where one can." His smile was bland, though Douglas heard innuendo and warning in his words.

"You are, of course, most welcome," Douglas said, lying graciously. "I'll have Mrs. Kitts prepare you a bedroom, and you must join Guinevere and me on the afternoon's outing. I'm sure Rose will want to see you as well."

"Might I see Miss Rose now?"

"Of course," Guinevere replied—damned easily. "I shall take you up, but let's also order a tea tray, and perhaps you'd like to freshen up before we greet the children?"

Fairly's visage underwent a subtle change, shifting gratifyingly in the direction of consternation. "Children? More than one?"

"Half a regiment," Douglas assured him, and being female the little dears would adore the viscount. "Noisy little heathen run thick on the ground here." May they run loudly and often, straight in Fairly's direction.

"They are the vicar's little girls," Guinevere interjected. "Their sister is Rose's nurse, and Rose has gone to the vicarage to play several times. Don't be hurt if Rose barely acknowledges you. These are the first real playmates she's had."

"Females seldom ignore me."

Rather than simper—which would have pained Douglas sorely—Guinevere rolled her eyes. "Come."

She headed for the door. "We'll leave Douglas to his ledgers and inventories, and let Mrs. Kitts know she has another guest."

Fairly grinned—or was that a smirk?—and followed Guinevere to the door. "Sorry to abandon you, *Douglas*."

❧

Dinner passed amicably, as had all the meals since David had joined the Linden household. Gwen excused herself at the conclusion of the meal, citing a need to check on Rose, though to David, the dear lady seemed a bit too eager to join her daughter upstairs.

"Shall we amuse ourselves with billiards?" David proposed. Though he wasn't going to waste his first opportunity to speak with Douglas alone on a silly game of billiards. When the footmen had a decent fire going in the billiards room, Douglas racked the balls and offered David the break. Choosing a cue stick at random, David took the shot, scattering balls in every direction.

"You should talk Gwen into playing," David said as he sighted on the cue ball and two others. Both went into the pocket, but unfortunately, so did the cue ball.

"Bad luck," Douglas commiserated, eyes glinting with humor. He lined up his shot and sank the ball easily. "Why should Guinevere learn billiards?"

Guinevere. She'd been Miss Hollister to David for a solid year, and Douglas was using her first name easily within a matter of days. A fraction of David's concern for his friends abated, but only a fraction.

At least they weren't going to kill each other, that much was plain.

"Haven't you noticed Gwen doesn't have much understanding of recreation? She plays, but only when

Rose can cajole her into it. She'd see this as a challenge, something to become proficient at."

"So that's what all your jollity over cards was about yesterday?" Douglas asked, missing his shot by a whisker.

Intentionally? Or could a friend hope the topic of Guinevere Hollister ruffled Lord Amery's legendary composure?

"Some of my jollity was for Gwen's benefit," David allowed, eyeing the table. He sank a ball but left himself little in the way of follow-up shots. "I also simply enjoy children, and Rose in particular. I was an only child, and I've always enjoyed children as a result."

Douglas stared at the table, probably seeing shots and figuring odds while David was trying to have a civilized conversation over a casual game—at least to appearances. David made what was intended to be a spoiler shot, leaving Douglas with no good options.

His lordship sidled past David and hunkered to view a tricky misalignment of balls at eye level. "Most adults have more to worry about than whether they can get away with cheating at children's games, Fairly."

"Most adults," David countered, "would worry less if they paused to play a few more rounds of some silly game—like billiards. Are you going to leave me anything to work with?"

"Not if I can help it." He stalked around the table again, his footfalls making not a sound on the polished oak floor. "And you might as well get on with the scold, Fairly."

Douglas's ball bounced off two bumpers and careened with lazy grace directly into a corner pocket.

And David was *not* scolding. "When a fellow is concerned, he occasionally journeys through the autumn chill and pouring rain to assure himself his friends and relations are faring adequately."

A pontification worthy of Douglas himself.

With balls still scattered over the table, Douglas put up his cue stick. "Surely you intend to lecture me at some point for developing a regard for Guinevere, particularly given what you know of my family history. My late brothers—with their womanizing, gambling, and indebtedness—do not recommend me to anybody's notice."

"You are ridiculous," David said, putting his stick up as well, lest he cosh dear Douglas stoutly with it. "I am far more likely to lecture you because you are not getting adequate sleep, you don't indulge in the occasional extra bottle, or you've yet to pinch that cheerful nursery maid in locations that will make her giggle and you smile."

Douglas lined up the cue sticks with a precisely uniform space between every one.

"I am a physician, Douglas." David offered the reminder as gently as he could. "What you tell me regarding your personal circumstances goes with me to my grave."

Douglas stopped fussing the cue sticks but did not turn to face his guest. "There are things…" He ran a hand through his hair. "I am doing better. I have nightmares regarding my brother's deaths, I can't stand the sound of gunfire, and I am dreading the first snow, but I am functioning."

He crossed the room to pour himself a brandy, and even at that distance, David could see Douglas's hand shook slightly. Henry, the younger brother, had come to a bad end on a snowy day the previous winter, while Herbert had reportedly been the victim of an accident while hunting.

"How much are you drinking?"

"Little," Douglas replied, pouring a second drink for David. "I never drink alone, and I limit myself to what is socially expected. My brothers both drank to excess, frequently."

"Do you sleep?" David asked, accepting the drink.

"Sometimes badly, but yes, I sleep." Douglas sipped his drink and wandered over to the dart board. "I can never recall a time when I did sleep particularly well, though, so you can't attach much significance to that."

"Are you eating adequately?"

"What is this?" Douglas set his drink aside, toed the line, and thunked a dart into the board. "An interrogation?"

"This is a medically knowledgeable inquiry, motivated by appropriate concern," David replied, *pleasantly*.

"I eat."

"But?"

"But Guinevere pointed out I wasn't tasting my food, wasn't enjoying it, and she was right." He fired off a second dart, harder than the first.

"Are you prone to fits of weeping?" David asked in the same brisk tone.

"None of your goddamned business." The third dart might have been a bolt from a crossbow, so hard did it hit the board.

"It's relevant business when a man is flirting with melancholia." Though who would not be melancholy to lose both brothers in rapid succession, and inherit a financial mess along with those griefs?

"Here is my advice to you, Douglas Allen, and you had best heed it, because I will only continue to needle you, haunt you, and generally harry you until I am satisfied with the state of your well-being. When you are trying to cope with difficulties, they are best met a bit at a time and in the company of people you trust to have your best interests at heart. Your late elder brother was married to my sister, and that means you have family now, in me, in Greymoor, in Heathgate, and in their lovely spouses. If you need anything, you have only to indicate, and we will leap to provide it."

Douglas pulled the darts from the board. He offered them to David, who really did not want to fence any further over darts. As he took aim, it occurred to him that his concern for Douglas had long since blossomed from the clinical interest of a physician into the more visceral, burdensome anxiety of a friend… perhaps even of a brother.

"I am not finished," David said, tossing the first dart and hitting nearly the same spot Douglas had. "You are also well-advised to put something in your future that you will look forward to, something perhaps, like salvaging this potentially beautiful estate. Gwen thinks it would suit you, and she is both sensible and well-informed."

Also quite pretty, lonely, and quietly brilliant regarding management of the land. David tossed the second dart, landing it as close to the center as the first.

"Finally"—he fired the third dart at the board, temper giving him particular accuracy—"your time is too precious to waste, Douglas. Rather than whiling it away, showering your company manners and congenial hospitality on me and the staff, if there is something you would truly, deeply enjoy, then I suggest you be about it sooner rather than later."

Douglas was silent a moment, regarding the cluster of darts in the center of the board.

"Thank you," he said, sketching a bow. "I'm off to heed your advice."

He turned on his heel and departed, leaving David in solitude, silently toasting the good intentions of friends and family.

Six

"Douglas, is that you?"

"Let me in, Guinevere," came the impatient reply, "lest I'm seen malingering outside your door by the staff, or worse, by Fairly."

Seeing the wisdom in that observation, Gwen admitted Douglas to her bedroom. She was covered from neck to ankles in a thick flannel nightgown as well as an equally sturdy flannel dressing gown, while her feet were inelegantly covered in wool stockings. His lordship deserved to see her thus if he was going to be so cavalier in his timing.

Douglas sauntered into the room, hands in his pockets, and took up a stance by the mantel. "I've been missing you."

He offered this greeting in the same tone most people discussed the exiled Corsican or the rising price of bread.

"You can't be missing me," Gwen retorted, closing the door behind him. "We see each other all day."

"True." His expression was faintly scowling as he perused her evening finery. "Though since Fairly arrived, we've had nothing but decorum and propriety between us, and that leaves me… missing you."

Decorum, propriety, a few subtle innuendos, and an... *ache*.

"Douglas, this is not a good idea. Tonight is not..."

He stepped up to her, right up to her, and peered down his aquiline nose. She caught a whiff of his cedary scent and made no move to put distance between them.

"Hush," he admonished, leaning in to kiss her cheek. "I've missed you. Now tell me you've missed me too."

Oh, *God*, she had missed him. Missed his scent, missed the casual touches throughout the day, missed the hours closeted with him or riding the countryside with him. Missed his exclusive company at meals, missed the anticipation of his next subtly veiled flirtation.

"Tonight is not a good time," she tried again, while her eyes had drifted shut without her willing them to. Douglas slipped a hand to her nape and cupped the back of her head.

"Not a good time for what?" he murmured, cruising his mouth over her eyelids, her eyebrows, her forehead.

"You shouldn't be in my room," Gwen whispered, "and I can't be with you." In fact, she shouldn't be with him, not the way he intended, not ever. But here in Sussex, with none to know, both the common sense and the fear that had kept Gwen trapped at Enfield no longer aided her judgment.

"You are with me," Douglas replied, letting his lips settle over hers. He took his time, refreshing her memory regarding the taste and feel of their mouths together. Gwen let herself slide under the spell his wove with his mouth and hands and sighs, losing her emotional balance in the pleasure of Douglas's kisses.

Hummingbirds took flight on the wings of eagles.

She marshaled her resolve and broke the kiss, using her palm to push on his chest—which moved him something less than an inch. "I meant what I said: I can't be with you tonight."

He put his hands back in the pockets of his breeches and regarded her curiously. "Are you expecting someone else then?"

Manners be damned, he ensconced himself in the chair beside her fireplace and propped his chin in his hand. Gwen liked the relaxed look of him all too well, gilded by the firelight and lazy male confidence.

"I wasn't expecting anybody, and you know it." She did *not* know what to do with herself. If she paced, he'd sense she was nervous. She absolutely could *not* sit on the bed, and yet she felt foolish, standing in the middle of the room, trying not to gape at him in his waistcoat and shirtsleeves.

"So why can't we spend some time together now?" Douglas asked, all reason.

"Because we can't," Gwen replied, all banked annoyance.

"Come here, Guinevere." Douglas held out a hand, and against her better judgment, Gwen crossed to the warmer side of the room to stand before him.

"Come here," he repeated, taking her hand and tugging her toward him. When she stood right next to his chair, he gave her wrist a stout tug and brought her tumbling into his lap.

"Douglas!" Gwen tried to get up, only to find his arms looped about her. Where she had expected him to be a candles-out, under-the-covers-in-silence sort of swain, he'd become the type of fellow who toppled a woman into his lap.

"We can be quite comfy here," he said. "The chair is large, well upholstered, and plenty sturdy. Now settle down, or I'll turn you over my knee."

She ceased her struggles.

"Oh, for God's sake, Guinevere, I don't care for that type of diversion. Now cuddle up, or I'll rethink my position on spanking."

Merciful saints. *Spanking?*

He nuzzled her throat, a friendly, reassuring sort of nuzzle that turned Gwen's spine and a few of her reservations about spanking to butter. "I'm too heavy," she said, swinging her legs over the chair's arm and tucking into Douglas's chest.

Douglas's chin rested against her temple. "Don't be absurd. You are a wonderfully abundant lapful, and please don't argue the point with me. I have held a few more women than you have—though only a few."

They fell silent, and Gwen relaxed against him. His right hand started a slow, gentle stroking along the bones and muscles of her back, and his lips brushed at her temple.

"I have missed you," she said, bundling herself more securely against him, for he had missed her and sought her out to inform her of it. "But, Douglas…"

"I *know*, Guinevere. I am not to ravish you tonight, though that was hardly my intention. How are you feeling?"

"What do you mean, how am I feeling?"

"Here." He rested his hand low on her abdomen. "How are you feeling, here?"

"How did you know?" She hid her face against his neck, lest he exercise his Douglas-tendency to look her in the eye at the most mortifying moments.

"I suspected when you decided not to join me and Fairly on our ride this afternoon and then when you excused yourself so soon after dinner. Are you very uncomfortable?" His arm encircled her shoulders, and he gently kneaded her tummy with his free hand.

"Where did you learn to do that?" Gwen closed her eyes, giving up tension she hadn't realized she'd been holding. The last of her good sense decamped for the Continent as well, along with a portion of… loneliness.

"You are teaching me how to do it right now, Guinevere," he said, kissing her temple.

That he had never comforted another woman thus pleased her, for herself, but made her wonder why it should be so for him. Though Douglas was composed of muscle, bone, and self-discipline, he was surprisingly good at cuddling.

"So," she said, eyes still closed, "you've abandoned Fairly, or did he retire early?"

"He is not yet abed, though he more or less excused me from providing him company. Does he harbor a *tendresse* for you?"

The question was detached, merely curious, in contrast to the comfort of Douglas's body all around Gwen's and his hand, both thorough and gentle on her belly.

"I don't know." But what a marvelous, surprising notion. "If he does, it's the kind of *tendresse* he would never want either of us to acknowledge. I believe it more likely he has befriended me out of sympathy for his in-laws, and I do consider him a friend."

"I do as well. A good friend."

"I am glad you have a good friend." She shifted on his lap and felt the unmistakable evidence of his growing arousal. "Douglas?"

"Miss Hollister?"

"Are you…? That is, did you want to…? Oh, hell and the devil…"

"I am not here to importune you, Guinevere. I came to see how you fare and because I missed you."

"But you're… aroused." And he'd become aroused simply holding her in all her voluminous night clothes.

"Are you uncomfortable because you had to say the word aloud or because I clearly desire you?"

The damned man sounded *amused*. Gwen tucked her face back against his shoulder, the better to sniff at him without getting caught at it. "Both."

"Ah, Guinevere." He grazed his nose along her hairline, inhaling audibly. "Your modesty is sweet, but for the love of God would you put from your mind the notion I will fall upon you like some ravening beast?"

"Eventually," she muttered. "Maybe." Douglas as a ravening beast, though… as a soaring eagle, rather. That she might inspire him to such a state was much too intriguing.

"I shall make you pay for your lack of trust, you know," he whispered. "One fine day—or night—you shall fall upon *me* like a ravening beast." And didn't he sound pleased to contemplate such a notion?

Gwen drew back to assess his expression. "Isn't it uncomfortable to be aroused without expectation of fulfillment?"

"As a boy of fourteen, yes. At that age, a fellow can be perpetually aroused and never have a realistic expectation of fulfillment. As he matures, a man learns to control himself and to find gratification when needs must. I, however, am in anticipation of eventual fulfillment, so arousal can be seen as inchoate pleasure."

"Inchoate pleasure." Gwen tried the phrase on, finding it vintage Douglas Allen. "That sounds like a particularly masculine point of view."

"Allow me to enlighten you."

He bent his head to kiss her, but paused, closing his eyes and inhaling her fragrance first. Gwen watched the sensual pleasure of it suffuse his features and traced his jaw with her fingers. Douglas turned his cheek into her palm, then with her fingers drifting into his hair, set his parted lips to hers.

She tasted brandy sweetness on his tongue as he traced her lips, limned her teeth, and dared her to explore him in return. He smoothed the hair back from her temple and brought his hand to rest again on her abdomen. While his mouth feasted on hers, she let her hands trail over his shoulders and winnow through his hair. As she grew more and more involved in his kiss, Douglas moved his hand stealthily *up*, one rib at a time.

The instant Gwen recalled that he had a hand and that his hand was on her person, and that, more specifically, his hand was on her *ribs*, she went immobile, as if she might hear the sound of that hand sliding along her flannel dressing gown. Douglas stilled his hand as well, allowing her the opportunity to pull away, to protest, to stop him.

He had, Gwen reminded herself, been so utterly daft as to promise her control.

But Gwen's courage and curiosity carried the moment, and when she made no demurrer, Douglas lifted his palm and brought it to rest, gently, over the fullness of her breast.

He gave her time, let her become accustomed to the weight of his hand on that intimate and precious part of her person, to the warmth of his fingers and palm through the fabric of her bedclothes. He'd touched her thus previously, but she'd been properly clothed and upright.

What was he waiting for?

Not a what, but a who. Gwen arched her back, pressing her breast against his hand. Douglas lifted his face, his gaze hooded as he explored the lush abundance of her in his hand. Gently, he kneaded, and Gwen sighed a moan of mingled longing and satisfaction.

She continued to arch into his grip as Douglas eased his fingers and thumb around her nipple and applied a hint of pressure. In response, Gwen seized his face between her hands and brought her mouth up to his in fierce demand. Her tongue sought his, her breath quickened, and her whole body writhed in slow, seeking movements.

Revelation poured through her along with riotous satisfaction. She *could* be a ravening beast, she *did* arouse a man's passion, and here in the privacy of this isolated estate, she *would* share pleasure with her lover. Six years of self-doubt Gwen had never admitted to another save Douglas evaporated on a sigh.

Douglas eased his hand back down to Gwen's tummy and rested his forehead against her temple, and eventually Gwen realized he was not giving her another pause to gather her courage; the dratted man had the self-possession to call a halt to matters.

When Douglas lifted his head, she saw humor in his eyes, and regret—more than a hint of regret.

"Inchoate pleasure. Any other questions?"

Gwen's schoolmaster's hair was rumpled, his breathing deep, and his eyes lit with desire. "Yes. What in the world have I got myself into?" And by what means could she delay their return to Enfield indefinitely?

"How about we get you into bed?" Douglas suggested. "I did not want to deprive you of your rest, and it's late."

"I am supposed to sleep after that?"

"You are." Douglas rose with her cradled against his chest, as if she weighed no more than Rose. "And you are to dream of me and of pleasures no longer simply inchoate."

Gwen did not protest that she was too great a burden, because clearly—for Douglas—she was not. Douglas laid her on the bed and lifted the covers over her.

"You are almost more lovely than I can bear,

Guinevere," he said, perching at her hip. "I shall visit you again tomorrow evening, if you'll allow it."

He regarded her with such gravity, she suspected his words were reluctant, an admission or concession of some sort. "I'll allow it."

Which was a concession from her, one she could make only because his discretion was absolute and their privacy considerable.

He rose, though he scowled down at her for a moment, his hands on his hips. "If I don't leave now, you will find yourself in the company of a ravening beast, and that won't do."

"No," she said, smiling up at him. "That won't do—yet."

Douglas nodded in brisk approval. "That's the spirit."

He bent to kiss her lips, a quick parting kiss that brooked no further mischief, and then he left the room.

Before his footsteps in the corridor had even faded, Gwen was back to… missing him.

∽⁂∾

"Let me walk you up to the nursery, Gwen," David offered when dinner concluded. "Amery can meet me over the cribbage board later." Amery would likely trounce him, of course, not that David minded so very much.

"Of course," Douglas said, following them from the room.

As Douglas headed off in the direction of the library, Gwen watched him go with a curious blend of fondness and despair in her pretty green eyes.

"I've been meaning to ask you something," she said.

Yes, she should marry the man. The sooner the better, damn it. "Ask. My discretion rivals that of the tomb, dear lady."

"Was Lady Heathgate truly indisposed?"

Tricky ground, for it was entirely likely even Lady Heathgate—Greymoor and Heathgate's mother—was conspiring to foster a match between Douglas and Gwen.

David infused his words with a physician's clinical confidence. "Lady Heathgate nearly died of lung fever following that long-ago boating accident. Her constitution would be more susceptible to ailments than other people's, and flu is tricky. I've seen it carry off hale adults in a matter of days, and the only nursing to be done is essentially to keep the patient comfortable. Willow bark tea and cool baths for fever, hot toddies, the usual tisanes, and so forth. I don't believe she's ill, so much as avoiding becoming ill, but that is not why I asked for your escort up to the nursery."

"What was it you wanted to discuss?" Her tone suggested if David meant to lecture her about propriety, when the entire family knew he owned a brothel, she'd slap him, friendship be damned.

"As I was packing today," David replied, winging an arm he half-expected Gwen to ignore, "I came across some papers Heathgate and Greymoor wanted me to pass along to you."

Papers he'd been ignoring for the duration of his visit.

"This sounds serious."

Already, without an inkling of their contents, she was fretting over the documents. "Gwennie, when will you believe your family loves you and wants to see you happy?"

She took his arm, a victory of sorts, though more of a victory for Douglas than anybody else.

"When I have title to my own property and can support myself and Rose thereupon, and my cousins still attempt to meddle. What kind of papers are they?"

She hadn't remonstrated him for his familiar address, hadn't bristled at taking his arm as they wandered up the stairs. Truly, Douglas was effecting miracles in the wilds of Sussex.

"These documents describe the terms upon which Greymoor established a trust for Rose, and name you as trustee for as long as you choose to serve. The trust holds a substantial sum, provided by the family, and is disbursable at your discretion for any purpose that would serve Rose's well-being."

Gwen stopped at the head of the stairs and dropped his arm. "Did you put them up to this?"

David took a leaf from Douglas's book and resorted to cool politesse. "I do not believe that constitutes a thank you."

Gwen paced ahead of him, skirts swishing. "I do not want to be beholden to them, or to you. Rose doesn't need anything that I can't—"

She stopped, her hems settling around her ankles.

"You were saying?" Gwen had been working up to a rousing tantrum, which David was rather relieved he would not see. He sauntered up to her but did not offer his arm.

"Rose needs options."

She recited this, eyes closed, fists clutching folds of her skirt.

"We all need options." But Gwen's pronouncement sounded like a grudging concession to common sense.

"Many by-blows of titled gentlemen can occupy a place on the fringes of Polite Society," Gwen said, gaze fixed on the flame of a mirrored sconce. "Rose will not be one of those so blessed, and if some decent fellow ever does take an interest in her, she can't have her old mother's wicked past standing between her and a happy future."

David positively hated the determination in Gwen's tone, hated the ruthlessness with which she relegated herself to the status of nuisance-at-large in her daughter's life.

He put Gwen's hand on his arm and patted her knuckles. "Rose will have options. Her titled relations have seen to it." All three of her titled relations had seen to it, for David in particular knew what a child raised without a father faced when coin was in short supply.

"Thank you."

Now he did not want Gwen's thanks. He wanted to pass her his handkerchief, shake his finger at her, and tell her to damned marry Douglas for everybody's sake.

"You're welcome," David murmured as they approached the nursery door. "I'll leave you here, but I won't depart so early tomorrow Rose can't wish me well on my journey."

"Good night, then."

David Worthington had traveled much as an apprentice to a ship's surgeon, seen much as the owner of a high-class brothel, and experienced much as a wealthy young man might when plagued by both curiosity and boredom.

Nothing in all that experience prepared him for the shock of Gwen Hollister going up on her toes to kiss his cheek. For God's sake, the woman didn't even kiss her cousins, or she hadn't—prior to making this journey with Douglas.

"You will make some woman a wonderful husband. For your sake, I hope it's soon." Gwen left him standing in the corridor, David's smile becoming not exactly sad but certainly thoughtful.

Did Gwen's cousins know Rose was the offspring of a wealthy, titled gentleman? Did the gentleman himself know he had a daughter?

Did Gwen know she'd admitted more to David about Rose's paternal antecedents than she'd ever allowed her aunt or her cousins to know?

And what confidences, if any, was Douglas teasing from Gwen when his lordship ought instead to be wooing the lady?

❧

"Did you take your nightgown off for me, Guinevere?" Douglas's words, just above a whisper, were followed by the sensation of his hand cupping Gwen's buttock as she lay drowsing in her bed. His chest curved against her back, creating warmth wherever they touched.

"What are you doing here?" She scooted over onto her back and found Douglas propped on an elbow, regarding her by the light of the dying fire.

"I was holding you," he said, smoothing her hair back from her forehead. "Now I suppose we're going to indulge in that favorite female pastime, *talking*."

By the light of the fire, he looked tired. Tired and burdened, like the Douglas she'd first met nearly three weeks ago. "You can hold me, and we can talk."

"A compromise." Douglas touched his mouth to hers. His hand rested on her abdomen, while his lips parted over hers. "I've missed you," he murmured between kisses. "Missed touching you." He brushed his mouth over hers again. "Missed your scent." Gwen began to enjoy his litany and his manner of punctuating it. "Missed kissing you." Her hand wandered up to caress his face. "Missed being kissed by you."

Something warm and blunt nudged at her hip.

Gwen yipped and jerked away. "Douglas!"

"I have not missed startling you." Douglas rolled onto his back and stared at the ceiling. "It's only me, and only a part of me you've known to achieve this state before. All it means is I desire you, not that you will allow me to act on my desires."

"I wasn't…" Gwen forced herself to take a slow, steady breath. "I'm awake now."

"So you are," Douglas replied, still staring at the ceiling. Gwen laced her fingers through his, though he at first did not acknowledge the gesture other than by turning his head to regard her. "How flustered are you, Guinevere?"

"I am not panicked."

"What reassurances do you need?"

"Oh, the usual: You won't rape me. You won't demand from me things I'm not ready to give. You'll allow me to stop you." She'd tried for a flippant tone, as if she woke up to a man—a naked man—in her bed every night. Tried and failed. "Douglas?"

"Hmm?"

"This is hopeless. I am hopeless."

"Nothing," Douglas said with tired resolution, "is hopeless, and certainly not you. If I'd told you a month ago you'd find yourself naked in bed with me, how would you have reacted?"

"I would have slapped you. At least."

"You're not slapping me. There is hope, yes?"

Gwen didn't share the humor. She wanted more than dogged hope, a function of Douglas's stubbornness more than any real expectation. She rolled to her side and considered the bleak, set line of Douglas's face.

"Are you angry, Douglas?"

"God, no," he replied, frowning at her. "Never that. I should not have presumed a willingness to talk to me in your bedroom was the same as a willingness to have me naked in your bed."

"You are unexpected in my bed, not unwelcome."

"That's something." Douglas turned his gaze back to the darkness overhead. "Guinevere," he recited patiently, "I will not importune you for favors you are unwilling to grant, I will stop when you ask it of me, and I will not cause you pain."

He'd recited his oaths calmly, and she believed he meant them, but to Gwen, he also sounded unhappily resigned to having to offer them to her yet again.

"May we try something, Douglas?"

"If this something involves either one of us putting our clothes back on and leaving the room, then no, I cannot endorse it." Douglas's fingers curled around hers gently, for all his tone was brusque.

"I want…"

"Just say it, Guinevere. I cannot see you blush in the dark."

"I want to hold you."

"Any particular part of me?" Douglas asked, a note of anticipation in his voice.

"You," Gwen said again. "I want to hold all of you, in my arms, in this bed, now."

No rejoinder, no further interrogation, no further questions. Douglas rolled up against her side and laid his head on the slope of her shoulder. She wrapped an arm around him as he hiked a hairy, muscular thigh across her legs.

His hand drifted over her belly again. "Is this what you wanted?"

"Yes." What she wanted and what she needed. His eyes drifted shut as her fingers feathered over his features—eyes, eyebrows, lips, the contour of his ears.

Could a man have aristocratic ears?

Gradually, he relaxed against her and the sexual tension abated. His cheek was pillowed on Gwen's breast, though, and desire would recede only so far.

"David says I have money." She could discuss this with Douglas, in the dark. "Rose has money, rather, and I am to manage it for her."

"You sound forlorn, Guinevere, but you are in truth blessed in your family. Rose is blessed."

He had no family, save for a mother reported to be growing frail and half-daft at the family seat. Gwen cuddled him closer, and his sigh feathered over her chest. Did Douglas ever discuss his family, or his lack of family, with anybody?

"If you'd like to be intimate, Douglas, I think might be able to manage it."

He nuzzled her breast. Gwen suspected she'd made him smile. "We are intimate now, Guinevere. Or do I mistake the matter?"

"I meant—"

"One grasped your meaning." He grasped her hand, too, and brought it to his lips to kiss her knuckles. "We can couple throughout your cycle, but the risk of pregnancy exists even if I withdraw."

Withdraw. From Gwen's body. Rose's father had used a Latin term for it, which Gwen could not recall. "You can do that?"

Douglas's fingers wandered up to her ribs, a strange, ticklish caress. "Of course, though it rather spoils the moment for both of us."

"Conceiving another child would spoil more than the moment." And create complications on top of complexities in addition to difficulties. "Did you mean to touch my... to touch me just then?"

"Touch you here?" Douglas let his knuckle brush the underside of her breast again. "Why, no, I didn't. An accident, I'm sure. Beg pardon."

"You are distracting me," she complained, but he no

doubt heard the smile he'd caused too. "How do we go about this if I don't want you to… withdraw?"

"We have at least two choices." Douglas's words were businesslike, though his hand now grazed her breast again and again. When she made no protest, he graduated to caressing the soft skin on the underside of her breast. "We can copulate in the next day or two, or wait until you are no longer fertile, which would be in about two weeks."

"You sound very matter—" Gwen's mind went blank as Douglas gently lifted her breast in his hand. "You sound very matter-of-fact."

"The decision," Douglas said, "is entirely up to you." Then he shattered her focus beyond recall by slipping his palm over her bare breast.

"Douglas…"

"I'm here."

"Touch me." He was a bright man. She was being as specific as she could be.

"I'm touching you."

"*Touch me*," Gwen insisted, arching her back.

He kneaded gently, he stroked, he let her feel, for the first time, the exquisite pleasure of having her bare nipple pleasured by a knowing, firm touch. As her body began to undulate and soften with passion, Gwen closed her eyes lest Douglas see how desperate she was becoming.

Gwen at first did not comprehend the additional sensation. Her left breast was in Douglas's hand, his touch sending spirals of restless pleasure through her body to her womb. He was taking her beyond the previous night's inchoate pleasure to something hotter, darker, needier.

And then another heat introduced itself. A subtle wet, sinuous heat near her right nipple. Not his fingers.

The heat touched her fleetingly, a flicker of warmth and dampness, too quick for her to sort out.

His mouth. His beautiful mouth was committing such naughty, lovely mischief on her person. "Douglas…" She clasped his wrist then pressed his hand more firmly against her.

"I'm here," he murmured. For long moments, he explored her responses with his hands and his mouth, sending heat ribboning down into her vitals.

"Douglas…" Gwen's voice held wanting and bewilderment. She was engulfed in the sensations he created, in the strangeness and intensity of the pleasures he showed her. With her hands and her body, she tried to tell him she wanted more, not less.

Finally, he took her nipple into his mouth and suckled strongly in a rhythm mimicked by his fingers on her other breast.

"Oh God, Douglas," she hissed. Her hips shifted restlessly, and her hand moved over the smooth muscles of his chest.

Douglas slipped a knee between her legs, and she instinctively clamped her thighs around him. He snugged his thigh against her damp sex and gave her the pressure she craved.

"Ride me," he whispered. "Ride me hard, Guinevere."

He applied more pressure to her nipple, pinching and rolling in counterpoint to the strong pressure of his mouth on her other nipple, while Gwen ground her slick flesh against him with desperate strength.

"Harder, love," Douglas whispered. "You're almost there."

He punctuated his words with a particularly sharp tug of his lips and teeth, and Gwen pressed herself all the more firmly against him. The sensations he brought her robbed her of speech, wit, and everything but a sense of driving need, need for him. He repeated the sharper pressure on her nipple, and Gwen moaned with frustration.

"Douglas, merciful… *Douglas*…" Her voice rose in consternation and then…

Unthinkable, unbearable, unimaginable pleasure, deluging her from within her own body. Her intimate flesh spasmed in a great welter of heat, surprise, and profoundly shocking sensation. Just as she thought the pleasure had crested, Douglas drove her up again by wedging himself more tightly against her.

Through it all, she clutched at him desperately with her thighs and hands. When he sealed her mouth with his, she suckled at his tongue and lifted her shoulders from the mattress in an effort to get closer to him.

To be one with him.

"What on earth did you do to me?" Finding the wit and will to voice a simple question had taken two full minutes of lying in Douglas's arms, *panting* in his arms, while the vortex of sensation gradually slowed and Gwen again became capable of thought.

She gave no resistance when Douglas rolled onto his back and wrestled her up to snuggle against him, her head on his shoulder.

"I pleasured you a bit. Or assisted you to pleasure yourself."

Pleasured her *a bit*? "A hot cup of tea is a pleasure. That… That was… That was too much."

"That was just a start." His voice held no smugness, no humor, no arrogance.

"You are serious."

"Your breasts, my dear, are exquisitely sensitive to erotic stimulation. With a little practice, you could bring yourself off just by stimulating your own breasts."

Bring herself off. The phrase needed no explanation. "Are you saying I am wanton?"

His chest moved, as if he might have chuckled. "Of course not. You are the next thing to a virgin, Guinevere, but your body understands sexual pleasure more easily than most. You are to be envied."

"This is complicated." Gwen's wits were resisting every order to reassemble themselves. "Is this the same pleasure a man experiences when he spends?"

"Comparable, I should hope."

"You were *that* aroused when you got into this bed tonight?"

"My dear Guinevere," Douglas said on a patient sigh, "I am nearly that aroused now."

"I do not comprehend this." Some sort of upset was trying to coalesce amid all the sensations still burbling through her body. "You had me so bothered, so utterly beside myself, I could not have told you my own name. But you are content to lie here, cuddling me, while you… while this…" She reached under the covers, found his erect member, and gave it a little flip against his belly. "While this *part* of you clamors for attention."

In the next instant, she had cause to remind herself that Douglas was a bright man. His hand snaked around hers, keeping her fingers clamped on his shaft.

"Some attention would not go amiss."

Gwen let him caress himself with her hand. "Douglas… I don't think I'm quite… I still can't manage…" She fell silent rather than attempt more untruths.

She wanted to. Was dying to.

Douglas used his free hand to toss back the covers. He apparently cared not that he was revealed to her, but instead thrust against the sleeve of her fingers and palm in a languid, unhurried rhythm.

"Only some attention," he assured her, closing his eyes. His breathing deepened, and his thrusting changed, becoming stronger, even while his pace did not quicken.

Watching his face, seeing his naked body gilded by firelight and passion, Gwen's arousal stirred again. But something else was at work as well. Something to do with trust, and protectiveness toward the man in her bed.

The notion was as novel as the pleasure Douglas had just shown her.

"Hold me tighter," Douglas whispered. He used his hand to show her how much tighter, and the muscles in his neck corded with tension. This was pleasure for him, though he looked to be in pain. His jaw clenched, his neck arched, his breathing became labored.

Gwen didn't want to touch him with only her hand. She wanted to be with him in this experience as he had been with her moments ago. On impulse, she leaned over and took his earlobe in her mouth.

"Dear God…" he rasped, arching his back in pleasure. Gwen buried her face against his shoulder as his free arm came snugly around her.

"Ah, Guinevere," he breathed. His hips jerked as he thrust hard against her hand. He did not sigh or moan or make any of the sounds Gwen had, but she could not doubt he was experiencing profound pleasure. The tension in him eased and he cupped the back of her head with his palm, maneuvering her face to rest against his chest. He lay with her thus, gently stroking her hair, her back, her face, until Gwen felt herself slipping toward sleep.

"You have unmanned me," he said, not sounding the least perturbed.

Gwen roused herself, leaned over him, and retrieved a handkerchief from her nightstand. She mopped at him gently, but was surprised when Douglas took over the task from her.

"Immediately after I've come," he said, swabbing at himself briskly, "I can be quite sensitive, but thereafter"—he balled up the linen and tossed it on the nightstand—"you needn't handle me so delicately."

He was so matter-of-fact, even about this—maybe especially about this. "Come?"

"Spent my seed, taken my pleasure." He lifted the covers over them both and settled back against the pillows. "Now, I really must hold you."

"Must you?" Gwen subsided against him, wondering if he'd use the same tone of voice to state a need for eggs with his toast. "Why must you hold me?"

"I cannot precisely say." He rearranged her in his arms, gathering her closer. "Usually, after I've tended to myself sexually, I am quite happy to move on to the next task. You provoke me to gratuitous displays of affection."

"Douglas?" Gwen wasn't sure she liked the sound of that. "Are you teasing me?"

"Whyever would I do that?"

"To distract me from all that has occurred," she said, flicking her tongue across his nipple.

"Hush," he admonished her sternly, "and behave yourself. I really do need to hold you."

Her lover was a bright man, but he was also—wonder of wonders—a *shy* man. Gwen wanted to interrogate him about these gratuitous displays of affection, but—in deference to Douglas's tender sensibilities—decided she really did need to be held, too.

Seven

THE FIRST THING GWEN SAW IN THE MORNING WAS
the handkerchief Douglas had used the night before.
She eyed it curiously, glad for some proof she hadn't
dreamed his presence in her bed but not wanting to
touch it, so different had the experience been from all
she'd known.

Different, but precious. For whatever else was true,
the experience had been shared with a man who would
protect Gwen's dignity, protect her person in every
regard. The relief of this realization was... astounding.

She snuggled down into her covers, content for once
to drowse a bit longer in bed, when memory rose up to
assail her.

"You knew it would come to this," Rose's father had
hissed as he'd fumbled with Gwen's skirts. He had never
used that tone of voice on her before, and the shock of
it had rendered her silent. "You'll soon crave it, you'll
crave *me*. Hold still, goddamn it—"

And then, humiliation and bewilderment, and discomfort just shy of pain. Oh, he'd been different when
they'd first met: coaxing, reassuring, dashing... But in
the end, he'd been brusque and inconsiderate in his lust.

Her disappointment—in him and in herself—had far eclipsed any fleeting physical hurt.

Gwen need not dwell on the memory. Then, as now, nobody could divine her experiences simply by looking at her.

So she went down to breakfast, head held high, determined to carry on as if…

As if the mere sight of Douglas at the breakfast table, in tidy, conservative riding attire, didn't melt her insides and provoke those damnable yearnings in the vicinity of her privy parts.

"Guinevere." He rose and studied her, his eyes unreadable as he held her chair. "You look well this morning. May I take it you slept well?"

She'd never slept better, which notion provoked a blush, though fortunately, no footman stood ready to serve her, no maid brought up fresh tea from the kitchen.

Which was very likely Douglas's doing. "I did, and you?"

Douglas poured her a cup of tea, a small, thoughtful gesture. He added cream and sugar, and when he passed it to her, he wrapped her fingers around the warmth of the cup.

"I slept better than usual, in truth, but then, I was tired." There was nothing—nothing—in his expression, voice, or gaze to indicate he'd been naked in Gwen's bed the previous night and shown her more pleasure than she'd known a female body could experience.

And this morning, he'd touched her. He'd touched her hand. He'd offered her a perfect cup of tea.

"Guinevere?" He set the rack of toast beside her plate. "Fairly was stirring in his room, so I expect he will join us shortly, but you must tell me"—he paused while he set the jam and butter by her plate—"how you fare."

She could meet his gaze only fleetingly, but that much she managed.

"I am well," she said, feeling he'd coaxed the words from her, for all their honesty. "What have we planned for the day?"

"First," he said, pouring himself a cup of tea, "we must see Fairly safely on his way. Cook said you asked her to pack him some victuals, and it seems the weather will hold dry for the next few days. Will you miss him?"

God bless Douglas, he was going to carry her into a normal conversation despite all odds to the contrary. "David is a good friend but he can be... trying. His mind is restless, and he is not particularly respectful of one's privacy. Inquisitiveness is how he befriends one, in part, but also a natural curiosity in him. With all of his quiet and reserve, it's rather disconcerting to find he is so intensely attentive to his surroundings and so audacious in his exploration of them."

"That is Fairly to the teeth, and I will miss him." Douglas looked puzzled to reach that conclusion. "Rose, I think, will miss him most of all."

"I'll fetch her down when I've finished breaking my fast." And why did the cup of tea Douglas had prepared taste particularly lovely? Gwen appropriated a section of the newspaper folded at Douglas's elbow. "She's been skipping her naps lately because Hester's sisters don't nap. Bedtime is earlier as a consequence."

The tea tasted lovely, the scent of bacon and toast was lovely, and this day—another wonder—also held the potential for loveliness.

"Would you like to ride out with Fairly? We could accompany him as far as the village if you like."

Out of habit, she'd appropriated the society pages, though Gwen had never been one for reading at the table.

Douglas was offering her the chance to climb on a horse, to make pleasant conversation with Douglas under David's watchful eye for two interminable miles over rutted roads on a cold day.

Gwen wrinkled her nose at that less than appealing prospect.

"I see." Douglas tapped his teaspoon twice against his saucer. "Perhaps today is a bit chilly for riding, and we were on horseback for most of the day yesterday. Ledgers, then, I suppose, and a long epistle to Greymoor, regarding our findings thus far."

"That would be agreeable." Gwen gave up on the paper and focused her attention on her toast, which was in want of sufficient butter and jam. "How much longer are you willing to wait here for the steward to return from Brighton?"

"I can wait several weeks at least, but what of you and Rose? How long can you spare for this errand of ours?"

Was that a double meaning? Lovely feelings faded as Gwen silently lamented a lack of facility with innuendo and subtle flirtation. She could deal instead in plain meanings and direct answers—also more butter.

"I was prepared to remain here at least a month," she said, making sure the butter covered one entire side of the toast. "But the whole journey will have been for naught if we don't get some answers from Mr. Tanner regarding his deplorable accounting."

"Will it truly have been for naught, Guinevere?" Douglas asked softly.

Oh, drat him, bless him, and drat him all over again. "That remains to be seen." Because there was no telling what comment Douglas might make next, Gwen pushed her chair back. "I'll fetch Rose."

She stood abruptly, bringing Douglas to his feet as well.

She was so intent on escaping him and his eyes and his veiled remarks and the lingering sense of a privacy she could not have described, that she collided with David at the door.

"Well, good morning," David said, steadying her by the upper arms. "Late for an audience with the Regent, are we?"

"I'm going to fetch Rose," Gwen said at the same time Douglas volunteered, "She's anxious to leave my dubious company."

"That's easily understood," David allowed, bending to kiss Gwen's cheek. "You look lovely this morning, Gwennie. But please do bring our Rose down to grace the table. It's what Douglas deserves for being rag-mannered so early in the day."

"You're a big help," Douglas groused as Guinevere fled them both.

"Turn loose of that teapot, old man, or you'll see just how charming I can be first thing in the morning. Gwennie didn't eat much." He took Gwen's seat and went to work on her unfinished toast.

"She's flustered this morning, no doubt in anticipation of your departure." Douglas picked up a section of the three-day-old *Times* Guinevere had been pretending to read, though it struck him as odd that she'd been perusing the society pages.

"Flustered?" David studied a piece of thoroughly buttered toast. "She looked more peeved to me, but then, what do I know?"

"More than you should," Douglas muttered from behind the paper. He was staring at some inane piece about the Duchess of Moreland's daughters all appearing attired in pastels on the occasion of the Windham family hosting a hunt ball at the ancestral seat in Kent—*who reads this drivel?*—when Rose bounded into the breakfast room.

"Cousin David!" She greeted Fairly with an exuberant hug, which his lordship obligingly bent at the waist to accommodate.

"Morning, Poppy," he said, holding his toast away while she embraced him.

"Cousin Douglas!" Rose bounced around the table and headed for Douglas.

"Good morning, Rose." He felt a twinge of smugness when she scrambled up onto his lap, scooting around until she was facing the table.

Well, more than a twinge, really. Fairly frowned at them then went back to reading the paper without making a single comment, while Douglas spread butter and sprinkled cinnamon and sugar on Rose's toast, then cut off the crusts and sliced it into triangles.

"Mama fixes my toast exactly like this. I love my toast."

"Your mother's guidance in all things is to be treasured," Douglas said. He poured a slosh of tea into a cup, added a significant amount of cream and two sugars, and set it within Rose's reach, but not so near she might spill it by accident.

While Fairly pretended to peruse the newspaper, his expression bemused and possibly a bit puzzled.

⤫

As Guinevere and Rose hugged Fairly good-bye, Douglas stood a short distance away, wanting nothing more than for the moment to be over. There was work to be done, for God's sake, and it wasn't as if Fairly were going off to war.

"Safe journey, Fairly." Douglas extended a hand as his lordship at last prepared to mount. Fairly took the proffered hand and used it to pull Douglas against him in a hug.

"See to our womenfolk, Amery," Fairly said before thumping him once on the back—rather stoutly—and releasing him. "And send word if you need anything."

"Of course," Douglas replied, deciding it was a mercy the idiot man hadn't kissed him.

"I'm off." Fairly swung up onto his mare. "I'll see you all at Christmas, if not before."

He touched the brim of his hat with his crop and cantered down the drive.

"He rides well," Douglas observed. Rose, perched on her mother's hip, was waving her handkerchief and bellowing further good-byes to Cousin David, who had disappeared past the curve in the drive.

Guinevere surprised Douglas by shifting to stand directly at his side and resting her head on his shoulder. Grooms in the stables and all manner of people at the house might see her leaning against him, the child in her arms, but Douglas understood the emptiness parting left for those remaining behind. He slipped an arm around her waist and pulled her against him more snugly.

They had stood like this the day they'd met. To feel her body close to his now, to know the strange void left by Fairly's parting was not Douglas's singular burden, was a novel and profound comfort.

"I miss Daisy," Rose said. "And Cousin David and my other cousins."

Guinevere put Rose down, shot a rueful smile at Douglas, then tucked one hand into his and the other into Rose's.

"That's the trouble with loving people, Rose," Guinevere said. "You miss them sometimes. But you will see all of your cousins again soon." She began walking them toward the house. "Do you also miss Hester's sisters?"

"A little."

"Then it's a good thing you'll get to go play with them again this afternoon."

Rose brightened. "I may? I promised to bring paper with me when I visited, so we can make snowflakes for the windows."

"I'm sure they'll enjoy that." Guinevere chattered on, distracting her daughter from the sadness of dear Cousin David's absence, and offering to bake some biscuits to send along to the vicarage.

"Biscuits!" Rose dropped her mother's hand and scampered ahead of the adults, leaving Guinevere and Douglas walking hand in hand.

"Do cousins normally hold hands?" Douglas asked.

"I don't know." She kept her hand in his and sounded toweringly unconcerned. "Andrew often takes my hand, though Gareth isn't as demonstrative. I am still not quite comfortable with all of Andrew's hugging and so forth, but he is attempting to provide me what he thinks I need. I accept that, and understand, as you pointed out, I hurt his feelings when I don't try to meet him halfway."

"I'd say you're a bit past halfway," Douglas observed, squeezing her hand. "And I daresay Fairly, whom I saw kiss you three times this morning, would agree."

"He did, didn't he?" she said, looking thoughtful. "And you have yet to kiss me even once today. Fancy that."

She strolled off toward the kitchen, leaving Douglas in her wake—unkissed but proud of his lady nonetheless.

❧

"Douglas?" Gwen came upon him, boots propped on the corner of his desk and a pair of reading glasses perched on his nose. She drew the glasses away and tried them on herself when he rose.

"Gracious. These would spare the eyes considerable effort." She took the spectacles off and handed them to Douglas. "They make you look professorial. Even more distinguished and proper than usual." They called attention to his eyes, too, which were a gorgeous, piercing shade of blue.

"But you know better, don't you, Guinevere?" He abruptly seemed about as professorial as a great golden jungle cat, as if he'd moved closer without shifting his feet. "You know I am not always so proper, hmm?"

"I know no such thing, Douglas Allen," she retorted, unwilling to step back when proximity allowed her to inhale the spice and starch scent of him. "You are a gentleman under all circumstances."

He raised an eyebrow then handed her a sheet of foolscap covered with elegant, flowing script. "My report to Greymoor, to which you may append any editorial comments you deem appropriate."

"Duly noted." Gwen withdrew to the sofa and not entirely for the cushions it offered. "Cook said something odd in the kitchen just now. The staff supports your purchase of Linden, thinking you would be an improvement over Andrew's absentee efforts, but Cook also said, regarding the steward, 'That one didn't know as much as he thought he did.' She used the past tense, as if the man has left his post."

Douglas sat at the desk and twiddled a white quill pen in elegant hands—elegant hands capable of endless tenderness. "That might explain why the books are in such disarray, but it leaves us with the question of who made the peculiar entries if the original steward has departed."

Douglas's fingers brushed softly over the feather, which sight did queer things to Gwen's middle.

"You mean, whom is Andrew paying to lie to him and falsify his records?"

"Precisely. I would rather we came across a steward who was lax in his bookkeeping than a liar."

"You won't buy the property now?" And did she want him to? This corner of Sussex was not close to Surrey, not as close as London was.

"I don't know," Douglas said, scrubbing a hand over his face. "Have you considered buying it?"

"Me? I haven't the money, and Andrew isn't offering it to me."

Douglas regarded her steadily. "As trustee of Rose's funds, you could certainly use them to provide a home for her."

"Good heavens." Was he exhorting her to put the money to that use? Was he relieved to think she might be distant from him when their task—journey, whatever—was complete? "I could. But I won't."

He tossed the quill on the desk. "Why not? If not Linden, then why not find some nice, pleasant little estate and become not simply its steward but its de facto owner?"

"I've never considered such a thing." Dreaming about something was not the same as considering it. "Enfield is our home, and Rose can use the money to choose her own home, or for her settlement, should she marry."

"By the time she marries, *if* she marries, that trust will hold far more money than Rose would need as a settlement, and you have more expertise than she will have at choosing and maintaining a valuable property."

Gwen wanted to argue—she also wanted to kiss him. Douglas was relentlessly rational but also not… not wrong.

"What you're politely implying is that I, as the fallen woman, will have more need of the funds than Rose, who may find a decent man to overlook the shortcomings of her antecedents."

But being a proud fallen woman, a stubborn fallen woman, she'd made it impossible for her cousins to provide her any wealth directly.

Douglas picked the feather up and stared at it as if he'd no notion how it had fallen to his blotter. "And if I offered to marry you?"

The question was quiet—Douglas dealt his most telling blows quietly. "I've already told you I have no interest in even discussing the word. None."

How convincingly she lied, for the notion of marriage to Douglas fascinated her.

Douglas took a seat beside her on the sofa, hunching forward so she saw his face only in profile. "I'd be a bad bargain, anyway, though I don't like to think of you alone for the rest of your days, subsisting through your daughter, serving the Alexander family business without reaping much reward from it."

She rubbed his back between his shoulder blades, a gesture she'd never offered a grown man. "You would not be a bad bargain, and my life at Enfield is good. I have security and meaningful employment, and the Alexander family business is what has allowed Rose's trust to be so generously endowed. You are in a strange mood."

"That feels good," Douglas said, his shoulders relaxing under her continued touch. "And I am feeling a bit off. Fairly was good company, but he has a disconcerting habit of seeing one too clearly and wanting to discuss what he sees. Still, I had expected to be relieved at his departure."

"One misses one's friends," Gwen said. Like she was going to miss Douglas. "Particularly when they are few in number."

"And then what does one do with the… loneliness?"

Douglas asked, the note of bewilderment in his voice suggesting the question had taken even him by surprise. "I was defined for so long by the conviction that if I were a decent fellow and occupied myself with the family's finances assiduously, then my life would unfold as it should."

He would describe the archangel Michael as a decent fellow, and refer to slavish devotion as mere assiduousness.

"And now," Gwen said, "despite your efforts, the family finances are in difficulties, but what do they matter, when you have essentially no family left worth claiming?"

Douglas glanced at her over his shoulder, a self-mocking acknowledgment of her question in his gaze.

"Somewhere, Douglas," Gwen said, her hand drawing slow patterns on his back, "you lost sight of, or were not permitted to keep in sight, the person you are. You like animals and sweets and taking care of things. You have a good, rational head for business, and you are shy, but people like you too. You are a gracious host and inspire loyalty in your staff. You are patient, kind, and honorable, every inch a gentleman."

His shoulders dropped on a sigh. "I don't know this paragon you describe, for he exists only in your imagination. I'm trying to get under your skirts, so you must attribute virtues to me I don't have."

And sometimes, he was not so rational after all. She tugged on his earlobe.

"That's my point. You don't know this paragon, you don't appreciate him, you don't take pride in what he has accomplished and in what he plans to accomplish. You don't love him; you don't protect him from the abrasiveness and carping of your more critical self."

Gwen dropped her forehead against Douglas's back, wondering where on earth such blunt words had come from. "I'm sorry, Douglas, I have no right to speak to you thus."

He drew her arms around his waist.

"Don't stop now, Guinevere. Whoever this fellow is, he sounds like an improvement on your present company. I should like to meet him."

"Oh, Douglas," she whispered, squeezing him tight. "You are an awful man, an awful, lovely man. And you are not trying to get under my skirts."

"Not at the moment, no. Though we could lock that door and remedy the oversight." He sounded utterly serious—but then, Douglas always sounded utterly serious.

"In broad daylight, in the *library*?"

Douglas got up and locked the door. He turned, his expression… *exceedingly determined*.

"I will not importune you for favors you are unwilling to give," he said as he stalked closer. "I will stop if you ask it of me, and I will not cause you pain."

"Here?" Gwen repeated, her insides going to riot. "Now?"

Though why not? She'd surprised her menials in all manner of unlikely locations—also her married cousins.

"Not here," Douglas replied, sitting on the low table before her, "and not now, because I won't have our first consummation in one of the public rooms of the house, when anyone could knock on that door."

"Then why…?" Gwen glanced meaningfully at the library door.

"I want to kiss and cuddle a bit."

"You don't look cuddly, Douglas." Many a baby had no doubt been conceived in the midst of *kissing and cuddling a bit*.

"Then you shall have to help me acquire the knack."

~~

"Fairly claims there's billing and cooing going on in rural Sussex, though he saw no direct evidence of it." Andrew passed the letter to his brother, a proposition made dicey when his horse refused to stand still in the chilly air of an autumn afternoon.

Heathgate stashed the epistle in the pocket of his riding jacket and nudged his gelding forward. "If there's no direct evidence, then how does Fairly reach his conclusions?"

Andrew's horse, Magic by name, chose to passage along next to Heathgate's less athletic—or excitable— mount. "Gwen kissed him good-bye."

A low-hanging branch momentarily interrupted conversation.

"If kissing Fairly would inspire him to leave, I might have to try it myself," Heathgate said. "One does worry about our Guinevere, though."

Heathgate was head of the Alexander family, which position gave him a warrant to worry about all and sundry, though he'd seldom admit as much in words.

"One worries about Douglas, too, but mostly, one worries for Rose." Andrew could say this only because of the little blond, blue-eyed sprite ruling over his nursery—and over his heart. "Do you realize that in five years on earth, Rose has probably never been to Sunday services, never been farther from home than the village on market day, never galloped her pony beyond the bounds of Enfield?"

"She's too young to gallop."

"She's our kin," Andrew said, slowing his horse to a point approaching the trot in place known as piaffe. "She's not too young to gallop, though Daisy is too old." And getting older as the days turned chillier. Andrew had cleaned his horse pistol even as he'd also prayed fervently for a mild winter.

"Children raised in the country often stick close to home until they're older," Heathgate said. "Will you stop showing off?"

"Piaffe is not showing off," Andrew said, then he collected the horse further, into a few seconds of the crouching rear called pesade. "*This* is showing off." When Magic's front hooves dropped to the ground, Andrew petted the gelding soundly on the neck, which only provoked the beast back into passage.

"To look at that animal, one would never suspect him of the potential you've found in him," Heathgate said. "Well done, baby brother."

Heathgate had seen the horse first and given him to Andrew, though if Andrew made that point, an argument would ensue. Magic was a sensitive fellow and did not care for argument of any kind.

"Magic puts me in mind of Douglas," Andrew said as they approached the fork in the trail at which his path would diverge from his brother's. "One tends to underestimate them both."

"We're back to the billing and cooing," Heathgate said, bringing his chestnut to a halt. "A crooked pot needs a crooked lid, and if Felicity says Douglas and Gwen would suit, then I believe her."

"Douglas and Gwen are not crockery. Fairly says Gwen kissed him good night too, readily took his proffered arm, was heard to laugh when playing cards, and has allowed Rose to make the acquaintance of the hooligans from the local vicarage."

Heathgate was a papa too, several times over. Also a quick study. "Rose hasn't had playmates before, has she? Not from outside the family."

"No, she has not, and Heathgate, that is not right. Gwen is a good mother, but the longer I think on it, the more remiss I believe we have been in caring for our cousin. Astrid agrees with me, too."

"Good mothers allow their children to form friendships," Heathgate admitted. "Good mothers take their children to services. Good mothers know that a child needs to see more of the world than one rural estate. Why didn't we notice these things sooner?"

The obvious answer—that both brothers were more at ease focusing on their wives and families than on Gwen's uncomfortable and lonely existence—need not be stated. Then too, Gwen had kept Rose a secret, even from them, until the girl was several years old.

"What is Gwennie afraid of?" Andrew wondered aloud. "What is she so terrified of, that she can allow herself to flirt and smile only when she's off with Douglas, visiting an estate I've barely kept staffed?"

Heathgate turned his horse toward the left fork in the bridle path, while Andrew aimed Magic toward the right. "And how will Douglas fare when dear Gwen drops him flat at the end of their rustic idyll?" Heathgate asked with a wave good-bye.

On that unpleasant question, Andrew urged his horse into a flowing canter as Heathgate's gelding disappeared around a bend in the bracken and bare trees.

Before Andrew reached the comforts of home, his musings had circled back to their origin: Gwen and Douglas were billing and cooing now, but Andrew doubted that their attraction, no matter how strong, could overcome Gwen's determination to resume a life of rural obscurity.

Someone had stolen from Gwen the future she was entitled to, and unless Douglas could earn a permanent place in Gwen's heart, Rose would also be victimized by that larceny.

❧

Douglas poured Gwen a glass of red wine midway through dinner. He knew exactly how to twist his wrist so not a drop spilled, and he absently served her the exact portions appropriate to her appetite.

His attention to detail—his competence—impressed Gwen in a way she would not have noticed had she not embarked on a more intimate acquaintance with him. Thoroughness was a part of him, a vigor of the mind and spirit that could also be a bit intimidating.

Maybe more than a bit, at times.

Over the fruit and cheeses and more expertly poured wine, they planned a reconnaissance mission in the village for the next day, and finished the evening with Douglas escorting Gwen to her room and accompanying her into her chamber.

"If I get into the bed with you, Guinevere," he said as he lit her candles, "I will not answer for the ensuing events."

Gwen did not want to deny him, and yet she was also not ready for the events he alluded to. She needed to be alone, to think, to come to some understanding of what was passing between them. Douglas must have seen something of her thoughts on her face, because he drew her into his arms and pressed her head to his shoulder.

"We are in no rush, sweetheart," he reminded her gently. "I know you are accustomed to doing without a lady's maid, but would you allow me to brush out your hair?"

Douglas's surprising request restored some sort of balance for Gwen, and she suspected it did for him as well. They touched, they talked, and they spent time together without enflaming each other's passions—as they had earlier in the day in the library—or tempers.

To which the selfsame library had been witness

when they had debated the virtues of wheat versus oats. Marvelous rooms, libraries.

Gwen closed her eyes and wondered if Douglas would offer this attentiveness to his viscountess when he married—for a man with a title must marry, eventually.

"Your hair," Douglas mused as he drew the brush in sweeping strokes from her crown to her bottom, "is almost as lovely as your eyes."

"I've always wished I had my cousin's blue eyes."

"You are partial to blue eyes?" Douglas asked, putting the brush down to braid her hair.

Gwen watched him in the mirror, and in this as in many things, his competence was easy to miss for its very quietness and lack of fuss. "I like your eyes, Douglas. They are honest and kind—and a very handsome blue."

An unforgettable blue.

In response, he busied himself with the considerable length of her hair.

"I recall the first time I did this," he said after he'd organized three skeins. "I had walked in on you at your bath, and suffered paroxysms of mortification over my equally intense paroxysm of lust."

"Lust?" Gwen couldn't turn around to look at him askance, which was likely why he'd chosen this moment for his surprising disclosure—or confession? "I would never, ever have guessed. You braided my hair and bid me a pleasant good night, all the while lusting for me?"

"A man of sense learns to curb his impulses." He finished her braid and tied it off with a green hair ribbon, then bent over Gwen and wrapped his arms around her shoulders from behind and above her. His forearms, strong, male, lightly dusted with blond hair, rested along her collarbones.

"I'll dream of you," he whispered in her ear, and those were not the sentiments of a man of sense.

"You need your sleep. You didn't get enough last night."

"I seldom enjoy a whole night's sleep, though I seem to be doing better since coming to Sussex. The air must be salubrious."

Gwen brushed her lips over his forearm, wanting to give him something as mundane and necessary as a good night's sleep, and sentiments much less mundane than that. "Douglas Allen, I would be your friend."

"And I would be a friend to you."

She remained in his arms a few moments longer, treasuring the gift of a mere embrace. When she rose, she indulged in a kiss to his cheek. "Good night, dear man. Pleasant dreams."

"Sweet dreams," Douglas replied, returning her kiss with lingering tenderness.

When he'd left, Gwen sat wrapped in a blanket by the fire for a long time, thinking about the day's events, and about the man who'd just left her room.

Today, he had begun to use endearments— "sweetheart," and when cuddling "a bit" in the library, he'd called her "love." Gwen had known few endearments in her life, and she hugged Douglas's to her soul with jealous zeal. Better still, when they weren't on Douglas's lips, the endearments were in his serious blue eyes.

When the time came to leave Sussex, Gwen would miss those endearments sorely—miss them, too.

Eight

WHEN DOUGLAS INQUIRED AS TO WHEN MISS HOLLISTER would be coming down to dinner, Mrs. Kitts informed him Miss Rose was "a mite peaky," and that the girl's mother was still in the nursery.

Douglas himself was feeling "a mite peaky," having spent the day tramping from shop to shop with Guinevere and Rose, calling on the vicar, the curate, and several of the Linden tenants.

And on the bakery—twice, owing to the excellent quality of their apple walnut muffins and to Rose's flagrant ability to wheedle.

Which had saved Douglas the trouble of finding an excuse to make a second stop.

"Hullo, Cousin Douglas," Rose greeted him as he entered the nursery. She sat in her mother's lap in a rocker pulled close to the hearth. Realizing he was to be spared—or denied—the usual enthusiastic hug, Douglas took the remaining rocking chair.

"You're reading 'Hansel and Gretel'? I never did fancy that witch. Whatever could she have been about, snatching up children for her pudding?"

"Children are sweet," Rose informed him. "That's

why my big cousins like to nibble on me. Mama says I'm sweet too."

"Sweeter than Christmas pudding," Guinevere assured her. "Also quite tired. I think we've had enough story for one night. Time for prayers."

"Yes, Mama." Rose slid off her lap and repaired to her bedroom, leaving Guinevere standing in the bedroom door to monitor Rose's exchange with the Almighty. Douglas stayed in his rocking chair, having no wish to intrude.

Rose was apparently comfortable enough with her Creator to prattle on at some length. By the time she got to "…and God bless Daisy," Douglas's stomach was growling. He did notice, however, Rose had included him in her litany. "And God bless our friend Cousin Douglas…"

On what basis had the child decided he was her friend?

"There," Rose said. "Time for beddy-bye."

When Guinevere returned to the outer room, Douglas was sitting in near darkness, waiting for her and enjoying this peek at a routine very different from his own nursery days. She took up the second rocker and appeared content to spend a moment enjoying the cheery fire with him.

"Do you put her to bed every night?"

"I do. When a child has only one parent, that parent needs to be rather in evidence if the child is to feel safe and happy in this life. I think David suffered from his parents' inattention, and I would not wish that on any child, much less my daughter."

"Her father, then," Douglas said, nudging the screen closer to the flames with his toe. "He had nothing to offer a child?"

Nothing to offer the child's gently born mother?

"He had wealth and position and certainly could have given Rose some advantages, had it been consistent with his wishes. It is hypocritical of me, I know, but I did not want Rose exposed to his character. My own character, certainly, was lacking to the point that I conceived the child, but having the ability to exercise hindsight, I choose to hold him in lower esteem than I do myself."

"As well you should," Douglas concurred, rising. "Shall we go down to dinner?" He offered her his arm, wondering if she would have answered more questions regarding Rose's father, had Douglas had the inclination to ask them.

Which he did not, not given that he wanted to end the evening in Guinevere's bed.

Throughout the day, Douglas's body had been in happy anticipation of consummating his relationship with Guinevere. Helping her in and out of the carriage, taking her arm while they strolled the shops, sitting beside her in various parlors and drawing rooms, had been tantalizing. Her scent, her warmth, her glancing touches had Douglas frequently forcing his thoughts off certain paths.

But now that the hour was drawing near, an odd reluctance had taken hold, not of his body, but of his spirit. Guinevere deserved not only the pleasure of a passing affair, but also marriage with all the trimmings—respect, security, affection.

Love.

"You are quiet," Guinevere remarked as they arrived to the dining parlor.

"Tired," Douglas replied, seating her.

"You did not sleep well again last night. Grandpapa would say you looked jug-bitten."

Not a sanguine conversational direction, so he tried for

a distraction. "Guinevere, I know it isn't exactly on topic, but why were Rose's eyes so... they were odd tonight."

She paused in her consumption of a savory beef and barley soup. "Odd, how?"

"Her eyes looked shiny, as if she were teary, though I know she wasn't."

"I know what you mean, and it's a look she gets when she's under the weather. I suspect she's coming down with wee Ralph's sniffles."

"Delightful."

"You were charmed by wee Ralph."

Douglas held up a hand. "Not at table. How anybody has any hearing left at the vicarage is a wonder." Wee Ralph, despite his poor health and tiny size, had been possessed of a marvelous set of lungs and tremendous stamina.

"Don't you think it odd, Douglas, everyone in the village was friendly and polite, but little information was forthcoming about our missing steward or the estate's business in general?"

Yes, he rather did think it odd and a much worthier topic than wee Ralph. "I agree with your assessment," Douglas said, setting his soup spoon aside. "I also think we had to investigate, and the continued lack of information suggests we are dealing with someone local when it comes to the crooked books."

"How so?"

"The merchants and tenants were politely evasive, though they apparently favor my purchase of the estate. They wouldn't risk my ill will for just anyone. They have to be protecting one of their own."

When the dishes were cleared, Douglas placed his hand over Guinevere's—a simple touch, but gratifying in the way a skillfully prepared meal never could be.

"You, madam, look exhausted. Shall I escort you directly to your room?"

"You may," Guinevere said, rising and accepting Douglas's arm. And thank whatever lucky star was beaming down on Douglas in a forgetful moment, the servants were not in evidence as he escorted her through the house and up the stairs.

Her steps were slow and weary, as if she genuinely needed an escort to lean on.

"Guinevere, if you are too tired, I would not inconvenience you with my company tonight."

She paused on the landing under the flickering light of a wall sconce. "In my life, Douglas Allen, I have had… intimate relations, and we have the evidence thereof. I have waited my entire adulthood for someone to *make love* with me, someone I could *make love* with. You are that man, Douglas, and tonight is when my waiting will end. I want to be with you in this way."

Such fierce, generous, remarkable words—from a woman who did not want to marry him. As glad as her declarations made him, that last thought—that she would not accept him as more than a passing comfort—troubled him, for himself and for her, too.

Douglas tucked his hand over Guinevere's and resumed their progress. They had reached her door, and Douglas's fingers were on the latch, when Hester appeared from the servants' stairs.

"Oh, ma'am," she said, trotting toward them. "I think you'd best come to the nursery. Wee Rose is sickening, and she wants you."

A beat of disbelieving silence went by as Douglas watched Guinevere shift in a blink from a woman anticipating lovemaking—with him—to a mother focused on the welfare of her child to the exclusion of all else.

Sexual *grief* lashed at him, along with a single question: How would Douglas's life have been different if he and his brothers had had such a mother, rather than the vain, selfish debutante whose fortune had preserved the family from ruin three decades ago?

"Go to your daughter, Guinevere. I'll check on you before I retire."

She gave him a look conveying gratitude for his understanding, but also—surely he did not imagine it?—disappointment that their evening was ending thus.

❧

"How is Rose?" Douglas set down a tea tray he'd brought to the nursery and took the second rocking chair.

"Ill. Probably flu." Gwen nearly choked on those few words. David had said influenza could carry off a healthy young adult in a matter of days.

Douglas passed her a cup of tea. "You don't seem alarmed."

She drained the cup and passed it back to him empty. "I am not, yet." Except she was. In a quiet, determined way, Gwen was settling in for a fight, a fight she would not lose.

"What can I do?" Douglas asked, reaching for her hand.

If she hadn't been in love with him before, that simple question and that simple gesture sealed her fate.

"You're doing it," she said, squeezing his hand. Some of the grimness left her, and she rested back against the rocker. So many of her fights had been solitary battles, for she hadn't wanted even her family to know of Rose's existence.

Hadn't wanted to burden them, hadn't wanted her troubles to become theirs.

"Why don't you have another cup of tea and try a

scone, then see if you can't nap on the daybed?" Douglas suggested. "I'll call you if Rose stirs."

"You're exhausted," Gwen protested, "and she's my daughter."

"And you are my Guinevere," Douglas replied, regarding her sternly. "I am used to doing without much sleep. It's you she'll want, and it's you who must rest now."

Gwen saw worry in his eyes—worry *for her*—and something else, something steady and solid and good.

You are my Guinevere.

She had been nobody's Guinevere. Lately she'd been Cousin Gwen and Gwennie... none of it added up to the tender concern Douglas offered with his lecture.

She accepted his help and sought some rest, falling asleep gazing on his solitary profile as he rocked slowly by the fire. It felt like only moments later that Douglas was gently touching her shoulder.

"Sweetheart?" His hand brushed her hair back from her forehead. "Guinevere? Rose is awake."

His words got through the fog of Gwen's fatigue and had her swinging her legs over the side of the daybed before her mind was fully alert. Somebody—Douglas—had removed her slippers and stockings and loosened the top buttons of her dress. The fire had died down, and in the dim light, Gwen could see Douglas had gathered up the tea things and taken off his boots.

"Tell me what I can do, Guinevere." In the other room, they could both hear Rose whimpering.

"Fetch the white willow bark tea. The kitchen made up what was available, and I'll need some cool water. Hester already brought up a basin and towels."

The resolute set of his shoulders as he departed made Gwen smile, but Rose's plaintive voice had her hurrying to her daughter.

"Mama?" Rose struggled to sit up in her small bed. "I'm hot, I have to pee, and my head hurts."

"Poor girl. Let's deal with the chamber pot first, shall we?" *Please God, could those remain the child's worst problems.*

By the time Douglas returned with more of the bitter tea, Rose was back in bed, in a clean nightgown, her hair brushed and rebraided.

The night wore on, with Gwen grabbing naps and Douglas fetching and carrying. He brought Gwen her nightgown and robe, and helped her change out of her dress, braiding her hair, and pushing biscuits, hot tea, and occasional hugs at her. He brought her a pair of his thick wool stockings to wear as slippers, made several more trips to the kitchen, and stood watch while Gwen catnapped. By dawn, he was sitting on the daybed, his back propped against the wall, Gwen stretched out beside him, her cheek pillowed on his thigh.

And Rose was no worse, but she was certainly no better either.

❧

Tired as he was, Douglas's mind wandered into corners he usually avoided. As he stroked Guinevere's hair, he considered once again the prospect of marrying her. The notion was forbidden from many perspectives. Firstly, the lady herself forbade it.

Secondly came Douglas's own reservations about offering himself to any decent woman, and he did, most assuredly, consider Guinevere a decent woman. When he'd said he was a bad bargain, he'd meant it. Though his personal finances were improving gradually, by the standards of Guinevere's family, he was not wealthy. He was not—Douglas cast around for a word—lighthearted.

He could not offer a woman much in the way of cheerful companionship, flirtation, and flattery.

"Douglas?" Guinevere struggled to sit up, the absence of her sleepy weight a loss. "How's Rose?"

"She's been quiet for the past hour." He trailed his hand down her braid. "Would you like to sleep some more? I know I don't make the most comfortable pillow, but I grew a little lonely in that chair."

A lot lonely.

"You are a wonderful pillow." Her smile was both tired and sweet, not a lover's smile, though Douglas might have described it as a *loving* smile. "You must be exhausted. Why don't you catch some sleep?"

"I would rather get you some breakfast," Douglas replied. "I'm not that tired, but we're almost out of the willow bark tea. I wonder how the medical supplies are here generally, when the medicinals are typically the domain of the lady of the house, and this house has no lady at present."

Guinevere flipped her braid over her shoulder before a yawn claimed her. "Mrs. Kitts would know."

"Should we send for Fairly?" Douglas asked, slipping his arm around her.

"I hadn't thought of that."

For which she would no doubt castigate herself.

Douglas rested his chin against her temple. She looked tired, rumpled, pale, and to him, achingly dear. "What, love?"

"Sending for David." She turned her nose into his shoulder. "You said 'we.'"

Ah, Guinevere. Such a noticing sort of woman. "Did I misspeak?"

She shook her head but did not look up, so he sat holding her and wishing he could understand the great, fathomless mystery that was the female mind—or at least her mind. Eventually Guinevere scooted to the edge of the bed, though when she rose, her eyes were suspiciously moist.

He hadn't meant to hurt her, for God's sake. *Never* that.

"David will probably have just arrived home," she said, "and he likely couldn't return here inside a week. By then, Rose should be better. We can always consult a local physician if we must, or send word later."

Douglas did not argue, it being exclusively Guinevere's decision whether to seek reinforcements from family. "Perhaps a note would be appropriate?"

"If you wouldn't mind writing one?" She sank into the rocker, weariness in her every gesture.

"Certainly." Douglas crossed the room to stand before her chair, wanting nothing so much as to scoop her into his arms and carry her to her own bed, there to stand guard over her while she enjoyed some decent rest. "I can post a note for you, and I shall at least find the local physician and some more of that tea. Is there anything else I can do, Guinevere?"

She rose and wrapped her arms around his waist. "Not for now, but Douglas, I cannot thank you enough."

"No thanks are needed. I would not see you distressed for anything."

"Nor I, you," she said, stepping back and looking pleased with the exchange—daft woman. "When you've dispatched your errands, you'll get some sleep, please?"

Douglas did not reply other than to kiss her cheek before he left her to entertain her sick, grouchy, bored child for several more hours, may God have mercy upon his dear Guinevere.

Outside, the weather went from sunny, if cold, to wet, windy, and bitingly chilly as the morning progressed. Riding fourteen miles round-trip to the nearest apothecary was not a pleasant undertaking, but Douglas at least returned with a goodly supply of the willow bark tea. He'd also learned on his travels that the area's only physician had expired the year before, and the local herbalist was herself ill with the flu.

He'd posted a short note to Fairly, informing him of Rose's impaired health, and one to Greymoor, reiterating that news and updating him regarding the steward's continued absence.

By the time he'd completed his errands, Douglas admitted to both exhaustion and gnawing hunger, but when he returned to Linden, he went directly to the nursery, not bothering even to change out of his wet riding attire.

"Hullo, Cousin Douglas." Rose smiled up at him from the daybed, the picture of pale innocence as she played cards with Hester.

Douglas bowed slightly. "Miss Hester. Miss Rose. How are you feeling?"

"I'm sick. Hester has to play with me 'cause I have the flu."

"I *get* to play with you," Hester interjected. "Ma'am went to her rooms, your lordship."

He left the nursery and rapped softly on Guinevere's door but received no reply; when he peeked past the door, she was nowhere to be seen. He reined in his mild sense of distress and decided to change his clothes before searching for her.

Douglas sailed into his own room, knowing he was running on false energy, and had his cravat off and one cuff undone before he noticed his bed was rumpled.

His bed was, in fact, occupied.

Guinevere lay curled on her side, lips slightly parted,

chest rising and falling in the breathing pattern of sleep. Her eyes looked bruised and her face pale, but to Douglas, the sight of her at peace in his bed was more dear than words could say. He let her slumber on, stripping off his wet clothing as quietly as he could. Shrugging into a dressing gown, he sat in the chair by his hearth and beheld the woman in his bed.

He could not trust himself to simply cuddle up with her now. Despite fatigue and misgivings of the spirit, his desire for her was unabated, and his self-restraint not improved by exhaustion. Something had passed between them during the night, something precious. Seeing Guinevere with her child, seeing the concern and bottomless wealth of love she bore for that little girl had left Douglas… defenseless, vulnerable somehow, and beyond sense.

He had told himself and even told Guinevere that what he sought with her was a brief, exclusive, intimate affair, but what he'd done was fall in love with a woman whom he could never deserve—one who wasn't interested in marrying him, besides.

So, this is love.

Love was the farthest emotion from duty, he mused, scooping her up against his chest. No one saw him carry her to her room, tuck her into bed, and kiss her cheek, but she stirred when he would have left her in peace.

"Douglas?"

He propped a hip on the bed, ready to tie her to the posts if she tried to rise. "Here, love."

"Why didn't you join me?" She was confused, half-asleep, and not pleased with him.

He brushed her hair back off her brow, unable to keep his hand to himself. "I couldn't trust myself not to fall asleep beside you and risk us being discovered in the same bed when we failed to appear for dinner or at Rose's bedside."

"Go sleep," she said, caressing his jaw. "Bring me your pillow first."

"My pillow? If you wish." He'd bring her his heart on a silver tray if she'd ask it of him.

"I want the scent of you on me as I sleep," she murmured as she closed her eyes.

What an erotic, revealing thing to say. Douglas retrieved the top pillow from his bed and brought it to his lady. He traded it for her top pillow, kissed her cheek, and sought his own bed.

As he drifted off, he allowed that Guinevere had been right: with her pillow beneath his head, the scent of her was on him as he slept.

How lovely. How very lovely.

❧

"This is worse than last night," Douglas said as Guinevere poured more bitter tea down Rose's throat. Rose was apparently too uncomfortable and hot to protest, merely lying against her mother's chest, weak and whimpery. "What can I do?"

"She has to fight through it, Douglas. We're doing what we can to keep her safe and comfortable, and she's sturdy."

She is not, Douglas wanted to shout back. *She's only five years old and tiny and dear and too sick.* But even in his fatigue, frustration, and inexperience, he knew panic and tantrums would help neither Guinevere nor Rose.

Guinevere sang lullabies as she rocked her child, and when her voice fell silent, Douglas offered a half-dozen verses of "O Waly, Waly" in a quiet baritone.

When he finished, Guinevere gave him another soft, tired smile. "What a lovely voice you have."

As if a lullaby could cure the flu? "I enjoy music, though in my family, the arts were generally considered unmanly."

"Did you at least sing in the chorus at university?"

"No, I did not. Because I was only eleven months younger than Herbert, he was there for the first two years of my matriculation. And by the final year, I was more focused on my studies than on any social activities."

"No wenching and gambling for you?"

If only Rose were well, Douglas might use this exchange to ask her mother some questions of his own. "No gambling. I did make the acquaintance of a rather sweet, tolerant tavern maid named Dorcas in my final year. When she realized how little experience I had, she took it upon herself to educate me lest I go out into the world unprepared."

"And I'll just bet you hated attending her classes." This smile was knowing, female, and every bit as precious to Douglas as the softer versions.

They put Rose to bed then, and Guinevere repaired to the daybed, but Douglas could barely allow her an hour's rest before he was shaking her shoulder again.

"Guinevere?"

"I'm awake." She sounded anything but, though her eyes were open.

"Rose is uncomfortable, and she feels very hot to me."

He'd avoided touching the child since she'd taken ill, but a brush of the back of his hand against her forehead had told him the fever was spiking again.

"I'll need a basin, rags, and cool water." Guinevere slipped on a pair of Douglas's wool stockings as she issued orders. "Some towels as well, and I'll need you to lift Rose so I can get some of the towels under her."

Douglas located the basin and towels, poured cool water into the basin, and joined Guinevere in Rose's room.

"She's never had a fever this high before." Guinevere's voice held a thread of terror. "She'll go into convulsions if I can't bring her fever down. Lift Rose up, *please*." As if to emphasize Guinevere's fears, a tremor passed through Rose, shivering over her arms, legs, hands, and feet.

Douglas lifted Rose up in his arms, and gently replaced her on the bed once the towels were spread. Guinevere dipped a flannel in the water and handed it to Douglas.

"You take that side."

And so they worked together, bathing Rose from head to toe repeatedly in an effort to control her fever. She did not go into convulsions, but her temperature remained high. At three in the morning, Douglas suggested immersing her in cool water, and hauled six buckets as well as the small copper bath up two flights of stairs.

The house boasted only two footmen, and Douglas could not see Guinevere allowing them in the nursery. Hester needed her rest, and Mrs. Kitts could not risk falling ill herself.

When Rose had been drowsing in the tub for about fifteen minutes, Guinevere put a hand to her forehead. "I think she's cooler."

Douglas laid the back of his hand where Guinevere's had been. "She is. For now."

He changed the linens on Rose's bed and hung the damp towels up to dry while Guinevere dried Rose off and tugged another nightgown over her head.

Douglas considered mother and child, unable to decide which of the two was more pale. "I'm thinking the tub should stay up here until we know her fever's broken."

"It helped more than the sponge baths," Guinevere agreed tiredly.

"Lie down. I'll fetch us some tea and sustenance."

Guinevere didn't argue, which was vaguely alarming.

Douglas was surprised she was still awake when he arrived back to the nursery, bringing sliced apples, cheese, hot cider, and buttered bread with him. And he was more intensely relieved than he could say to see Rose sleeping peacefully.

"How do you manage to forage so effectively?" Guinevere mused, sipping her cider.

"Growing boys," Douglas replied, taking a loud bite of apple, "learn to scavenge."

"I am so glad I had a daughter."

Douglas paused in mid-reach toward his mug of cider. "Should I be insulted?"

"Of course not. I would not know how to go on with a son, but with a daughter I at least have a little relevant knowledge. As I grew up, there was nobody to pass along certain things to me. That caused no little upset, I can tell you."

"What sorts of things will you tell her?"

"That it's normal to bleed, for one thing," Guinevere said, considering an apple slice.

Perhaps it was shared fatigue, or the nature of the care they'd provided Rose, but Douglas felt only curiosity at Guinevere's reply, and regret—for her. "No one told you that?"

"I was still living with my father." She glared ferociously at her apple slice. "Douglas, I thought I was dying. Just when I gathered my courage to ask the vicar's wife what was killing me, it stopped. A few weeks later, it started again. It went on like that for six months, until I went to live with Grandmother, who at least passed along the rudiments and a stack of cloths."

"You have been too much alone with the burdens females usually share. Was your grandmother at least a help when Rose was born?" *Please, God, let her say yes.*

Guinevere shook her head. "She had just died, and the midwife was a nasty old crone who believed the suffering of childbirth was a woman's penance for tempting Adam to sin. She wouldn't even change my sheets, and for two days…"

She shook her head again, something about the gesture reminiscent of a fighter shaking off a stout blow.

Douglas stopped rocking. "Guinevere?"

"It does not matter now."

"It matters to me."

"Childbirth is a messy business. If my grandfather hadn't told the woman a foaling stall smelled better than my bedchamber, she would probably have left me to die in my own filth. That, and the housekeeper eventually stepped in out of sheer Christian duty. But you mustn't breathe a word of this to Andrew or Gareth."

"I would not betray your confidences, Guinevere." Though he'd lecture both her wealthy, titled cousins at length about their neglect of her, and damn the consequences. For good measure, Fairly—a physician, no less—would get the rough edge of Douglas's tongue too.

"I don't suppose you would betray anybody's confidences, but if you did mention to Heathgate and Greymoor that Rose's birth was not well attended, they'd probably wonder first how you came by the knowledge, and draw some accurate conclusions."

"So how did I come by the knowledge?"

"I trusted you with it."

"Will you also trust me with some details about her father?" Douglas asked the question in the most casual tone, prepared to be gently rebuffed. He'd rebuffed his own curiosity on this topic repeatedly, until seeking information seemed the easier course.

"It wasn't complicated," she said in a low, humorless

voice. She'd resumed rocking, and that allowed Douglas to relax a bit too. "He was a dashing young lordling, though he held only a courtesy title. I was in my first season, nineteen unworldly years old. Grandmama had wanted to bring me out, but she was elderly, and then Grandpapa went through a bad spell."

Her rocking slowed. "In hindsight, I've concluded Rose's father believed me to be more sophisticated than I was, and when he proposed an elopement, I thought it romantic and adventurous. I was in love, you see, but had told the fellow firmly he would be granted no liberties outside of wedlock."

She paused to consider a pale slice of cheddar. "To my mind, suggesting we elope meant he truly, truly valued me above all others and wanted desperately to have me for his own, though my immediate family was little better than gentry and his so very exalted."

Douglas said nothing, though he was fiercely glad the man was titled, for it meant Douglas could call him out.

Guinevere popped the cheese in her mouth and chewed for a moment. "I was an idiot, but a clever idiot. I concocted a credible tale of going to stay with a friend, dodged my aunt, left Town with my so-called fiancé, participated in a wedding that was so ramshackle and clandestine that now I don't understand why I thought it was real. The 'church' was some shabby little chapel north of Richmond, and the vicar was not much older than my betrothed."

Another bite of cheese was inspected then dispatched, while Douglas waited and kept an entire magazine of questions behind his teeth.

"In the morning, my supposed husband's older brother caught up with us and raised three kinds of Cain, until my spouse informed him it had been a sham wedding.

The brother was inclined to force him to marry me, but by that point, I realized what kind of man I had given myself to. I begged the brother to forget the incident, and he seemed, reluctantly, to follow my reasoning."

The tale wasn't that unusual. False weddings were considered sport among the more debauched roués of the aristocracy, and young ladies were cautioned against same from the time they put their hair up.

Though who would have been on hand to caution Guinevere?

"Does either the father or his brother know of Rose's existence?"

"I don't know." Guinevere spoke softly, as much bewilderment as fatigue in her voice. "The older brother was not the heir then, but among Polite Society, a man's responsibility for his own by-blows, much less his brother's, is a matter of whim and honor. I have not contacted him or Rose's father."

And like a thunderclap can shake even a sturdy structure, Douglas understood what drove the woman beside him to her reclusive and unsocial tactics. "You are more concerned his family *would* take an interest in Rose than that they wouldn't?"

She did not dither over any more cheese, but rather, studied her hands—sensible, unpretentious hands that could convey such caring.

"You gather correctly," Guinevere said. "By law, being illegitimate, Rose is my daughter, not his, and no amount of money or influence could convince me to allow him any say over her. Because the Season was mostly over, my return to Enfield didn't cause unusual comment. I can only guess Rose's father was persuaded to keep his indiscretions quiet."

Through his own fatigue, through his concern for

Rose and his equal concern for Rose's exhausted mother, Douglas felt two emotions erupting: rage, understandable and pure, for the way Guinevere had been treated by a supposed exponent of the Quality, and... a tenderness toward Guinevere that included respect, compassion, and protectiveness equal to the task of keeping the rage silent.

"You are not an indiscretion, Guinevere."

"The worst thing," she said, her hands balling into fists in her lap. "The worst thing about the whole business..." She took a slow breath and let it out while Douglas mentally chose swords over pistols, for a contest of swords was bloodier and more protracted.

"He consummated our farce of a union standing up," she said in quiet misery. "He tossed my skirts over my back, bent me over a chair, and went at me. It hurt, Douglas, though not physically. Physically he was probably trying to be careful, but it hurt anyway. It hurt my spirit endlessly. When he finished, he went to the common below and spent the rest of the night—my supposed wedding night—gambling and bothering the tavern wenches. In the morning, he told me I'd disappointed him, and then—only then—did I cry. If his brother hadn't come, there's no telling how long I would have suffered his attentions before he confessed his venery."

Douglas rose, scooped Guinevere up in his arms, and sat back in his rocker. He arranged her across his lap and rested his cheek against her hair.

"Right now," he said, his voice oddly tight, "I am ashamed to be a man. That you could have been treated thus and borne the consequences so singularly... Of course it broke your heart, for it breaks mine simply to hear of it."

He set the chair to rocking slowly, wanting both

peace for her and revenge in her name on the man who'd so casually wrecked her life. Douglas let her cry, felt the heat from her body, felt the tension, and then the easing of muscles and emotions held in check for years. When she was breathing evenly again, she turned her face up to his and kissed him gently on the mouth.

"What a friend you have become to me, Douglas Allen," she said before nestling back against him.

He continued to rock her gently, to stroke and soothe and *console* as best he could, but his mind was reeling at the magnitude of the insult done her.

The scoundrel's brother had faced a real dilemma. Marriage would have addressed the public harm to Guinevere's reputation, but it also would have condemned her to a lifetime of private misery, bound by law to permit a mendacious near-rapist intimate access to her for all of her days, to bear as many children as he chose to get on her, to perhaps stand by while he seduced and toyed with other innocents.

And behind those charged conclusions, another thought intruded: for Rose's father to have both a courtesy title and an older brother, the man had to be the son of a marquess or a duke.

As silver linings went, that one was thin and tarnished, but it meant the man was likely possessed of family who would shudder at the thought of scandal, be it scandal in the form of a love child or a challenge on the field of honor.

None of which would be of any use to the woman falling asleep in Douglas's arms or to the little girl in the next room.

Nine

WHEN GWEN SAW DOUGLAS NEXT, HE HAD CHANGED his clothing, shaved, and otherwise put himself together for the new day, but to her maternal eye, exhaustion was taking a toll on him. Nonetheless, when Gwen entered the breakfast parlor, the stubborn man rose, bowed, seated her, and carried on as if he'd enjoyed a full night's sleep.

"Douglas Allen, you *must* get some rest today. Promise me. I can't have you falling ill now that Rose is on the mend." Though would Rose *be* on the mend without Douglas's vigilance and support in the nursery?

"I will rest today," he replied, which Gwen took for a polite, cheeseparing, Douglas-like prevarication. "Yesterday's post brought us an interesting letter from one Loris Tanner, who purports to be writing from Brighton."

Gwen laid her serviette across her lap, wondering when Douglas had had time to read his correspondence. "The name Loris Tanner is familiar."

Douglas swirled his spoon slowly in his tea. "Her father is Meredith Tanner, our errant steward. She claims Mr. Tanner took ill in Brighton, malady undisclosed, and his illness has delayed his return to Linden.

Miss Tanner will join us here soon, while her father
remains behind to recuperate. A reply to the lady is in
order, expressing our fervent hopes that her father will
make a speedy recovery, and our cheerful anticipation
of making her acquaintance."

"Cheerful and fervent, are we?" And clearly, Douglas
would not bring up the topic of last night's exchange,
which Gwen took for much appreciated consideration.

"We are nigh ebullient," Douglas assured her gravely.
He passed her the note, a polite little epistle in a pretty,
feminine hand. Gwen studied it for a moment, but fell
to consuming her breakfast in silence shortly thereafter.
Douglas occupied himself similarly, though he wasn't
eating nearly enough to suit Gwen.

"Now that we've broken our fast"—Douglas drained
his teacup—"if you'll excuse me, I'm off to the library,
there to immure myself in the ledgers. I'm thinking
a reply to Miss Tanner, indicating we'll await a call
from her two days hence, would be appropriate, if you
wouldn't mind drafting same."

"I'll see to it."

Gwen let him go, not surprised that by the light of day
and under the weight of what had to be crushing fatigue,
Douglas was less approachable than he had been rocking
by the fire in the dead of night.

It mattered not. Gwen reviewed their breakfast
conversation and wondered if Douglas realized how
liberally he had begun to use the terms *we*, *us*, and *our*.
To Gwen's ears, they were strange and beautiful, but
ultimately, sad words.

❧

"Rose is ill, though reported to be on the mend."
Andrew passed Fairly two letters from Douglas. "And

my steward is nowhere to be found, or larking about Brighton for weeks, right when I'm trying to convince Douglas the damned place is well enough run he should be able to make a profit off of it in his sleep."

"And why would you want to do that?" Fairly, looking handsome and golden by the windows, scanned the letters while he posed impertinent questions. "My grasp of commerce is admittedly shaky, but I seem to recall one retains the profitable enterprises and jettisons the others."

"Aren't you hilarious," Andrew retorted, lounging in a comfortable chair behind a scarred desk that had belonged to his grandfather. "My dear wife—that would be your very own darling baby sister—has taken it into her head Douglas is in need of a home, and we own several thousand sheep too many. Ergo, Douglas should have Linden."

"But?"

"But Linden didn't get quite the attention from its present owner it should have. Shall I ring for tea, or would you care to join me in a drink?"

"Tea would give your brother endless opportunities to mock—we are gentlemen outside the supervision of our ladies, after all. Brandy it is."

They were in the baron's study at Enfield, Andrew having agreed to meet Fairly here on Gwen's turf, where Heathgate could join them and the women and children would not. Andrew had wanted to look in on the property, and didn't think it quite sneaking behind Gwennie's back to neglect to mention he'd do so.

He was, after all, owner of the damned place.

"Someday," Andrew said, "I am going to own one property, and I am going to live on the property I own, and I am going to raise horses there, and children, and have enough time each day to see to the happiness of my spouse."

"Speaking of your spouse, how is Astrid?"

"Queasy," Andrew replied, unable to hold back a smile, "but happy. She's blooming with this pregnancy in ways she couldn't with Lucy. And because she is trying to wean Lucy, I am getting to spend more time with my daughter. Suppose I should have thought of that several months ago."

Fairly scowled, sliding down to sit against the wall, his knees bent before him. "My sisters are not rabbits to be kept perpetually gravid by their idiot spouses."

"One of whom would be me," said Gareth, Marquess of Heathgate, strolling through the open door and closing it behind him. He was a slightly larger, darker version of Andrew, complete with sable hair and snapping blue eyes and—according to Andrew's exceptionally discerning countess—a trifle less handsome. "Who is perpetually pregnant?"

Andrew bounced out of his chair to shake his brother's hand.

"Congratulations are in order, Brother." Andrew grinned as he stepped back. "You are to be an uncle again."

Heathgate shot a sheepish look at Fairly, who had risen and gone to the decanter. "As are you two, possibly."

"Fucking rabbits," Fairly muttered, handing Heathgate a drink. "Can't either of you keep your bloody breeches on?"

Andrew and Heathgate exchanged a look of self-conscious glee, a look that confirmed that keeping one's skirts down had as much to do with events in anticipation as keeping one's breeches up.

"May we turn our attention to the matters at hand?" Heathgate asked.

"Here." Andrew passed him the letters. "Read for yourself."

"Don't suppose there's much we can do for Rose," Heathgate said a few moments later, "short of prayer. Mother is still not entirely recovered from her go 'round with flu. And where in the hell is your steward, Brother? I thought you hired the fellow yourself."

Heathgate sank onto the edge of their grandfather's desk, tossing the notes down on the blotter.

"I don't know where Tanner has hared off to," Andrew replied. "I have no business I can think of that would take him to Brighton, and he didn't send me word he was traveling from the property."

"Is that unusual?" Fairly asked.

Fairly excelled at the insightful question, may he choke on his brandy.

"Yes," Andrew replied. "Tanner has been all that's conscientious when it comes to sending along the reports, giving me the information I need to make decisions, and so forth. I wrote to him that Douglas and Gwennie were going to look the place over, and told him to be as forthcoming as if Douglas were already the new owner."

Though that outcome—*damn and perdition*—looked increasingly unlikely.

"I wonder if your man met with foul play." Heathgate was the local magistrate. Foul play in its various forms was his idea of a diversion and frolic.

"The neighborhood didn't strike me as a foul play kind of area," Fairly commented. "The estate is well run, but—forgive me, Greymoor—has substantial problems."

Douglas had delicately alluded to the same notion, but Fairly would be blessedly blunt. "What kind of problems?"

"Your pastures are overgrazed, according to Gwen. You've made no headway on an irrigation and flood control system, for another. The fences are falling into disrepair, and the land is tiring. It's salvageable, but in another few years it will become expensive to turn around."

Andrew glowered at his drink when what he wanted to do was toss it back and immediately pour himself another. "I thought I was offering Douglas the property at a more than fair price, and now we shall have to haggle. When I last saw the place, it seemed as lovely as ever. But as for this situation with Gwen and Douglas…"

Which was what they really ought to be discussing, but what did a concerned cousin say, when all and sundry had been more than half-hoping both Douglas and Gwen would turn up smitten?

"I don't know as there is a situation," Fairly said. "Gwen won't have him as a spouse, which was made clear to Douglas when he approached her honorably. They seem to be getting on better though, and he calls her Guinevere, so make of that what you will."

"Swiving her," Heathgate predicted. "Or she's swiving him, poor sod."

"Ungentlemanly, Heathgate," Fairly said, which did not go to the accuracy of the observation. "What I want to know is why Douglas, whom one wouldn't exactly term impulsive, would offer for a woman he's known only a few weeks."

"Because Gwennie is lovely and lonely, and Douglas is nothing if not discerning and persistent," Andrew said. "Why do you think we suggested Douglas avail himself of her expertise?"

Though a decanter had figured in the discussion he and Heathgate had had when the idea had been hatched, and possibly a few hints from Astrid and Felicity. A decanter and a rotten headache the next morning.

"Rabbits," David muttered. "Perishing damned

rabbits, with only one rabbiting thing on your little rabbity minds."

"I rather think," Heathgate said, making a study of the cupids cavorting about the crown molding, "they are both lonely and discerning, and further speculation on their personal interactions does not respect their privacy."

"Perhaps not," Andrew said, "but it's fun, and the women would have gossiped circles around us by now."

"And this," Fairly mused, "would help us figure out where your steward is?"

While Andrew cast about for a witty rejoinder that wouldn't start a round of fisticuffs, a knock sounded at the door.

"Enter," Andrew barked.

"Milords." The butler bowed, exposing the top of a shining pink pate. "A visitor for Miss Hollister."

Andrew plucked the proffered calling card from the butler's salver. "Westhaven?" he asked, glancing from Fairly to Heathgate.

"Gayle Windham, Earl of Westhaven," Fairly supplied. "Heir to the Moreland dukedom, sober fellow to all appearances, considered a prime catch, spends most of his time at the family seat avoiding the ladies or holed up with his man of business in Town. Was the spare until the more dashing older brother got himself killed in Portugal."

"I did some business with him once," Heathgate added. "No complaints, but he isn't the most cordial of men."

"That honor would likely go to you?" Andrew asked.

"Receive him in the front parlor," Fairly instructed.

"For God's sake, I know where to receive a guest on my own property."

"Children, please," Heathgate tut-tutted.

"Show my guest into the visitor's parlor, Denton. A tea tray with some decent food would also be in order." Andrew grabbed his coat, buttoned it up, and prepared to look genial and harmless, for glowering was Heathgate's forte, and being shrewd and silent, Fairly's.

While Andrew made introductions, he also sized up Gayle Windham, Earl of Westhaven. Westhaven was of a height with the rest of them, a few inches over six feet, with dark chestnut hair. His eyes were a startling green and fringed with thick, dark lashes long enough to fascinate debutantes and dowagers both. Those lashes gave an otherwise austere countenance a touch of the exotic.

Andrew launched the protocol of inquiring after one another's health and family, and remarking on the weather and the unfortunately virulent strain of flu going around. Throughout that trial, Westhaven gave no hint that he found the trivialities a test of his endurance. He was even well mannered enough that he couldn't be caught staring at Fairly's peculiar eyes—which only made Andrew watch his guest more closely.

The small talk paused when the tea tray appeared. "You're a distance from Town," Andrew said. "I thought some sustenance might be appreciated. Shall we sit?"

Westhaven flicked an odd glance at him but took the proffered seat on the sofa, while Heathgate and Andrew took the flanking padded chairs.

When tea and sandwiches were disappearing down four male gullets—and where were the cakes, for God's sake?—Westhaven made his first bid for information. "I trust Miss Hollister is in good health?"

"She is," Andrew replied, "as far as we know. She's from home today on a short holiday with other family members. Join me in another sandwich, would you, so these two"—he gestured with his chin toward Fairly and Heathgate—"do not remark my greed."

"You're just a growing boy," Heathgate said. "And the kitchen serves sandwiches sized for a lady's hand." He picked up his third and smiled blandly. "So, Westhaven, how was the harvest at Morelands?"

They fenced verbally, Westhaven probing delicately regarding Gwen's location, her expected date of return, and the identities of the others in her party, while Andrew and Heathgate parried with hints and insinuations aimed at determining the nature of Westhaven's business with her.

Eventually, Fairly, who had wandered off to a window seat—the man had a penchant for lurking near exits—spoke up.

"Gentlemen, I see we have demolished the fare provided by our host, and I am soon to leave for Town. Perhaps we might spare our guest further games and simply ask him what his business is with Miss Hollister?"

Westhaven's answer came easily enough, for it turned out to be no answer at all. "I am not at liberty to disclose the exact nature of my dealings with Miss Hollister. I can assure you, however, I wish her no ill, nor do I believe she has reason to be… uncharitably disposed toward me. I hope you would be good enough to let her know I have called, because unless Lord Greymoor forbids it, I will call again."

A pretty speech, delivered with a determined glint in the man's eyes. Gwen was technically under Andrew's protection, though Heathgate was head of the Alexander family, so Andrew provided a response.

"We will tell her you called, and you may await her here upon her return," Andrew said, because if she didn't want to deal with the fellow, Gwennie should have the pleasure of rejecting him herself. "Please send word first, and be warned she might not receive you. Gwen lives a retired life, and we would, each of us, go to great lengths to protect her privacy and peace of mind."

Andrew pinned his guest with a look: *pistols, swords, or fisticuffs being great lengths in the opinion of some.*

Westhaven—canny fellow—apparently decided his errand was complete. "I'll take my leave of you then, gentlemen." He rose, bowing to each in order of precedence. "I am grateful Miss Hollister's family takes her interests so to heart."

A small, assessing silence followed that pronouncement.

"If you can wait for my horse to be saddled, I'll join you for the ride back to Town," Fairly said.

"Certainly." Westhaven had no choice, manners alone preventing any escape from Fairly's generous offer.

Andrew and Heathgate saw them off, then Andrew headed back to the stables, Heathgate at his side. Heathgate said nothing as Andrew opened a stall door and approached the little white mare who stood listlessly nosing at her hay.

"She's failing," Andrew said. "I've asked the lads to dig a hole, because the ground will soon be frozen."

"You want me to shoot her?" Heathgate offered. "You needn't tell Gwen or Rose the details."

Andrew considered the offer—a peculiar manifestation of fraternal concern, for ages ago, Daisy had been Andrew's first mount—and considered the pony nuzzling his ribs. She pawed the straw then creaked into a bow, apparently still willing to earn the treat Andrew always kept on hand for her.

"Not yet, but thank you. She's stiff, though not in severe pain. She's also dropping weight, but the older ones do that when the weather gets colder. It's more the look in her eye that bothers me. When she doesn't have company, she's starting to go away."

Douglas Allen had sported some of the same look, not long ago.

"She may surprise us."

Andrew made no reply, for this too was brotherly love. He gave the pony a good long scratch on her shoulders and another bite of carrot.

"We have some time before Gwen is due back," Andrew said as he latched the stall door behind him. "There's no need to make a decision today."

"Of course not." Heathgate looped a casual arm across Andrew's shoulders, and Andrew made no protest. "I'll clean my gun just in case. Now, how do you suppose Fairly and Westhaven are managing?"

❧

David parted from Westhaven when they reached Park Lane. As his mare plodded on toward home, he considered how to summarize the exchange for Heathgate and Greymoor, and what, if anything, ought to be passed along to Gwen regarding her visitor. He was not inclined to burden her with this development prematurely, thinking that her hands were full with a sick child, a troubled estate, and the company of an equally troubled, if relentlessly polite, man.

David did not believe Westhaven was Rose's father, nor did he suspect the man was trying to blackmail Gwen regarding details of her past. More likely, Westhaven came as the emissary of Rose's father, which raised the question: Why didn't, or couldn't, that man present himself? One rather hoped he was still extant, so that somebody— Greymoor, Heathgate, even Amery—might have the pleasure of killing him, if that was Gwen's preference.

Of course, such an outcome might make explaining the situation a bit difficult when Rose was of an age to ask awkward questions.

David took himself into his study, poured a neat finger of whiskey, and sat down to think through the conversation with Westhaven on the way back to Town. In hindsight, he realized that for all his probing and fencing, and even in his direct questions, Westhaven had never once asked about a child.

On that thought, David trimmed his pen and started writing. His first epistle was to Greymoor and Heathgate, his second to Thomas Jennings, his man of business. The Alexanders would make their inquiries regarding the handsome earl, and David would make his. Between them all, they would come to learn whom the man swived, in what position, at what time of day or night, and on which days of the week.

❧

"Please have some more tea, Miss Tanner," Douglas coaxed. "The weather is so very unpleasant, you must fortify yourself."

Loris Tanner was tall, dark-haired, and blessed with slate-gray eyes Gwen characterized as serious more than pretty. Her face comprised a graceful set of feminine features: a wide, full mouth; a straight, even haughty nose; dramatically arched eyebrows, and bones that would age well. She was quite attractive and of an age with Gwen. Gwen was struck, however, by a sense of stillness in Miss Tanner's features, a quality of watchful repose, not unlike the expression Douglas often wore.

"Thank you, my lord, but I should be going." Miss Tanner stood and began pulling on plain gray gloves as if to leave.

Douglas did not rise when she got to her feet, but rather remained in his chair sipping tea and looking pensive. "Before you leave us, Miss Tanner, if you could appease my curiosity on one small point?"

"Of course." She did not sit back down, and unease flitted across the woman's otherwise calm features.

"You have described for us your stay in Brighton and your father's business there and his subsequent illness. We have your very polite note explaining same, and now we have your charming presence among us."

"Yes, my lord?"

Gwen had no idea what Douglas was about, but her stomach knotted in anticipation of the trap he would inevitably spring.

"My question is this," he said, putting his teacup down, and still looking preoccupied. "How is it you could be in Brighton a week or so ago, and yet also be purchasing sweets in the village baker's shop at the same time?"

Miss Tanner dropped to the settee she had just vacated, her expression going blank. Gwen did feel sorry for her, but how many times had Gwen told herself: Douglas is a man who notices details.

"Miss Tanner," Douglas went on, "if you are in difficulties, then we will render you assistance. If you have committed a wrong, we will not turn you over to the magistrate posthaste, but try to settle matters between ourselves. We have been at Linden these past weeks, you see, and we know things here have not been as carefully managed as one might hope."

Miss Tanner shot a beseeching look at Gwen, who gave a slight shake of her head.

"This matter must be resolved to Lord Amery's satisfaction, Miss Tanner, though if he says he will try to do that without involving the magistrate, then you may rely on his word. I would trust my life to his honor."

Perhaps it was that dramatic endorsement of Douglas's integrity, or perhaps Loris Tanner could see no other option, no dodge, no ploy, that would serve in the present circumstances.

She stood and went to the window, where a miserable, cold rain pelted the glass and whipped the dead leaves from the trees. "My father disappeared shortly after Lord Greymoor's last visit here. The circumstances of his departure were consistent with a lifelong inability to resist strong spirits. When he was sober, Papa was the best of men and the best of stewards. My father knew his business, but he was dismissed from one post after another because of his drinking.

"He was well liked," she went on dully, "for he wasn't a mean drunk, but when he drank, he'd carouse for days, even longer. He would drink himself insensate, not recalling what he'd done, where he'd been. A local woman accused him of taking liberties with her during one of his drunken spells, and he left before charges could be laid. I believe our magistrate, Squire Belmont, claimed he had to research the exact charges to be brought to give my father time to depart the area, for his accuser is not particularly well regarded."

"And do you know your father's whereabouts?" Douglas asked. "The truth, if you please."

Miss Tanner turned from the bleak day to face Douglas. "I do not. My father knows I am not an accomplished dissembler. He is either dead, or he is trying to protect me from those who would seek information from me."

"Or he has descended into the bottle, there to drink out his days in reckless disregard for his responsibilities to you," Douglas concluded. "Are you of age, Miss Tanner?"

"I am," she replied, giving him a curious look.

"And what of your mother?"

"I do not know who she was. I have always been with my father."

"And in your father's absence, Miss Tanner, who has managed this estate?"

For the first time, the lady paused before giving her answer. She raised her chin, adopting an attitude Gwen had seen Rose employ in her frequent righteous moments. "I have managed Linden.

"And do not scoff, my lord," she added. "Lord Greymoor is a good man, but he's a horseman first. He has not the knowledge to run a sheep operation or to husband the land. Father thought to impress him with profits and wealth, and Lord Greymoor allowed it, even as the toll that took became increasingly apparent. We once went for almost four years without even seeing Lord Greymoor, and still my father ran this estate to the very best of his ability."

"So what happened, Miss Tanner?" Gwen posed the question because a look from Douglas suggested he'd rather she be the one to force this recitation. "From what you've said, your father's drinking did not preclude him from managing this place to Lord Greymoor's satisfaction, but your father is gone, and the estate is suffering."

Miss Tanner drew herself up, spine ramrod straight, and turned again to face the nasty weather.

"That woman happened," she said. "My father became infatuated with Mrs. Pettigrew, and lost all reason over her. Nothing would do but she must have his advice, and Papa must have finery to escort her about in, and a blooded gelding to come courting... what?"

"Mrs. Pettigrew's reputation precedes her," Douglas said in tones of distaste. "I am most sorry for you that your father took up with her. But let us keep to the matter at hand, Miss Tanner. What do you know of the estate books?"

"I know they are a mess."

Plain speaking, for which Gwen had to respect the woman. "Perhaps you could explain that mess to us, and please, join us in another cup of tea." The small civility of another cup of tea must have reassured the woman that she wasn't to be shot at dawn. She resumed her seat and accepted another cup of tea from Gwen.

"Have you embezzled from the estate?" Douglas asked almost pleasantly as Gwen added a third sugar and a tot of cream to his tea.

"I have not," Miss Tanner said, "but I honestly can't tell you what Papa did. He simply stopped keeping the books about two years ago. My efforts to create a fiction of order probably struck you as laughable."

"Certainly ineffective," Douglas replied. "What was your plan?"

Her shoulders drooped, reminding Gwen how tiring estate management could be, particularly by the end of the growing season.

"I planned to hold things together until Papa came back, but then it was planting and lambing and shearing, and on and on, and we had nobody to provide direction. Linden is adequately staffed, and the people here have been on the land for generations. They'll do their part, but somebody has to lead them. They looked to me because they knew, for all his drinking, my father was competent and I was his right hand in all things."

The story could have been Gwen's own, but Loris Tanner had had no wealthy cousins to support her, no grandfather happy to turn his acres over to her, no doting aunt to send the occasional chatty note.

As Douglas studied his teacup, Gwen suspected the very same thoughts were occurring to him.

"I will contemplate your situation, Miss Tanner," Douglas said when the last round of tea had been consumed. He stood, drawing her to her feet and laying her hand on his arm. "I will consult with Miss Hollister, who is also considering purchase of the property, and we will make a recommendation to Lord Greymoor regarding what should be done. Some provision will be made for you. Lord Greymoor does not shirk responsibility for his dependents."

He'd escorted her to the front hall, with Gwen on her other side.

"You won't be notifying the magistrate?" Miss Tanner asked, though it was clear the question cost her pride significantly.

Douglas peered down at her, his expression one Gwen recognized not as mild distaste, but rather, Douglas's version of concentrated regard. "That would not be appropriate. If the weather is dry the day after tomorrow, can you ride out with us?"

"I can," Miss Tanner said, relief jeopardizing her composure.

"We will look for you then." Douglas bowed over her hand and signaled for the butler to open the door.

"Thank you, my lord. Miss Hollister."

The butler, who had heard Miss Tanner's last question, closed the door behind her, caught Gwen's eye, and winked.

If Douglas saw that exchange, he made no mention of it, but offered his arm to Gwen. "A moment of your time in the library, if you please, Miss Hollister?"

So formal, and yet Gwen was learning a different side to Douglas, too, one that suggested shyness was a part of his formality.

"Interesting development," Douglas observed, taking Gwen by the hand and leading her to the library sofa. "Do you believe she's telling the truth?"

"I do," Gwen said, settling herself in beside him. "If she were bent on mischief, she could have sold every animal on the property and absconded. She could have continued to dodge us. She could have posed as Tanner's wife, that sort of thing. I don't envy her."

When Douglas slipped an arm around her shoulders, Gwen tucked herself into the curve of his body and marveled at how comfortable their proximity was.

And... comforting, too. Not simply because the fire crackled cozily and Douglas's cedary scent tickled Gwen's nose. The comfort was purely a function of being with Douglas—touching him, and sharing with him the dilemmas and duties of the day.

Douglas leaned his head back against the cushions, closing his eyes. "We have solved our mystery, and I must now decide whether to buy the property or not."

Abruptly, Gwen understood they were on boggy ground—ground she hadn't foreseen while Douglas clearly had. "Is Andrew pressing you for an answer?"

"He is not, yet. I like this property well enough. I like this house. I love, most of all, the memories I have here of time spent with you. The decision will be... difficult."

Love. Douglas would not love casually, would not even use the word casually.

A shaft of pain lanced at Gwen's heart, to hear Douglas talking in the same sentence—already—of both love and memories.

"You would be good for this place, Douglas. The people here would do well by you."

"Are you so anxious to get rid of me, then?"

Gwen turned her face into his shoulder. "I most

assuredly do not want to be rid of you. I wish it were not so, but there it is."

"You still don't trust me?" he asked, something resigned in his voice.

Gwen drew back to study him. "What do you mean? You heard my endorsement of you to Miss Tanner."

"Guinevere, *why won't you marry me?*"

The clocked ticked, the fire roared softly in the hearth, and the raw wind soughed around the corner of the house, and there was nothing—not one word Gwen could think of to say. Douglas deserved the truth, but she hardly knew what that truth was herself or how to give it to him. She stood, keeping her back to him as she moved toward the door.

"It isn't a matter of I will not marry you, Douglas. It's that I cannot."

She slipped from the room in a flurry of skirts, leaving Douglas to stare at the fire and consider at significant length why a woman *couldn't* marry the man who was in mortal peril of loving her beyond all reason.

Ten

"LADIES." DOUGLAS INTERRUPTED A FIERCE DEBATE over plow designs, the most recent of many fierce and exuberant debates between Guinevere and Loris Tanner. "I am tiring more rapidly than I had predicted. I don't want to leave you without escort, though. Shall I send a groom out to join you?"

"I apologize, Douglas," Guinevere said, turning her horse to walk along beside his. "I had not realized the time we've passed in the saddle. Why don't we ride by Dove Cottage and then continue to Linden? We've seen plenty for one day, and the afternoon grows chilly."

"Miss Tanner?" Douglas inquired politely, though judging by his aching fundament, chilly was a vast euphemism.

"I am a bit cold."

"Then we shall ride in." He urged Regis into a rocking canter, the ladies fell in behind him, and they soon reached Dove Cottage.

Douglas assisted Miss Tanner to dismount, but when she turned to lead her gelding to her stable, he stopped her with a hand on her arm.

"I think you should know, Miss Tanner, I wrote to Lord Greymoor today."

She said nothing, her expression indicating she expected press gangs and constables to swarm her property at any moment. Douglas knew that expression, for it closely resembled Guinevere's view of the world not so long ago.

"I suggested to Greymoor he might want to retain you in the capacity of steward," Douglas said. "Andrew Alexander is one of few titled gentlemen—perhaps the *only* titled gentleman in the realm—who could be persuaded to accept a female in that capacity, thanks to Miss Hollister's excellent efforts at Enfield and your peculiar circumstances here at Linden. Should he offer the position, and should you decline it, he will forward to you a sum commensurate with the salary you have earned since you assumed the post informally."

"Thank you," she said, looking away. "Lord Amery, thank you."

Her grip on the reins looked perilously tight, though her sturdy gelding was in no danger of bolting off when his supper waited in the nearby barn.

"You are welcome, though you have Miss Hollister to thank for putting this option to Lord Greymoor."

"Miss Hollister." Miss Tanner turned and curtsied deeply.

"It is getting chillier, isn't it?" Douglas observed, gaze going to the gray clouds overhead. He bowed crisply to Miss Tanner and swung up on Regis before one or the other female became overwhelmed by sentiment. "Miss Hollister, shall we be off?"

Upon reaching the Linden stables, Guinevere handed her horse to a groom and shot a quizzical look at Douglas as he led Regis into the barn.

"What did you say to her?" she asked, lowering herself to a bench while Douglas removed Regis's bridle and saddle.

"I told her I took your advice." He stepped back so Regis could shake his big dark head from side to side, and that turned into a whole body shake such as a sound, sturdy mount could best enjoy when free of saddle and girth.

"And that had her in tears?" Guinevere inquired, watching the horse.

Regis, completely unconfined, stood his ground while Douglas retrieved a coarse towel from the saddle room and laid it over his own shoulder.

"I didn't know she was crying," he said, stepping up to the horse's face.

What followed was part of a ritual between man and horse Douglas had never intended for another—much less his lady love—to observe. Regis lowered his head to rub his face blissfully against the towel on Douglas's shoulder, Douglas having to plant his feet and lean into the horse simply to stay upright. When Regis lifted his head away from Douglas's shoulder, Douglas switched the towel to his other shoulder, and let the horse repeat the exercise on the other side of his face.

"Will that do?" Douglas asked the horse when Regis appeared to have tended to his itches. Regis turned an innocent eye on his owner, clearly a beast in need of treats.

"Shameless," Douglas muttered, producing a small apple from his coat pocket, taking a bite out of it, and offering the rest for Regis to chomp to bits.

"What has you frowning?" Douglas asked Guinevere as he folded the pad over the saddle. Regis hung his head and shook all over again like a half-ton wet dog.

"I am thinking of how affectionate you are."

Daft woman. "I don't believe I've been described as affectionate before."

"Ask Regis. He'll tell you who's affectionate."

Guinevere rose and took up scratching the horse's withers, and really, the damned beast had no dignity. "So why, sir, haven't you been affectionate with me lately?"

Douglas found a brush and focused on the flank of the horse he was grooming. Even over the scent of horse and barn, he picked up Guinevere's floral, feminine fragrance, and his body became subtly more alert to her nearness.

"I have not wanted to impose," he said. "It has been more than a week since the household was healthy enough for us to… disport, and you have rebuffed my offer of marriage yet again. I'm not sure where that leaves us."

He brushed his horse, but had to pause to recall if he'd started on the beast's neck or quarters—neck, most likely—and on which side.

"Douglas."

He straightened and regarded her levelly across the horse's back. "Yes, Guinevere?"

"That leaves us with *me* still desiring *you*, very much."

Douglas had one hand on Regis's withers, the other on the gelding's croup. He braced himself against the horse and studied the muddy toes of his boots. Guinevere made this pronouncement in a blasted barn, where any groom might chance upon them, and where Douglas could *not* drag her up into the haymow—

"Are you sure that will be enough?" he asked, though he knew the question was pointless—also hopeless. "You want only my body, Guinevere? Only coupling? You would not rather have my name, my companionship, my honorable attentions, my future?"

"I may want all of that, Douglas Allen. What I want and what I can have are two different things."

Oh, and wasn't that lovely? Regis, having an unfortunate history, had gone tense at the note of temper in

Douglas's voice. He offered the horse a reassuring pat, and spoke with careful civility. "We are in the same position then, for what I want is apparently ñot what I will get either."

She said nothing but took to stroking her hand over Regis's neck in a slow pattern that Douglas found any-thing but soothing to watch. The horse, however, was calmed to the point of half closing its fool eyes. Douglas put the beast away and escorted Guinevere up to the house, pausing before they went inside.

He was not a complete simpleton. He might not win the lady's hand in marriage, but he would console himself with whatever crumbs of intimacy she'd allow, and hope those might lead to greater possibilities.

"Tonight, then, Guinevere?"

She did not pretend confusion. She beamed a smile at him, a naughty, lovely smile such as every woman ought to aim at some hapless fellow at least once in her life. "Tonight."

Then she sashayed through the door, pronouncing herself in need of a soaking bath. Douglas shut himself in the library, ostensibly to deal with his correspondence. In truth, he sat on the sofa, listening to the ticking of the clock, staring at the fire, and thinking.

❧

When Gwen arrived in the family parlor, Douglas greeted her in the same cordial, well mannered tones he always did, offered her wine, which she declined, and made polite inquiries regarding Rose, Hester, Mrs. Kitts, and even wee Ralph. He offered his arm when the butler announced dinner, and seated her in the same unerringly polite sequence he always observed.

But after the soup had been brought, he indicated to

the hovering footman they would serve themselves for the balance of the meal. When Gwen was alone with him and several courses had been consumed, Douglas regarded her over the rim of his wineglass.

"You are unusually quiet tonight, Guinevere."

"I am preoccupied." Douglas was a clever fellow. She need not be more explicit than that, though she did appropriate Douglas's wineglass from his hand and gulp down a healthy measure of Dutch courage.

Douglas took the wineglass from her and set it out of her reach. "If you do not look forward to this as much as I, Guinevere, if you do not feel some joy in the anticipation of our joining, if you do not desire me as I desire you, then we shouldn't do this. Not tonight, perhaps not ever."

God in heaven, how could the man be so calm, so articulate? Neither feat was within Gwen's grasp, though she could be honest. With Douglas, she could manage that much.

"I am flustered," she said, indulging in a monumental understatement. "We were becoming quite *involved*, and then Rose got sick, and our situation changed." She reached for her water glass this time, thoughts completing themselves as she spoke. "Now Miss Tanner has come forth, and the decision to buy or not can be made, and circumstances have changed again. I am flustered, and I have lost track of you."

"I am still here," Douglas said, covering her hand with his. "I still desire you, and I still offer you my intimate attentions, but only if you still want them."

"I do." He had such beautiful hands, and he offered his for her to hold, when she could offer him so little in return.

"Is there a but, love?"

"But then we go home," she murmured, mustering

her courage, "and it will change yet again, perhaps for the last time."

Douglas's chin dipped as if he'd taken a blow. "If that is what you deem must happen, but we are not home yet, Guinevere, and tonight things will change between us yet again."

She declined to argue, was *unable* to argue. When Douglas left her at her door, he leaned in to kiss her cheek, his lips near her ear.

"Leave your hair up for me." His words sent a shiver of anticipation down her spine, so she ducked into her room, lest she drag him directly to bed that very moment.

❧

The bath Douglas had ordered was waiting for him in his bedroom, and he quickly divested himself of his evening clothes. He wanted tonight to be perfect for Guinevere, and he debated the merits of masturbation as he soaked in the tub. Anticipation had him sufficiently aroused that he decided to indulge, hoping it would take the edge off his lust and allow him to show Guinevere greater restraint.

But damn and blast, onanistic gratification only left him hovering nearer to the edge of arousal.

As he toweled off and donned a dressing gown, he tried to prepare for what lay ahead. He and Guinevere would make love, more than once if God were merciful to a fool in love, and then… what?

Then, he most assuredly wanted *more*. Guinevere Hollister had been rebuffing even the possibility of suitors for five years. She wasn't going to marry anyone else, and Douglas wasn't going to give up on her. He set his mind to that resolution and made his way to her bedchamber.

He knocked twice then let himself in. Clad in her

dressing gown, his lady love sat before the fire, her hair still up in an elegant twist. She was neither reading nor working on her embroidery, but simply sitting on the carpet, knees drawn up, toes peeking out from the hem of her dressing gown.

He'd never made love on the floor before, and did not entirely favor the notion for the consummation of his dealings with her—nor did he entirely reject it. "Guinevere?"

She looked up and smiled at him, a warm, beneficent welcome that erased whatever doubts he'd been holding at bay. He'd go slowly and ease her into passion. He *would*.

He might have joined her before the fire, but she stood, crossed the room to slip her arms around his waist, and tucked her forehead against his chest.

"You want this?" Douglas asked for what his swelling cock hoped was the last time. She nodded without looking up. "Feeling shy?"

She nodded again, and when she laid her cheek against his chest, he could feel the heat of a blush on her skin.

"Guinevere." He took her face between his hands, feeling her embarrassment against his palms. "I will not cause you pain. I will not importune you for favors you are unwilling to give. I'll stop if you ask it of me."

Her response was to go up on her toes and press her lips to his, a tender sealing of his vows to her. He gathered her against him, sent up a silent prayer of thanks, and opened his mouth over hers. For long minutes, they stood thus, kissing, holding each other, and exploring ground they hadn't visited for days. When Guinevere's hands began to roam his body, Douglas eased his mouth away from hers.

"I want to take down your hair," he whispered against her neck. "Will you allow that?"

"Of course." She would have moved away, but Douglas laced his fingers through hers, and walked with her to her vanity. She handed him the brush, and he stopped her as she lifted her hands to start removing the pins.

"Let me." *Please, God, let me.*

He removed hair pins and loosened thick, coppery coils, strands of golden red sliding through his fingers like wishes on the wind. Soon her hair was streaming down her back, and Douglas was using the brush gently, in long rhythmic strokes. When her unbound hair shimmered by the firelight, he buried his nose in a fistful of lavender-scented curls.

"Time to undress you," Douglas murmured to the pulse that beat in her throat. "Please."

Guinevere stood and unbelted her night-robe, while Douglas watched from several paces off, lest he tear her clothes from her body.

"The nightgown, Guinevere." He was begging in all but the most technical sense.

She stepped over to him and unbelted his dressing gown. He understood. She would not be the only one to be naked and vulnerable, so he slipped the dressing gown off, purposely turning his back to her to drape it across the foot of the bed. She had seen him naked, or parts of him, but this complete undressing now symbolized an intimacy of more than the body that he very much wanted to share with his Guinevere.

He turned to her and waited, his arousal clearly evident, desire coursing through his mind and body. Guinevere did not approach him, but rather, keeping the distance between them, lifted the nightgown over her head and laid it beside his dressing gown on the bed.

This disrobing by stages, unveiling themselves by turns, struck Douglas as a sartorial exchange of further vows.

He held out a hand. Guinevere was so lovely, his breath caught simply to behold her like this, naked, proud, and for tonight at least, *his*. "Come to me—please."

And he was proud of her, too, for Guinevere walked into his arms, bringing her body flush up against him, breasts to chest, belly to belly, thigh to thigh. She was no longer that nineteen-year-old innocent, nor was she a woman held captive by that innocent's experiences.

Douglas's erection lay snug between them, the feel of her warm flesh against him a completion of some journey for him as well.

Were he given to poetry, he'd have the words. Instead, he treasured the sensations.

Guinevere's hands sliding down his back.

Her fingers sinking into the muscles of his buttocks as she pulled him closer to her still.

Her hair brushing his arms as he anchored her against his body.

Guinevere was strong—physically strong. Why had he not realized this? She raised one long leg and wrapped it around his hip.

She managed this while Douglas focused on a kiss that burned into near violence within moments. His mouth over hers was ravening, his tongue plundering, arousing, and more wicked in its forays than he'd known he could be.

"I want my hands on you," Douglas whispered. "I want to be inside you. Bed. We need to get on the bed."

Douglas unwrapped Guinevere's leg from his hip and walked her back until she bumped into the bed and sat abruptly. He sat beside her, naked, aroused, and breathing heavily. It was not too great an exaggeration to allow he was a trifle dizzy as well.

"I want to go slowly." He honestly did. Slowly and often.

"I just want to *go*," Guinevere replied, her breathing ragged. God bless the woman, she looked like years of sexual deprivation were riding her to the limit. While he still could, Douglas sorted through their options.

He climbed onto the bed and stretched out on his back. "Straddle me. We'll go at whatever pace you set."

"I want you on top of me. I like your weight."

She *would* argue about this, and he loved her for it. "I am endeavoring to be considerate, Guinevere. Can we try it this way, and if it's not to your liking, we can move on to something else?"

She frowned, but thank a merciful Deity, relented. "We can." She crawled onto the bed then swung a leg over his body. "Shall I touch you?"

God, yes.

"Soon." Douglas brushed her hair back from her shoulders, resisting the urge to lash his arms around her and drive up into her feminine heat. "For now, kiss me."

She brushed her lips against his in a languorous caress, one that helped Douglas dampen the loudest of his body's clamorings. He liked it when she gave him her tongue, he liked it even more when she took his hand and fitted it around her breast, and he liked it nigh unbearably when she settled her hips firmly over him and slid her sex across the ridge of his erection. Just a few minutes of that was enough to leave them both slick and undulating against each other.

"I want to be inside you," Douglas managed, arching up off the bed to get his mouth on a succulent nipple.

"Want you inside," Guinevere panted.

"Guide me. Take me slowly."

He fitted Gwen's fingers around his shaft and let his

hand fall away, leaving control of the moment entirely with her. She went still, and so did he, subsiding onto the bed and letting his hands rest on her hips when what he wanted was to be anything but passive.

To take control of the moment from her would be easy, and she might even thank him for it. It would also be wrong in a way that had to do with respect and caring rather than mindless swiving. Douglas waited, stroking his thumbs over the crests of her hips and praying for patience.

Guinevere took a steadying breath then brush-stroked the head of his cock along her sex, using him to paint herself with her own lubrication. She did this several more times, while Douglas fought not to grind his teeth.

When he thought he'd explode with frustration, she leaned up a little, used her free hand to brace herself against Douglas's chest, and positioned the tip of his cock against the opening of her body.

"Easy," he warned. "Go easy."

Her expression said she didn't want to go easy. She was anxious, aroused, and uncertain. He suspected in some way the dear lady even wanted this over with, but an abrupt invasion would not serve her well.

"Shall I move?" he asked when Guinevere seemed unable to manage it.

"Please."

Lovely, useful word—particularly when whispered as a desperate plea.

He lifted his hips minutely, and Guinevere flinched away. Her gaze was focused on the place where their bodies would join, her eyes holding equal parts worry and passion.

"Guinevere, I need you to kiss me."

She leaned down obligingly and treated him to

another languorous, sanity-robbing assault on his mouth. As her tongue traced his lips, Douglas shifted his hips up again, the merest fraction of what his body sought. She didn't flinch, and it was enough that—thank all the gods—he was threaded into her body. He added to this a soft caress to her breast and felt her relax above him.

Her breasts, he finally recalled, were exquisitely sensitive. He kept his cock shallowly embedded in her slick warmth and brought both hands up to her breasts.

"Move on me, love," he coaxed. "Pleasure yourself." She broke the kiss momentarily and flexed her hips slowly. "That's it, but give me more."

He experimented with adding his own flexion to Guinevere's undulations, and when she arched her breasts into his hands, he concluded she was pleased with his efforts.

As, by God, was he. And beyond pleased with her.

Sliding one hand to the small of her back, Douglas anchored himself and settled in to penetrate his way to her depths with slow, steady strokes.

"Douglas Allen, you feel *sublime.*" She curled down to his chest, her breathing deep and a trifle unsteady. They left off kissing, both apparently more interested in this other, newer pleasure, the overwhelming pleasure of intimately joining. Douglas's free hand cupped her breast, and Guinevere arched into his hand, her hips writhing in counterpoint to the pleasure of his thrusts.

Seeing her face suffused with arousal and feeling her body succumb to passion, Douglas allowed himself to escalate the speed, force, and depth of his thrusts.

"I want you to have your pleasure of me." Longed for it, and desperately hoped he could manage it for her.

"Douglas…" Her voice held wonder and yearning. Also some bewilderment.

"I want to be inside you when you come," he whispered, closing his fingers in firm rhythmic pressure around her nipple. He let himself thrust harder, then harder still, watching all the while for any sign from Guinevere that she was unreceptive to his efforts.

"Douglas…" The longing in her voice had become more intense as her hips began to meet his with strength and purpose. "I want… so much."

"I know." He nipped at her breast. "Let go for me, love, just let go…" He took her nipple in his mouth, inspiring Guinevere to a soft, keening moan. Driven by his mouth, his hands, and his cock, her body began to spasm around him in great clutching shudders of pleasure that tested Douglas's resolve to its limits. When she would have flinched away from the intensity of the sensation, he drove her forward into its depths, thrusting relentlessly, slowing his hips only when he felt her pleasure subside.

In the aftermath, Guinevere lay sprawled on his chest, her fingers tracing his features.

Douglas kissed her temple. "My love, tell me you are all right." *Tell me I am your love, too.*

She flicked her tongue over his nipple.

"Ah, love…"

Guinevere repeated the gesture then traced his sternum with her nose.

While she drowsed on his chest, Douglas barely moved inside her, minutely gliding in, and then partly withdrawing, but the pleasure of it was exquisite. He'd not shared erotic intimacies this way before, not ever, and the sheer glory of Guinevere cast away with passion soon had him lost to restraint. He thrust hard and deep, and she met him exuberantly.

"Come for me." He heard her whispered exhortation

just before she opened her mouth on the meat of his shoulder. And then… "Dear God, Douglas…"

Her pleasure sent him hurtling over the edge, tossed headlong into endless moments of profound bliss. Before it was over, Douglas's vision wavered, his ears roared, and even lying twined tightly in Guinevere's arms, he felt a sense of breathless vertigo. So he held on, and in that moment, could not have let her go to save his own life.

"You are all right?" Douglas whispered some moments later.

"Better than all right. You?"

"Lovely." The word felt strange on his lips, strange and… well, lovely. "Beyond lovely—though becoming a bit untidy." He was, in fact, slipping from her body. "Flannel, sweetheart. Sooner rather than later."

She reached over to the nightstand and slapped a cloth into his hand.

"Lift up and forward."

"But I'll…" How could she argue? How could she be Guinevere and not?

"Yes, you will," he said, "onto me. Better me than the sheets." He patted her bottom—why had he never patted her lovely bum before?—and she eased forward. Douglas swiped at her gently with the flannel and blotted it against her sex before guiding her off of him altogether. He tidied himself up as well, then wrapped an arm around Guinevere's shoulders.

"You want to talk?" he asked, drawing her head to his shoulder. Quite possibly, *he* needed *her* to talk to him, if even a little.

"I don't know what to say. The sensations are indescribably intense, the pleasure overwhelming, the emotions beyond description. I am in awe, bewildered, and completely incapable of comprehending this."

Were he asked, Douglas might have admitted to the same list, though he might also have been carried away enough to have gone a step further. *I love you too.* "Do you have any physical discomfort?"

"No. None."

Douglas relaxed fractionally at that assurance, but as she heaved a sigh he waited, prepared to hear any criticism, any demurrer.

"Is it always like this?"

Ah. A brilliant question—and something he could work with. He kissed her temple, and if he'd been able, he might have kissed her very thoughts. "No. I have never, Guinevere, not *ever*, enjoyed a sexual experience as much as this. I think between us, it would always be wonderful, though not always in the same way."

"This is what my cousins have, isn't it?" She sounded puzzled and wistful. "Their wives *thrive* on their affections."

"I suspect this is a substantial part of their marital joy." For which his envy was without limit.

She snuggled closer, the fit of their bodies nothing short of marvelous. "And this is why you want to marry me, because you knew it would be like this?"

"One can't know how matters will progress with a prospective lover, but yes, this is part of why I want to marry you." *Want desperately to marry you.* This time he kissed her brow.

"I wish you could." The wistfulness shaded closer to misery, or perhaps closer to sleep.

"I wish we could too." Wished, prayed, importuned the Almighty without ceasing… the yearning Douglas felt to spend the rest of his life with this woman beggared description.

He stayed with her until her breathing was even and her body relaxed in slumber. As much as he wanted to remain with her through the night—through every night—Douglas dared not. He sensed she would not marry him, even if they were found scandalously entwined in the morning, but regard for her reputation alone wasn't what sent him back to the cold comfort of his solitary bed.

He left Guinevere's bed because he feared if he allowed himself to spend the entire night in her arms, he would never be able to let her go.

※

Douglas poured a fresh cup of breakfast tea for his lady and for himself, having shooed the footman off and suggested that worthy fellow shoo the maids off as well. "How are you this glorious morning, Guinevere?"

"Glorious?"

The tiniest hint of uncertainty in Guinevere's eyes only warmed Douglas's heart. "For me, it is glorious. *You* are glorious."

She found her tea fascinating at that remark, and Douglas felt a surge of affection for her that made him want to scoop her into his lap and... by God, he wanted to *tickle* her.

He settled for laying a hand on her arm, but wondered if he could tickle her out of her shyness—and if she might tickle him back.

Which thoughts suggested he had misplaced his sanity the previous night, and happily so.

His lady was shy this morning and, he suspected, vulnerable. "Is something amiss, Guinevere?"

"You left me," she murmured.

Without penning her a note, without plucking a rose from some hothouse bouquet for her pillow, without a whispered farewell. He had much to learn about being her lover, and hoped she'd allow him the time to learn it.

"I did not want to drift off in your bed and be discovered there come morning."

"Douglas, you needn't be concerned with the servants' opinions of me. Your discretion is appreciated, though I'm already quite the fallen woman and hardly—"

He stopped her with a finger to her lips.

"You are fallen—into my arms, and while you are there, I will protect you with every resource I possess, including my very life."

She declined to argue, thank the Deity.

"You haven't answered my question, Guinevere." Douglas added cream and sugar to her tea, for the small indulgences were what she permitted him to give her.

"I am... well," she said, as Douglas stirred her tea, passed it to her, and wrapped her fingers around the warmth of the teacup.

"I am well," she repeated more strongly, "and you are a bit glorious yourself."

She was so brave, and he was in such trouble. Such glorious trouble. He took a steadying sip of his tea, though the case was hopeless.

"Am I really, now? Good to know. A fellow likes to hear these things from time to time. Would you prefer cinnamon for your toast? And you've some letters from your lady cousins. I brought them down for you in hopes they'd make a pleasant start to your day."

They passed the remainder of breakfast in companionable silence, parting so Guinevere could check on Rose—the letters unread on the sideboard—and Douglas could steal off to the library. He set himself to the task of drafting projections of the income and expenses needed to put Linden in good enough repair that it could serve once again not merely as a gentleman's country retreat, but as a home where dreams could be shared.

✐

Douglas Allen had been *whistling* when he'd jaunted off to cavort in the library with his abacus. As Gwen made her way to the nursery, she realized that whistle might mean Douglas was leaning toward buying the property.

This notion *hurt*.

Gwen had hidden away at Enfield, burying herself in the agricultural cycles of land and livestock for more than five years. She'd been close to no one, save Rose, and she'd managed to convince herself it was a good life.

Compared to the lot many faced, it was a very good life.

But compared to the prospect of becoming Douglas's wife—his viscountess—the years stretching before her at Enfield loomed bleak, lonely, and empty. More bleak and empty to think Douglas would choose Sussex and this pretty property.

Though he should. Absolutely he should choose Linden, and she would encourage him to do so.

Douglas was her miracle, a reserved, burdened man who nonetheless brought her caring, joy, and passion. She would not seek his like in another. She would not hope for other affairs to alleviate her loneliness. The price of Douglas's regard was that Gwen saw, in stark relief, how far gone into isolation and despair she'd fallen.

And when Douglas left her…

She reversed her steps, slipped into the library, and stood just inside the door, watching Douglas at the desk. He had his spectacles on and scratched away with a pen in one hand, while he flicked at an abacus with the other.

"Are you spying?" Douglas did not look up but frowned at the paper before him. "I am stuck on a column of figures. You must come pull me out of the morass."

Gwen shifted to stand beside him, to look over his shoulder while he wrapped an arm around her waist.

"I can't get the columns to tally the same across and down," he said, nuzzling the underside of her breast, "but you should look them over anyway, because I have the nagging suspicion I've left out myriad expense categories. Come here."

He levered her around to sit between his legs, her weight braced on one of his thighs.

"You're right—you've left out all kinds of expenses and revenues, that I can see." Gwen pretended to study his figures for another few moments, though she also examined the way Douglas's golden hair grew in a swirl from his crown. "And you've no contingency fund."

"Do your worst," Douglas challenged. He let her go to perch on the corner of the desk, which was fortunate for the remnants of Gwen's wits. "Will you allow me to come to you again tonight, Guinevere?"

Gwen glanced up and then went back to his figures, or tried to.

"Guinevere?" He'd moved silently and stood beside her as she sat on the corner of the desk. A little hint of his cedary scent teased her nose, and the numbers on the page blurred. He leaned in, and by virtue of a hand on her shoulder urged her to rest her weight against his chest.

"I didn't know how to ask you," she said, putting the figures aside.

He let go a sigh that Gwen suspected meant he was relieved—as if she *could* have refused him—and then his lips cruised over her temple, and it was her turn to sigh. Some moments and several more sighs, groans, and caresses later, Douglas went to the door, locked it, and returned to the desk to stand immediately before her.

He was gentle with her, drawing her skirts up, letting her be the one to unbutton his falls. He slid into her body easily while he kissed her insensate, and despite the novelty of the location and the position, Gwen felt as if this coupling in the broad light of day, in a public room of the house, completed them somehow. She watched the place where their bodies joined, watched the thick column of his erection glide into her, and then back out, wet, glistening, virile, and to her eyes, beautiful.

A few minutes of that, a few minutes of knowing Douglas watched her as she watched *him*, and her desire began to gather in anticipation of more intense pleasure. Her last coherent thought was that this joining was different from its predecessor, intense but deliberate too, like a deep, rumbling roll of thunder rather than a sudden, sharp crack. Douglas joined her on a soft groan, and she felt wet heat when he spent deep in her body.

She drowsed on his shoulder, unable to speak, think, or move while Douglas tidied them up and restored their clothing, all without moving away from her. She was drifting somewhere toward sleep or pure oblivion, when Douglas scooped her up off the desk and carried her to the sofa. He sat them down such that the arm of the sofa supported Gwen's back, and tucked her head against the crook of his neck.

"Douglas?"

He kissed her temple then laid his cheek against her hair. "Right here, love."

"I slept."

"In my arms," Douglas replied softly. "I wore you out—you may be sore."

"Sore?"

"Intimately," he clarified. "I was rather exuberant."

"I know." Gwen arched her back and tried not to start

wishing and wishing. "One would not suspect Lord Amery capable of such lovely, decadent, *gratifying* exuberance."

"Nor Miss Hollister," he agreed, nuzzling her again. "But if one doesn't get the library door unlocked fairly soon, the entire household will promptly begin considering the possibility."

"Blast." Gwen kissed his jaw. She loved the angle of his jaw, finding it metaphor for his personality in general: resolute, clean, strong. *God help her.* "Just when I've a mind to inspire you to exuberance again."

When Mrs. Kitts came bustling in with the tea a while later, Gwen was ensconced on the sofa, chewing the end of her pencil and sitting amid a sea of foolscap. Douglas sat at the desk, his booted feet propped on one corner, the only sounds the crackling of the fire, ticking of the clock, and the clicking of the abacus.

"So serious, you two," Mrs. Kitts remonstrated. "It can't always be work, work, work, you know." She set the tea tray down as Douglas abruptly went looking for something in the bottom drawer of the desk. "Well, it can't," she repeated, nodding for emphasis.

Gwen recovered enough from her coughing fit to thank the woman and shoo her on her way, but when the door had closed behind the housekeeper, she dissolved into fits of laughter. It took two cups of tea—and keeping several yards between her and the hardworking Lord Amery— before she felt sufficiently composed to leave the library.

"I'm going to see Rose," Gwen announced, standing and stretching and sounding—she hoped—like she couldn't possibly have been thinking of straddling Douglas's lap as he sat ciphering away at the abacus. "Shall we have luncheon in here or in the dining parlor?"

"Why not in the dining parlor, and why not invite Rose to join us?" Douglas suggested as he got to his feet.

"Rose?" If Douglas had suggested Gwen ride naked through the town, she could not have been more surprised.

He peered down at her. "Well, all right. Mr. Bear, too, though I understand he might be under the weather."

"How do you understand that?"

"I usually stop by the nursery for the daily report on my way to breakfast, and then again before I change for dinner. Rose is most informative. My judgment is reserved about that bear, however." He kissed her nose then returned to the desk.

"I see."

"I will look forward to the company of you ladies at lunch." Douglas had his feet propped and his spectacles back up on his nose before Gwen had left the library.

As she made her way to the nursery, Gwen decided it didn't matter *when* she'd fallen in love with Douglas. It might have been when he rescued Rose from the hornets, when he'd first grasped Gwen's hand, when he'd been sufficiently interested in her to win her intimate trust, when he'd fought so hard to keep Rose well, or when he'd casually announced he made regular visits to the nursery.

But fallen, she had—into his arms, as he'd said, but also in love.

"Guinevere Hollister, you are in such trouble." She'd probably fallen in love with Douglas on each of those occasions and a few more besides, and there was not one blessed thing she wanted to do about it.

Eleven

"I miss Daisy," Rose announced at lunch. "Cousin Douglas, will we go home soon?"

"We shall," Douglas replied, which was fortunate, for Gwen could not think of a response. "Your mother and I have almost completed our business here, but we must now wait until the weather is promising to make our journey home. You could write Daisy a letter, and I'm sure your Cousin Andrew would read it to her."

"Mama? Can I?"

"May I," Gwen corrected automatically, though thoughts of home did not bring the joy and relief they ought. "Yes, and I commend you for not pelting off without asking to be excused."

"Can I be excused?"

"May I," both adults chorused. Gwen followed up with permission for Rose to leave the table, after which Rose rocketed out of the dining parlor, intent on her correspondence.

"So we're soon to leave for home?" She did not meet Douglas's gaze while she posed this question. A leaden feeling settled in Gwen's stomach, having nothing to do with Cook's excellent meal.

"I'd rather tarry here and let the rest of the world go hang."

He looked as morose as Gwen felt, which was some consolation. "Is that an irresponsible sentiment from Douglas, Viscount Amery?"

"Irresponsible, selfish, lascivious, and heartfelt. What becomes of us when we return, Guinevere?"

Us—troublesome, wonderful word. "I don't know." She dreaded the exchange that must ensue, even as she was grateful that Douglas, at least, had the courage to face it. "I can't see beyond the fact that we must leave."

Douglas propped his elbows on the table—which astounding breach of etiquette Gwen found endearing—and turned the teapot in a steady circle by its handle. "As I see it, we have several options. We can continue our liaison, though it will be more difficult with family underfoot and familiar retainers about. We can allow this aspect of our dealings to come to a close and trust each other to behave civilly when our paths inevitably cross, or we can make an effort to disentangle our lives, ensuring we need not interact in future."

So rational, so blasted logical. "None of those options appeal."

"Indeed they do not," Douglas agreed, still twirling the teapot thoughtfully. "There are others."

"Others?"

"I can buy this property, and you can accompany me here as a nominal cousin, acting as my hostess and lady of the house, or you can marry me, though I understand you do not regard that possibility as realistic."

Douglas was persistent. Bless him and damn him, he was persistent. "Do we have to have this conversation now?"

"We need to start it, Guinevere," Douglas said, his tone painfully gentle. "We face a difficult business, and if we cannot come to some understanding of our preferred outcome, we could part in anger or distrust. I could not abide that."

"Nor could I." Though assuredly they would part in sadness. "I have no answers, Douglas. I do not want to part from you, but neither can I see smiling pleasantly through little Lucy's birthday party, treating you as if you were simply her dear godfather and uncle. Nor, however, can I conceive of a future without you in it, though in some ways, a clean break might heal most easily. This idea of living together here at Linden had not occurred to me, honestly, but I will give it thought."

She would likely think of little else.

He left off twirling the tea pot and seemed to come to some decision. "Why, given how you say you feel, would you not allow me to marry you? Your position makes no sense to me, and I am a man who must have his plain answers and commonsense explanations. I believe you care for me, and whatever holds you back is real to you, but I wish you could share it with me. I *beg* you to share it with me."

Oh, wretched, dear man. He would offer that—that *too*. "The reason is very real to me, and all I can say is I am abjectly sorry. If you cannot continue to offer me your affections, I will understand."

Because of this much, she was certain: if Douglas knew her circumstances, he would end their liaison immediately—would never have embarked upon it, in fact.

Douglas was silent for a moment, no doubt shifting the beads on some internal abacus.

"I want to shout at you, Guinevere." Douglas spoke very softly, a note of bewilderment in his tone. "I feel like shaking you, like galloping away on Regis and never looking back. This vacillation of the emotions—from ecstasy to despair in the course of a morning—is beyond what I can bear, yet bear it I shall. I sense defeat looming, though, and without even being able to name my foe. I can't bear that either."

He scrubbed a hand over his face. "I will have any place in your life you'll allow. As Lucy's uncle, as your former lover, as your friend, as your cicisbeo. I will leave you in peace if that's what you ask of me, but Guinevere, it will be the loneliest, most pointless peace either of us has ever known."

"I know," Gwen said, tears trickling down her cheeks. "Douglas, I know."

Gwen got up so quickly Douglas barely had time to get to his feet before she snatched her cousin's letters from the sideboard and quit the room.

What she wanted was to throw herself on the bed and dissolve into tears—except that bed was where she and Douglas had first made love. The vanity was where Douglas had taken such care with her hair. The hearth rug was where she had waited for her lover...

She took the letters to the escritoire by the window, promised herself a good cry later, and tried to focus on the words her cousins' wives had penned to her. When she'd read the first, never mind the second, she climbed onto the bed and cried as if her heart was broken and would never mend.

⁂

"You didn't see her?" Victor Windham asked again, though Westhaven's note had been clear enough, and several days of rereading it hadn't changed the brief contents.

"No, I did not, and neither did I see portraits of her hanging about the place that would tell me how her looks have changed in six years," Westhaven said, drawing open curtains to let cold autumn light fill the small parlor. "She is surrounded by a phalanx of concerned, titled, wealthy, and protective male relatives now, and a butterfly on a pin would have been more comfortable than I was taking tea with them."

Victor's older brother paced the confines of the smallest family parlor in the Moreland ducal mansion, a distaste for both confinement and secrets part of his nature. Westhaven was a good sort, duty bound and conscientious about the land—also possessed of vibrant animal health, for which Victor gave thanks every night. God knew, Westhaven would make a better duke than their late brother Bartholomew would have, and he was by far a better brother than Victor deserved.

"I appreciate that you tried," Victor said, staring at the blanket on his lap. He was often cold of late, and their sister Jenny had knitted him the blanket. She'd used a blend of wool and angora, and the blanket's soft, plush feel was a tactile reminder of her love. "I hope you're willing to try again."

"I'll see her, Victor, and I'll put your request to her." Westhaven squeezed his shoulder gently.

Everyone handled him gently these days. Everyone except his father, His Grace, the Duke of Moreland. The duke, a hale, bluff curmudgeon of a former cavalry officer, expressed his disappointment in his remaining—*woefully unwed*, according to His Grace—sons at every opportunity.

Westhaven paused to straighten a frame that held a sketch Jenny had done of her five brothers years earlier. "I will not fail you on this. Fairly seemed confident Miss Hollister would admit me, though I suspect it would be to give me a royal dressing down."

"She has nothing to castigate you for," Victor retorted. "I'm the one who used her badly and made no reparation." None at all, though he'd intended his distance as a kindness—not that Gwen could understand it as such.

Westhaven made another circuit of the parlor, boots thumping in the confident rhythm of excellent health. "At the time, she truly did not want to marry you, and I think you'll find her mind unchanged. If she has any sense, she regrets trusting you. She does not regret her unwed state."

Guinevere Hollister had had buckets and bales of sense, and if Westhaven hadn't met with her, he could hardly speak to the woman's regrets. "I have to try, Westhaven."

The earl did not argue—Westhaven was the soul of discretion and courtesy—but instead summoned a footman to wheel Victor's Bath chair from the room.

Gayle Windham watched his brother's departure with a sinking sensation that had become reflexive where poor Victor was concerned. This quest—for in Victor's eyes, it was a quest—to offer reparation to Miss Hollister seemed to be the main reason Victor clung to life.

And while their parents hovered around Victor, Westhaven was left to manage the vast acreage of the ducal estates. Their youngest brother, Valentine, chose to rusticate, and kept an eye on matters at the family seat in Kent, but Val was typically so lost in his music, Westhaven relied on him as little as possible. As the fourth legitimate son by birth, Valentine now approached the status of presumptive heir to a dukedom. If the title befell him, he'd have little enough time for his music.

While Devlin, God love him, continued to jump at shadows and hear the cannons of Waterloo in his dreams.

And God help Guinevere Hollister, because diligent, discreet searching had turned up no evidence that she'd married a man of her own choosing these past six years, meaning Victor's scheme for her faced no impediment. No impediment whatsoever.

~❧~

Astrid and Felicity's letters said the same thing, no matter how long Gwen stared at them, no matter how many times she reread them: Gayle Windham had come to call, and he'd introduced himself as the Earl of Westhaven. Six years ago, he'd not assumed one of the duke's lesser titles, that being the privilege of his older brother, Bartholomew, Marquess of Pembroke, the duke's heir. Why had Westhaven—now the ducal heir—called upon her all these years later? Where was Victor?

And what did it all mean for Rose?

Dread congealed in Gwen's stomach, and her imagination threatened to gallop away with her reason. She curled on the bed, desperate prayers winging up as despair threatened to swamp her.

When a knock on her door interrupted her flights of panic, Gwen dragged herself from the bed and opened the door to find Douglas standing in the corridor in waistcoat and shirtsleeves. He took one look at her, stepped into her room, and closed the door behind him.

"Guinevere, what in God's name is wrong?"

She threw herself at him, and his arms wrapped around her, without questions, without hesitation.

And without hope. "He's going to take Rose," she moaned into his shoulder. "Oh, Douglas, after years of leaving us in peace, he's going to take Rose."

"Nobody is going to take Rose without a damned nasty fight," Douglas replied, tightening his embrace. "I won't allow it. Now breathe."

She gulped a breath, the scent of him calming her as much as his embrace.

"Again," Douglas ordered, "and let it out slowly."

He held her for long moments while she literally caught her breath, then walked her over to the bed, where he sat her down, fetched her a glass of water, then sat beside her.

"From the beginning, if you please," he instructed, taking her free hand and holding it in his lap.

"I did not want to tell you, not ever. I've never told *anybody*."

Douglas looped his arm across her shoulders. "Sooner or later, we are given an opportunity to trust again, Guinevere. Whatever misery looms over you, I suspect it affects me as well, and probably every person who cares for you and Rose."

Before anxiety could claim the last shred of Gwen's coherence, she made herself start speaking. "Rose's father—"

The words hurt. Even those two small mundane words hurt unimaginably.

"Guinevere, I might not like what you have to tell me, but I will not judge you, and I most assuredly will not judge that dear little girl for matters far beyond her control. I am, and ever shall be, your friend."

Such a stern friend, though a true friend, one who would listen. The thought gave Gwen emotional ballast, as Douglas's physical presence calmed her bodily.

"Victor Windham," she began again, "is a younger son of the Duke of Moreland. Victor is Rose's father. His brother Gayle came to call on me at Enfield last week. Fortunately, David, Andrew, and Gareth were there at the time, and they received him without disclosing my whereabouts or Rose's."

Douglas held up the water glass, as if he'd known this recitation had left her mouth dry, then passed her a handkerchief with three simple letters monogrammed at one corner in black thread.

Gwen took a sip of fortitude and soldiered on. "Gayle is the brother who found Victor and me when we eloped. He knows Victor dishonored me. At my request, and then Victor's, he did not go to his father with the tale. Gayle, however, is now using the title Earl of Westhaven, and is the Duke of Moreland's heir."

"You believe they know of Rose's existence?"

"They easily could."

"I would not be so sure, Guinevere. Your own cousins weren't aware of Rose until she was almost four. You didn't live quietly at Enfield, you were an anchorite."

"This is why," Gwen cried. "Because I didn't want Victor's family finding out about Rose."

"If she is illegitimate," Douglas reminded her, "the father and his family have no claim on her."

"But what if she's not?" Gwen wailed, five years of uncertainty loading her question with panic. "What if the damned wedding was real? What if they can *make* it real? Then they can take her away and I have nothing to say to it and I won't even be able to s-s-see her."

She dissolved into tears, great, noisy, terrified sobs that robbed her of dignity. Douglas laid her back on the bed, straddled her, and crouched over her, sheltering her with his body. Gwen clung, wept, and clung more tightly still, while Douglas comforted her with his touch, and with his very presence. When she lay spent and boneless, and her breathing calmed, Douglas brushed her hair back from her forehead and regarded her solemnly.

"Better?"

To Gwen's surprise, she was. Not as choked with fear, not as paralyzed. "A bit."

Douglas sat up, swung his leg over her, helped her sit, and passed her a second handkerchief, this one sporting not even a monogram.

"I am mortified."

"Terrified," Douglas countered—accurately. He settled on the bed beside her, and Gwen could feel his mind clicking away, adding facts and supposition on an internal abacus.

"You won't marry me because you are afraid you might be married?" he hazarded. "And any children you bore me would then be the legal issue of your first husband, Victor Windham, while he remains extant, and my union with you would make you a bigamist."

How calmly he referred to a felony offense.

Douglas did not take her hand, did not wrap his arm around her, but his insight afforded a curious relief. *Sooner or later, we are given an opportunity to trust again.* Douglas was her opportunity, and Gwen did trust him.

"You may add that I have possibly inveigled you into an adulterous liaison—for which I apologize," Gwen said.

"*If* you have a husband, then surely his apologies to you are the only ones that matter."

I love you. Gwen reached for Douglas's hand rather than offer that sentiment now.

"You did not want to return to the shabby little chapel where the ceremony was held for fear word of your inquiry might get back to Victor, who seemed content to leave well enough alone, but you've always wondered about your marital status and Rose's legitimacy. Victor has not married in the past six years?"

"I've watched the Society pages. He has not married or announced any engagements." She hadn't watched the Society pages, she'd read them religiously. "I took that as evidence Victor was also reluctant to commit bigamy."

Douglas kissed Gwen's knuckles in a manner she might have described as fierce. "Why do you believe the ceremony was genuine?"

"I saw the marriage lines, Douglas." Gwen unclenched her free hand, which had wrinkled his handkerchief beyond hope. "I signed a registry, and I saw our names on something that looked like a special license."

Douglas took a drink from Gwen's glass. "Those things can be forged. A special license is merely writing on parchment with a seal attached.'"

"They can be forged," Gwen agreed, "but when Victor joined me in the morning, he told me in no uncertain terms I was going to make a poor wife for the rest of his life, I had about as much passion in me as a dead fish, begetting children on me was going to be more work than any man should have to endure, and so forth."

Those spiteful words had wrought devastation at the time, though now they struck Gwen as petty and unimaginative.

"I'm sorry. Victor Windham was mean, stupid, and wrong."

Given the utter conviction in Douglas's tone, Gwen pitied Victor Windham should his path cross Douglas's—and pity was one emotion she'd never thought to feel about any duke's son.

"I know he was wrong—now—but until his brother showed up and rang a peal over his head, Victor behaved convincingly like a disgruntled bridegroom, when he could easily have told me we weren't really married. He saved that revelation for when Gayle barged in and found me in tears, and Victor railing against the fate he'd consigned himself to."

"Confusing at best," Douglas mused. "If you are married to Victor, then it must be dealt with, Guinevere, but how you deal with it is up to you."

"Douglas, if I'm married to him, I am his chattel, as is the produce of my body."

"That is the law, but Rose is a girl, not a potential heir

to anything, and you have at least four titled relations on your family tree, including present company, who would gladly take on Moreland over this. Then too, there may be issues of consent, validity of the documents, or other legal stratagems to consider. You were not of age."

She'd not been of age, but she'd given her consent to the so-called minister, and had had no guardian at the time to protest in any case, making even consent a potential legal morass. Gwen wanted to kiss Douglas for his unequivocal support and to throttle him, because legal stratagems were tedious, expensive, and no match for a duke said to be among the most powerful men in the realm.

"I cannot stand to be that man's wife. If Victor is the only Windham son to marry, then I could represent the sole means for a Moreland grandson to inherit the dukedom. I simply cannot abide the thought—"

Douglas kissed her into silence, but swiftly, distractedly.

And that might well be the last kiss they ever shared. Gwen fell silent and willed herself not to succumb to tears yet again.

❧

Guinevere's voice trailed off into miseries too numerous to count, and the situation was worse even than she knew. Douglas had spent enough time in the Lords to know that His Grace, Percival, the Duke of Moreland, was an old-school aristocrat, and worse yet, Moreland was an old-school aristocrat whose five sons—four extant—had not yet provided him a single grandchild.

As far as Douglas knew, none of Moreland's progeny had married, and discovery of a grandchild, any grandchild at all, would likely bring out His Grace's most autocratic, possessive streak.

Douglas gathered Guinevere closer and tried not to think about their proximity to Brighton and ships bound for all manner of exotic places. "We will ponder this development, Guinevere. You might well not be married to Victor Windham, or he might be willing to pursue an annulment if you are."

"But you aren't going to let me run from this, are you?" Guinevere's head came to rest on his shoulder, a weary weight.

Douglas said nothing rather than admit that running right now was appallingly attractive, if dishonorable in the extreme.

"I won't let myself run," she muttered. "I've been hiding for six years. I cannot run for the next fifteen, too."

"I thought not." He could admit to neither relief nor disappointment at her decision. Of course she wouldn't run, not when Rose might enjoy all the privileges of ducal progeny for the rest of her life.

"Hold me, Douglas. Please, hold me. I was hardly ready to part from you on any terms, and this, this…" She heaved a great, burdened sigh. "This development means I must acknowledge between us that a part of you was lost to me from our first meeting."

As opposed to carrying that truth as a private burden. He weathered her bald sentiments as best he could, though "lost to me" rang with all the warmth of a death knell.

"Does it help at all," Douglas said quietly, "to know my regard for you will never abate?" Nor would his desire for her, and for what they'd shared so briefly here at Linden.

"That assurance only makes me angrier." An encouraging spark of rage shone through in her tone. "To think that Victor has taken the freedom to choose you from me, too."

"And it angers me," Douglas said, lacing his fingers through hers, "to have finally found a woman with whom so much that is good is possible for us both, and I might have to yield all this promise to another, and to one undeserving of the privilege."

"I would never yield to Victor again the gift he has already spurned." The spark of rage was catching in the tinder of Guinevere's determination, and while that was a good thing, Douglas could not allow anger to guide her decisions exclusively.

"Death before dishonor, Guinevere?" He kissed her knuckles, as a knight might kiss his lady's hand. "That would hardly serve Rose, now would it? Besides, we aren't truly angry, are we? We're merely hurt, disappointed, and just possibly, afraid."

He recognized the fear because it was new and mightily unwelcome. Douglas had worried about the family finances, grieved his brothers' passings, and resented his mother's whining, but his only *fear* had been that his honor might not prove equal to his responsibilities.

That honor might require him to relinquish Guinevere to her lawful spouse evoked rage, bewilderment, grief and—fear.

"Douglas, I am so sorry. I thought—"

He put a finger to her lips. "Hush. You owe me no apologies, nor would I make any decisions differently had I known they led us to this moment, Guinevere. Were you free to accept me, you would still reject my suit?"

He should not have asked her, should not have sought selfish reassurances from her now of all times, but her answer mattered to him.

"No," she said with weary conviction. "No, I would not reject you. I'd marry you and be joyous to do so and so grateful to you for the honor you did me. I'd be the best, most loving, most lovable wife to you and mother to our children this earth has ever seen. You deserve no less, Douglas, and I won't dissemble to the contrary in hopes of sparing your feelings."

"Well." Reassurances, indeed. "That is something, isn't it?"

He kissed her open hand before cradling her palm against his cheek and closing his eyes. She did not have the petal-smooth hands of the debutante; she had the hands of a woman who cared for the land and loved a child.

Even her hands were dear to him.

"So what shall we tell your family, Miss Hollister?" he asked without opening his eyes. "They will need some time to adjust to your news, and to snort and paw and threaten until their wives and sisters can appeal to their reason."

"They will not understand." She was certain of her conclusion, and miserable with it. "They will not understand why I would rather bring shame to the family, raise Rose as a bastard, and live the life of a fallen woman. They will not understand why I refuse to acknowledge the possibility of a marriage to the son of a duke. How can they?"

Douglas opened his eyes and stood so he was no longer touching the woman he loved.

"I disagree with you, my dear. When your cousins learn you were indeed ill used, lied to, and abandoned by the man who promised you his love and protection, it is Windham's behavior they will not understand. Nor will they excuse themselves when they realize you needed their protection and they were too self-absorbed to offer it. Six years ago, both of your cousins were in England and unencumbered by a spouse or children."

"But I lied to them," Guinevere retorted, head

bowed. "I hid Rose from them and carried on at Enfield as if I owned the property outright. They've been kind in the past year, but I have exceeded all bounds now. I am not their responsibility. I am Windham's, if anyone's."

Damn it to bloody hell, the woman was using reason to torture herself. Had she perfected this skill on her own or acquired it from him?

"Windham has failed you, Guinevere, repeatedly, and failed his daughter as well. Is it so hard for you to accept that your cousins love you? They are decent men, and if they've kept a distance from you, it's because you've demanded it, not because they disdain your company."

He did not want to raise his voice so much as he wanted to weep. Guinevere went into his arms and turned her face into his shoulder, the feel of her in his embrace both a consolation and a torment.

"I shall tell my cousins the truth," she said. "And if they have advice to offer, I will listen to it—ask for it, even. And if they have influence or stratagems to employ, I will thank them for that as well."

"They don't want your thanks, Guinevere," Douglas said, feeling a faint thread of humor at how *determined* she was in her humility. "They want your love and your trust."

She made no move to leave his arms. "Will you write to them for me?"

"I'll draft something tonight. You can edit it before we post it tomorrow."

"Thank you. How much longer can we stay here?"

That she put her question thus gratified, even as the answer rankled. "At least a week, I should think." Douglas propped his chin on her crown, the better to consider their options. "I want time for this letter to reach your family. I want time to accustom myself to the situation and its ramifications."

"You want time to grieve."

Time to grieve with the only person who could share the loss.

When he did not argue with her, Guinevere went on speaking. "Unless all my suspicions are ungrounded—the wedding was a sham, Victor knows nothing of Rose, he seeks nothing of meaning from me or Rose—you and I will have to become those polite strangers to each other, nodding cordially at the occasional family function. And some day, I will see you marry another woman, a woman who can give you legitimate heirs."

The dispassion in her tone cut him to the bone, and the accuracy of her prediction tore at his heart. She was a strong woman, an indomitable woman who had already borne far too much loneliness and hardship with too little support. If because of him her heart was broken yet again, Douglas was not sure his reason would survive.

"Hush," he said, kissing her temple. "Just hush, and someday I will tell you all you have given me."

He tugged on her hand until she was again seated next to him on the bed, then he shifted so his back rested against the headboard, and tucked her against his side. She fell asleep there, her head on his shoulder, while he stared at the afternoon shadows advancing across the ceiling.

And thought.

⟡

"Good God." Andrew blew out a breath as he passed Gwen's letter to Fairly. "When Gwennie decides to disclose, she doesn't spare one's sensibilities. Our Rose could be the legitimate granddaughter of a duke."

Harsh wintry light came through the windows of the Enfield study, falling on a bedraggled bouquet of yellow asters on the sideboard. Andrew's inclination was to set the whole arrangement on the table in the hall for some obliging footman to deal with, but how did one even move such a thing without creating a worse mess?

"And Rose's mother," Heathgate added, scowling over by the hearth, "could be the object of the duke's ire. Moreland takes the protection of family, particularly his womenfolk, seriously."

Fairly lounged against the estate desk and scanned the letter. "I should think Moreland might be protective of Gwen, given how Victor comported himself."

"He might," Heathgate allowed, swiping a finger along the mantel as if examining the premises for dust. "The best Gwen can hope for is that she'll be permitted to continue raising her daughter on the Moreland property of the duke's choice. And Moreland will have no patience for a wife who doesn't tolerate her husband's attentions. His other surviving sons are not married, and there is doubt the youngest ever will. Gwen is the only broodmare in the ducal stable at this point."

For once, an equestrian analogy made Andrew wince. He went to the sideboard and poured a round of whiskeys, ignoring the pond-muck scent emanating from the spent bouquet. "Westhaven must have understood how badly Victor behaved on his wedding night, or he would never have allowed Gwen to flee the marriage."

"Or maybe," Fairly suggested, folding the letter and setting it aside, "Westhaven hoped the damned wedding was indeed a sham. Gwen is the mere granddaughter of an obscure earl who came very late to his title."

"But what is Westhaven up to now?" Heathgate wondered aloud, accepting a drink from Andrew. "And where is Victor?"

"In Town," Fairly supplied. "His social calendar has

become increasingly inactive over the past few years, and it is rumored he does not enjoy good health, though the details are vague. If he's given Gwen the French compliment, I will be hard put not to hasten the man's death."

On that lowering thought—when was any conversation improved by mention of syphilis?—Andrew took a bracing swallow of his drink.

"If I find my cousin has been raped, lied to, and abandoned to raise a child on her own," Heathgate said, "I will at the least challenge the man responsible."

And those whom Heathgate challenged tended not to enjoy a pleasant old age.

"As would I," Andrew said, though he favored winging his opponents—usually.

"But if the bastard doing the abusing turns out to be her lawful spouse," Fairly said, "then what you propose is murder in the eyes of the Crown."

As if that mattered?

"And we would be tried in the Lords and acquitted," Heathgate growled.

"Only to be subsequently drawn and quartered," Fairly countered pleasantly, "by my sisters."

"And there, my logic fails." Heathgate tossed back his drink and handed the glass to Andrew. "We're left with nothing to do but bide our time until Gwen and Amery return, and then take our cue from Gwen. Then too, the ladies might have some ideas."

"I'll put it to Astrid," Andrew said, collecting Fairly's glass.

"And I will arrange a jaunt out to that chapel near Richmond," Fairly said, looking thoughtful—which generally boded ill for somebody. "Shall we return at week's end?"

"Plan on it," Heathgate replied. "And attend to a bit of target practice and swordsmanship in the meanwhile."

Before departing, they chose a time to gather again, and on his way out, Fairly paused by the spent bouquet. "Best tell the staff to tidy up in here. Gwen will not appreciate a mess like this in her study, much less that foul odor."

He touched a tired blossom, and petals showered the sideboard and the carpet. Andrew bellowed for a footman and hoped a passing stink was the worst of the problems Gwen would face.

Twelve

Breakfast passed quickly, with both adults complimenting Rose on the progress she'd made with her attempts to improve her company manners. When all had finished eating, Gwen bade Rose to retrieve Mr. Bear and her small traveling satchel.

"So how much did you hear?" Douglas asked, topping off their teacups.

"Hear?" Gwen had a suspicion about what he was really asking.

"You lurked in the doorway to the nursery this morning when I stopped off to listen to Rose's final report. You heard some of our exchange."

"I heard you tell Rose you loved her," Gwen said, feeling an ache in the center of her chest. "For that, I will always be grateful."

"It's the simple truth, Guinevere." Douglas added sugar to his tea and stirred at exactly the same tempo he always stirred his tea. "She's too bright to accept anything less."

His tone was brisk, but Gwen wasn't fooled. Douglas didn't merely love Rose, he was attached to her, and he dreaded the possibility she too might be taken from him.

"I love you, you know," Gwen said, wishing she'd given him the words under more auspicious circumstances.

Douglas set his teacup down and closed his eyes as if in pain. "Must you, Guinevere?"

"It's the simple truth," she quoted him. "You are too bright to accept anything less."

He opened his eyes, and Gwen found humor and regret in his expression. "You are braver than I, and I thank you for the declaration, untimely though it may be. The sentiment is, of course, reciprocated."

"Say it," Gwen said, ready to beg if she had to. "Just once, Douglas, please?"

He considered his tea. He folded his serviette and placed it near his plate. He arranged his cutlery just so, then he stood and went to where the bright, chilly sunshine streamed in the window.

"Come here, Guinevere, if you please." When she joined him, he wrapped his arms around her and pulled her against him.

"The weeks spent with you here have been the happiest I can recall. You have put warmth, affection, and meaning in the empty places inside me. You have challenged me, touched me, teased me, and confounded me by turns. Your generosity and strength put me in awe of you, your integrity and determination put me to shame. I love you, I will always love you, and I will always be glad I love you, come what may. Because of you, there is a joy in me, Guinevere, even as we face separation, difficulties, and unknown challenges. You have no idea how much you have restored to me, and all I can do in return is offer you my love, little comfort though that may be."

His sentiments, offered so quietly, buffeted her with the strength of an emotional gale. "Douglas, how will we ever bear what lies ahead?"

"You shall. *We shall.* I can bear it because I know even though we might part, we bear it together."

Gwen simply held him, unable to respond. She didn't share his sense of optimism, didn't believe they could have any kind of life together, at least not without it costing her—costing them both—Rose. Maybe Douglas could have faith enough for them both.

Or maybe even Douglas's great determination would not be equal to the challenges they faced.

❧

The journey home started with the entire estate staff turning out to see the travelers off. Douglas rode out on Regis, and Gwen and Rose contented themselves with talk of home—particularly talk of Daisy—throughout much of the morning. They made good time, the roads having no traffic and the lanes being frozen rather than muddy.

The morning set the tone for the entire journey. Rose was pleasant and easily distracted by short jaunts on Regis's back, the weather was cold but dry and sunny. Douglas parted from them after supper at night, and met them the next day over breakfast. Part of Gwen resented the separation; another part of her understood it was preparation for the greater separation to come.

All too soon, the heavy coach lumbered up the drive to Willowdale, where Gwen planned to spend a night before traveling on to Enfield the next day. Abruptly, the prospect of facing her cousins, most especially the marquess, was not the insignificant detail she'd tried to label it.

Neither was facing her cousin, the earl, or their in-law, the viscount—much less the ladies.

So Gwen climbed down from the coach and took Douglas's arm with her chin held high. Rose fell silent beside her, clutching her mother's hand as a cold wind whipped up the drive.

"The prodigal returns," Heathgate growled, stepping down off the front terrace and striding up to the coach. Gwen dropped Douglas's arm and raised her chin another fraction of an inch.

"I am back," Gwen countered. Gareth wouldn't upbraid her before Rose; he was enough of a parent himself to behave better than that. Her cousin studied her for long moments, his expression stern and unreadable.

"About time," Gareth said, putting his hands on her shoulders and pulling her against him. "About damned time you came back to us, Guinevere Hollister."

Gwen returned his embrace with a sudden, fierce joy. "I am back," she said again, hugging him tightly, both laughter and tears threatening.

"Cousin Douglas," Rose whispered, "Cousin Gareth is squashing my mama."

"That I am." Heathgate stepped back from Gwen and scooped Rose up. "And now I'm going to squash *you*." He hugged Rose against his chest and made loud papabear noises as he pretended to squash her in his arms.

"Gareth," Felicity's soft voice chided from behind him. "Put the poor child down before you make her ill."

"Shall I squash you too, my dear?" Heathgate asked, as he did, indeed, carefully return Rose to terra firma.

"What?" Douglas inquired. "No threat of violence for me, Heathgate?"

The marquess pulled Douglas into a quick hug and thumped him between the shoulder blades, perhaps the first time Gwen had seen Douglas surprised.

"You'd leave too big a mess were I to squash you properly."

Felicity followed up her husband's greetings with more

ladylike hugs and kisses to cold, rosy cheeks, then ordered everyone inside, where hot drinks awaited. To Gwen's delight, Andrew, his wife Astrid, and David waited for her in the entry hall, and more hugs and greetings were exchanged before Felicity had Rose on her way to the nursery and the adults ensconced in the library.

Gareth took up his seat on the desk, Andrew and Astrid perched on the hearth, and David lounged against the French doors, while Gwen and Douglas sat beside each other on the long couch facing the hearth.

Without touching, because that was how it must be.

"You will wait until I at least have some hot tea in these people before you begin your inquisition," Felicity warned her husband.

"Yes, my love. Douglas takes all the sugar you have in the house in his, but it won't sweeten his disposition one bit."

"I will buy the property in Sussex," Douglas said, "if only to ensure my neighbors are not also my relations."

Gareth looked around the room when Felicity had everyone's teacup filled. "Any more obligatory insults? All right then, Gwen, prepare yourself, for we're no end of confused regarding this little contretemps you're in."

This contretemps was huge, but Gwen loved her cousin for referring to it otherwise. "Ask me anything. I'll tell you what I know."

"Well, for starts, are you married or not?" Andrew tossed out the question then followed it up with an apologetic smile.

"I honestly don't know," Gwen said—and how oddly simple it was to admit something she'd kept bottled up inside for years. "Victor claimed the ceremony was a sham, but only after he complained at length to me about what a dismal spouse I was going to make. The revelation that we were not truly married was withheld until his brother came upon us the next morning."

"Did Victor have a license?" Gareth asked.

"I saw something that certainly looked like a license, but I haven't seen any other to compare it to."

"The registry of that little chapel north of Richmond has had the last few pages carefully excised," David said. "My guess is the facility fell into disuse shortly after your visit there, or that it already had. Somebody got there before I did and removed any evidence that could support—or undermine—the legitimacy of your nuptials."

And he had made this journey without Gwen having to ask it of him.

"Are you suggesting the marriage is legal, but Victor wants to suppress evidence of that?" Gareth looked none too pleased with the notion.

"It's one theory," David said. "Perhaps he's met another lady. Perhaps he's sired another child, and he's hoping for a boy this time. Perhaps in a surfeit of well-deserved guilt, he sought to support the outcome Gwen said she wanted."

Did David have to have such a facility for hypothesizing? "This grows complicated," Gwen said, and yet the urge to reach for Douglas's hand was so simple.

"It does," Gareth replied. "Did you know, Gwen, that Gayle Windham is now heir to the Moreland dukedom?"

He put the question so casually, and yet, it was not a positive development. "I believe that makes Victor the spare and the only one of the remaining brothers to marry, *if* he married me." And the spare's first duty was to see to the succession. Also his second, and his third.

"I don't suppose Westhaven is considering matrimony any time in the near future?" Douglas posed the question to the room at large.

"He is not," Gareth said. "My mother has checked her trap lines and found no gossip to that effect in any quarter. He's considered eligible, if dull, and unenthusiastic about his marital responsibilities."

"So what does Gayle Windham want with me?" Gwen asked. "And does he know he's an uncle?" The library was warm, and the support of Gwen's family also a comfort. Douglas's quiet presence beside her was the dearest comfort of all.

"I doubt Windham knows about Rose," Andrew said. "We've had no casual inquiries of the household staff regarding a small child. Nobody has seen strangers about the property, not even in passing. Hell, Gwen, if we didn't know about Rose until last year, you can bet any member of the Windham family, ensconced in Town and socially in demand, would have no clue as to her existence."

From there, the discussion moved on to speculation regarding the purpose for Westhaven's call, and Gwen's next move. After much consideration, Gwen penned the earl a note stating that she would anticipate a call from him at his convenience. She agreed with her cousins nothing would be gained by dodging the confrontation Westhaven sought, and much could be learned. Gwen handed the epistle off to Gareth for delivery, and Felicity declared the war council at an end.

For now.

❧

"You and Rose are home. How does it feel?"

As conversational gambits went, Douglas didn't consider his question particularly inspired, but it served to gain Guinevere's attention as he escorted her through the dead gardens to the Enfield manor house.

"Coming home isn't the relief I thought it would be,"

she said as they reached the entrance hall. "I thought Enfield was my sanctuary, but with Westhaven's visit looming, this place no longer feels as safe. It's still home, though."

"So you and Rose have both had your peace cut up with this homecoming," Douglas observed, slapping his gloves on his thigh.

"You aren't going to stay for a bit?"

He wanted to stay. He wanted to stay for the rest of his life, building walls and barricades to keep the Windhams of the world away, and to keep one mother and her child safe from all of life's difficulties. "I will come in, if you think it advisable."

"I do," Guinevere said, her chin coming up. "I'll ring for tea. Now off with that coat, and stop looking so dour. You've already told Rose her pony died, surely nothing could be more onerous than that."

They'd handled that chore on the ride over, with Rose sitting up before Douglas on Sir Regis—and a miserable, damned, two-handkerchief business it had been, putting positively grim overtones to a situation already ominous.

"I can think of at least one thing worse than Rose's pony dying," Douglas said. "Saying good-bye to you." At the stricken look in Guinevere's eyes, he regretted his words. They were true, of course they were, but one needn't utter every inane, painful truth that came to mind. "I am sorry. My remark was thoughtless."

"Perhaps you don't want to stay for tea?" she retorted, her voice carefully controlled.

Oh, lovely. Now she was aiming her ire at him. "It is more the case that I dare not stay for tea, but I will not allow us to part in anger or confusion, Guinevere. I'd rather make my good-byes to you in private, however."

Her bravado wavered, and she led him to the small informal parlor where she'd first agreed to journey with him to Linden.

"It hits me now, it has been hitting me for the past few days, really, that we truly are going to part." She spoke with her back to him, looking out the window facing the stables. "My mind won't accept the reality of it, but my heart is breaking all the same."

She'd closed the door, which saved him the trouble. Douglas locked it then slipped his arms around her waist without turning her to face him.

"I would never have engaged your affections had I known how painful this was going to be for you. I am more sorry than I can say, Guinevere."

"If I hurt, Douglas Allen, it is only because I understand the magnitude of the loss I will suffer when you walk out that door."

Did she have to be so damnably brave? "I will walk out the door, Guinevere. I am not yet ready to walk out of your life." As a gentleman, he ought not to have said that last part, not to a woman who could well be married to the son of a duke. As a man who had made love with her and who loved her, he had to give her the words— the assurances.

She turned in his arms to face him. A shaft of sunlight fell across Guinevere's brow, revealing fatigue as well as beauty. "So what will you do now, Douglas?"

Weep, possibly. Get blind drunk, very likely.

"I am to be a guest of the marquess for the next week or so," Douglas replied. "All of my properties in Town are for sale, and because my solicitor has had no luck finding a purchaser, Heathgate has put his man of business to the task. I didn't want to return to Town only to find prospective buyers interrupting my morning tea." And he'd been damned sure he wasn't going to repair to his own family seat, there to be harangued by his aging mama about the need to secure the damned succession.

"I see."

Two innocuous words imbued with a full complement of female censure, making clear she did not want to hear about his real estate. Well, neither did he.

Douglas stepped back, leaving Guinevere alone in the sunlight. "I would rather a thousand times tell Rose her pony died than let you face Westhaven alone, but were I to openly defend your causes, it could only redound to your discredit."

"I would hardly go that far. You are as much family as David, and he certainly feels comfortable tilting at windmills on my behalf—or he would if I'd allow it."

Which left Douglas feeling both respect and consternation toward Fairly. "But you are not allowing it—yet. I almost feel sorry for Westhaven, Moreland, and Victor Windham."

"That's the spirit. I shall be quite formidable." She smiled at him, the saddest smile he'd yet to see from her. "Before you go, tell me your thinking regarding Linden."

This, Douglas concluded, was a bid for mutual composure. He seized it not quite gratefully, but with a sense of inevitable duty, and—hang noble intentions—took Guinevere's hand, too. "I don't know what to think of Linden. The house itself is captivating, but the estate is troubled, as you know, and I can hardly like the idea of relying on Loris Tanner to implement the restoration of the place when she's been taken advantage of by her errant father already."

"So you are thinking of declining it?"

Douglas kissed her knuckles, though he stood with

her before a window, and he ought to have been halfway down the drive by now. Also half-drunk.

"I can think of nothing, Guinevere, save resolving matters between us. Until I know for a certainty you are wedded to another, I will make no commitments elsewhere. If you were to accept my suit, the decision whether to buy Linden, or some other property, would be one made by both of us."

This bit of honesty caused his lady—*the* lady—to withdraw her hand. "If you didn't buy Linden, where would you look?"

Her tenacity was one of the things Douglas admired most about her—usually. "Heathgate mentioned that property was available locally, between Enfield and Oak Hall. The neighbors might be a slight drawback though." He tossed out that sally despite the mood, the circumstances, and the untruth his comment conveyed. "I see a smile on your face, Guinevere, so it's time I take my leave of you."

She went into his arms, a dear and familiar comfort against the ache threatening to break Douglas's heart.

"Leave me with something, Douglas. I need a token, something to reassure me you are real, that we really did lo—that we really did spend time together."

That her composure slipped to this degree was a relief, and her request a blessing—for they truly had spent time *together*. Douglas stepped back and withdrew his penknife, a plain, serviceable little blade he kept razor sharp.

He freed his hair from its old-fashioned queue, then sliced off a curling lock about three inches long and laid it across her palm.

"Not very original," he commented, taking out a monogrammed handkerchief—how he wished he had something prettier to give her. He folded the linen around the lock of hair and then closed her fingers around it. "Your token."

"You are such a sweet, romantic, dear man, everything I dreamed of as a girl and thought I would never find." She threw her arms around his neck and hugged him tightly. "I will miss you."

"You will likely see me by Wednesday," Douglas replied, his lips against her temple. Wednesday was ages and ages away to a man staring at a dying dream. "I'll want to know what Westhaven has up his sleeve, and I will not allow you to keep it from me."

"I wouldn't. I won't."

"Good. Until Wednesday then."

She framed his face with her hands and turned his head so she could kiss him—not a tender, wistful parting kiss, either. Guinevere's kiss was ravenous, hot, demanding, and arousing—also both heartbreaking and reassuring. Douglas at first simply let her have her head, accepting what she bestowed without either inciting or denying her passion. When she slipped her hand around the back of his neck and molded her body to his, however, arousal stirred in earnest.

For a moment, he allowed himself to reciprocate, to plunge his tongue into her mouth and press himself tightly to her curves. To acknowledge the heat that flared between them still, to revel in it however briefly, was as much relief as agony.

Douglas eased the kiss back to something sweet and tender, to the parting kiss it should have been, and Guinevere accepted his decision—for once without argument.

"Until Wednesday," she said, leaning against his chest. Douglas moved his hands on her back, soothing and caressing, but also memorizing the bones and muscles, the contour of her spine. And then he held her, but forced his hands to still, and eased his grip.

"It is so difficult, Guinevere, not to crush you to me, to wrap my arms around you as if I'd never let you go. I don't want to leave you."

As he'd intended, his admission was fortification enough that Guinevere could take the first step away.

"And I don't want to let you go," she replied, the sad smile curving her lips. "I'll tell Rose you'll come visit midweek." She took his arm and walked him to the front entrance, where she handed him his greatcoat and gloves.

"Until Wednesday." Douglas brushed one last kiss to her cheek and took his leave.

~⁂~

"A caller for you, madam." The butler offered Gwen the calling card, which—no surprise—bore the Earl of Westhaven's particulars engraved in black script on white stock.

"Show him in to the small parlor," Gwen directed, as the butterflies in her stomach threatened to upend her lunch. She tidied her hair—again—pinched her cheeks—again—and closed her fingers around the handkerchief she'd kept in her pocket since Douglas had left her side days earlier.

She made her way to the family parlor—the room she associated most strongly with Douglas—and opened the door to find herself perused by a pair of serious, even beautiful, emerald-green eyes.

"Miss Hollister." Gayle Windham, or rather, the Earl of Westhaven, looking altogether handsomer and more imposing than Gwen remembered him, made her a formal bow.

Gwen curtsied to an appropriate depth, no more. "My lord." She gestured to the sofa. "Please have a seat."

Westhaven resumed his inspection of her, but when Gwen took one of the rocking chairs, he sat himself in the other rocking chair, in closer proximity than the sofa would have afforded. Gayle Windham was more heavily muscled than he'd been six years ago, his dark chestnut hair a trifle longer, and his air that of a man preparing to assume a weighty title, however reluctantly.

"May I offer you tea, my lord, and perhaps something to eat?"

"Tea," the earl responded, still studying her.

"Have I a smudge on my nose, then?" Gwen asked when he seemed disinclined to take up the conversational reins.

"You do not. You look, in fact, to be thriving." He was not offering a compliment.

"How fortunate, for I *am* thriving." She willed Westhaven to hear the implication: *No thanks to your lecherous brother.*

"I am pleased to hear it." Then his handsome features creased into a frown. "No, actually, I am relieved to hear it. Quite thoroughly relieved."

His sentiment was genuine, and made Gwen recall something she'd forgotten. She had liked Gayle Windham, six years ago. He'd grown on her gradually, as Victor had promised he would. He was the personification of the dutiful son, and despite those lovely eyes and patrician features, he was without artifice. Though he had dignity in abundance, he wasn't an arrogant man.

And whereas Victor had been flamboyantly handsome, with green eyes, dark hair worn rakishly long, and the Windham height and grace, Gayle was quieter, his tastes sober, and his demeanor reserved.

Sitting in her parlor, all quiet self-containment, Westhaven reminded her fleetingly of Douglas.

Whom she would never stop missing. "You were concerned about my welfare?"

"I was," he replied, "but you did not invite continued interest from any member of my family, and because I understood and respected your reasons, I trusted to my brother to deal with you, should the need arise."

The tea tray arrived—the best service in the household, polished to a spotless shine—accompanied by pears, cheese, bread, sliced ham, and an assortment of cakes. The interruption was timely, for Gwen felt her temper flare higher at Westhaven's words.

"I see no need," she said as evenly as she could, "for any member of your family to *deal with* me. I am at a loss to explain your visit now, six years after our last, unfortunate encounter."

"I appreciate your curiosity," Westhaven said, not a hint of confrontation in his tone, "so I will be as plain-spoken as you. I am here at the request of my brother, who feared were he to approach you directly, you would not receive him."

Gwen could not imagine handsome, dashing Lord Victor Windham fearing anything. "Why in the world would I avoid Victor? He was a mistake, but one that has faded into obscurity with time."

"So you have forgiven him?" Westhaven asked, his regard intent for all his manner was nonchalant.

"To be quite honest," Gwen said, reaching for the silver teapot, "I haven't spared him sufficient thought to consider whether he's deserving of it."

My, how wonderfully mendacious she could be when provoked, though how wonderfully true the sentiment was of late.

"Was my brother so forgettable?" Westhaven asked, accepting his cup of tea.

"You speak of Victor in the past tense," Gwen pointed out. "He is a memorable man, but his actions regarding me are better forgotten. I trust he is getting on well?" She had wondered, mostly because Victor's behavior on their elopement had been so very out of character, then she'd castigated herself for caring.

Westhaven's brows twitched down. "Victor is not at ease with the way matters were left between you two, and he seeks to meet with you that he might address the issue."

There it was, the gently worded command, the ducal gauntlet so politely dropped on the table, the beginning of the end of her freedom. "And if I refuse to meet with him?"

"I wish you wouldn't," Westhaven said, looking less dignified and more… more bothered. "He will insist I continue to pester you, Miss Hollister, and I will comply with his wishes, until you capitulate simply to be rid of me."

The last was said with a small thread of self-deprecating humor. Gwen wasn't to be threatened overtly. At least not yet. She would instead—God help her and Westhaven both—be *charmed*.

"I don't want to meet with him." Douglas would have been proud of her for that understatement. "Nothing he has to say, nothing he can offer me, nothing he has, holds any interest for me. You may convey to him my complete forgiveness, if indeed there is anything to forgive. Victor and I were both foolish, selfish, and lacking in judgment, but I find no lasting harm, at least not to me."

Westhaven looked pained at that speech, but he'd at least heard her out.

He set down his teacup precisely in the middle of

its saucer. "How can you say you've suffered no lasting harm, when you had more than an understanding with a duke's son six years ago, but because of his stupid schemes, you've spent the rest of your youth buried here in the country, not even taken into the household of your relations? Being deprived of a husband and children of your own constitutes harm in itself."

Gwen parried out of instinct, though Westhaven's condemnation of his brother was interesting, and his words confirmed that he knew nothing of Rose. "Where is it written, my lord, that a person, a woman, can be happy only with a spouse and children?"

"Probably in the Bible, for starters, and certainly in my father's personal lexicon under the heading 'contented females,'" Westhaven replied, the humor again evident in his eyes. "I hope I do not offend when I observe you are more strikingly lovely than you were six years ago, Miss Hollister, and you deserve to have a fellow about who can appreciate that. To the extent my brother stole such a future from you, you are an injured party."

Such was the charm a man in expectation of a duke-dom could dispense, so subtle, so casual, that the flattery felt deserved.

Gwen had neglected to pour herself a cup of tea, and remedied the oversight while she gathered her wits. "I appreciate your assessment, Lord Westhaven," she replied, her voice gratifyingly steady, considering she wished he'd choke on his aristocratic charm. "Any harm I suffered at your brother's hands was fleeting and easily rectified. I simply did not enjoy what I learned of Polite Society. My presence there was more a function of my aunt's ambitions than any choice on my part."

"So you won't see him?" Westhaven asked, rising and ambling to the mantel, over which a portrait of

Grandfather's favorite bitch with a litter of puppies held pride of place.

"What can Victor Windham offer me, or want from me, that would improve our situation now? If he needs my forgiveness, he has it, though I've explained it isn't necessary."

Westhaven perused the portrait, and Gwen had the sense he was in truth inspecting the artistry with an educated eye. "I believe Victor intends to offer you marriage of a sort, but he hasn't confided in me specifically."

"Marriage of a sort?" Wasn't "marriage of a sort" already the state of things between them?

Westhaven left off appraising the painting and turned to face her. "Victor is not the impulsive, reckless young man you knew. If he's offering you marriage—and I don't know for certain that he is—then he has reasons for it, well-thought-out reasons. He would provide for you generously, of that I am sure."

"I have no need of his generosity," Gwen shot back. "You can see I am quite comfortable in my home."

"This is not your home," Westhaven said gently. "This property is entailed with the barony that passed to your cousin Greymoor. Victor can offer you your own home, Miss Hollister, and security for the rest of your life."

Gwen struggled not to let the strength of that blow show on her face, but it was difficult. A life estate here was one thing, but Westhaven had stated the truth. She might live at Enfield, but it wasn't *hers*.

Just as Douglas was not, in the ways that Society valued, *hers*.

"I am sorry," Westhaven said in the same quiet voice. "I do not seek to distress you, but rather to prevail on you to grant the favor I ask."

"You want me to meet with Victor. Is that all?"

"That's all he is asking, as far as I know." Westhaven was dodging. He was doing it politely and subtly, but he was dodging.

"Does your father know anything of our dealings six years ago?"

This question had the earl glancing at the hound above the mantel again, and at the litter of eight fat pups cavorting around her. "I said nothing, and I doubt Victor did either. One word to His Grace, and you would find Victor here in my stead, on bended knee, ring in hand, and a horse pistol at his back."

Bad, if predictable, news. "Your father is that old-fashioned?"

Westhaven's smile was rueful. "To put it mildly, though Her Grace would be the one to make sure the gun was loaded. Victor behaved dishonorably toward you, and I colluded with him after the fact."

Such self-castigation—now, when it did no good whatsoever. Gwen shoved to her feet. "Is it you who seeks forgiveness, my lord? If so, then hear me well. Had you forced me to solemnize that farce of a wedding with your brother, you would have earned my undying enmity, not to mention that of my cousins. One thing you need to be very, very clear about. Your brother's intimate attentions were rendered with an abominable lack of consideration for me, and the prospect of suffering similarly at his hands for the rest of my life would indeed be enough to put me to flight."

Westhaven's expression had gone from stunned to stern to impassive.

"I suspected as much," he said when it was clear Gwen had finished. "And for that reason, I respected your wish to return quietly to your aunt. Victor behaved abominably, but this merely makes his request to see you that much more emphatic."

"What aren't you telling me?" Gwen asked, resuming her seat. Sparring with Westhaven, a man who shared Douglas's ability to keep his own counsel, was draining. The oppressive, unhappy fatigue she'd struggled with since coming home from Linden and parting from Douglas abruptly robbed her of the energy to argue with his lordship further.

"Victor must tell you some things himself," Westhaven said. He took his seat next to her and examined his teacup. Gwen would not have been surprised had he upended the thing to inspect it for a maker's mark. "Let's try it this way. Under what circumstances would you consider meeting with Victor?"

"I don't understand." He was attempting to *lawyer* her now, though if asked, he'd no doubt say he was being *reasonable*. Gwen dropped her head against the back of the chair and closed her eyes. Had she permitted Gareth, Andrew, or David to attend this interview, they would simply have tossed the man out for her, earl or not. "I do not want to see Victor. How much more blunt can I be?"

"But he does want to see you, and I would not be carrying his request to you did I not think it was made in good faith."

Gwen opened her eyes, and of course, Westhaven was still seated beside her. The earl was not going to go away, but perhaps—it was a silly hope—perhaps if Gwen met with Victor, he might be willing to leave her in peace thereafter. Victor was, after all, the only person who knew if they were truly married.

"Fine. I will meet with your brother, accompanied by you and the escort of my choice. I will not set foot in any of the ducal residences, and this meeting will be within the next week or not at all. Victor is not to accost me here at Enfield in the meanwhile, and he will have no more than one hour of my time. Now, *will you please go away?*"

She had rattled off her conditions with admirable ease, but they represented hours of thought and second-guessing.

"If I promise to leave soon, will you at least let me have a bit of cheese and a bite of apple before I go? It's a two-hour ride out here and another two hours back to Town."

Gwen resigned herself to more civility. Six years ago, she'd thought him the dull older brother, good-looking enough, but without joie de vivre, humor, or even much conversation. Now, she saw him as undeniably handsome, unpretentious, and *safe*—an impressive set of characteristics on the unmarried heir to a dukedom.

"Why aren't you married?" Gwen asked as she set about fixing him a plate.

"I haven't met the right lady," he replied, watching Gwen's hands as she piled his plate with sustenance. "I am considered eligible, but I suspect I'm too much of a chore for the sweet young things to bear. I dance well enough but cannot abide inane gossip. I am also lamentably indifferent to fashion, and I only come up to Town when His Grace insists upon it. These are egregious shortcomings, even in the son of a duke."

"I danced with you," Gwen recalled, pouring him another cup of tea. "You dance as well as Victor ever did."

Westhaven looked preoccupied as he demolished his apple. "I led you out for your first waltz. I remember thinking it a pleasure to dance with a tall woman for a change."

"How flattering, to be memorably tall."

"And graceful," the earl said, moving on to a slice of cheese, "and blessedly willing to simply enjoy the dance rather than chatter your way through it from start to finish."

Something in the way he looked at her—wistfully?—made Gwen think he did recall dancing with her, and it was a pleasant memory for him. How odd that now, after six years, she should become aware of it.

Though the memory was no longer pleasant for her. The best that could be said was that the dance hadn't been *un*pleasant. "When shall I meet with Victor, and where?"

"You can use my new town house, though I'm not yet residing there," Westhaven suggested, wrapping his second slice of cheese in ham. "I'm assuming you will bring one of your cousins, so we should have no problem with the proprieties."

Gwen found that comment ridiculous, but if it comforted Westhaven to think she was still within the ambit of the proprieties, she'd allow him that fiction.

"When?"

"What about Saturday?" More food disappeared, making Gwen wonder if anybody ensured Westhaven had proper meals. "My parents will have taken my sisters off to a hunting party by week's end, and Victor will be able to maneuver with more privacy."

"Is he ashamed of me?" Oh, drat. She hadn't meant to ask that. Hadn't meant to think it—ever again.

Westhaven paused on the verge of inhaling another wedge of cheddar. "I think it rather the case he is ashamed of himself, as well he should be."

Gwen frowned at her tea, trying to come to peace with the bargain she'd made.

"Am I making a mistake?" she asked, even more

appalled at herself, but sensing Westhaven's counsel would be honest.

"The mistake was made six years ago, I should think. All you are doing now is meeting with the man and hearing what he has to say. I cannot see how that can compound the earlier error in judgment."

"It still feels like a mistake." And an imposition and an intrusion, though the opportunity to confront Victor also held an odd, powerful appeal, and it was a chance to learn the truth of their marital situation.

"Bring both your cousins, then," Westhaven suggested, passing her back his empty plate. "Heathgate could intimidate the devil himself, and Greymoor is doubly lethal because he charms as he moves in for the kill."

"You know my cousins?" For his description of them was deadly accurate.

"Mostly by reputation," Westhaven answered. "They are impressive men, even in my father's eyes."

Probably because neither would care a fig for Moreland's estimation of them. "They weren't so impressive six years ago."

"They were impressively naughty," Westhaven suggested, draining his teacup with the dispatch any yeoman might show his ale. "But they have accepted the civilizing influence of matrimony admirably, in His Grace's opinion. Neither one has been seen misbehaving since speaking his vows."

This exchange bore the pull of Town gossip, where everybody knew and commented on everybody else's business. For herself, Gwen did not care that she might soon be the subject of such speculation, but for Rose, and for Douglas...

"Both of my cousins are thoroughly besotted with

their spouses," Gwen said. "Absolutely, thoroughly devoted, and their wives are lovely, lovable women."

"Sounds as nauseating as His Grace and Her Grace," Westhaven replied, smiling openly. The change in expression was remarkable, making him younger, lighter, and altogether breathlessly attractive.

Gwen scowled at him as a consequence. "You should smile more often, Westhaven. The sweet young things would be more inclined to overlook your many shortcomings."

Westhaven's smiled dimmed, becoming… wistful? Pained? "That leaves us with the question of how I am to overlook theirs, and why I would want to. Hmm?"

"A dilemma," Gwen conceded. But not her dilemma. "Have some more tea, or if you need fortification for your journey, I have brandy about here somewhere."

Westhaven let her fill his traveling flask and walk him to the front hallway.

"You have been more than gracious," he said. "And I don't think you'll regret this decision."

She already did. "I certainly hope not. Safe journey, my lord."

"Until Saturday, then." He bowed the same formal, correct bow he'd offered her in greeting and then was blessedly gone.

Gwen's relief was accompanied by profound, inexplicable fatigue, and a longing for Douglas's embrace so intense it made her ache. She was tempted to ride over to Willowdale simply to see him, but knew such behavior would merit her nothing but another sorrowful leave-taking.

Her thoughts were interrupted by a footman bearing a note. "This arrived from Willowdale, madam."

Gwen opened a missive sealed with the marquess's

crest, but addressed in Felicity's hand. Douglas would not write to her unless it was a dire emergency, and yet, Gwen was disappointed. The proprieties were back in place between her and her lover—her former lover—and they rankled more than ever.

"Thank you." She sent the footman to make sure the messenger was offered hot food and drink in the kitchen, then took herself into the library.

Felicity hoped Gwen's meeting with Westhaven had gone well, and warned her to expect both of her cousins after breakfast tomorrow. She added that Lord Amery had been called to Amery Hall, his mother having suffered an apoplexy, and her prognosis being dubious.

At the bottom of Felicity's note were two lines in a beautiful, flowing script:

> *Madam,*
> *I hope you are faring well, though you have my abject apologies for being unable to keep our appointment later in the week. Until next we meet, I remain,*
> *Your devoted servant,*
> *Amery*

A devoted servant was not a lover, and likely never would be again.

Gwen added to her aches and miseries not only the desire to feel Douglas's arms around her, but also the need to comfort him, though anything that prevented Gwen from further intimacies with Douglas Allen was a good thing.

A miserably difficult, unfair, painful, hard thing, but a good thing.

Thirteen

DOUGLAS HAD BEEN SURE HE WAS CAPABLE OF hating her.

Looking down at his mother's shrunken form, he admitted his error, for all he felt was pity and a vast regret. Pity for himself, that this was the mother he'd been given, but pity and regret for her.

When had she become elderly? When had she grown so small and frail and gray?

"She wakes occasionally," the nurse informed him. "Say something to her, and she might stir a bit."

Douglas pulled a chair up to the bed and took his mother's cool hand.

"Mother." The word came out much less resolute than he'd intended. He tried again. "Mother."

Her eyes opened, and a ghastly, lopsided caricature of a smile pulled at one side of her mouth. "Da…" she said softly, lifting her right hand toward his face.

"She can get initial consonants," the nurse observed, "and that's encouraging."

"Please do not refer to Lady Amery as 'she' within her hearing."

"Da…"

Douglas captured his mother's hand and returned it to the bed. "I'll stay a bit," Douglas assured her. "Would you like something to drink?"

When his mother looked confused, Douglas scanned the room for a pitcher.

"She can't…" The nurse, a stout older woman with tired eyes, caught herself. "Drinking from a cup can be difficult after an apoplexy."

"Then how do you ensure your patients are getting sufficient liquids?"

"Sometimes a drinking straw will help, but it's difficult, your lordship."

Difficult. A monumental understatement. "When did you last offer her water?"

She smoothed a hand over a starched white apron—a spotless, starched white apron. "Before tea."

"That was almost six hours ago." He tucked his mother's hand against her side and crossed the room to the pitcher and basin on her dresser. Pouring a small amount into a glass, he brought it to the bed and set it on the nightstand. When he had Lady Amery propped against her pillows, he held the glass against her lips, scowling mightily when it became apparent she was desperate to drink.

Some of the water dribbled over her chin, but enough of it made it down her throat that her eyes reflected gratitude. When Douglas returned to his chair by her bed, she reached for him again.

"Gi…" she said, her gaze trained on him beseechingly. "Gi… me."

"Give you?" Douglas asked, feeling her frustration keenly.

"Gi… me."

Douglas wracked his brain but could not discern her

meaning. *Give her.* Give her what? She refused more water, so he gave her his hand and sat with her thus, holding her thin, cold fingers in his until she'd drifted back to sleep.

Douglas spoke for a few minutes with the nurse, ensured his mother would not be left alone through the night, and took his leave of the sickroom.

He'd stopped by his town house long enough to gather several days' worth of clothing, and had paid a call on David Worthington, Viscount Fairly. The purpose of that visit had been to educate himself regarding apoplexy and some other relevant medical issues, Fairly being the only thing approaching a trustworthy physician among Douglas's acquaintances.

The information Fairly had shared regarding apoplexy was daunting. Victims of apoplexy often became incapable of clear speech or incapable of moving an entire side of their bodies. Their prognosis was grim, particularly if the ability to speak, chew, and swallow was affected. Those who survived a massive seizure often died of its consequences or in a subsequent attack.

So Douglas had ridden hard the entire day, prepared to arrive in time to arrange his mother's funeral. The relief he'd felt to have her still on this earth, albeit speaking gibberish and looking a hundred years old, had shocked him. But she was his only adult relative, and she was his mother. That apparently counted for something, despite Douglas's unbecoming wish that it did not.

He took himself downstairs, past the formal parlor, the music room, the estate offices, breakfast parlor, and dining room to the kitchen. The kettle was warming on the hob, so he rummaged until he found the fixings for a cup of tea, some cheese, and a red apple.

Sitting at the scarred plank table in the middle of the

room, he assembled his simple meal and added sugar—
and cream—to his solitary tea. The sound of his spoon
clinking against the teacup reminded him of Guinevere,
stirring his tea before passing it to him, perfectly prepared
on every occasion.

He missed her with a relentless, bone-wracking ache.
The hours he'd spent in the saddle allowed him to consider, at length and in detail, their situation. Two things
had become obvious: First, if Guinevere were married to
Windham, the situation was grave, indeed. Married was
married, in his eyes, in Guinevere's, and in the eyes of
the law. Second, regardless of the legalities, he did not
see how he could build a life without Guinevere in it.

More tired than he could recall being in many a
month, Douglas climbed the stairs, stopping to check on
his mother. She lay as if asleep, a maid curled in a chair
by her bed. Douglas withdrew without alerting the maid
to his presence and found his bed.

He drifted off to sleep, hoping he would dream of
Guinevere. To see her, even in his dreams, would be a
comfort—or, more accurately, a welcome torment.

When he awoke early the following morning, he
hadn't dreamed of Guinevere, but he had puzzled out an
understanding of what his mother had been trying to say.

Not "give me," but rather, "forgive me."

❧

"Your escort is here." Guinevere's hostess for her stay in
Town, her aunt, the estimable dowager Marchioness of
Heathgate, said this a bit loudly, as if Guinevere might
have lost some hearing since Douglas had last seen her.

"My escort?" Guinevere perched on the middle of a
green velvet sofa, looking tired and severely pretty as she
went through the motions of a game of solitaire.

Lady Heathgate shot a glance of maternal exasperation over her shoulder at Douglas and took two steps into the room. "You are in another world completely. I'll fetch your cloak and bonnet while you greet his lordship."

Her ladyship brushed past Douglas, leaving him in full view of the little sitting room. "Guinevere?"

Her head came up, and where her posture had been diffident and listless, at the sound of his voice, she came alive. "Douglas!" She flew across the room in two strides. "Oh, Douglas, I have missed you so." She buried her face against his shoulder, burrowing into his embrace.

And even as Douglas reveled in the feel of her in his arms and positively wallowed in her flowery scent, somehow, he missed her still. Missed her and resented bitterly that he'd had to leave her alone, because he and Guinevere both knew what it was to remain alone, even when surrounded by family.

"I've missed you, too." He made himself step back, made himself leave the parlor door open, though such propriety would soon render the room chilly. "You look fatigued."

"I am," she said, keeping a grasp of both of his hands. "I can't seem to keep my eyes open, and I am a veritable watering pot of late."

Her hands were cold, and to Douglas's unending dismay, she teared up again as she spoke.

"This will not do." He offered her his handkerchief, inadequate though the gesture was. "If you are not inclined to go forward with this meeting, Guinevere, I will convey your regrets to Westhaven."

She paused between dabbing at the left eye and dabbing at the right. "*You* are my escort? I asked David to attend me."

"He would, except he has come down with the flu

and has asked that I serve in his stead. He explained to me that you wanted neither Heathgate's glowering nor Greymoor's splenetics on hand for your meeting with Lord Victor."

Though why in the bloody perishing hell hadn't Fairly observed the courtesy of sending Guinevere a note? And what sort of flu was it that left a man capable of summoning a friend from the wilds of Kent and suffering no fever whatsoever?

"I can't ask this of you," she said, fresh tears welling. "Douglas… This won't be civilities over tea. You of all men should not have to listen to the conversation between Victor and me."

"I disagree." He had to put some space between them though, or Lady Heathgate might be scandalized by what she found going on in her parlor. Douglas clasped his hands behind his back and paced over to the fireplace. "I will protect your interests with my last breath, Guinevere, and I would have no secrets between us. If you are to be Victor Windham's wife, then all that remains is for me to serve as your friend and very distant relative."

For soon, distant relatives would be all that was left to him. Lady Amery had not rallied in the least during Douglas's tenure in Kent, but her condition had stabilized sufficiently that Douglas could heed Fairly's summons—thank God.

Guinevere clutched his handkerchief as if her firstborn child were threatened—which, in effect, was the case. "Don't refer to me as that man's wife. Don't say it, don't think it."

Douglas spoke as gently as the miserable truth would allow. "You have been thinking it for at least the past week."

His handkerchief was summarily jammed in a skirt

pocket, as if a sword had been sheathed. "Thinking it and accepting it are not the same thing."

Just as saying it and accepting it were worlds apart.

Lady Heathgate appeared with a brown velvet cloak and a plain straw bonnet. Douglas escorted Guinevere to the coach, but only lasted until they'd pulled out of the mews before he shifted to the place beside her and took her hand in his.

"We need a signal."

Guinevere ceased tracing his knuckles with her free hand, though she really should not have removed her gloves—and neither should he. "A signal?"

"You need a way to tell me to get you out of there in a hurry, something that won't be obvious to Westhaven and his brother. And you need a way to tell me you want privacy with Windham as well."

Her fingers went still. "Why would I want privacy with Victor?"

"To state your terms if he reveals you are in fact married?" The words lay between them, making a verbal corpse of hope.

Guinevere took her hand away and jerked on her gloves. "Married—I cannot contemplate such a thing. I'm hoping he doesn't know about Rose, and I'm not inclined to tell him."

"You must trust yourself to do what is appropriate when the moment arises," Douglas said with a calm he did not feel, and then conscience, honor, or some damned fool penchant for martyrdom prompted him to let his idiot mouth yammer on. "If she were my daughter, I would most assuredly want to know."

Guinevere glowered out the window as they passed a flower girl standing in the bitter chill, bedraggled yellow chrysanthemums in pots around her.

"If she were your daughter, I would not have been lied to and mistreated, then left alone for the past six years to muddle along with her as best I could."

Douglas cracked the window enough to toss the child a coin. "If you want privacy, you mention that life at Enfield is prosaic. If you want to leave immediately, you mention the dreary weather. Privacy—prosaic; depart—dreary."

"Privacy—prosaic; depart—dreary."

"That will serve." A few minutes later, Douglas reached past her to open the door. "Now, chin up, and on your dignity."

For he surely intended to be upon his. He preceded her out of the coach, exemplifying his own advice by showing her the greatest courtesy as he helped her alight and tucked her hand around his arm. A footman opened the door to the quietly impressive Mayfair town house, and Westhaven himself was on hand to greet them.

"Westhaven." Douglas returned the man's formal bow while Guinevere's cloak and bonnet were taken by a servant.

Westhaven's consternation was lovely to behold. "Amery? I wasn't expecting you to serve as Miss Hollister's escort."

Gratifying, to be a ducal heir's inconvenient surprise. "Despite your expectations, I appear to have that honor. It's been some time since our paths crossed in Kent. I trust your family is well?"

He offered the small talk because civilities were Douglas's specialty, and because Guinevere was peering around while trying not to look intimidated.

"My parents and sisters thrive, while Lord Valentine rusticates. Miss Hollister, I've taken the liberty of ordering tea for us in the small parlor. Shall we get out of this drafty hall?"

"By all means," Douglas replied, winging his arm at Guinevere before Westhaven had the chance. Their host led them through the house, pausing outside a closed door and turning a grave expression to Guinevere.

"Victor is not… as you knew him. I would ask, out of decency, you not dwell on his infirmity."

Guinevere shot Douglas a puzzled look, but Westhaven had already turned to open the door.

"Victor?" Westhaven led the way into the room. "Our guests are here."

To Douglas's eye, the brothers bore a resemblance to each other, though Victor's bow to Guinevere was *careful*, not the casually graceful display his brother made. "Miss Hollister. Thank you for paying this call."

"Douglas Allen, Viscount Amery joins us today," Westhaven said by way of introduction. "Amery, my brother, Lord Victor Windham."

"My lord." Douglas bowed, trying to keep his conflicting emotions from his expression. Victor was slender to the point of gauntness. His eyes were tired beyond mere fatigue, his complexion was pale—even his lips were pale—and his mouth was bracketed by grooves suggesting chronic pain.

Part of Douglas wanted to howl with frustration, because Guinevere would not turn her back on this weary, hopeless man. She would accede to his wishes, hear him out, offer him her sympathy, and even her complicity.

Because it was plain to Douglas the poor bastard was dying.

A dying husband was better than one in the pink of health. Only the merest scintilla of guilt accompanied the thought. Perhaps two scintillae, or three. And a wagon-load of pity.

"Shall we be seated?" Guinevere suggested after making the requisite curtsy.

"Will you pour, Miss Hollister?" Westhaven asked.

Guinevere made a pretty picture over the shining silver tea service—a far finer display than even the best available at Enfield, the tray itself being approximately half a cricket pitch in size.

"You look well, Miss Hollister," Victor observed.

"I am. I confess, I do not recall how you like your tea." *First point to the lady.*

"I don't believe I've had the pleasure of having you pour for me before. I like it plain, if you can believe that."

"Certainly. And perhaps while we're enjoying our tea, you might share your reasons for requesting this gathering? Our time is limited."

Douglas silently applauded Guinevere's directness. She realized Victor was gravely ill, but she wasn't letting sentiment sway her.

"I wanted to see you," Victor said, "so I might resolve to my satisfaction matters that arose between us when last we encountered each other. My conscience is not at peace, and I am quite honestly running out of time to address the situation."

"Victor—"

"Hush, Westhaven," Victor said, rueful humor in his expression. "My brother is protective of me and would prefer I not acknowledge the extent of my illness. I am consumptive, you see, and quite near the end of my rope."

"You don't know that," Westhaven said, his tone losing a measure of its reserve.

"I do know it," Victor countered. "My family does not accept it, but I know it just the same. Consumption is tiresome beyond all telling." As if to emphasize the point, he was seized with a fit of coughing.

When Victor regained his breath, Guinevere handed him his tea and gestured with the pot toward Westhaven, who shook his head.

"I am sorry you are ill." Her tone was sincere, and Douglas could see in her eyes that she was measuring the present Victor Windham against the more robust, charming version she'd eloped with years earlier. "How long have you been unwell?"

"I have been ill since before we last had dealings."

"I see."

Douglas also silently refused tea, lest he miss some innuendo or expression relevant to the conversation.

"I don't think you quite do see," Victor said, all humor leaving his expression. "This is difficult to put into words, particularly with others on hand, but you deserve to know the truth."

"And I want to hear the truth," Guinevere said, picking up her teacup. "My existence at Enfield is prosaic, to say the least, and your summons is quite the most extraordinary thing to happen in years."

Well. The damned signal had been his own brilliant idea, hadn't it?

"Westhaven," Douglas said, getting to his feet. "I've heard your teams are exactly matched. Perhaps you'd offer me a tour of your stables?"

"Delighted," Westhaven said, looking vastly relieved as he bowed to Guinevere. "If you'll excuse us?"

"Of course." Guinevere rose and bobbed a curtsy. Victor had risen as well, but the move had cost him and was executed mostly by pushing himself up with his arms, as if he were elderly.

"This way," Westhaven said, moving off toward the back of the house. "And mind you, my cattle can't hold a candle to the Moreland teams."

◆❧◆

When she was alone with Victor, Gwen resumed her seat, allowing him to do likewise.

"They certainly cleared out in a hurry," Victor said as he settled back in his chair. "Are you comfortable unchaperoned with me?"

Gwen regarded him over her teacup and struggled to balance honesty with compassion. "Not entirely, though I believe you are frankly too unwell to do me bodily harm, and you'd rather discuss certain matters without an audience."

"Kind of you," Victor said, brows knitted. "Now I don't know where to begin."

"Find a place, because you have only forty-five minutes left to conduct this business, Victor. If you've left your explanation this late, the least you can do is deliver it well rehearsed."

"Ah, Gwen." He gave her a sweet smile that harkened back to all of the charm and appeal he'd had when in good health. "I have missed you so."

The sentiment and the affection of it were honest, which was a bewildering surprise. "I have not missed you." Also quite the truth—lately.

"Well, good. I did not want you to miss me."

He sounded sincere, and Gwen was reminded that part of what had upset her so about their elopement was that Victor had never, previous to that night, struck her as capable of unkindness. "Why wouldn't you want a former amour to miss you?"

Amour. Vapid, silly, innocent word—and it had applied, six years ago.

"The place to start this explanation," Victor said, "is where it is ending, with my illness. I was aware of my condition when I courted you, Gwen. Although three different physicians had confirmed the diagnosis, I did not accept their judgment."

"You didn't seem ill." He'd been the picture of dashing young manhood, blast him and the fate that had befallen him. Gwen reached for her drink then drew back, something about the blinding shine on the service rendering the tea unappealing.

"The illness is worst in the autumn and winter, when the coal fires are lit," Victor explained. "The spring of your come-out, I rallied, as I do every spring and summer. I threw myself into every entertainment available to a duke's younger son, and that included flirting with the debutantes."

"I was long in the tooth for that designation."

"You were not yet twenty and so lovely—you're still lovely, of course, even more so—but you were different from the simpering widgeons and scheming bitches haunting the social scene. You were bright, shy, beautiful, graceful… I fell for you harder than I've fallen before or since."

"And I fell for you," Gwen said, which was only part of the relevant truth. "I have since remedied that misstep, lest you harbor any delusions to the contrary."

"No delusions, my dear," Victor murmured, regarding her wistfully. "I courted you then, sincerely, intensely, and with a burning awareness my time with you would be limited."

"So you proposed that we elope?"

He shifted in his chair, the way an old man does, one who has so little flesh to pad his bones that even a cushioned seat becomes uncomfortable. It occurred to Gwen that if he tried to sip his tea—even that—he'd likely be afflicted with more coughing.

"I proposed an elopement, yes. I didn't want my more

sensible siblings talking me out of something as selfish as taking you to wife when I knew I would not be a healthy spouse. I had not disclosed the nature of my affliction to them, but Westhaven in particular is canny. I knew I could provide for you well, of course, though I would make a widow of you all too soon."

Gwen put a tea cake on her plate—chocolate, Douglas's favorite—mostly to distract herself from the emotions flitting across Victor's ravaged face.

"Victor, what business would it have been of your brother's if we married or not? Many couples don't have even five years together before one or the other of them dies, goes off to war, perishes in childbed, or otherwise leaves."

"True, but I did not tell you I was ill, Gwen, and in that I wronged you."

"That is hardly to the point"—especially considering the further transgressions he committed on their wedding night—"and I can't think, as infatuated as I was with you, it would have made a difference."

Victor smiled faintly. "I do note you used the past tense."

Gwen scowled at him, tempted to dump the teapot in his lap, illness notwithstanding. "I am not in the habit of remaining enamored with people who treat me badly, deceive me, and then disappear from my life for years on end."

His smile vanished. "Nor should you be. If you believe nothing else, though, believe I regret the manner in which we consummated our vows."

Gwen got up and paced away from him, unwilling to hear his damned manly *regrets*. "You all but *raped* me," she said, whirling to skewer him with her gaze. "*Why?*"

He still had beautiful eyes—a lovely, perfect green, capable of mirroring such sincerity, his gaze alone could have destroyed the common sense of her nineteen-year-old self. And those eyes were so sorrowful now. Not angry, not defensive, but... profoundly sad.

"I was losing my nerve, hence the state of semi-inebriation," he said. "I wanted to seal your commitment to me as quickly as possible, but I couldn't look into your eyes while I did it. It certainly wasn't healthy for you to be in close face-to-face proximity with me, either."

"You hurt me," Gwen said bitterly. "And I do not refer to the physical discomfort some women experience on the occasion of their deflowering. You abused my sensibilities, Victor, and that..."

He waited, his gaze unflinching.

He wanted her to administer a sound tongue lashing, to excoriate him with her words, and she simply hadn't the heart for it. Hadn't the energy.

"I was so disappointed," Gwen said. "Then you railed at me for being disappointing to you. Victor, I was as ignorant of how to please you as a grown woman can be. *Why did you treat me that way?*"

This was why she'd consented to meet with him. Not because he'd asked, but because she needed to have answers, however painful or difficult it was to put her questions before him.

"I cannot excuse my behavior in any way, Gwen, but I have had years to reflect on it, and I've arrived at an explanation of sorts."

To her horror, Gwen's eyes had filled with tears, and she was too upset to reply. She visually cast around the room for something interesting to glare at while she blinked away her lachrymose impulses.

Victor held out one thin, pale hand. "Come sit with me, Gwen, lest manners require I struggle to my feet. You are entitled to cry, so let's have no stiff upper lip nonsense."

He was charming still. He was winsome, urbane, and thoroughly self-possessed, even as death stalked him. She hadn't stood a chance with this man. His social skills, his intensity, the driving needs originating in his illness—they'd all conspired to render her powerless in his unfolding personal drama.

"So explain," she bit out, using a handkerchief—*Douglas Allen's handkerchief*—to blot at her tears. The little scrap of linen bore Douglas's scent, a significant comfort.

"I wanted to live," Victor began. "Being a young fellow, raised in the ducal household, I thought I was entitled to live my three score and ten, of course, and so I was angry. I was also, understandably, terrified. I wanted to live, and I did not want to be alone with my illness. The solution, it seemed, was to find a devoted bride, in whose arms I would be able to at least forget my condition for moments at a time. When I was with you, Gwen, I did forget—or almost forget."

"When I was with you I forgot what day it was." In no way did she intend that as a compliment.

"You can't imagine what a tonic that was for me, to be found absolutely fascinating by someone as vital and attractive as Miss Gwen Hollister. But the nasty thing about consumption is it can be contagious, or so some physicians believe. As we made our plans and then journeyed from London, that began to prey on what remained of my conscience."

Consumption could be contagious, and yet it also often wasn't. "Victor, you should have told me."

"No doubt, I should have. You would have had two choices then, Gwen. You could have left me, showing the good sense to put your longevity ahead of your infatuation, or you could have agreed to stay with me, as my wife, and run the risk of infection to both you and any children we might have had. Neither choice had much appeal from my perspective—recall, please that I was a younger man, in many regards."

"So when it was all but too late, and the opportunity presented itself," Gwen said slowly, "you gave me a third option: I could part from you enraged, happy never to see you again, and you could tell yourself you had done me a favor. You never had to suffer the fear you would indirectly cause my death, but neither would you see my regard for you fading as you grew more ill."

And—Gwen admitted this only silently—he'd ensured she could abandon him without guilt on her part, a kindness as backhanded as it had been profound.

Hence his bad behavior and insults had been an effort to drive her away even before Westhaven had arrived. The scheme was stupid, desperate, and yet credible, for Victor had been young, scared, and given to dramatics.

He was not being dramatic now. He looked disgruntled, as if Gwen had divined in a moment of hindsight what might have taken him years to put together.

He twiddled a gold cuff link in a gesture reminiscent of the younger man, though the cuff was woefully loose on his wrist. "With the benefit of hindsight, I conclude I tried to control the terms of our parting because I was too immature, selfish, horrified, and inebriated to allow you or my illness that prerogative—and I succeeded, may you and God forgive me."

I will not allow us to part in anger or confusion, Guinevere... Oh, Douglas.

"When your brother showed up the next morning, you simply turned coward," Gwen summarized, though this honesty—and oversimplification—offered no gratification.

"I did," Victor acknowledged, head bowed for a long

moment. "I would not give you the chance to reject me
for a good reason when I could make damned certain
you would for a bad one, and I told myself I was acting in
your best interests at the time. I cannot think," he paused
again, "I cannot think how you can stand the sight of
me even now. I can barely stand the sight of myself
when I consider how terribly hurt and angry you must
be, all because I could not cope with the sadness every
grandfather faces when his chest pains him, or he can no
longer see to read stories to his grandson."

Gwen considered him, while somewhere in the house,
a clock chimed. The sound was a portent to her, not a death
knell yet, but a reminder that her opportunity to make
peace with the father of her child was also slipping away.

Douglas's words, about wanting to know Rose had
the honor of her paternity befallen him, rang in Gwen's
ears, and as much as she wished it were not so, she had
things to atone for too.

"Victor," Gwen said gently, "I have something to tell
you, something dear and happy and precious…"

∾

"I told him about Rose," Guinevere said from her place
beside Douglas in the coach. "I hadn't realized Victor
was dying… Well, of course, how could I have realized?
Oh, God, Douglas… he's Rose's father and he's *dying*.
What difference does it make if our marriage was valid
when he's dying?"

Douglas shifted to wrap an arm around her, even
while he fished for his spare handkerchief. He would
have to order more at this rate, lest he be without one
when he himself had tears to dry.

"I'm sure there's time to sort out the legalities,
Guinevere." Though precious damned little of it.

"Douglas, he wants to meet her. I could not deny him."

"Of course you couldn't," Douglas soothed, though the meeting had better be soon. When he and Westhaven had returned to the parlor, Victor had looked worse than ever—exhausted, haggard, and emotionally spent. Victor hadn't even been able to walk Guinevere to the door when it came time to leave, but had used all his strength merely to rise from his seat.

"You are not upset?" Guinevere asked, shifting to regard him warily.

"I have no right to be upset," Douglas replied, but as he canvassed his emotions, he found he could be more honest than that. "I am not upset you would want Rose to have some memory of her father, or that you would want Victor to meet the unlikely blessing to result from his past bad behavior."

"My bad behavior too," Guinevere said. "He asked endless questions about her, until he was too exhausted to talk and the coughing overcame him."

"So how are you?" Douglas asked, loving the feel of her snuggled against him, regardless of the circumstances—regardless of anything, God help him. "Are you upset your former love is dying?"

"How can you ask me that?"

"I am your friend, Guinevere. Even if I were your husband, I would inquire after your emotional well-being."

"You shouldn't have to hear me prosing on about Victor, regardless of his illness."

Douglas took her hand in his, wondering with whom Guinevere would talk if she could not talk with him. She had her cousins thoroughly cowed, and she would never burden her daughter with inappropriate confidences.

"Since you ask," she said after a pause, "yes, of course I am upset Victor is dying. As a younger man, Douglas, he was passionate in all things. He did nothing by half measures, he lit up the whole room with his good moods, and raged without limit when he was angry. He was devoted to his sisters, and woe to any who did not treat a Windham daughter well. For all that, he wasn't a spoiled young man, particularly, he was simply dramatic. He takes after his father in this regard. They are men of... of presence."

While Douglas was a man with wrinkled handkerchiefs, who at that moment would not trade places with anybody for any amount of money, charisma, or familial consequence.

"And you told him about Rose." Which disclosure made Douglas both proud of Guinevere, and nervous for her—and for Rose.

"I told him, and I agreed to bring her to meet him in the park the day after tomorrow. And the look on his face, Douglas... it was as if he'd been given complete, unconditional absolution for every misdeed he'd ever committed. I have never seen a man look so pleased, as if he comprehended the mystery of life itself."

Maybe Victor had done just that. While the idea of this meeting sat ill with Douglas, that Guinevere would allow it was perfectly in keeping with the fundamental fairness, the graciousness, of her character.

And in Victor's shoes... Douglas shied away from that uncomfortable thought.

When he ushered Guinevere into Lady Heathgate's kitchen, they were greeted by Rose, who was having Mr. Bear join her for a tea party at the worktable while her cousin Gareth cadged biscuits from the plate before the bear.

"I see you are entertaining," Douglas said, scooping Rose up for a hug. "How fortunate for Mr. Bear someone made a batch of biscuits."

"Cook made the biscuits and Mr. Bear and I helped," Rose reported, squeezing Douglas's neck hard. "I have missed you, Cousin Douglas. You must stay right here while I get you your snowflake."

"I have a personal snowflake," Douglas marveled, settling on the bench with Rose in his lap and a secure arm around her precious person. "How fortunate am I. Do you hear that, Bear?" Douglas cocked his head as if to listen, then frowned. "I don't believe he's speaking to me, Rose. Perhaps his feelings are hurt?"

"I can make him a snowflake, too." Rose scrambled off Douglas's lap, and the effort it took simply to let her go nigh robbed him of speech. "I made one for everybody who loves me." She was up the stairs in a flash, leaving three adults staring at a plate of biscuits in her wake.

"Tea, anybody?" Heathgate said between bites of his sweet. "And don't think to avoid an interrogation just because there's a bear present. How did matters go with Windham?"

The marquess, like any fellow in his own mother's kitchen, put the kettle on and ate half the biscuits. Rose handed out personalized snowflakes to the adults, then repaired to her room to fashion one for Mr. Bear. Slowly, Guinevere explained to her cousin what had transpired with Victor, and that she had agreed to introduce the man to his daughter.

Douglas was ready to defend her decision to her cousin, but as it turned out, there was no need.

"You are kind, Gwennie," Heathgate said, rising to put the tea things away, "but you are also tired. Why not lie down for a while, as I'm sure the day has been trying? I'll make certain the damned bear's snowflake is not costing us a year's worth of paper."

He shot a look at Douglas, a look portending future discussions outside of Guinevere's hearing, then disappeared in the direction of the nursery.

Fourteen

"I WANT COUSIN DOUGLAS TO CARRY ME," ROSE SAID, the smallest whine creeping into her voice as she peered around the empty park.

"Nonsense," Douglas said. "I carried you out to the coach, Rose Hollister. It is your turn to carry me."

Rose looked momentarily confused, then chortled merrily. "Cousin Douglas is silly," she told her mother, taking one of Douglas's hands in hers. "He's a very silly gentleman."

"He is that," Guinevere said, smiling over her daughter's head. "He's a very silly, serious gentleman."

The humor in her expression died as they neared the duck pond and caught sight of two men seated on a bench. Both were dressed well, but one sat with a cane across his knees.

Guinevere drew to a halt and knelt beside her daughter. "You see those handsome fellows there, on that bench, Rose?"

Rose nodded, eyes riveted on the pair her mother had pointed out.

"Your papa is the man with the cane. Your uncle is the other man."

"Uncle who?"

"Why, Uncle Gayle."

Rose must have heard the uncertainty in her mother's voice, for the child clutched her bear more tightly. "I don't want to meet my papa."

"Rose…" Guinevere bit her lip and cast a helpless look in Douglas's direction. Douglas hunkered down and tipped Rose's chin up with his finger until their gazes met.

"It's all right to be scared, Rose. Your papa might be scared too. Will you feel more brave if I carry you over there?"

Rose stared at the ground, allowing the smallest nod in reply.

"I will carry you then, though only as far as the bench. Then you must carry me back to the coach when we are finished."

He lifted Rose up to his hip and caught the look of relief Guinevere gave him. It was all he could do not to wrap his free arm around her shoulders, giving both Guinevere and Rose the protection of his embrace as they met Victor. Unbidden, the memory of the morning Douglas had met Guinevere rose up, a moment carried by courage and sentiment that had indirectly started them all on the path toward this meeting.

"Westhaven." Douglas bowed as best he could without turning loose of Rose. "Lord Victor."

Victor rose slowly, aided by his cane, his gaze on his daughter. The adults exchanged appropriate greetings, while Douglas surreptitiously inventoried Victor's appearance. His lordship looked if anything more pale and gaunt than he had two days earlier, though his gaze was warm, happy even, and he was smiling a damnably winsome smile.

"And who, may I ask, is this lovely young lady?"

Rose, suffering a rare attack of shyness, buried her nose against Douglas's shoulder.

"Lord Victor," Guinevere said, her smile as genuine as Victor's, "may I make known to you our daughter, Miss Rose Hollister."

Something crossed Windham's features, a sadness mixed with surprise, but he recovered quickly, sketching a labored bow.

"Miss Rose? May I introduce you to my brother, your uncle Gayle?"

Westhaven, to his credit, reached up and grasped Rose's hand gently in his. "Miss Rose, the pleasure is all mine." He smiled at her, a beamish, warm smile that reminded Douglas that even Moreland himself was reportedly capable of great charm. As Westhaven bowed over Rose's hand with mock formality, the child thawed a bit.

"You are a silly man," Rose pronounced. "Cousin Douglas is a silly man, too."

"Cousin Douglas," Douglas said, "is also a man whose arms are getting tired. Down you go, young lady."

"I have to carry him back to the coach," Rose informed her recently introduced relations.

"You are that strong?" her papa asked in wondering tones. "Could you carry me?"

"You have to carry me first," Rose explained. "Cousin Douglas carried me here, so now I can walk. Do the ducks bite?"

"I don't think so," Victor replied, "unless you are particularly sweet. They might appreciate some of the crusts of bread I've brought, though."

"You can *feed* them?"

"We can. If you'd like to join me?"

"Mama?" Rose was all but hopping up and down, so accurately had her father guessed her nature.

"I'll wait right here with Cousin Douglas. Perhaps your uncle Gayle might like to join you?"

"In a moment." Westhaven handed his brother the cane. "Careful on the slope, you two. It's slippery, and one doesn't want to come a cropper."

"Why is it slippery?" Rose asked, bounding along beside Victor as he made slow progress toward the pond. His answer was lost amid a flurry of honking and quacking as the waterfowl left the bank for the safety of the pond at Rose's approach.

"Shall we sit?" Guinevere suggested.

"If you don't mind," Douglas addressed himself to Guinevere, "I'll stroll for a bit. I won't go far, but I feel a need to stretch my legs."

He felt no such thing. He felt a need to snatch Guinevere and Rose up and spirit them far away from these charming fellows whose family was wealthy and whose papa was an autocratic old duke. Because Gwen and Rose did not need Douglas acting like that self-same, curmudgeonly old duke, Douglas took himself a short way down the path.

❧

Westhaven bowed slightly as Gwen gave Douglas leave to hare off. Douglas was not abandoning her, though. His casual stroll was about trust and consideration, even though Gwen was hard put not to call him back before he'd gone less than ten yards away.

"I should have known there was a child," Westhaven said when they had some privacy. "In hindsight, I recall seeing that stuffed bear sitting on the landing at Enfield, and Amery mentioned asking at Tatt's about a pony when we were in the mews. Little Rose will at least have a happy memory of today. It's more than some people have of their fathers."

"And speaking of fathers, what will you tell yours about Rose?" Gwen had neglected to negotiate a vow of silence from both Victor and his brother before she'd revealed Rose's existence, and that oversight haunted her.

Westhaven's lips quirked, not with humor. "Rose isn't mine to tell about. Their Graces should be told, though."

"Why?"

"So they can love her, of course," Westhaven shot back, his tone for once showing irritation. "They have lost one son and are soon to lose another, while a third is reeling from too many years murdering the French, and the fourth hides on any handy piano bench from the people who love him and worry about him. They need grandchildren to love, and I, for one, don't understand why the patronage of such grandparents would strike you as undesirable."

"Don't you?" Gwen's need to call Douglas back escalated, though he hadn't gone far at all. "When one hears at practically every turn how *old school* your dear papa is? How do you think I'd fare, Rose's unworthy mama, should my dictates as her parent conflict with His Grace's as her grandpapa?"

Westhaven sat forward and dropped his forehead to his palm.

"His Grace isn't... *terrible*," Westhaven said over his shoulder, "but he's ferocious, very protective, and convinced he knows best. To make matters worse, he is sometimes right, and on those occasions when he isn't, only my mother seems able to confront him with the evidence of his humanity and survive unscathed."

"Your description puts me in mind of my cousins."

The realization was uncomfortable. "They are both quite, quite stubborn, and equally besotted with their wives."

"That sounds lovely, doesn't it?" Down by the pond, Victor handed Rose one bread crust after another, the honking, flapping geese waddling closer as Rose shared her treats. "To be besotted with one's spouse?"

"In that, at least, your parents have set an inspiring example."

"They have." Westhaven sat back, the picture of a handsome gentleman at ease, though Gwen could not find his company relaxing. "Victor fretted terribly about this meeting. I see that he needn't have."

"I fretted," Gwen retorted. "Rose fretted, and my family fretted into the bargain. Why shouldn't Victor fret as well?"

"Your family fretted?" Westhaven glanced at Douglas, lounging against a tree some distance off. "Your family has been kind to you and Rose these last five years?"

"To the extent I allowed them to be. Suffice it to say there have been challenges, but that is all water under the bridge, my lord. How much time would you say Victor has left?"

"Weeks, maybe less," Westhaven said, a wealth of grief and acceptance in a few syllables. "After your visit on Saturday, he's done little but sleep, such as he can sleep when he coughs constantly."

"He doesn't seem to be coughing much now."

"He's distracted, in part, and he's stubborn as hell. He doesn't want Rose to remember him as an invalid."

"She knows he's dying." Anybody beholding Victor would conclude as much in a single glance.

"However did you tell a child such a thing?" The question was curious rather than accusing.

"I explained that Victor did not want to risk exposing

Rose to his illness, but now he is not likely to get better, so he is more worried he might get to meet Rose only in heaven."

"God help us," Westhaven spat. "The pain that must be endured by all as a result of this damned illness has no end. I hate it."

Westhaven's words bore a rare heat, and Gwen would have responded to his comment, but Rose was leading her father by the hand back toward the bench. Westhaven was on his feet immediately, offering his seat to his brother.

"Are the ducks going to sink for all the bread you've fed them, Miss Rose?" Westhaven asked his niece.

"No. The bread floats on the water, so it must float in the ducks as well."

"A scientific conclusion," Westhaven allowed. While Gwen monitored this exchange, from the corner of her eye she saw Douglas striding toward them with uncharacteristic haste. Foreboding tickled up her spine when a cultured voice spoke from the turn several yards up the path.

"I see our boys have captured the attentions of two fair ladies, my dear. Westhaven, introduce us."

Percival, Duke of Moreland, stood smiling expectantly at his heir, a dignified blond lady of mature years on His Grace's arm. Victor had introduced Gwen to Moreland years ago, and the duke was yet a handsome, lean fellow with snapping blue eyes and a full head of snow-white hair.

"I'm Rose." The bright, childish soprano sailed across the brisk air like so many arrows aimed for Gwen's heart. "This is my papa, and this is my uncle Gayle. Papa wanted to meet me before he went to the Cloud Pasture, but it's all right, because he can visit Daisy there."

A moment of stunned silence followed before the duchess asked, "And who, dear, is Daisy?"

"She was my pony, but she was very old. My papa is not very old, but he is quite, quite sick, and so he didn't know me. But we came here today, and so now he knows me. We fed the ducks."

"Westhaven." Douglas's voice cut into the next thick silence. "You will provide the introductions?"

While Westhaven managed that task, an expression of profound regret suffused Victor's face. Obviously, he hadn't told his parents anything of Rose, and consequences that might have been avoided—unpleasant consequences—were now going to rain down on Gwen from his ducal papa in torrents.

"Percival"—the duchess spoke with low urgency to her husband—"there is a child present. An innocent child." Her reminder seemed to steady the duke, whose jovial demeanor had gone from stern to thunderous the longer Rose chattered.

The duke turned a gimlet eye on Victor. "You, sir, have much to answer for, as do you." The last phrase was directed at Westhaven, who stood unflinching at his brother's side.

"This is neither the time nor the place," Westhaven rejoined. "Might I suggest Miss Rose be taken home, and the adults assemble at my town house two hours hence?"

"You may not," Gwen interjected, glaring at the duke. "I will take Rose home and await word from *her father* regarding *his* pleasure. If he has anything to answer for, Your Grace, then Rose and I are the ones to whom he need answer, and *we* were having a perfectly pleasant visit until we were rudely interrupted. Lord Amery, if you don't mind?"

"Not at all," Douglas replied, bowing civilly to all,

lifting Rose to his hip, and offering Gwen his arm before he led the ladies away. He handed them into the coach and sat down between them, an arm around each.

"Are we upset?" he asked the air in general.

"We are," Gwen said, offering him a watery smile.

"Who was that old man?" Rose asked. "He was mean to my papa and to Uncle Gayle."

"He was your papa's papa," Gwen explained, "and I think His Grace's feelings were hurt."

"He hurt my feelings," Rose countered, "and the ducks ran away."

Gwen tried again. "Your grandpapa was upset to think we tried to hide his granddaughter from him. That hurt his feelings."

"Nobody tried to hide me," Rose protested. "I was right there."

"That is the perishing truth," Douglas muttered.

"Your grandpapa hadn't met you before, Rose, and you are already five years old."

Rose had fixed her gaze on Mr. Bear, her expression guarded. "Don't they want a granddaughter?"

"Of course they do," Gwen said. Probably wanted her tucked up in a ducal nursery, never to see her mother again.

When Douglas passed his handkerchief into Gwen's hand—she was gathering an entire collection of Douglas's handkerchiefs—she repeated the words more softly. "Of course Their Graces want you."

❧

"You should consider going through a marriage ceremony with me, immediately."

Guinevere stepped back, out of Douglas's embrace, and from her expression, his suggestion had not struck her with a strong, immediate appeal.

Well, damn, what had he expected?

"Why should I do that?" she asked, wrapping her arms around her middle and pacing a few steps closer to the fire warming Lady Heathgate's parlor.

Douglas reminded himself they were both tired. The day had been long, including explanations to Guinevere's elder cousin, polite if strained conversation over Lady Heathgate's dinner table, more strained and not-so-polite discussion with the marquess over drinks, and now this.

Douglas resisted the urge to wrap his arms around Guinevere again. If you are not married to Victor, then marriage to me puts any other marriage for you out of consideration, at least during my lifetime."

Guinevere shook her head, and even that gesture looked tired to Douglas—tired and defeated. "Marrying you might make me a bigamist—don't you think the duke will pounce on that, bring charges, snatch Rose, and so forth?"

Would Moreland brand Rose's mother a criminal? Douglas considered the peer who'd verbally court-martialed two grown sons in the park, and came up with an answer between maybe and quite possibly.

"That is a risk. But I suspect the duke will have you marrying one or the other of his sons directly. I can think of no other way to spike his guns."

And not for lack of trying, and trying, and trying yet again.

"One or the other of his sons?" Apparently Guinevere hadn't allowed herself to consider that there were three ducal sons yet in whacking good health. "I may already be married to one of his sons. Whatever are you talking about?"

He was talking about a fate he could not countenance,

not for Guinevere, not for himself. Douglas also could not stand to have this conversation at a distance, so he settled for taking both her hands in his.

"Assuming you are unwed, the duke will likely be unable to force Victor to marry you, Victor's health making it harder to bully him. That leaves Westhaven, with whom you get on well enough, whom Rose has met, whom we both know to be a dutiful, marriageable son. It also leaves Valentine Windham, who, if rumors are to be believed, would have little objection to a white marriage if it allowed him to remain in the country with his music. And there's a firstborn bastard, Devlin St. Just, who served honorably against the Corsican."

She scowled up at him but did not drop his hands. "Where do you get such notions? The duke would not…" But her protest died, perhaps as she recalled the scene in the park. "I was worried before," she said, going back into Douglas's arms. "I am terrified now."

"Don't be terrified. You have allies, and for whatever it's worth, you have me." She nodded, but Douglas knew his words had provided little comfort.

To either of them.

"You need rest, Guinevere."

"Will you be here when I wake up?"

"I will be in my own quarters, as they've yet to sell," Douglas said. "I'll be with you in spirit until I collect you for our meeting with the Windhams. Tonight, you must sleep, and things will look less daunting in the morning."

The door opened, admitting Heathgate. The marquess raised a sardonic brow. "Am I interrupting?"

"Yes," Douglas replied, not removing so much as a finger from the person of the lady, for his hands upon her person had been intended for her comfort. He was immensely gratified that Guinevere also made no move to leave his embrace. For good measure, he kissed her cheek then forced himself to step back.

"Good night, Guinevere." He looked down at her, troubled by the fatigue and upset he saw in her eyes. "Sleep well."

He let her go and waited while her cousin wrapped her in a fierce hug before bidding her good night and sending her up to bed. An hour later, Douglas and Heathgate had each won a hand of cribbage, the brandy decanter had been soundly defeated, and yet—even aided by the brandy decanter—neither man had come up with one hopeful or encouraging thought regarding Guinevere's dealings with the duke.

❧

Westhaven had the dubious honor of moderating the discussion among the group arranged in the ducal formal parlor, and Douglas didn't envy him the job.

His Grace wanted to bluster and rant as befit a cavalry-officer-turned-duke, Her Grace looked like she wanted to cry, Guinevere clearly wanted to leave, while Victor...

If Victor hadn't exactly looked forward to death before, he was probably contemplating it a bit more fondly as the morning progressed.

"I am here," Guinevere said, "at Victor's request, and I would like to hear what *Victor* has to say."

"What *Victor* has to say," the duke barked, "is of no moment, young woman. You and he have conspired to drag the name of this family through the mud, to deprive my only grandchild of the loving care I would see her provided with, to *upset my duchess*, and to render what little honor remains to your own family a joke in very poor taste."

"Victor?" Guinevere asked pleasantly in the pause while the duke gathered momentum.

Victor tugged at the cuff of a beautiful dove-gray morning coat that had likely stopped fitting him two years ago. "I'd spare you this if I could."

"If that's all you have to say, Victor, then I can spare myself," Guinevere said, rising.

"Miss Hollister," Westhaven interceded, "please have a seat. His Grace is understandably upset."

"We are all understandably upset," Guinevere shot back, "but only His Grace is behaving with less decorum than a five-year-old." A look that contained both humor and foreboding passed between the brothers, but it was perfectly translatable to Douglas as well.

"And that," the duke volleyed, "is *precisely* the kind of disrespectful, impertinent influence my granddaughter should no longer be exposed to."

Firing his big guns early in the battle, typical of a man who was used to getting what he wanted.

"If I might be so bold?" Douglas kept his tone deferential.

The duke looked surprised Douglas could speak, but Victor looked hopeful, and Westhaven relieved.

"The duke and duchess have every right to feel their trust has been abused," Douglas began, "but Miss Hollister has come here, has in fact entertained Westhaven in her home, and introduced Victor to his daughter in an attempt to create trust, not destroy it. It is unfortunate Their Graces learned of Rose's existence in the manner they did, but Miss Hollister was quite appropriately leaving the determination of how to tell them to Victor. And he," Douglas finished in the same tone he'd use on a skittish horse, "has not had time to absorb the news of his paternity before finding a way to bring the situation to the attention of others."

"He had time to tell his damned brother," the duke

groused, but Douglas's diplomatic homily had mollified him, no doubt to the relief of all present.

"The question before us," Douglas went on, "is how we might each, as adults who care for Rose, work together in her best interests."

"That is a pretty speech, sir," the duke said, "but when the girl's mother keeps her existence from her father until she receives his deathbed summons, then we've established such a woman cannot act in her daughter's best interests."

"Westhaven," Guinevere said icily, her gaze trained steadily on Victor, "Their Graces remain ignorant of certain facts, and it is not my place to malign my daughter's father to his parents."

"Victor?" The duchess spoke up for the first time, her tone gently bewildered.

"It's complicated, Your Grace." Victor's expression had become stoically blank and fixed on the toes of his shiny boots—Hoby, if Douglas weren't mistaken.

"Then you had best begin your explanation, boy," the duke blustered.

"I did not behave honorably," Victor said. He directed his words to Guinevere, and Douglas heard both apology and profound regret in his admission.

"We damned well know that much," the duke expostulated. "But why shouldn't I have this woman arrested for prostitution?"

"Because I didn't pay her one farthing?" Victor replied, a flush suffusing his pale features. "Because I used her badly indeed, lied to her, abused her good name, broke my word to her as a gentleman, and then convinced myself my abandonment of her had no lasting consequences to her, but was, in fact, the best I had to offer her?"

Victor dissolved into a fit of wracking coughs, and the

duke fell silent, watching his son with eyes that abruptly looked old and tired.

"I raised you to be a gentleman," Moreland said. "And you are a disappointment to me and to your mother."

"Moreland," the duchess reproved. "You are not a disappointment, Victor."

"He is," huffed the duke.

"Disappointment I may be," Victor said, seeming to find some resolve, "but I am also Rose's father, and I have behaved in a manner that does not allow you to cast aspersion on her mother. Miss Hollister would have been within her rights to have me called out, and the marquess, I am sure, would have cheerfully settled the matter for her."

The duke blinked. "Marquess?"

Guinevere raised her chin in a manner that did not bode well for the civility of the proceedings. "My cousin, Your Grace. The Marquess of Heathgate, my other cousin being the Earl of Greymoor, my cousin by marriage being Viscount Fairly, and through those connections, I am also family to Lord Amery."

"And none of 'em could keep your virtue safe," the duke pointed out with satisfaction.

"The only threat to her virtue," Westhaven countered implacably, "was raised in the ducal household, Your Grace." The duke looked chagrined at his heir's reproof, but Guinevere—bless her, damn her—seized the opening.

"So what is it you want of me, Your Grace?"

"Nothing," the duke snapped. "From you, nothing. All I want is my granddaughter. She is to be raised with the privileges and standing of a duke's granddaughter, and that is all there is to say on the matter."

Moreland had raised two by-blows with his eight

legitimate progeny. Douglas gave the man credit for not even mentioning the question of Rose's legitimacy—fleeting credit.

"And how do you hope to gain possession of Rose, when she has both mother and father able to care for her?" Guinevere parried.

"Her father"—the duke shot a pitying look at Victor—"is not able to care for himself, though it pains me to say so before either my sons or my duchess. Her mother is a female. Unavoidable, but there you have it."

"Your Grace has spoken in haste." The duchess looked less concerned and more affronted. "Guard your tongue, if you please."

Startled, the duke turned to his wife, perhaps realizing too late he'd blustered past the lines permitted him by his bride. "Apologies, my dear. Meant no offense—to you, that is."

"You just offended mothers the world over, Moreland. Rose has known only her mother's care, and she is clearly a delightful child. You cannot expect Rose will appreciate the grandpapa who tore her from her mother's loving arms. If the child has one-tenth of her grandsire's stubbornness, you will have lost the match with your opening moves."

"But, Your Grace," the duke retorted, "our only grandchild must have *every* advantage, particularly when the same has been denied her for the first five years of her life."

In the duke's words, Douglas heard an interesting—an *encouraging*—note of wheedling.

"Your granddaughter has never known material want," Guinevere said. "She has been raised at Enfield, my grandfather's baronial estate, where within the limits of proper discipline, she has been given everything a child needs to thrive, excepting perhaps, the love of her father. For that last, I have already apologized to Victor. I apologize to you and Her Grace as well, for having denied Rose the benefit of association with you. Given the circumstances of her birth, however, I could not be sure you would welcome her into your lives, or that you wouldn't try to wrest her from me and my family."

In the silence that followed, a look passed between the duke and duchess, one that spoke of love, understanding, and decades of shared life and loss. This silent communication fascinated Douglas even as it broke his heart. From the tenor of the discussion, it was clear Douglas and Guinevere were not going to have the opportunity to develop such a depth of understanding with each other.

"I would like to meet my granddaughter," the duke said, "and under propitious circumstances, if you please."

The entire room breathed a sigh of relief, because the duke's reasonable request—albeit stated as anything but—signaled a departure from the name-calling and posturing.

"I'm sure Rose would like to meet you too," Guinevere said, giving the duchess a look of gratitude. Somehow, when Her Grace had expressed her displeasure with Moreland's disparagement of motherhood, the duke had become human. He'd become capable of acting like a loving, if high-handed, grandpapa.

"Your Grace," Westhaven addressed his mother, "I'll ring for tea, if you'd pour. I'm sure you have questions for Miss Hollister about our Rose."

Our Rose. Douglas didn't know if Westhaven made a diplomatic overture with his words, or a bid for possession. He did know another cup of perishing tea would be a trial.

"Miss Hollister," the duchess began in tentative, if

pleasant, tones, "perhaps you could tell us a little more about the child?"

"What would you like to know?"

"Anything," the duchess said quietly. "Anything at all."

∽✦∾

Two hours later, the farewells were observed with the protocol necessary in the presence of such exalted company—protocol that struck Gwen as ludicrous given how Moreland had comported himself.

Almost as ludicrous as Douglas taking the backward-facing seat in the coach.

"For the love of God, would you please sit beside me?" She wanted him to do more than that—much more, even in a moving vehicle, but contented herself with his arm around her shoulders when he shifted seats. "Can you imagine what a Tartar the duke was as a younger father?"

"He might have been less autocratic," Douglas replied, "but even half the current complement of self-assurance would be a difficult thing in one's sire. The duchess is delightful, however, and your ally."

In Douglas's calm assessment of the situation, Gwen gained a measure of peace, but only a measure.

"She is not my ally. She is the duke's ally, first, and maybe Rose's, second, then her sons—though that's a near thing—and with whatever kindness and civility is remaining, she will not oppose me."

He did not argue with Gwen, when she wished he would. Heathgate met them in the mews, which meant Gwen had to keep her hands more or less to herself when she wanted to cling to Douglas and not let him out of her sight.

"How did you fare?" Heathgate asked.

"The duke was perfectly obnoxious," Douglas replied, "but he calmed down when the duchess put a firm hand on the reins."

"I trust you were ready to add your whip and spurs if necessary?" Heathgate patted his horse on the rump as a groom led it away.

"Guinevere had him in check. A bit of the home brewed and he was more humble." Douglas sounded proud of her, which gave Gwen an odd pleasure.

Heathgate's gaze shifted from the mare's quarters to Gwen. "Is that how you'd characterize matters?"

"Close enough. Rose is to meet Their Graces at their home on the day after tomorrow. I can't help but fear, however, that I'm being lulled into a sense of security I'll come to regret."

"What do you mean, Gwennie, and don't think to spare my sensibilities?"

"The duke all but called me a strumpet, and made it clear he wants Rose but has no use for me. He did turn up sweet when Her Grace went to work, but I do not trust Rose's grandpapa."

Douglas whipped off his gloves. "He's a wily old devil and wields considerable charm, though only when it suits his purposes. I don't trust him, and given what we saw, I do not trust his sons to hold him accountable for his actions."

Heathgate smiled an unpleasant smile. "Then you both might be interested to hear what Fairly had to say over breakfast this morning."

As they made their way into the house, and Gwen absorbed what Heathgate had to pass along, she felt relief that David had located leverage to use against the duke.

But beneath the relief of having put the meeting with the duke behind them, beneath the fatigue dragging at her constantly, and beneath the comfort of knowing she was well supported, Gwen still felt a persistent sense of foreboding, a sense that if she blinked, her entire world would be knocked on its pins.

And she was increasingly certain when that happened, she would have to choose between her child and the man whom she loved more with each passing hour.

Fifteen

"HELLO, ROSE." THE DUCHESS DIPPED GRACEFULLY TO her haunches. "How are you today?"

"My stomach feels funny," Rose said, gripping her mother's hand while Douglas observed the exchange in silence. "Are you my grandmama?"

"I am. I am your papa's mother, and this is his papa."

Rose scowled up at the duke and dropped her mother's hand to plant both small fists on her hips in a posture reminiscent of Guinevere in a taking. "You had better not say mean things to my papa or my uncle Gayle," Rose admonished His Grace. "It isn't nice."

To Douglas's unending surprise, the duke blinked then came down beside his wife.

"I apologize. I was very unhappy with your papa." The duke cleared his throat and looked beseechingly at his wife, who seemed to be stifling a smile.

"You needed a nap," Rose pronounced.

"I very probably did," the duke allowed. "But I am quite well rested today, and I would like to introduce you to someone."

"Another uncle?"

"No, not another uncle." The duke rose and assisted

his wife to do likewise. "Not yet, though you do have another uncle named Valentine and one named Devlin. You also have a proper gaggle of aunties, but they will have to wait their turn to make your acquaintance. This person I'd like you to meet lives in the stables, and he's a very lonely fellow."

The old reprobate was cozening his granddaughter, and he was a natural at it. Beside Douglas, Guinevere's lips had flattened, and her expression had gone mulish.

"We have lads at Enfield," Rose said, "so does Uncle Andrew. He has lots of lads and grooms."

"Let's fetch your cloak so you can meet this lad, shall we?" the duke suggested conspiratorially. "Her Grace will remain here, but your mama will want to come along. Westhaven"—the duke's expression lost its genial quality—"you will entertain Amery in our absence, if you please."

Westhaven bowed his acquiescence, a look of resignation crossing the Moreland heir's face. Douglas accepted Guinevere's cloak from a servant. As he fastened the frogs at her throat—doubtless a presumption in present company—and he presumed further by whispering, "courage," just loudly enough that only Guinevere should have heard him.

She smiled faintly and trailed dutifully after her daughter, who was now holding the duke's hand with every evidence of trust.

"Unscrupulous old buzzard," Westhaven muttered when he and Douglas were alone. "I realize it's early, but shall we fortify ourselves?"

"It's late enough, and the day has been challenging," Douglas allowed. "I suppose he'll offer to give her that pony and then lament that Guinevere won't have any room here in Town to keep the beast?"

"Oh, probably," Westhaven said, handing Douglas his drink. "I love him, though I find it increasingly difficult to like him. He is upset about Victor's illness, feels guilty for having been caught unawares by a grand-daughter several years old, and is likely to behave badly as a consequence." Westhaven stared out the window of the Moreland formal parlor as Rose traversed the back gardens, one hand held by her mother, the other by her grandfather. "He also no doubt feels guilty because he permitted my late brother Bart to join the military, and he is certain I will make a miserable excuse for a duke."

"That's rather harsh." *And what were all these confidences in aid of, anyway?*

"The miserable part is accurate enough," Westhaven rejoined. "In truth, I don't think my father is as hale as he once was, and his own death looming before him while a second son shuffles off this mortal coil has put him rather out of charity with the Almighty."

"I'm sure God will muddle through somehow." His Grace, Rose, and Guinevere disappeared into stables that looked as clean and tidy as the Moreland mansion itself.

"Amery," Westhaven said, all humor gone. "Mad George and the Regent both know not to cross my father. Though I do not consider my interests the same as yours, I cannot warn you clearly enough you're underestimating him."

"Perhaps I underestimate His Grace," Douglas said, eyeing his brandy, "and perhaps he underestimates the support available to Miss Hollister should she find herself in difficulties. Your father's finances are dangerously overcommitted, my lord, and the funding for his linch-pin canal project will be withdrawn, without notice or mercy, should he overstep his role of doting grandpapa. I trust you will advise him of this development should the need arise?"

"I would honestly rather not," Westhaven said, tossing back his drink far too easily for the early hour. "Were that man to publicly fall flat on his arse even once, it would appease every instinct for justice in the known world. And then, just perhaps, I might wrestle the ducal finances into my own hands, where I can begin to put things to rights."

What a curious disclosure to make to a virtual stranger—or was this where the posturing attendant to any negotiation became convincing? If so, Westhaven was both a brilliant strategist and a talented actor.

"Then I will have to convince His Grace either that he is not giving up on Rose by becoming merely her grandfather, or, in the alternative, that it will cost him something more dear than his wealth to pursue this beyond what Miss Hollister will tolerate."

"You are not threatening to harm my father, I hope?" Westhaven asked with soft menace.

"Oh, for God's sake. You, yourself are threatening to withhold information he would find quite useful, Westhaven. I am no more a threat to your dear papa than he is to Rose or Miss Hollister." And that was nothing more than fact.

Douglas took a sip of brandy, the very quality of which suggested the ducal resources would be formidable too, despite what Fairly had passed along regarding the Windham family finances.

"I hope your intentions are benign," Westhaven said, staring out the window toward the stables, "for I have no wish—no wish whatsoever—to assume Moreland's place."

That much was obvious, and Douglas did not envy the man what lay before him. "Yours is not a happy family." Though compared to the Allen family, the Windhams seemed to muddle along adequately. Douglas spared his mother a silent prayer, though whether for recovery or for admittance to the celestial realm, he could not say.

"Would you be happy were your brother dying?" Westhaven asked.

"My brothers are both dead," Douglas said, "and yet happiness is within my abilities." He wasn't boasting— the words were a surprise to him, and yet they were true.

They had become true when he'd made a certain journey to Sussex.

"I shall be inspired by your example, then," Westhaven said, refilling his glass. Westhaven might well be slowly getting himself drunk, though seeing the despair in the earl's green eyes, Douglas felt not disgust, but compassion.

"If it weren't for the way His Grace dotes on my mother and sisters," Westhaven began, but he caught himself and offered Douglas a rueful smile. "Shall we join the others in the stables, Amery, or philosophize away our afternoon over cards and liquor?"

"I would prefer to keep an eye on His Grace, if you don't mind."

And on Guinevere.

And Rose.

When they got to the stables, Rose stood on a box, grooming a fat, furry bay pony known as George. George was in equine transports to have the attention, and the duke stood by, beaming at one and all.

While Guinevere was pale, tense, and making a visible effort to hold herself together. Douglas took a position beside and slightly behind her, standing a trifle closer than propriety allowed.

"If you groom him much longer, Rose," Douglas said, "you will have more of his coat on you than he has on himself. I believe there's a playroom in the house your grandmother would like to show you."

"Cousin Douglas," Rose caroled, "this is George, but I am going to call him Sir George, and he looks just like Sir Regis. He's a bit shorter, so I might be able to ride him by myself. Grandpapa says I may have him, because George is lonely, but I will have to come here to visit him."

"How lovely," Douglas remarked, larding his comment with sufficient irony to penetrate even the duke's thick skull. "I'll bet George will canter for you, too, won't you, George? But George doesn't have to live here in his lonely stall, Rose," Douglas went on. "You have plenty of room for him at Enfield, or even at your cousin Andrew's stud farm at Oak Hall. We could also keep him on one of your cousin Gareth's twenty-two different properties, or at a holding of dear Cousin David's, who has land on at least three continents."

Douglas met the duke's glare and charged on, heedless that he was engaging in tactics as childish as the duke's. "Of course, I can only add my few properties to the available list, but they are all close at hand, and each has adequate mews as well. If your grandpapa has truly given you this pony, you may choose from one of many, many other places to keep him besides this *lonely* stall here at your grandpapa's."

Rose's hand stilled. "George can stay at Enfield with me, like Daisy used to?"

"If he is truly yours." Douglas shot a cool stare at the duke, daring His Infernal Almighty Grace to take away the equine bait he'd dangled before Rose.

"Is he truly, *truly* mine, Grandpapa?" Rose asked, heart in her eyes.

The pony's grooming having been interrupted, the little beast stamped an impatient hoof.

"I suppose he is," the duke conceded. "I gave him to you, so he's yours. Shall we go tell your grandmama?"

And so back to the house they went, Rose tugging on her grandfather's hand, Guinevere silent on Douglas's arm, and Westhaven sending Douglas brooding looks from Guinevere's other side.

"And when will you be coming back to visit us again?" the duchess asked her granddaughter as the party gathered later to say their farewells.

"Mama?" Rose asked, swinging her mother's hand. Guinevere's glance slid furtively to the duke's bland smile before she met the duchess's eyes.

"Any time Your Grace would like," she said. "Rose and I have unlimited welcome in my aunt's households, and estate matters at Enfield are quiet this time of year."

If Douglas hadn't been looking directly at the duke, he would have missed the gleam of satisfaction in the older man's eyes. It flickered, unnervingly bright, and then disappeared.

As soon as Douglas had mother and daughter ensconced in the coach, Rose began to blather merrily about her new pony, though Guinevere looked almost haggard. Her complexion was pale, her expression taut, her eyes shadowed with fatigue and nameless dark emotions.

When they got to Lady Heathgate's stables, Rose hopped out and bounded down the barn aisle, squealing her delight to find her cousin Andrew unsaddling his tall black gelding.

"Magic!" Rose crowed to the horse.

Magic, not the steadiest of fellows generally, nonetheless met the oncoming charge by lowering his big head to Rose's level and sniffing at her delicately.

"Greymoor." Douglas nodded a greeting to Guinevere's younger cousin. "Guinevere and I would be in your debt were you able to keep Miss Rose occupied for a few minutes."

"Hullo, Gwennie." Greymoor swung under his horse's neck to greet them. He hugged Guinevere with one arm around her shoulders, then stepped back and frowned, surveying her. "Town life is not agreeing with you, sweetheart. Shall I take you and Rose back home with me?"

To Douglas's shock, that simple, barely teasing comment shattered Guinevere's control. She turned and fled, tears falling, leaving Rose, Greymoor, and Douglas to gape after her.

"Why is Mama crying?"

Douglas lifted Rose up and tossed her onto his back.

"She needs a nap, Rose," Douglas improvised. "She very badly needs a nap."

As do I, preferably in the same bed at the same time.

"Greymoor, until later?" Douglas bowed low enough to provoke giggles from the child on his back then followed Guinevere into the house. A nursery maid took over the job of putting Rose down for a nap, and when Douglas caught up with Guinevere, he found her in her bedroom, sound asleep.

He debated the kindness of waking her when she clearly needed rest, but it simply wasn't in him to wait for an explanation for her tears, for her brittle mood, for the despair he'd glimpsed in her eyes. Anxiety nagged at him, a sense that doom was closing in on them even as death stalked Rose's father.

"Guinevere." He spoke her name quietly and got no result. Thinking to do no more than hold her, he eased his coat, boots, and stockings off and slid onto the bed beside her, and thank a merciful God, she was at least wearing her chemise.

"Guinevere," he murmured, lips near her ear. "My dear, we must talk."

He sensed when she drifted up from sleep before her eyes opened. Lying on her back, she gazed up at him with such hopelessness, Douglas's sense of foreboding nudged toward panic.

"What?" He brushed his fingers across her forehead. "What did Moreland threaten you with? Tell me, Guinevere, and I will see him held accountable."

Brave words from a penniless viscount, when it was a powerful duke whose actions were in question.

She brought her hand up to cradle his jaw. "Make love to me, Douglas. I need you to make love to me."

Sixteen

GUINEVERE GAVE DOUGLAS NO TIME TO THINK OF A reply to her demand, much less to push common sense or scruples from his brain to his lips, before she was kissing him desperately.

"I need you so," she whispered, tears in her voice even as her hands went plundering under his shirt. She was frantic to touch him everywhere, and Douglas's ability to think dissolved in moments.

She kissed him, nuzzled him, breathed him in, and in every way possible seemed bent on consuming him with her senses.

"Clothes off," she begged. "Please."

A diabolical moral conundrum clamored for Douglas's attention. He shoved it aside on the realization that, as much as he might wince at the notion that he was making love with a woman legally entangled with Victor Windham, he would regret more denying Guinevere what she sought—what she needed.

And Windham had not, in fact, asserted the status of husband, despite many opportunities to do so.

Douglas obliged Guinevere's request as readily as he could while the woman was assaulting him bodily. He peeled off his breeches without leaving the bed, and got his cuffs open while Gwen's chemise went sailing to the floor. She had his shirt over his head in the next instant then resumed her ravenous kisses.

She was on fire, and even as the fire ignited an answering passion in Douglas's blood, he couldn't help but sense the desperation in her touch. This was more than passion, more than intense arousal.

Many emotions could drive a woman beyond all reason. Anger, certainly, and fear, and Guinevere was entitled to both, but in her relentless questing hands and her wild eyes, he recognized an old and very personal adversary.

What Guinevere's body was expressing, in addition to passionate arousal, was intense grief.

That insight allowed him to harness the firestorm of desire burning through his veins, and to gentle his kisses. He caught her hands and held them still above her head.

"Easy," he whispered. "We have time for this, Guinevere. We *do*."

As he slowly nuzzled and kissed his way across her chest, over her face, and around her neck, her breathing slowed. She heaved a sigh, and Douglas felt her desperation wane.

"Better," he said, looking down at her. She was pale, tired, and troubled—very, very troubled. He sensed she *could not* talk to him now, except to communicate with her body.

"You will explain yourself to me later," he informed her, rolling them so she was on top of him. Guinevere curled down against his chest to rest her ear near his heart.

The grief still had her in its grip, but she was mastering it. He moved his hands in slow circles on her back, feeling the supple muscles and elegant bones under her soft skin. When he slipped his hand down to knead her derriere, she began to truly relax against him.

Better still, and if this was all she wanted of him, a bit of cuddling and petting, then from some untapped well of self-restraint he'd manage—

Gwen's tongue touched the pulse at his throat, and Douglas closed his hand around the feminine abundance of her backside.

"Please, Douglas."

"My love, I can deny you nothing."

He would regret this—regret the intimacy, the endearments, the ambiguity of their situation, all of it— but he would regret it *later*.

Guinevere arranged her hips so her sex cradled his erection, and she began to move.

The slow sweep of her damp, intimate flesh over his breeding organs put patience almost beyond Douglas's reach, but at least he could distract her. He slid his hands from her back to her shoulders then trailed caressing fingers across her throat and sternum. When Guinevere's eyes fell closed, he slipped his hands between their bodies to gently palm both breasts.

Her eyes flew open. "I seem to be inordinately sensitive."

Wonderfully sensitive. In Sussex, her breasts had been sensitive, but not quite *this* sensitive—not that Douglas was complaining. He lightened his touch to a near whisper and kept his gaze on Guinevere's face. Her expression said she felt what he was doing, felt it keenly, and thrust along his erection more firmly.

"Douglas?" Her breathing was accelerating, her voice not quite steady.

"Yes, love?"

"I want to be… I want to be on my back," she got out, head falling back.

"Why?"

She blinked, as if Douglas had posed the question in a foreign tongue. "Why?"

"Yes, why." Douglas brushed a fingertip across each nipple. "I am reasonably comfortable where I am, you see."

"No."

"Yes," Douglas countered. He was, in truth, not comfortable at all. He was dying, burning, and screaming to be inside her. If he kept her above him, she could control the nature and pace of their joining as she had the only other time they'd had the luxury of a bed. In his present state of near-mindless need, Douglas frankly did not trust himself to show her sufficient consideration if the deed were left exclusively in his control.

"No," Guinevere repeated, lurching to the side. She flopped down beside him on the mattress, then—with surprising strength—tried to wrestle him into position above her.

"This once," she said as he gave up and settled above her, "just this once, I want your weight on me. I love the feel of you, all around me, inside me. Especially inside me."

And what more might she have told him had they had time to talk and touch at leisure? On the strength of that small grief, Douglas gradually gave her more of his weight, the feel of her breasts against his chest sending tendrils of glory through his body. He sensed she wanted to be *covered*, blanketed with his body, protected by him and yet open to him all at once.

Douglas probed at her sex gently, almost languidly, even as he felt the tension in Guinevere's body rocket back up. But she must have had some notion of their destination, for she permitted his deliberate pace without protest. When he had achieved a shallow penetration, she moved with him in slow, hungry lunges.

"Hold back," he coaxed. "Enjoy it a moment at a time."

She no doubt tried, but her body was too intently focused on its goal, and within moments, she was writhing beneath him, bucking greedily and clutching his wrists as gratification overcame her.

Douglas, from somewhere, found the strength to hold to his deliberate, relentless pace even as Guinevere battered herself against him in the throes of pleasure.

He gave her no time to recover, but added power to his slow, deep thrusts.

"I'll make you come again," he whispered, "harder, Guinevere. Hold me, wrap your legs around me and hold tight."

She did as he bid, and it changed the angle of her hips, allowing Douglas to drive her more steadily toward the next peak.

"Douglas…"

"I know, love." He thrust into her with a studied intensity that had her flying apart, leaving her keening and helpless in his arms. He sent her further into the maelstrom with deep, powerful thrusts, then fitted his mouth to hers and echoed the rhythm of his hips with his tongue. She drew on his tongue, whimpering her pleasure into his mouth and clinging to him with arms, hands, legs, and… even her sex.

When pleasure had wrung her into boneless torpor, Douglas remained inside her, matching his breathing to hers, nearly afraid to move for the tenuous grip he had on his self-restraint. Gradually, Guinevere's limbs eased from around Douglas's body, her fingers went slack in his hand, and her breathing evened out. He lifted his face from the crook of her shoulder to see her slipping into sleep beneath him.

Sleep—or complete oblivion, a mercy to which she was entitled.

Leaving her was difficult, heart wrenching, sexually frustrating, and possible only because she did not rouse. When Douglas stood fully clothed by the side of the bed, he unfolded a comforter from a rocking chair by the fire and tucked it around her. Guinevere slept on, drifting further toward dreams, and—Douglas hoped—real rest.

He left her room, boots in hand, and sat on the top step to put them on.

"Now what am I to make of a man who steals from my cousin's room without his boots on?" Greymoor's tone was pleasant, aggravatingly so, as he sat on the steps next to Douglas, his expression innocently curious.

"You don't know I was in Guinevere's room," Douglas replied, "and I defy any man to remain comfortable with a pair of well-fitted boots on his feet all day, particularly when it is this cold out."

"The temperature is dropping," Greymoor agreed. "At least outside."

"Do you have a point, Greymoor?"

"My wife seems to think I do, but its substance defies my recollection. Now, what had Gwennie so out of sorts earlier in the stable?"

"I am honestly not sure." Douglas pulled on his second boot but did not rise. "She went to her room and fell asleep before we had a chance to discuss it." He had not quite lied for his lady, though it was a near thing. "I suspect the good duke threatened her somehow."

"She didn't strike me as angry. Coercion would anger her."

"She is terrified," Douglas concluded, certain of it in his very bones. "I suspect the duke threatened her through Rose."

"Moreland threatened to take Rose?"

"At the least. He had given Rose a pony by the time I got down to the stables, but alas, she was supposed to keep her pony at dear Grandpapa's, of course."

"Are we to threaten the duke right back?"

"We already did." *And who was this "we," and when had Douglas become part of it?* "I explained to Westhaven the ducal finances would be summarily unraveled were his father to misbehave. Fairly offered to see to that."

"The good viscount comes in handy. Has good taste in sisters, too."

Was the man never serious? "He does at that. I put the message into Westhaven's hands, though I'm not sure it will reach the duke with sufficient clarity."

And this bothered Douglas. Like a loose tooth, his mind couldn't leave this niggling, irksome thought alone. He felt the pull of it, the same way he'd rifled the morning's correspondence, half-searching for a carping, whining letter from his mother, despite knowing her incapacity.

"What do you mean, the threat won't be made clear to Moreland?"

"The duke and his surviving sons have an odd relationship. They love him. They also despair of him, and at times, despise him. I don't know Moreland's sons well, though if I had to guess, I'd say Victor's life has been made a misery by the duke, and Westhaven's and Lord Valentine's not much better. Part of Westhaven would dearly love to see his papa brought to heel by financial difficulties."

"The duke sounds like a right pain in the arse. Nonetheless, I don't see what we can do about him until Gwennie tells us what he's up to."

"Guinevere is fast asleep. She's sleeping a lot lately."

"Probably tossing and turning all night," Greymoor

reasoned with apparent unconcern. "Missing Enfield, away from her routine, worried about Rose. She has a lot on her plate."

He gave Douglas a pointed look, which Douglas returned with a bland stare.

"How is my darling niece, anyway, and her dear mother?" Douglas asked, rising and heading down to the first landing.

"Thought you would never ask. My Lucy is the most intelligent female ever born to man, or, I suppose, woman, technically speaking…"

While Greymoor trailed Douglas down the stairs and prattled on about his prodigy step-daughter, Douglas paid attention with only half a brain. Something was stuck in his mind, something more unsettling than Guinevere's pallor and fatigue and her reticence about the duke's mischief.

He sorted through his recollection of their most recent encounter, all the while nodding and agreeing at the appropriate moments in Greymoor's panegyric about the Incomparable Infant Lucy, and then it hit Douglas.

"This once," Guinevere had said. "Just this once" she had wanted the experience of Douglas loving her while she lay beneath him on her back.

This *once*? The sense of roiling panic that had taken up residence in Douglas's middle condensed into something closer to full-out riot. Why this *once*? Had the duke stooped to threatening Guinevere's life?

"My lords." A liveried footman stood at the bottom of the stair, holding a salver bearing a sealed letter. "For you, Lord Amery."

Douglas tore open the missive, scanned the brief contents, and passed the epistle to Greymoor. Curses welled, along with hopeless frustration and grief.

More grief.

"Come." Greymoor took Douglas by the arm and led him into the cozy family parlor. "Your countenance is more serious than usual, Amery. Has Victor stuck his spoon in the wall?"

Behind the insouciance of Greymoor's question, there lurked... concern. It steadied Douglas, and comforted.

"I will be returning to Amery Hall." Greymoor did not start in reading the letter; he instead watched Douglas with an alertness that belied all the man's usual drollery. "I'm off to bury my mother, it seems."

Now Greymoor scanned the letter. "She may yet rally."

Douglas wanted her to, wanted her to regain all her faculties and survive to whine and complain at him for years to come. "She won't. I have forgiven her whatever missteps she holds herself accountable for, and Mother would not want to linger as a helpless invalid. I must make haste for Amery Hall in any case."

"Not tonight, you won't." Greymoor went to the sideboard and poured a stout two fingers into a glass. "It's cold as hell out there, and you just traveled that distance on Friday. Get a good night's sleep, set your house in order, and start out at first light. I'll alert Fairly and Heathgate that we'll all need to keep an eye on Gwennie, and you get back as soon as propriety allows."

Greymoor's suggestions made sense, and yet Douglas felt he ought to argue with the man, protest the need to repair to the family seat even in the dark of night. "I am abruptly both cold and tired."

Also, apparently, bereft of dignified self-restraint.

"You're in shock." Greymoor passed Douglas the drink and glowered—the man looked much like his older brother when he glowered—until Douglas took a hefty swallow.

"Decent libation. My thanks."

The whiskey was far better than decent, probably from Heathgate's private bribing stock. Douglas sank onto the parlor's sofa and wasn't surprised when Greymoor came down beside him.

"I am not in shock. I am, to be honest, more than a little relieved." Though why Douglas had to share this sentiment with Greymoor was a mystery.

"Oh, of course," Greymoor replied. "You are relieved to be staring at the loss of the last surviving member of your immediate family. You can be officially inducted into the Distinguished Order of Relieved Orphans."

"I am not an orphan." The whiskey, though superb, was making his throat constrict most peculiarly.

"You are a bloody orphan," Greymoor said from immediately beside Douglas. "But then, you always were."

Fools rush in, Douglas thought, taking another bracing sip of excellent potation. When the spirits were gone and the fire had begun to burn down, Douglas realized Greymoor would wait with him all night, if need be.

"I should be going." Douglas rose, putting his glass on the sideboard.

"What shall I tell our Gwennie?"

Our Gwennie. "Tell her…" *Tell her I love her?* Not the sort of sentiment one should convey through third parties. Tell her not to be worried about Moreland? She bloody well should worry about the infernal damned duke.

"Tell her I will return as soon as I can, and for God's sake, Greymoor, keep an eye on Moreland. A close eye. Don't let her be alone with him, and do remind Westhaven that the Moreland purse strings could easily be pulled shut."

"I can manage that. Will you be all right?"

Douglas knew a fleeting temptation to reply in the

negative, to ask that Greymoor tend to the details of the dowager viscountess's burial. Douglas's every instinct screamed at him to stay near to Guinevere and Rose, to ensure their well-being personally, without relying on the best efforts of family.

Except it wasn't Greymoor's mother who had suffered another apoplexy, and Douglas's duty was clear. "I will manage. I will be cold, tired, and saddle sore, but I will manage. Just hold the line in my absence."

"We can do that."

As Douglas reached the door, he felt Greymoor's hand on his shoulder. When he turned an inquiring eye, Greymoor pulled him into a quick, tight embrace.

"Safe journey. And you may be an orphan, but you have family nonetheless. Don't forget it."

Warmth curled through Douglas at Greymoor's words, at his gruff affection. He nodded a farewell and took his leave, but the reassurance in that hug and in Greymoor's final admonition stayed with him as he went out into the cold, dark night.

❧

"Why in God's name would you expect me to marry Victor's castoff?" Westhaven's tone was civil—barely.

"She is the mother of my grandchild," the duke shot back, and in a private parlor at the back of the Windham manor, there was no need for His Grace to moderate his volume.

"If I marry her, Your Grace, she could well be our next duchess of Moreland. While I don't judge her for her past, the rest of Society will raise an eyebrow for the liberties she allowed Victor, and they will make the lady's life hell."

"For your information, my boy, Society takes its cue

from your dear mother. If she says the girl is a widow and a distant cousin, then a widowed cousin she shall be."

The inane argument raged on—Gwen had been introduced to Society as Heathgate's cousin, for God's sake—Westhaven's generally quieter tones punctuating the duke's bluster. The open flues of the chimneys carried each word to Victor's ears, though the exchange was hardly surprising.

Victor had sent for his solicitor the day after meeting his daughter, his affairs were in order, and he'd said many, many good-byes. Still, he suffered a lingering sense of unease regarding not his daughter, per se, because he'd provided well for her, but for the girl's mother.

As the angry shouting from below increased in volume, Victor realized he could do one more thing for Gwen Hollister, and for their daughter. Though it might be done with his dying breath—such as he was able to breathe these days—he was going to do it.

While Victor made a few more arrangements in the privacy of his sick room, one floor below, Westhaven considered the man he called Father.

Like a dog with a bone, the duke would not rest until he'd achieved his goal of legitimating Rose Hollister's status as a Windham. Mere grandfatherly meddling would not do. Moreland was determined that Gwen marry Westhaven, and that Westhaven assume guardianship of the child. The earl would be more impressed with his father's goal were it not necessary to make several other people miserable to satisfy it.

"This is what I am prepared to do," Westhaven said. "You can take or leave it, Your Grace. If you leave it, I will make certain Victor, Her Grace, Valentine, Devlin, and the Marquess of Heathgate are all apprised of your scheme." Amery, as well, though Westhaven kept that to himself.

"So what is your proposition?" the duke asked with a good show of indifference.

"Pay attention, sir," Westhaven snapped, "and do not attempt to negotiate this offer…"

To Westhaven's deep unease, the duke paid attention, did not attempt to negotiate, and—most unsettling of all—left the room with a satisfied smile on his face.

❧

"The Earl of Westhaven to see you, ma'am, and Lord Valentine Windham," Lady Heathgate's butler announced.

Rose's little brows drew down, and Gwen's stomach sank as well. With the discipline that was second nature to any parent, she kept her expression bright as she got to her feet.

"I do believe your uncle Gayle has brought another uncle for you to meet. Would you like that?"

Rose wrinkled her nose. "I like my cousins better than I like Uncle Gayle."

"You also know your cousins better than you know Uncle Gayle." Gwen held out a hand to her daughter. "Maybe when you know Uncle Gayle better, you might like him better."

"Or I might like him worse."

"You might." Though Gwen had reason to fervently hope otherwise. She walked with Rose from the family parlor to the formal parlor, letting the child dawdle to her heart's content. Gwen paused outside the parlor door to order tea from the waiting footman, and knew it wasn't only the child dawdling.

She had no more interest in the perishing damned tea than she did in the Duke of Moreland's sons.

"My lords." She curtsied upon entering the parlor, noting Valentine Windham had the family height and good looks, but not in quite the same mold as his brother. Whereas Gayle had emerald green eyes, wavy dark chestnut hair, and a fairly muscular build, Valentine's frame was leaner, his eyes a startling pale green, and his hair straight, sable, and longer than fashion preferred.

"Miss Hollister." The earl bowed. "May I make known to you my youngest brother, Lord Valentine Windham. Val, Miss Guinevere Hollister, and Miss Rose."

Lord Valentine bowed to Gwen with perfect formality; to Rose, he offered an exaggerated, old-fashioned court bow, which had Rose giggling and hiding behind her mother's skirts.

"Mama," Rose stage-whispered, "he's silly." .

"He's your uncle Valentine," Westhaven corrected the child. "I am woefully out of practice with silliness, so I hope you will appreciate him."

"Shall we be seated?" Gwen gestured toward the conversational grouping near the hearth and took a large cushioned chair. Rose stood by her mother's seat, still clinging to Gwen's hand.

And now, for reasons that Gwen could barely perceive for missing Douglas so badly, she would make small talk with these handsome men whom she wished she'd never met.

"Lord Valentine, it is a pleasure to make your acquaintance. I understand you are the pianistic talent in the family."

He smiled with more charm than any one man ought to possess, particularly a man with the name of Windham. "Thank you. My mother is quite proficient, but because I have no other accomplishments, I will admit to an affection for the instrument."

"I'd love to hear you play sometime. My grandfather was a devoted keyboard amateur, and he despaired of me."

Conversation went on in the same superficial vein,

with Rose gradually wandering away from her mother's chair. Lord Valentine exchanged a humorous look with his brother and declined a second cup of tea.

"I see Miss Rose has grown bored with her uncles," Lord Valentine remarked. "Westhaven and I brought reinforcements, but left them in the stable. Perhaps Rose would like to see who has come with us?"

Rose looked up, her finely honed sense of adult conversation apparently alerting her to a change in topic.

"Rose? Would you like to visit the stables with your uncle Valentine? He's making hints you might like to see someone who's waiting out there."

Rose brightened. "My uncles have horses?"

"We do," Westhaven answered, smiling at her enthusiasm. "You have your own mount now too."

"Did you bring Sir George to call?"

Valentine waggled his eyebrows mischievously. "Perhaps we did. Would you like to come and see?"

"May I?" Rose fairly danced, she was so animated at the prospect of seeing her pony.

"You may," Gwen said. "Fetch your cloak and see Cook about a carrot or two."

"Treats!" Rose yodeled. "Sir George is ever so fond of treats!" She grabbed her uncle's hand and dragged him from the room, his bow toppling sideways as he left.

"My father will be enthralled with Rose's love of horses," Westhaven said.

Mention of the duke caused the single sip of tea in Gwen's belly to curdle. "Did *he* send you to schedule another visit for Rose?"

"He did not," Westhaven replied. "I wanted you to meet Valentine, and for Valentine to meet Rose. I thought Rose's familiar turf might make the introduction more comfortable for her. Victor requested it."

"How is Victor?" Gwen asked, though she dreaded the answer.

"Failing rapidly. Supposedly Valentine is up from the country to join the rest of us for the Christmas holidays, but we all know he has come because Victor won't last much longer. Val and Victor have been particularly close, and it would take something like Victor's death to make Val spend time under the same roof as my father."

"That bad?" And how reassuring, that Gwen wasn't the only one who found the duke so irksome.

"They tolerate each other for my mother's sake." Westhaven accepted a second cup of tea, though Gwen heartily wished she might lace it with hemlock. "The duke, however, has been busy, and I wanted to warn you."

"You have my attention." And please, God, might that be all he ever had from her.

"His Grace and I have struck a bargain." Westhaven rose and paced to the hearth, his tea untasted. "For some time now, my father's choice of investments, his entire management of the ducal finances, has been less than... prudent. Parliamentary matters, he handles with utmost shrewdness, but the business of the duchy he finds tedious, to a point approaching neglect. Our financial situation will soon grow intolerably parlous—"

Westhaven fell silent for a moment and clasped his hands behind his back. He probably did not realize he made a handsome picture of gentlemanly pulchritude standing by the hearth, though Gwen wanted nothing so much as to never see him again.

The earl turned and appeared to consider Gwen the way a barrister might regard a hostile jury. "My father has agreed to give me an irrevocable financial power of attorney over the ducal and familial assets in exchange for something he wants. I've been angling for that power of attorney for three years, and for the sake of my family, I have seen it executed."

The sense of foreboding murmuring through Gwen's veins escalated to a shriek. "What have you offered Moreland in exchange for financial control?"

"I have agreed to make a fool of myself," Westhaven said, his expression anything but foolish. "I merely have to ask you to marry me, though I have every confidence you will decline my suit."

Gwen *felt* the blood draining from her face as she rose to face Westhaven. "You will ask me to marry you?"

"Miss Hollister—or shall I call you Gwen?" Westhaven took her by the arm and led her back to the settee. "As I said, we need not be alarmed. You can simply refuse me, and there will be no harm done. I will have kept my word, and you will have been duly flattered at the great honor and so forth."

"I was counting on you not asking me," Gwen moaned in misery. "I promised him if you asked me, I would accept. I thought—I hoped—you'd refuse such a ridiculous proposition."

"Well, I didn't," Westhaven muttered, lowering himself to sit beside her. He shot a speculative frown at Gwen. "We have to think."

"There's no thinking," Gwen fired back. "Your father will see this done, and I'll bet he's already presented you with the power of attorney, so you are bound by your word."

Westhaven rubbed his chin, looking like his father in a scheming moment. "I am. You are not."

"Of course I am," Gwen retorted. "He had something you wanted, Westhaven, so you struck a bargain. I have something—*someone*—he wants, so he struck a bargain with me."

Those green eyes narrowed on Gwen, making Westhaven look even more like his father, which reassured Gwen not one whit. "What's your bargain with His Grace?"

"That is between His Grace and me."

"You are not of a mind to marry me?"

"Merciful heavens." Gwen shot back to her feet. "I hardly know you. Why on earth would I want to spend the rest of my life as your duchess?"

Westhaven looked *thoughtful*, which made Gwen want to slap some sense into him.

"I do believe that is the most backhanded compliment an heir to a dukedom has ever received." He stood, manners requiring it of him since Gwen was now the one pacing. "I appreciate the honesty, though I find it hard to imagine a tiara couldn't compensate you for the arduous burden of becoming my wife."

"A *tiara*?" Gwen nearly shouted. "You think a *tiara* compensation for subjecting my daughter to the likes of your father? His grown sons barely tolerate him, and if it weren't for the duchess, he'd be an unbridled shame. What chance will a little girl have against a man like that? What chance, for that matter, will I?"

"When you walk around the backside of a skittish horse," Westhaven said, his tone cooling, "the safest place to be is right up against its quarters."

"What is *that* supposed to mean?" Because the back of the horse was where the most odoriferous... missteps might occur as well.

"If you fear the duke's influence on Rose, the safest place to be is married to me."

The idiot man spoke in perfectly civil tones.

"You are *advocating* for this match?"

"I am considering it in the best possible light," Westhaven replied, "because it seems inevitable."

"There is no best possible light," Gwen wailed. "If I marry you, that wretched old man will expect me to produce your heir. I am *not* willing to do what that implies. I have already been ill-used by your brother, Westhaven, which was more indignity than one woman should have to suffer."

"I would not use you ill," Westhaven said quietly, giving her a hooded look that even in her panic took Gwen aback.

Westhaven regarded her as a man looks at a woman he *could possibly desire*. He was conducting a speculative, considering, thoroughly masculine, sensually inquisitive assessment that made it apparent, for all his reserved demeanor, Gayle Windham was a healthy, red-blooded male.

"Stop that," she hissed, "or I shall be ill. You will not use me *at all*, do you understand?"

"I shall not force you. You should trust me at least that far."

"You are speaking in the future declarative tense, my lord." She flopped back onto the settee, a tightness in her chest requiring that she get off her feet. "Are we then betrothed?"

"Not yet," Westhaven said, resuming his seat beside her and giving her a puzzled look. "Soon, I'm afraid. His Grace agreed with me that while Victor is extant, it would be beyond ill-bred to propose to you. Victor is dying, but he is neither stupid nor insensate. His Grace accepted my suggestion, but extracted my promise we would be wed by special license within a week of Victor's demise. His Grace is of the mind that this wedding—and Rose—will cheer my mother despite her bereavement, and I cannot gainsay the notion."

His Grace would show the same consideration to

Rose that he showed to his duchess, which was no comfort to Rose's mama at all.

"One *week*?" Gwen whispered. "What is Rose to think of this? That it somehow isn't beyond ill-bred?"

"I would pray Victor rallies and we somehow muddle past this folly without a trip to the altar, but in truth, Miss Hollister, nobody who cares for Victor would wish more suffering on him. For that reason, I will not apprise him of this development, and I ask you do not either."

Gwen sat back, a sense of unreality overtaking her. *Oh, Douglas. Oh, my dear, dear love…*

"Miss Hollister?" Westhaven looked at her expectantly, when the dratted man ought to have been moving blunt objects out of the range of her grasp.

"Victor forbid me to visit his sickroom, and included Rose in that decision."

"I will have your word anyway."

"You have it."

He nodded, giving Gwen the sense that were she to marry this man, she'd become just another loose end for him to tidy up. The frown with which he regarded her reinforced that notion.

"If you insist upon it, madam, we can have a white marriage, though I reserve the right to try to change your mind on the matter."

Drat the man for his arrogance, his stubbornness, and most of all for his paternity. "You shall not change my mind."

"We are young, neither of us is ignorant of the pleasures of intimate congress, and providing the duke his heir would merit us both a significant measure of peace," Westhaven reasoned. "I would also show you *every* consideration."

Gwen gave an unladylike snort. "For heaven's

perishing sake, do you think to sway me with promises such as that?"

"What promises could I make that would enhance the appeal of such a marriage?" Westhaven asked, and damn the man, he seemed to be enjoying this negotiation.

Like duke, like heir, and even Victor had had a bit of this swaggering, heedless self-confidence.

"Promise me we could annul the rubbishing marriage the day your blighted sire went to his reward," Gwen retorted. "That we would never dwell in the same residence as he, and that Rose would never be under his control."

"I can live with those terms, assuming our marriage remains unconsummated."

Gwen knew what he was thinking: at house parties, when visiting family, and so forth, they would be forced to share a bed, and in his calculating, considering way, he'd make the most of those opportunities.

"This is a devil's bargain," Gwen muttered. "I curse the day I met your father."

"I sometimes curse the day my mother met him," Westhaven rejoined. "As do my brothers. Though make no mistake, Gwen Hollister, I shall love my niece as if she were my daughter, and thank you for giving me something of my brother. I will become her custodian and be a father to her so His Grace cannot have himself appointed her guardian."

Gwen heard him as if from a distance, but in his *I shall* and *I will*… he sounded exactly like his ducal sire.

"I cannot absorb this," she said. "I quite frankly dread the prospect of marrying you, Westhaven."

Though she could see no alternative. None.

"We are not wed yet," Westhaven said, rising. "If you can find a means of thwarting His Grace, feel free to do so. I am bound by my word, by my duty to my family, and by a sense that marriage to you won't be the disaster you seem to find the thought of marriage to me."

"I do not want to be your duchess."

"We've established that," Westhaven said, staring down at her. "I'd like to offer one more point for your consideration before we're off to admire Sir George."

He kept hold of Gwen's hand when she rose, which left her standing a bit too close to him. Then he dipped his head and softly brushed his lips against hers. Gwen was so startled she didn't move. Didn't protest, didn't haul back and deliver the slap she'd contemplated earlier.

He was a good kisser, probably as a function of assiduous practice. In a procession of instants, his mouth moved gently on hers, coaxing and promising. He smelled good, like shaving soap and mint, and he tasted clean. When his tongue slipped along the seam of her lips, Gwen gasped in indignation and pulled back sharply.

"Shame on you," she spat. "You do that again at your peril, Westhaven."

"My apologies." He bowed slightly. "I will note you took your sweet time locating that indignation, my lady. We could manage, you and I, if we had to." He went to the door and politely held it for her, meeting her glare with a bland expression.

"I will be damned," she said to him in low, venomous tones, "if I will *ever* allow another Windham male to inflict his intimate attentions upon me again. One incompetent, selfish lout in my life has been more than sufficient."

Seventeen

"Look!" Rose squealed from the depths of a stall. "Sir George gave me his hoof. Now what do I do?"

"You put it *gently* back down on the ground and pat his shoulder to let him know you appreciate his manners," Lord Valentine instructed. Gwen found them with Sir George, his lordship hunkered beside the beast to demonstrate the proper means of lifting the pony's foot.

"Hello, Rose, Lord Valentine," Gwen called, careful to make sure Sir George saw her as well. "Are you having a pleasant visit with Sir George?"

"Yes, Mama," Rose said, leaving the stall. "Uncle Valentine says our George can live with us at Enfield and stay with us at Aunt's house."

Our George? Gwen would have cheerfully handed the little beast over to the knacker. "Did he now? I suppose you want to move your bed out here to the barn if he does?"

Rose stroked a thoughtful hand over the pony's hairy shoulder. "It's still too cold out. Maybe in summer?"

"Maybe in summer when you are a grown-up. Did you thank your uncle Valentine for bringing you out here?"

Lord Valentine had been watching mother and

daughter interact, and Gwen had the sense he was typically a quiet man. The duke was downright noisy, while Westhaven was reserved, but lacking in this younger brother's quality of *stillness*.

"Thank you, Uncle Valentine." Rose snapped off a curtsy.

Her uncle smiled down at her with what looked like genuine affection. "My pleasure."

"Mama, may I get one more carrot for Sir George? He was a *perfect* saint."

"I'll take her," Westhaven offered. "Come, Miss Rose, and we'll nip a treat off Cook before she knows we're in the kitchen." Rose smiled hugely at her uncle's teasing and disappeared, her hand trustingly wrapped in Westhaven's.

"He leaves us alone," Gwen said when Rose and Westhaven had made their escape. "Is there some conversation you would have with me in private, Lord Valentine? Am I to marry you if ill fortune befalls two of your brothers at once? You have another brother, too, I'm told, though the circumstances of his birth likely preserve him from begging for my hand."

Lord Valentine closed the stall door and stood regarding the fat, happy pony within. "You are not what I expected. I thought to find someone... well, someone quite different."

An honest, forthright Windham—how novel. "You expected the loose creature your father believes me to be?"

His lips quirked. "Do you truly think I would rely on any characterization that originated with my father?"

"I don't know. What were you expecting?"

"Somebody ruined," he said, perusing her. "A defeated woman."

What an odd conversation. "I suppose my reputation

is ruined, but because I never joined the battle, I can't consider myself defeated."

"Thank the gods. You will be good for us, and Mother will love you. Rose is a treasure."

A treasure Gwen was going to have to learn to share, much as Douglas had predicted weeks ago.

"And in what capacity will I be good for the estimable Windham family?" Because they would certainly not be good for her.

George pawed at his straw, apparently of the mind that humans in his vicinity ought to be paying attention to him rather than petty affairs like death, marriage, and a doomed love.

"His Grace has worn us all down, Westhaven probably most of all." Lord Valentine reached forward and scratched the chubby pony getting down to business with a pile of fragrant hay. "I hide in the country as much as I can, and Devlin keeps mostly to himself, but Westhaven must do the pretty about Town as the heir. Mother mitigates damage in His Grace's wake, but since Bart's death, the strain has been telling on her. My sisters know how to placate His Grace, but when the duke has seen his sons married, my sisters will feel the dubious blessing of their papa's matrimonial ambitions."

"You make him sound harmlessly devoted, or perhaps even to be pitied."

Dark brows twitched down, as if this were some sort of insight. "Perhaps he is to be pitied, Miss Hollister, but rather like King George until recently, he holds a lot of power even in a pitiable state. You will be a bracing wind, one that gives the rest of us some new perspective."

Horse-fashion, the pony lifted its tail and casually passed gas, a fine response to Lord Valentine's mention of a bracing wind.

"I have no intention of joining the Windham family in any meaningful way." *Brave words, of course, nothing more.*

His lordship left off scratching the flatulent pony and straightened. He was tall, and hours on the piano bench apparently filled out a man's chest and shoulders considerably. "The entire household heard Westhaven railing at His Grace for this latest crack-brained scheme, but the entire household also knows Westhaven had little choice but to concede if we're not to end up in difficult circumstances."

"Moreland's indifference to financial matters is not my fault."

"Nor is it Westhaven's." Lord Valentine ran a hand through thick, dark hair. "I have antagonized you by mentioning my father. I do apologize."

"So why did you come here today?" Gwen asked, finding despite herself that she liked Lord Valentine—as much as she could like any Windham.

"I wanted to meet you and to let you know I do not approve of this scheme His Grace has hatched. Westhaven doesn't like it much either, but he has little choice."

"And Her Grace? What does your mother think?"

Valentine continued to study the pony shut up in its stall. "Sometimes, I believe my mother thinks as little as possible, but I know that is both unfair and untrue. She will be told you and Westhaven found you would suit, and a marriage between you will benefit Rose. In fact, Westhaven will be a good father to our brother's child, and were he to learn of it, Victor would likely approve too."

Gwen closed her eyes and forced herself to take a slow, deep breath. In her mind's eye, she saw Douglas climbing a tree to rescue a child who was small, helpless, and in very great peril. She saw Douglas in the dead of night, hauling bucket after bucket of cool water up to a nursery turned into a sickroom. She saw Douglas insisting she be treated with utmost civility as he escorted her into the ducal lion's den.

For Douglas's sake, she asked another question. "How can Westhaven contemplate marriage to a stranger at the duke's request—a stranger with whom his brother has been intimate, lest we forget?"

"Westhaven doesn't lack a sense of humor, though he certainly doesn't have the same sense of fun my other three brothers were born with. He'll marry you because he must marry someone. You are lovely in a way he can appreciate, and marriage to you will allow him to finally curb the duke's financial missteps. Why shouldn't he marry you?"

"Because," Gwen said through clenched teeth, "I do not wish to marry him."

Valentine studied her for a long, silent moment. "You poor woman," he said quietly. "You love another."

Gwen stiffened as if slapped. By reputation, Windhams were neither cowardly nor stupid.

"For pity's sake," he said in the same low voice, "do not let the duke catch even a hint of it, or you will regret it endlessly. Westhaven understands something about life and the workings of the heart, but the duke will torture you without mercy should he learn of it."

"Your warning is appreciated," Gwen said with bitter honesty, "though absolutely, entirely, completely unnecessary."

❧

Douglas closed his mother's bedroom door and found his way to the Amery Hall estate office by the light of a single, short tallow candle. Fatigue, worry, and sorrow hovered near, like the flickering shadows cast by the flame before him.

Correspondence sat in tidy stacks on the battered desk, all dutifully sorted, read, and replied to. Douglas lit a few more candles, sat down, and took out pen, paper, sand, and ink.

> My dearest lady,
>
> Mother yet lingers, and in the kindnesses I can do for her, I find a measure of peace and a measure of torment. Each hour I hold her hand, each sonnet I read to her, each sip of water I can provide her, makes me a more dutiful son, and more worried for you and Rose.
>
> For too many years, long before Rose's birth, you have lived as if alone, facing every challenge with only the wit and resources you yourself commanded. I know that strength, Guinevere, and I know the fears and worries that can drive it.
>
> Until I can return to your side, please do not receive a Windham male in private, despite such a course being your natural inclination. Do not, I beg you, allow His Grace to corner you and bludgeon you with his arguments and machinations. I commend the man's loyalty to family, but you already have family.
>
> And you have at least one friend. I can content myself with that role in your life if and only if I know you are content as well, free from coercion and worry, for yourself and for your daughter.

Douglas stared down at the neat script flowing over the page. More thoughts crowded his mind, thoughts about missing Guinevere, loving her, fearing for her happiness.

Thoughts about resigning himself to the choices Guinevere might make, to becoming solely her friend, if her marriage turned out to be valid or if her maternal heart required that she accept a place in the Windham family.

Would the thoughts Douglas had penned comfort her or make her decisions harder?

A swift, soft tapping on the door interrupted Douglas's brooding. "My lord, you're wanted above stairs."

The summons came at least twice a night, when Lady Amery's breathing became particularly labored, or she became restive and the nurse could not fathom her needs.

"Coming," Douglas replied.

He balled up the letter, tossed it onto the meager fire smoldering in the hearth, and returned to his mother's side.

❧

"Westhaven will propose to *Gwen?*" the Marquess of Heathgate all but roared, causing his wife to wince in unison with his brother. There were no children in the vicinity, however, and as far as Heathgate was concerned, some sentiments deserved a bit of volume.

"The duke's household is all abuzz with it," Fairly replied in maddeningly calm tones, "but Westhaven was able to convince the duke not to insist on a wedding until after Victor has passed to his reward."

The five of them, Fairly, Gareth and Felicity, Andrew and Astrid were gathered in Lady Heathgate's family parlor while Rose and her great aunt strolled in the park and Gwen napped—or fretted in solitude. While Felicity, Andrew, and Astrid were side by side on the sofa, Gareth paced, and Fairly looked on from a window seat that had to be a bit chilly.

Astrid spoke first, and with conviction. "You will not want Gwen to know you've been spying, David. We need to send for Douglas. If anyone can talk sense into Gwen, it's Douglas."

Douglas, who was at his mother's deathbed, while another sort of demise was in progress here in London.

"And what if he can't talk sense into her?" Gareth asked, pausing to pour a bit too much fresh coal on the fire. "Then you'd subject him to seeing Gwen led to the altar?"

"If somebody doesn't do something," Astrid retorted, "you, Heathgate, will be the one giving her away. Should Gwen accept this ridiculous match, you'll have to stall the duke with the negotiations."

Excellent tactic. As Gareth tidied up the mess he'd made at the hearth, he was equal parts relieved at Astrid's suggestion and chagrined not to have thought of it himself.

"Capital notion," Andrew remarked. "I also agree with Astrid that we should be sending for Douglas."

Heathgate's wife said with a glance she was in agreement with the others, though she'd never contradict her husband publicly—well, almost never. Not often, in any case.

"He can't very well leave his mother's side," Gareth pointed out. "If Lady Amery yet lingers, his hands will be tied."

"Heathgate." Felicity spoke quietly. "Douglas is our family, too. He will fret himself silly if he hears no word of the situation here. He's been gone almost a week, but my guess is not one of you has written to him. If we can't keep Gwen safe from Moreland's schemes in Douglas's absence, then we owe it to him to at least make sure he has notice of the nuptials."

Silly and the present Viscount Amery were not acquainted, nor likely to become so.

"I wrote midweek," Fairly said, "but only to say Valentine Windham had joined the family in Town, and Sir George now resides with Rose here. I can put this development in a letter as well, but I'd rather tell Douglas we're damned sure not going to facilitate this farce."

"We may not have a choice," Felicity said, sparing Gareth the trouble. "If Gwen decides marrying Westhaven is best for Rose, then she will not appreciate our opposition. She is Rose's mother, and we must respect her decision in this."

Gareth scowled, though his wife's reasoning was damnably sound. What she did not say was that this entire mess might have been avoided if Gwen's nearest male relation, one Gareth, Marquess of Heathgate, had moved promptly to assume guardianship of Rose upon learning of the child's existence.

But that cowardly bastard had not wanted to offend the girl's mother. He set the hearth broom back in its stand forcefully enough to nearly upend the lot.

"I will *appear* to support Gwen's decision while I stall the settlement negotiations," Gareth said. "Fairly will alert Douglas to the goings-on, and you ladies ensure Gwen has the benefit of your wisdom on this matter. How much longer is Victor expected to last?"

"That poor wretch is on borrowed time," Fairly said. "He could leave us at any moment, and would probably rather go sooner than later." As a physician, Fairly rendered an educated opinion, not a guess based on servants' gossip.

Gareth scrubbed a hand over his face, when what he wanted to do was raid the decanters on the sideboard, or better yet, smash them one by one. "I suppose it's the best we can do. Douglas was convinced the duke threatened Gwen somehow, but she's yet to intimate what the nature of the duke's coercion might be. We need more leverage over the old weasel, and the sooner the better."

"The old weasel is gathering intelligence on the lot of us," Fairly said. "If you want to worry about something, worry about that. We've each misbehaved at some point in the past, and he has the reach to discover all of it, given enough time."

Gareth did not *want* to worry, and yet…

"Whatever he finds has to be ancient history," Gareth said, fully cognizant that Society's memory for scandal went back approximately to the Flood. "Anything of a criminal nature would be tried in the Lords. They don't convict, as a rule."

Felicity's glance warned him his reasoning was In Error. "Whether you fellows are willing to endure whatever mischief the duke can rain down is not the point. The point is he can hold the threat of it over Gwen's head, and she, *of all people*, will not be responsible for bringing more shame to the family."

"Rose is not a shame." Fairly spoke quietly but firmly.

"In Gwen's mind," Astrid said in the same repressive tones, "she herself is a social liability to this family."

"Hang social liability," Andrew expostulated. "This is not an encouraging line of reasoning."

Marriage, or perhaps fatherhood, had imparted to Andrew the gift of understatement.

"The entire mess is discouraging as hell," Gareth said, "begging the ladies' pardon. For all we know, the duke may be rounding up six witnesses to charge Gwen with prostitution." That silenced the room for long, uncomfortable moments.

"Somebody had better keep a very close eye on

Gwen," Andrew said. "If the duke can't get to her, he can't threaten her."

"Douglas asked she not be left alone with His Grace," Fairly reminded them.

"I'll insist she spend time here with family once the marriage proposal is on the table," Gareth added, though Gwen would probably rather hare away to Enfield, there to suffer in solitude.

"And, David"—Astrid skewered her brother with a look—"you'll write to Douglas *immediately*."

❧

As Douglas watched his mother die, he found a slow, silent wasting had nothing to recommend it over the violent deaths of his brothers and father. His mother lay, day after day, unmoving and as if dead in her sickbed.

But she breathed, her chest rising and falling with lugubrious regularity, while her body grew smaller, older, and weaker. She was stubborn, the nurse said, or perhaps afraid to die.

Douglas rose from his mother's bedside, where he sat for several intermittent hours each day. The duty had been distasteful at first, but as he'd grown accustomed to his mother's appearance and made her final arrangements, the privacy had become welcome.

Welcome, except Douglas was afflicted with a burning sense he should not be away from Guinevere and Rose.

He was met in the hallway by a footman bearing a letter addressed from David Worthington, Viscount Fairly. An acid unease gnawed at Douglas's stomach as he dismissed the footman and found his own room. Fairly had written earlier that Lord Valentine Windham was in Town, perhaps for the holidays, but more likely to say his final farewells to Victor. Douglas had a passing acquaintance with Lord Valentine, having overlapped a year with him at Oxford.

He liked Valentine Windham well enough, liked that the man had developed his musical talent contrary to His Grace's preferences, but did not like *at all* the implication that the duke was massing his troops.

The letter was every bit as alarming as Douglas had feared, and Douglas was stuck at Amery Hall, waiting for his mother to die, just as Guinevere was likely sitting in Town, praying unceasingly that Victor would not.

~❧~

When Westhaven came to call, Gwen knew the purpose of his visit, for he'd buried his brother the previous day.

Westhaven bowed. "Miss Hollister. Or may I call you Gwen?"

Right down to business. The dratted man would likely approach consummation of his vows with the same brisk, unsentimental efficiency, which thought made Gwen *ill.*

"You have called me Gwen on previous occasions. I see no harm in it, but returning the familiarity may be beyond me."

"My name is Gayle," Westhaven said. "You have leave to use it, though even my family prefers addressing me by the title. Practice, I suppose, for when I am the duke. You understand the purpose of this visit?" He sounded prepared to provide her instruction on the matter should she answer in the negative.

"I suppose. Shall we be seated, and shall I ring for tea?"

For then she could at least scald a few of his more troublesome parts.

"Yes to both. Tell me again why you don't want to marry me?" he asked, seating himself on the end of the settee at right angles to Gwen's chair. He crossed his legs and straightened the crease of his breeches with a casual elegance that suggested he proposed to unwilling brides regularly.

"In the first place, I object to any marriage based on coercion, and neither of us would have chosen the other but for the duke's manipulation."

Westhaven perused her, though his assessment this time was dispassionate. "Allow me to doubt that. You are very pretty, Gwen Hollister, and as poised and lovely as any princess. Our paths might have crossed, and we might have noticed each other."

The violence of Gwen's frustration exceeded anything she'd ever felt parenting Rose, and that was saying something.

"*Don't do this.* Don't try to talk yourself into me, Westhaven. I am the granddaughter of a lowly squire turned earl, and our paths *did* cross in more than one ballroom, and you didn't take an interest in me when it would have been appropriate. We were coerced into this situation, but we both get something we want from it."

"So you will marry me?" He put the question as casually as he might have asked her to drive out with him later that day.

"I suppose."

"A ringing endorsement." His voice was laced with irony when the dratted man ought to have been fuming. "We will muddle along together well enough, but I am still at a loss to understand your reluctance. You gain the status of prospective duchess, I am not a bad specimen as a spouse, and you and Rose will be secure, socially and financially. What is it you think you are giving up in this awful bargain?"

"Gayle," she used his name intentionally, though it felt toweringly awkward, "I believe you are a good man, honorable, kind, and tolerant within the ambit of the responsibilities you bear. If we marry, I will do my best to be a good wife to you, but what I am giving up... I was happy, you see."

The realization sank in only as she formed the words. "I was finally happy. If I marry you, my family, *my loved ones*, will not understand. I will lose them, and I hold them more dear than I knew. And in exchange, I will have... the duke, a duchess whose life consists of managing the man she loves, a brother-in-law who would rather rusticate on a piano bench than face his father, another brother-in-law who hasn't bothered to introduce himself, and you."

"And me?"

"You are not happy. You are defeated." And where was the dratted tea tray when a woman was busy ruining any chance she might have had for a cordial white marriage?

She had used the word Lord Valentine had chosen. Defeated—the woman she'd been when Douglas had met her, the woman she would soon be again. The duke had defeated his entire family, and he had defeated her, too.

She was glad Douglas was not on hand to see the entire farce play out, even as she missed him with a bitter ache.

"Reserve judgment until we're married," Westhaven said, "and then you'll see just how undefeated I can be."

∽◦∾

Gwen's wedding day arrived, and she felt nothing. Somewhere beneath her immediate awareness she was grieving—not for Victor, who doubtless had embraced death like a friend—but for her dreams, her hopes, her carefully nurtured fantasies.

For her Douglas. She was marrying, all but behind

his back, while he dutifully kept a death watch by his mother's bed. David had likely informed Douglas of the goings-on, but what, really, could Douglas have done? Wished her well?

He likely would have, so genuine was his regard for her.

"Dearest cousin." Gareth broke into her reverie. "You might try to look composed instead of grim." His tone held a wealth of regret, though Gwen knew Gareth had tried mightily to drag out the settlement negotiations. His Grace, however, had cheerfully—and quickly—capitulated to every demand.

"Heathgate, Gwen is nervous," Felicity chided. "Wedding into a ducal family, however quietly, is a nerve-wracking business."

Gwen made no comment as Gareth handed her down from his emblazoned town coach. The duke had been willing to wait one week after his son's funeral to hold this wedding, and so, with the yuletide holidays looming, Gwen had endured social calls from her five prospective sisters-in-law, and the hasty assembling of a small if exquisite trousseau. Her hand sported an elegant emerald and diamond ring, and her daughter had flown into transports at the prospect of attending the wedding.

Until Rose had realized her mother was marrying Uncle Gayle, who would then be her step-papa.

The conversation had gone round and round, until Gwen had bribed Rose with the prospect of riding Sir George to the church, complete with hothouse flowers braided into his mane.

In the end, Rose's elegant little pink skirts did not arrange themselves to her satisfaction on Sir George's back. Andrew had taken Rose up before him on Magic, while Sir George had been tied ignominiously to the back of Gareth's coach.

Dealing with Rose's temper, however, had made them quite late to the church and only added to Gwen's sense of unreality. What ducal bride had to argue with her five-year-old regarding seating arrangements in the bridal coach?

"You don't have to do this, you know," Gareth said when he handed her from the coach. "Whatever the duke is threatening or implying, we can weather it, Gwen, but only if you'll let us help."

She shook her head, tears gathering when she ought to have cried enough for a lifetime already. Felicity and Astrid led her toward the church, knowing better than to assault her with small talk and false cheer.

The moment before she crossed the threshold into the pretty building where she would make vows that would ensure she never again held the man she loved in her arms, Gwen cast a longing glance in the direction of Commerce Street.

Douglas wasn't coming, the duke wasn't backing down, and there was nothing Gwen could do except marry the groom the duke had chosen for her.

❧

Andrew rode up on his big black gelding and stepped down to hand his reins to a groom, and Rose to a footman.

"Your beast is much quieter with town traffic than I thought he'd ever be." Gareth shook his brother's hand and looked the horse over. "You've done well with him."

Andrew patted the horse's glossy neck. "I spoil him rotten. How's Gwennie?"

"Other than looking like she's on her way to her own hanging, doing splendidly. Where's Fairly?"

"Sent along a note about having the flu again," Andrew said. "He seemed healthy enough to me, though

I suppose we can proceed without him. Probably did not want to be a party to this farce. Has the doting duke shown up yet?"

Gareth permitted himself a patently unpleasant smile. "I'm sure he'll want to make an entrance."

The ducal coach and six—snow white and all of a height—trotted down from the square, as if on cue.

The duke's footmen, postilions, outriders, and other assorted lackeys swarmed the coach before it disgorged its cargo. When the steps had been let down, the duke himself, in full regalia, assisted one pretty female after another from his carriage. Lord Valentine Windham, arrayed in courtly splendor, brought up the rear on a dark horse.

"Let the play begin," Andrew muttered.

When the Windham ladies were organized on the arms of various footmen, the party began its stately parade toward the church. Gareth watched this bit of ducal stagecraft, not surprised when Moreland detached himself from the procession to approach. His Grace was beaming, no doubt pleased his machinations were about to bear fruit. His youngest son loitered a few paces away, expression bored.

"Your Grace." Gareth bowed to the duke, Andrew following suit.

"Gentlemen, a fine day for a wedding," Moreland commented jovially. "I take it the blushing bride has already arrived?"

"Gwen is here," Gareth replied, though if Gwen were blushing, it was no thanks to any Windhams. "Westhaven awaits within, as do the appropriate documents, but I have to say, Your Grace, if this wedding goes forward, I believe we will all regret it."

Moreland's white eyebrows lifted, but his smile didn't falter. "You are mistaken, Heathgate. There will be regret all around if this wedding does *not* go forward. Now, shall we join the others? Miss Hollister is no doubt anxious to conclude the ceremony."

No, she was not. Gareth glanced up the street where Andrew's tiger was trying to quiet a restive Magic. Two horsemen came galloping around the corner, causing a general commotion. One did not gallop in Town, and certainly not at ten of the clock, and most assuredly not right up to St. George's very steps.

"Cavalry," Andrew muttered to his brother, nodding at the pair who had swung down off their horses and were approaching the church at a purposeful jog.

"We're not too late," Fairly said to Douglas as they came panting up the steps.

"You." Douglas shot forward toward the duke. "What have you done with Guinevere?"

"Amery?" The duke stepped back, his face a mask of disdain. "Miss Hollister awaits us in the church, where she will join with my heir in holy matrimony. Now if you will take your odoriferous, untidy self off, I've a wedding to attend."

"There will be no wedding," Douglas snarled, grabbing the duke by the forearm.

The duke looked down pointedly at Douglas's worn, sweaty riding glove gripping his coat, and then up at his footmen, postilions, outriders, and grooms.

"There has been an assault on a peer," His Grace snapped, "before witnesses. Seize this man and use whatever force is necessary to subdue him. Thoroughly."

Eighteen

NOT TOO LATE. NOT TOO LATE. WE'RE NOT TOO LATE.
Fairly's words beat against Douglas's sanity even as rage
threatened to crowd out reason.

Moreland's liveried army was closing in, preparing
to prevent Douglas bodily from entering the church
and stopping a wedding Guinevere should never have
consented to.

Douglas gripped Moreland's wrist with some notion
of hiking the man's arm behind his back when a muttered oath came from his left.

Lord Valentine Windham had donned court finery for
the wedding, and thus sported a gleaming sword at his
left side. Douglas lunged and appropriated the weapon,
which larceny provoked the youngest Windham son to
grin, sketch a bow, and hustle off toward the church.
The blade was more decorative than functional, but
sharp enough to do damage. Douglas saluted his thanks
to Windham's retreating back and waved the weapon at
the circle of ducal retainers forming around him.

"Your Grace," Greymoor said pleasantly from the
duke's immediate left. "That man"—he nodded at
Douglas—"is dear to my wife and therefore dear to me.

He is family to us, and you harm him at your peril."
The sound of a dagger sliding from its sheath filled the
ensuing silence.

"And he is dear to me." Fairly picked up the thread
of Greymoor's warning, unsheathing his own dagger on
the duke's immediate right.

"And to me and my marchioness," Heathgate informed
him, an ugly, very businesslike short pistol appearing in
his hand.

The duke's hauteur faltered at a quiet voice from
behind him.

"Percival?" The duchess stood at the door to the
church, leaning heavily on Lord Valentine's arm, her
pretty face wreathed in bewilderment. "Why aren't you
joining us inside?"

"There will be no wedding, Your Grace," Douglas
answered her.

"There most assuredly will be," the duke shot back.
"Seize him!" He turned to go but hadn't counted on the
reflexes of a desperate man. The tip of Douglas's sword
caught him under the chin, and the duke went still.

"You will listen to me, Moreland," Douglas instructed
with lethal quiet. "*And there will be no wedding.*"

"Percival," the duchess said, "hear him out. He seems
determined, though that sword is entirely unnecessary,
Lord Amery."

Douglas inclined his head toward the duchess and
dropped his sword a few inches to the right. "Thank
you, Your Grace.

"There will be no wedding," Douglas went on, "for
at least three reasons. First, a man may not marry his
brother's widow. The issue of such an invalid union are
not legitimate, leaving you without an heir, even were
Westhaven to get children on Miss Hollister. The second

reason there will be no wedding is that you will not know, Moreland, whether the child Miss Hollister bears in, say, eight or nine months is Windham progeny—*or mine*. While a man of different ambitions might long for his child to become duke in your stead, I could hardly wish it on any son of mine. The third reason there will be no wedding is that Her Grace will not permit it, knowing you somehow coerced Miss Hollister, bullied her, or threatened her into accepting Westhaven's suit."

Douglas's sword dropped farther, as the fatigue of having buried his mother the day before, then riding all night with Fairly at his side, found him.

"Her Grace," Douglas went on, "knows you are not a truly reprehensible man, for she loves you and is secure in your love as well. You deny Miss Hollister and your own son the same marital blessing when you force them to wed each other. *I will not allow it.*"

He watched the duke with eyes that promised unstoppable retribution. "There will be no wedding."

A few beats of silence went by, Douglas's arm burning with the weight of the ceremonial sword, his heart heavy with regrets. Guinevere's very presence in the church, her consent to a ceremony that would ensure she and Douglas had no future at all, rendered Douglas's hopes and dreams ashes.

"Percival St. Stephens Tiberius Joachim Windham," the duchess said quietly, "your duchess has developed a *blinding* headache, and requires your immediate escort home."

The duke heaved a sigh, looking much like a little boy whose nanny has caught him making mud pies in his Sunday best.

"But, Esther… Of course, Esther." His Grace waved a white-gloved hand in Douglas's direction. "Because there is to be no wedding."

As the duke departed, swords and daggers were lowered, and Heathgate's pistol disappeared.

"Well done, Amery," Heathgate muttered. "We were getting worried."

"I've about killed my horse," Douglas replied, "and Fairly as well. He made the journey to Amery Hall and back in less than thirty-six hours. You all"—Douglas looked around at people to whom he bore no blood relation whatsoever—"have my thanks."

Guinevere appeared at the church door, looking lovely, tired, and bewildered—*on Westhaven's arm*. "Douglas?"

"Miss Hollister." Douglas bowed slightly, lest fatigue and emotion both topple him. "My apologies for having disturbed your morning. The nuptials have been called off."

He turned and trotted down the steps, swinging up onto Regis without a backward glance. He left the woman he loved—the woman who had not even thought to inform him of her decision to marry another—standing before the church, pale as the white roses in her bouquet. At her side, Westhaven smiled faintly and saluted as Regis cantered off in the direction of the square.

∽৵৵

In the days following his return to Town, Douglas mostly slept. He managed this by imposing on Fairly's hospitality, Heathgate's man having found a buyer for Douglas's sole remaining London property.

Fatigue was only part of what plagued Douglas.

In his life, Douglas had suffered betrayal. His siblings had betrayed him at various turns, as had his parents. The society in which he lived, one that purported to value integrity, honesty, protection of the weak, and myriad other Christian virtues, had betrayed him in a general sort of way.

His body had betrayed him as well, as when he'd first seen Guinevere in her wedding finery and felt a flash of desire for her even as she prepared to marry another.

His heart had betrayed him, when in that same moment, he'd felt such an aching relief simply to see her again, he'd been nearly speechless.

Guinevere had betrayed him, profoundly, and that hurt in ways Douglas couldn't begin to label, much less describe.

But where he'd not once felt betrayal was from his reasoning mind. There, his survival instincts took up residence, turning the gears of his reason, provoking him into long staring spells and such fits of brooding that Fairly gave up lecturing him. Douglas was attempting to think his way through this latest grief, driving his host nigh to distraction with worry couched as all manner of medical lectures about humors and melancholia.

Greymoor called on Douglas, despite the butler's warning that his lordship wasn't receiving.

"Look, Greymoor," Douglas said, jamming his hands in his pockets when Greymoor had politely lectured him at length, "understand me, please. I do not bear Guinevere any ill will, but she was prepared to wed another and has not seen fit to explain her reasons to me, though I comprehend the advantages of the match for her and for Rose. You and the rest of the family should leave it at that."

Family whom Douglas shared with Guinevere, whether she liked it or not, whether there was a blood tie or not.

Greymoor prepared to take his leave, but before granting that signal mercy, graced Douglas with a sober, measuring look.

"Gwen says you owe her nothing and you probably regret the day you met her. I could live with such a sorry outcome, if true, because you are family too, and I can see you are miserable. What I cannot accept is seeing the light gradually fading from Gwen's spirit as she approaches the day when *she* regrets having met *you*. You gave her back something vital, Douglas, but now you are ripping it just as deliberately from her grasp."

"And Rose?" Douglas couldn't help but ask.

Greymoor shot such a look of pity over his shoulder, Douglas wondered how he'd ever mistaken the man for frivolous. "Rose is one very unhappy, confused little girl. She is at risk for growing up every bit as worried, careful, and self-reliant as her dear mother is, and may I point out, as you can be. For that looming tragedy, I blame you and Gwen both, for it is in your mutual power to prevent it."

He closed the door behind him, the sound reminiscent of the lid of a casket being lowered for the final time.

Douglas's first inclination was to return to his bed, but his mind would not let go of the things Greymoor had said, and so he poured himself another cup of tea and set to work brooding his way back over their conversation.

Guinevere had no doubt felt she had to marry Westhaven to protect Rose. He accepted that, and would, he trusted, eventually get around to admiring her for it. What he could not accept was that Guinevere would not tell him how the duke had intimidated her into that particular corner. *She hadn't even let him try to defend her.*

"Merciful saints." Douglas groaned as insight struck, and set his teacup down as he mentally stumbled over a different possibility, one that had his sluggish mind reviewing all the available data. He wanted to exonerate

Guinevere's betrayal of him, wanted to think he hadn't misplaced his sanity when he'd lain down with her, or on the several occasions when he'd asked for her hand.

But he was tired, confused, and wary, and he promised himself he'd wait out the week before putting action to his thoughts. The next morning found him sitting at the breakfast table with Fairly, hiding behind some section of the newspaper or other, when a footman brought in the post.

And, from a completely unsuspected quarter, Douglas's intention to consider matters deliberately and to proceed rationally were shot to hell right out from under him.

"This one's addressed to you." Fairly tossed an epistle to him, a small smile accompanying the gesture as Mine Nosy Host turned to the footman. "Have his lordship's bay saddled, to be ready in about thirty minutes, if you please."

Douglas wondered who could be writing to him, for he surely did not give a whit about keeping up with correspondence of late, nor did he recognize the very immature hand.

Five minutes later, he knew what it meant to be unable to form a coherent thought.

> *Dear Cuzn Duglis,*
>
> *No one helpt me rite this. Dentn will post it for me. I miss you. My papa died, and he is with Dazy in the Clowd Pastur. I do not miss my papa, and he said I did not have to, but I miss you. Mama crys when she thinks I don't see her. I talk to Sur Jorj a lot, but he is just a horse. He looks like Rejis. Can you bring Rejis to visit Sur Jorj? I love you.*
>
> *Miss Rose Hollister*

Something about Douglas's stillness must have caught Fairly's eye, because Fairly came around the table and went to his haunches to read the letter Douglas held in one hand. Douglas permitted it, unable to move.

Rose was, as she'd been the first time he met her: *little, helpless, and in harm's way.*

She was going to think Douglas did not love her, did not miss her, did not want to play a role in her life, all because her mother had hurt Douglas's feelings.

What mattered reason and deliberation, what mattered hurt feelings or dignity, compared to love? The poor child might even think Douglas did not love Guinevere, when the very opposite was true.

And *Guinevere* was going to think Douglas did not love her, when all that mattered, *all that would ever matter,* was that he did and that the lady should know it.

That revelation allowed Douglas to breathe with more ease than he had in days.

Fairly cuffed Douglas on the shoulder. "Godspeed, and mind you don't bungle this, or I swear I'll console the woman right into my own bed. The horse will be ready soon. I'll send hot water up so you can shave first."

The viscount smiled wickedly as he left the breakfast parlor, yelling for his own horse to be saddled next. Precisely twenty-five minutes later, Douglas was on Regis, his steed cantering off smartly in the direction of Enfield.

❧

"Cousin Douglas!" Rose met Douglas in the barn aisle, outside the stall where Sir George was crunching a carrot to bits. She started to run to Douglas, but her momentum died mid-pelt, uncertainty clouding her features.

"You remembered the no-running-in-the-barn rule,"

Douglas said, his voice far steadier than his nerves. "I don't believe there's a no-hugging rule." He closed the distance between them and swept her up in his arms. "I have missed you, Rose," he said, breathing in her wiggly, warm, sweet-little-girl presence. He held her tight, a lump rising in his throat before he set her down.

"I've brought Regis to visit with you as well," Douglas went on, wanting to pick the child up all over again. "Have you a carrot for him, perhaps?"

"No carrots left," Rose said, swinging Douglas's hand. "Sir George ate them all. We could get one from the pantry."

"Let's do that, and you can tell me how you're getting on."

"I will be six soon," Rose reported, and as they walked into the back entrance to the house, she launched into a detailed and enthusiastic recounting of her every activity since Douglas had last seen her.

"…And we planted the Holland bulbs for Daisy," she concluded, "just yesterday, because Mama said it was the January thaw and our last chance. Hullo, Mama."

Guinevere stood in a brown velvet dress, looking bewildered and lovely by the enormous kitchen hearth.

"Miss Hollister." Douglas forced himself to bow, though it meant momentarily parting with the sight of the woman he loved. "My apologies for my unorthodox arrival. Miss Rose and I met in the stables and thought to bring Regis a treat before I made a proper entry."

"Douglas."

A familiar blend of arousal and gladness suffused Douglas as he simply beheld her.

"Sit." Douglas gained her side in two strides and took her arm to lead her to a bench. "You are quite pale of a sudden, and I do apologize again for appearing this way. Rose, could you fetch your mama a glass of water?"

Rose scampered away on her mission, and Douglas busied himself removing his greatcoat, gloves, and scarf. When Rose reappeared with a half-full glass, Douglas handed it to Guinevere, who had yet to say anything besides his name.

"Shall we feed Regis his carrot?" Rose asked worriedly.

"May I ask you, Rose, to take him the carrot for me?" Guinevere's color still hadn't returned, and she looked to be in shock. "You will have to wait until Ezra has him in a stall, though I know the beast would appreciate it."

"I'll pet his nose and everything!" Rose trotted off, carrot clutched in her fist like a sword.

"You came to see Rose," Guinevere said, watching her daughter depart. "I should have known you would."

"May I fetch you a cup of tea?" Douglas leaned back against the wooden counter, arms crossed over his chest lest he use them to enfold the quiet creature before him. And tea would be no damned help at all in any case. "Or would you like something stronger? You still look wan to me." And more beautiful than ever.

"No spirits." Her smile was wan too. "I couldn't keep them down, I'm sure."

"I suppose a woman in anticipation of a blessed event can expect some digestive upset," Douglas observed, turning to rummage for tea, cream, and sugar, or perhaps to search for his wits.

"But, Douglas, I'm not in expectation of any—"

He turned back to her quickly enough to see her expression flit from diffident to bewildered, to utterly, fiercely joyous. Her hand flew to her mouth then drifted slowly, reverently, to her abdomen.

In those few seconds, profound relief coursed through Douglas from two distinct sources. Relief came first from the joy on Guinevere's face: *she was overjoyed to be carrying their child.* He'd harbored such a miserable load of fear—for her, and for *them*—fear that for Guinevere, pregnancy, any pregnancy, might carry so many negative associations the renewed prospect of motherhood could bring her only worry and resentment.

He'd been wonderfully, blessedly wrong. Her pleasure radiated from her like an angel chorus in full song.

The second source of Douglas's relief came from the momentary disbelief on Guinevere's face. *When she'd gone to marry Westhaven, she hadn't known she carried Douglas's child.*

More than anything, he'd wondered how she could have done that—allowed their child to be raised by another man. That decision had seemed so unlike Guinevere, so deceptive and just plain wrong.

The damned lump was back in Douglas's throat, so he turned to the counter and busied himself pouring hot water from the kettle into the teapot, then preparing Guinevere's tea. When he was once again in possession of himself, he brought the tea to her.

"Sit with me?" she asked, turning a hesitant smile on him.

Douglas lowered himself to the bench beside her, feeling abruptly unsure. It had never occurred to him Guinevere, having been through one pregnancy, wouldn't have put together the symptoms—nausea, fatigue, tender breasts, missed courses—though apparently she hadn't.

He wanted to take her hand in his, but didn't dare.

"I thought," Guinevere said, wonder in her voice, "I thought I was upset and overwhelmed. I *was* upset and overwhelmed. Very upset, and exhausted. I thought I was simply…"

"Yes?"

"Simply missing you," she said, some of the wonder dying.

"I've certainly missed you," Douglas muttered testily.

She bowed her head and addressed herself to her teacup, the self-same little green cup with white unicorns Douglas had seen her with the day they'd met. "I was to wed Westhaven. How could you miss me when I'd accepted another's proposal and rejected all of yours?"

The urge to touch her was overwhelming, but Douglas held back, needing truth more than comfort. "Did you turn to another, Guinevere, or were you simply trying to manage matters on your own, without the aid of those who love you?"

She dithered by consuming her tea, but her expression had become solemn. "I could not jeopardize Rose. Surely you did not expect me to let Moreland simply whisk her away?"

"Of course not, though surely *you* didn't expect *me* to let you and Rose walk out of my life?"

"I thought it for the best."

"Why?"

⤜⤚

Douglas was here in Gwen's kitchen, he was being civil and considerate, and she was going to bear his child. Gwen's mind could not grasp those three happy facts entirely, but she could hear his tone of voice.

"Why?" Douglas asked. He wasn't accusing. He was curious, as if he couldn't puzzle the situation out without Gwen's assistance. Gwen stood, took her empty teacup to the sink, then turned to face Douglas as he remained sitting on the bench a few feet away.

"Do we have to have this discussion?"

"We do," Douglas said, glancing at her waist meaningfully.

"Promise me something first," Gwen said, because Douglas's word was utterly reliable. "Promise me you won't seek retaliation against Moreland."

Douglas's expression cooled to that of the polite, distant viscount Gwen had met weeks ago. "You have my word."

"Moreland made a few casual comments when we were alone in the stables," Gwen said, shuddering at the memory. "He implied he would have David brought up on charges of maintaining a common nuisance for his ownership of the Pleasure House. He was also prepared to restart all the rumors about Gareth sabotaging the boat that sank with his family aboard years ago. For Andrew, recently back from years traveling abroad, the unhappy widow Pettigrew could be prevailed upon to stir up all manner of mischief. He's a very inventive fellow, the duke, very determined. He confided in me—the old wretch. Told me his heart is troubling him, and he's loathe to burden his family with that news, though he's desperate for grandchildren. Can you believe he cares not so much for the succession as he does for leaving his duchess with more children to love?"

Douglas closed his eyes for the space of several heartbeats, then stood and crossed to her, coming so close she could smell the cedary fragrance of his shaving soap.

"And for me, Guinevere? It took me days to fathom the real threat hanging over you. Your family was willing to weather scandal on your behalf, and that you might have allowed. But what did the duke have planned for me?"

She had hoped he would not puzzle this out, but Douglas was a man who noticed details, particularly when those details affected *her*. Tears spilled down her cheeks, tears not for herself, not even for Rose, but for Douglas.

"Guinevere, you have to tell me."

His scent wafted to Gwen as she stood a few inches and an ocean of regret away from him. Douglas hadn't said he loved her, hadn't said how he felt about the baby, hadn't said he'd forgiven her. She wanted to throw herself into his arms and rejoice with him that they were to be parents, but he had come for answers, and to see Rose, not for Gwen.

All she had left to give him was the truth.

"Moreland said"—Gwen controlled her voice with limited success—"he said he'd known your father, knew how hard he was on the horses and the help, how profligate with the family finances. Peer or not, His Grace would have seen you ruined. He implied that he knew the extent of your late brother's debts, knew how close to disaster your family had come. Not a passing scandal for you, Douglas, but complete ruin."

"Merciful God." Douglas's hands fisted at his sides, and when Gwen peeked up at him, his eyes were closed, his jaw clenched. The silence in the kitchen filled with frustration and suppressed violence.

"So you think Moreland would have carried out his threats?" Her worst fear was that the duke's intentions had been so outlandish, she'd been foolish to be swayed by them.

Douglas heaved a sigh and looked down at her, bringing his attention to her as if with great effort.

"He need not have carried out half of them. All he would have had to do," Douglas replied, "was grumble a few innuendos in his club, or mutter about his suspicions in the Lords, and there is no telling where the momentum of gossip and maliciousness would have taken things, particularly given the tenuous nature of my finances at present. Your fears, Guinevere, were more than justified. And were Heathgate, Greymoor, Fairly, and myself aware of the nature of his threats, somebody would have been settling matters on a field of honor. Probably several somebodies, not any of whom were guaranteed to survive."

"Thank you," Gwen said, letting out a long exhale. Douglas might not forgive her, but he at least understood why she'd done what she'd done.

"We need to talk, Guinevere. It isn't so cold outside. Will you walk with me?"

Gwen's heart sank. Of course they would talk, about the baby, about what to tell the rest of the family, about what to tell Rose, but Douglas still hadn't touched her, and that spoke volumes. She took down a worn cloak of brown velvet while Douglas shrugged back into his coat and left his scarf—a soft gray wool—dangling around his neck.

"Come," he said, holding the door for her. When they gained the out-of-doors, he surprised Gwen by not offering his arm, but rather, by taking her bare hand in his. He walked her through the dreary winter gardens, the sunshine doing what it could to soften the crisp air.

Gwen waited for him to do this talking he seemed to think was so important, but he merely led her to a bench and sat beside her, still holding her hand. He sat with her thus for long, silent minutes, and Gwen had the sense he was trying not to put his thoughts together but to find the courage to speak them aloud.

"Douglas," she said softly, "whatever it is, it can't be so terrible as marrying a man I do not love without giving you my reasons. If you cannot see your way clear to continue our dealings, I will find a way to accept that."

He glanced down at her, consternation in his eyes.

"Guinevere…" He brought her knuckles to his lips, then kept her hand in his and rested it on his thigh. He didn't look at her again but began speaking in the soft, reasonable tones she'd come to expect from him.

"My parents," Douglas said, looking out over the dreary landscape, "should not have had children. Moreland's innuendos were very likely based on truth. My mother no longer went about in Society because she was too mortified by our circumstances. My brothers' lives were monuments to self-indulgence and venality, which ultimately resulted in their untimely deaths." The strength of Douglas's grip on her hand was desperate. "My father and grandfather were no better. Before we traveled to Sussex, my thoughts dwelled on little else."

He paused and hunched forward, resting his elbows on his knees, shielding his face from her view. From his defensive posture, Gwen suspected he was battling mightily to maintain his dignity.

Still.

Gwen could not bear for Douglas to struggle so. "I vow, Douglas, Moreland should be pilloried for using such an unfortunate family history to get his hands on an innocent child. Perhaps his conscience plagues him, because he's since sent Heathgate a sum to be held in trust for his granddaughter's needs, and a florid little note about family misunderstandings and best intentions. You are free to give Moreland the rough edge of your tongue when next we see him."

He shot a look over his shoulder, as if she spoke nonsense, which she did. She'd say anything, promise anything, to keep Douglas from parting from her in anger.

"*We*, Guinevere? Is there still a *we* for us, when I have hurt you? When I have doubted you and convinced myself you had played me false, cast me aside for a duke's heir, when all along it was me you were protecting from the duke's machinations? Not Rose, *me*. You had given me back parts of my soul I was resigned to living without, and still I doubted you."

He was angry with himself, and that Gwen could not tolerate. "If you were truly convinced I'd thrown you over, you would not have stopped the wedding, and you would not be here today. And, Douglas"—she had to pause to swipe her knuckles over her cheek—"had *I* not doubted *you*, I would never have been at that church."

She felt him absorb this, for it was the truth, and Douglas Allen dealt most easily with truths.

"I could not let you wed another Windham under false pretenses," Douglas said. "You were legally married to Victor, and even when you eventually figured that out, you would not have repudiated Westhaven."

"How did you know I was legally married?"

"Small clues," Douglas replied. "I haven't seen proof. Victor was surprised when you introduced his daughter to him as Rose Hollister. In hindsight, I gathered he expected her to be Rose Windham. And Victor knew his father, knew if there were evidence of marriage the duke would search it out and either destroy it or use it for ducal ends. Victor no doubt found a safe place for the documents, but we might perhaps never know where he secreted them."

"He passed them to his mother," Gwen said, "sealed in a letter to Rose, which was to be given to her upon his death. The duchess was too distraught at the loss of a second son and the marriage of the heir to attend to that detail until several days after the intended wedding. She didn't know the letter to Rose contained the lines and the registry page."

"Have you told Westhaven?"

"I haven't wanted to see the man." Did not *ever* want to see him, unless Douglas was with her to endure such a trial.

"Did Westhaven misbehave, Guinevere?" Douglas asked with ominous quiet.

"Not in any substantial way. He treated me with every courtesy and promised me a white marriage if that's what I wanted." And what did one brief, presumptuous kiss matter when Douglas was holding her hand?

"How could you refuse such a reasonable gentleman?" Douglas mused. "It's as well he did the pretty with you, Guinevere, or he might have to consider some extended travel."

They fell silent until Gwen leaned back, Douglas's hand cradled in hers, though she'd no recollection of when their fingers had laced.

"Douglas?"

"Yes?"

She turned a question he'd once asked back on him. "Where does this leave us?"

"Where would you like it to leave us? You know I have wanted to marry you, Guinevere, and now you are carrying our child. If we marry, though, I can't promise you any understanding like you had with Westhaven. I want to be a husband to you, and I want you for my wife. I know you value your independence, but I simply can't allow…"

A tremor had crept into his voice, despite this flight of reason and articulation. Douglas swallowed and breathed out slowly before attempting to soldier on.

"For God's sake, Guinevere." He brought her knuckles to his lips again. "Please marry me. I don't want a future if I can't have one with you. I love you. I will always love you. Please."

He sat beside her, back straight, eyes forward, while more tears trickled down Gwen's cheeks. She rose from her seat beside him and knelt between his legs, wrapping her arms around his waist and resting her cheek on his thigh.

"Of course, Douglas," she said. "Of course I will be your wife."

"Thank you," Douglas murmured, wrapping his arms around her and folding his body down over hers. "From the bottom of my heart, from the depths of my soul, thank you."

❧

"Don't go out there," Fairly warned Andrew.

"What are you two doing here?" Andrew turned from the kitchen window to regard Fairly, who sat sipping tea on the counter beside Heathgate like a pair of giant, happy raptors.

"I came to hear the good news," Fairly said, "when they are ready to come in and tell us. I collected Heathgate on my way out from Town, he being the head of the family and entitled to be present. What are you doing here?"

"It was my turn to check on Gwennie," Andrew said. "And I owe Rose a riding lesson. I take it, from the way Ezra says they've been plastered against each other for the past twenty minutes, Douglas and Gwen are in charity with each other?"

"In charity." Fairly saluted with his teacup. "In love, in lust. Douglas suspects Gwen is breeding. We will have to find a truly impressive wedding present—perhaps the Miller property?"

Andrew paused in the act of pouring himself a cup of tea.

"What a fine idea." He went back to brewing his tea. "Astrid also suspected Gwen was breeding. When's the happy event?"

"One would hope a discreet interval after the wedding."

"One would," Andrew agreed, "if he wanted to avoid the sharp end of Heathgate's tongue."

Heathgate smiled. "I shall be the soul of avuncular tolerance, just as soon as Douglas gets the special license."

"Shame on you, Heathgate." Fairly's smile broadened as he hopped off the counter and appropriated Andrew's tea. "You aren't in a position to call kettles black, and neither are you, Greymoor, so leave Douglas in peace. He's earned it."

"Suppose he has at that," Andrew said, gazing out the window at Douglas and Gwen still entwined in each other's arms. "Though we may have a spot of trouble. Rose is heading out of the stables and charging straight for the scene."

∽∾

"Are you saying good-bye, Cousin Douglas?" Rose yelled as she churned across the gardens. "That's not fair. You just got here, and Regis and Sir George haven't visited yet. You can't leave already. Tell him, Mama."

The young lady was trying hard to maintain her dignity, but Douglas could see she also wanted to stomp her small, booted foot.

"I am not leaving, Rose." *Not ever.* No words, short of those declaring his love for Guinevere, had given him more satisfaction.

Rose did not appear in the least reassured. "Then why is Mama crying? She cried when you didn't come visit us. She cried when we went to visit the trout pond. She cried when we sang about the wide water."

Rose was so upset to relate these tragedies, Douglas knew with a certainty Guinevere had not been the only lady in need of a handkerchief. The idea that he might have imperiled the happiness of either was… would not do.

"Rose," Guinevere said, holding out a hand, "come here. We have things to tell you."

Rose, with the instincts of the young and determined, inserted herself between the adults on the bench. "I want to show Cousin Douglas where we planted the flowers. Then I want to show him my drawings, and all the snowflakes I made for him. He could ride out on Regis with me and Sir George, and you can come with us, Mama. Then we'll bake biscuits, because Cousin Douglas loves biscuits with his tea, and then Mr. Bear and Cousin Douglas—"

Douglas exchanged a smile with Guinevere as he placed a finger against Rose's busy little mouth. "Hush, child. You needn't find reasons to keep me here. Your mother has said I'm to stay."

Rose glanced up at her mother. "Stay? Forever? Like Sir George?"

Like Sir Gawain, if Douglas had anything to say to it. Slaying his ladies' dragons, eating biscuits, and admiring flowers and snowflakes until he was so old he creaked about the garden, his Guinevere on his arm, fragrant memories blooming around them on all sides.

"Cousin Douglas and I will be getting married very soon," Guinevere said, and her smile put to rest any lingering doubts Douglas might have harbored regarding her views on their nuptials. "He will become your step-papa, and live with us."

Rose sprang off the bench and spun around, her smile radiant. "I must tell Sir George! This is the best news ever! My very own step-papa!"

She bolted off, slipping onto the cold, hard ground as she rounded a bed of dormant roses, getting right up, and pelting for the stables, the entire time bellowing good news to her pony, the grooms, and the world at large.

"Ours might be a small family," Guinevere remarked. "And as parents, we might develop hearing difficulties at an early age."

Douglas scooted closer to her and tucked his arm around her waist. Guinevere's head rested on his shoulder, the feel of her beside him warming him as the sun alone could not.

"Guinevere, at the risk of arguing with a lady whom I esteem above all others, and always will, no matter the vicissitudes of married life, ours is unlikely to be a small or quiet family."

This was a matter about which, as the years and decades slipped by, Douglas's prediction proved to be the more accurate, if incomplete. Theirs became a large family, though not *always* noisy. They were, however, abundantly happy, even into those years when Douglas and Gwen strolled about their gardens, surrounded on all sides by loving memories and noisy, happy grandchildren.

**Read on for an excerpt
from *David*, the next book in the Lonely Lords
series by Grace Burrowes**

OWNING A BROTHEL, PARTICULARLY AN ELEGANT,
expensive, *exclusive* brothel, ought to loom as a single,
healthy young man's most dearly treasured fantasy.

Perhaps as fantasies went, the notion had merit. The
reality, inherited from a distant cousin, was enough to
put David Worthington, fourth Viscount Fairly, into a
permanent fit of the dismals.

"Jennings, good morning." David set his antique
Sevres teacup down rather than hurl it against the breakfast parlor's hearthstones, so annoyed was he to see his
man of business at such an hour—again. "I trust you slept
well, and I also trust you are about to ruin my breakfast
with some bit of bad news."

Or some barge load of bad news, for Thomas
Jennings came around this early if, and only if, he had
miserable tidings to share and wanted to gloat in person
over their impact.

"My apologies for intruding." Jennings appropriated a serviette from an empty place setting and
swaddled a pilfered pear in spotless linen. "I thought
you'd want to know that Musette and Isabella got into
a fight with Desdemona and are threatening to open

their own business catering to women who enjoy other women."

Not a spat, a tiff, a disagreement, or an argument, but a *fight*.

Please, God, may the girls' aspirations bear fruit. "I fail to see how this involves me." David paused for a sip of his tea, a fine gunpowder a fellow ought to have the privacy to linger over of a cold and frosty morning. "If the women are enterprising enough to make a go of that dodgy venture, then they have my blessing."

Though dodgy wasn't quite fair. London sported several such establishments that David knew of, and each appeared to be thriving.

"Bella told Desdemona you had offered to finance their dodgy venture," Jennings informed him, taking an audible bite of pear and managing to do so tidily.

"Not likely." Was there a patron saint for people who owned brothels? A patron devil? "Felicity and Astrid are the best of sisters, but they wouldn't understand my involvement in that sort of undertaking, and, worse yet, their spouses would find it hilarious. I'll suggest the ladies apply to *you* for their financing."

He shot a toothy smile at Jennings, who'd taken a seat without being invited, a liberty earned through faithful service that dated back well before David's succession to the Fairly viscountcy.

"I could," Jennings mused, "but having seen the challenges facing my employer, I will decline that signal honor." He saluted with his pear.

"Such a fate would be no more than you deserve," David said, pouring Jennings a cup of hot tea and sliding the cream and sugar toward him. "Those women positively fawn over you."

Jennings lounged back, long legs crossed at the ankles

as he devoured another bite of perfect pear. He managed to look more dangerous than attractive much of the time, but in his unguarded moments, his brown eyes and dark hair could be—and were—called handsome by the ladies. Then too, Thomas Jennings had a well-hidden protective streak roughly equal in breadth to the Pacific Ocean.

Jennings paused halfway around his pear. "Despite your strange eyes, the ladies are unendingly fond of you, too. No accounting for taste, I suppose."

"Their regard is a dubious blessing, at best. Will you at least accompany me to the scene?" Because the physician in David had to see for himself that matters had been resolved without injury to anything more delicate than feminine pride or the occasional crystal vase.

Jennings rose, pear in hand. "Wouldn't miss it. I have never been so well entertained as I have since you inherited that damned brothel."

While David had never been so beleaguered.

When he'd dispatched matters at The Pleasure House—a round of scoldings worthy of any headmaster, followed by teary apologies that would have done first formers proud—he departed from the premises with a sense of escape no adult male ought to feel when leaving an elegant bordello.

As cold as the day was, David still chose to wait with Jennings in the mews behind The Pleasure House for his mare to be brought around. Why David alone could address the myriad petty, consummately annoying conflicts that arose among his employees was a mystery of Delphic proportions.

"I've been meaning to mention something," Jennings said as David's gray was led into the yard. With a sense of being hounded by doom, David accepted the reins from the stableboy.

"Unburden yourself, then, Thomas. The day grows chilly." And a large house full of feuding women and valuable breakables sat not fifty feet on the other side of the garden wall.

"Do you recall a Mrs. Letitia Banks?"

"I do," David replied, slinging his reins over the horse's head as an image of dark hair, slim grace, and pretty, sad eyes assailed him. What had Letty Banks seen in David's late brother-in-law that she'd accepted such a buffoon as her protector?

"You sent me to advise her regarding investment of a certain sum upon the death of her last protector," Jennings went on as a single snowflake drifted onto the toe of David's left boot. "I did that, and she's had two quarterly payments of interest on her principle since then."

David swung up into the saddle, feeling the cold of the seat through his doeskin breeches. "All of which I am sure you handled with your customary discretion."

Jennings sighed. "I have."

Perishing saints. Thomas Jennings would scowl, smirk, swear, stomp away, or—on rare occasion—even smile, but he wasn't prone to sighing.

From his perch on the mare, David studied Thomas, a fellow who, on at least two occasions, had wrought mortal peril on those seeking to harm his employer. "This is a historic day. You are being coy, Thomas."

Jennings glanced around, making the day doubly historic, for Jennings evidenced uncertainty no more frequently than he appeared coy. "She spends it."

Coy, uncertain, and indirect was an alarming combination coming from Jennings. "Of course she spends it. She is a female in a particular line of business, and she must maintain appearances. Whether she spends the interest or reinvests it with the principle is no business of mine."

"She's not spending it to maintain appearances," Jennings said. "I believe, despite this income, the lady is in difficulties."

David masked his astonishment by brushing his horse's mane to lie uniformly on the right side of her neck. He wasn't astonished that Letitia Banks was in difficulties—a courtesan's life was precarious and often drove even strong women to excesses of drink, opium, gambling, and other expensive vices. What astonished him was that Jennings would comment on the matter.

"Thomas, I would acquit you of anything resembling a soft heart"—at least to appearances—"but you are distressed by Mrs. Banks's circumstances. Whatever are you trying to tell me?"

"I don't know." Jennings's horse was led out, a great, dark brute of a beast, probably chosen to complement its great, dark brute of an owner. "Something about that situation isn't right, and you should take a look."

"Might you be less cryptic? If there is looking to be done"—and Mrs. Banks made for a pleasant look, indeed—"then are you not in a better position to do it than I? I've met the lady only once."

Months ago, and under difficult circumstances, and yet, she'd lingered at the back of David's mind, a pretty ghost he hadn't attempted to exorcise.

Jennings's features acquired his signature scowl, which might have explained why the stableboy remained a few paces off with the black gelding. "I haven't your ability to charm a reluctant female, and my efforts to date meet with a polite, pretty, lusciously scented stone wall."

Had Jennings noted that the luscious scent was mostly roses?

"You mustn't glower at the lady when you're trying to tease her secrets from her, Thomas. You aren't really as bad-looking as you want everyone to think."

Jennings took the reins from the groom, and gave the girth a snug pull. "Since coming into that money, she's let a footman and a groom go, sold a horse, and if I'm not mistaken, parted with some fripperies. She's reduced to taking a pony cart to market."

"Thomas," David said gently, "she is a *professional*. She would likely accept you as her next protector, and her financial worries would be solved. In her business, these periodic lapses in revenue happen. She'll manage."

Though the soft-spoken, demure ones usually managed the worst.

Thomas sighed again, a sigh intended to produce guilt in the one who heard it. "I am *asking* you to look into her situation."

Jennings never asked for anything. He collected his generous pay, occasionally disappeared on personal business, and comported himself as a perfect—if occasionally impertinent and moody—man of business. He was both more and less than a friend, and David was attached to him in some way neither man believed merited discussion.

And really, David could not muster a desire to argue with Jennings on this topic, not even for form's sake.

"I will look into it," David said, touching the brim of his hat before trotting off to his next destination.

Acknowledgments

Douglas and Gwen's story has been lurking close to my heart since before *The Heir* came out in December 2010, and *The Soldier* in June 2011 (where Douglas plays significant supporting roles). This is the tale that acquainted me with the Windham family, and if you read closely, you can see the seeds of much that makes the Windham stories enjoyable.

I'm particularly indebted to my editor, Deb Werksman, who had the thankless and complicated task of reading manuscript after manuscript of mine, and spinning trilogies and series and sequels from an enormous pile of literary straw.

And I'm grateful to the many readers who contacted me to ask about the "missing" prequel to the Windham series. Douglas, Gwen, Rose, and I (also Regis, Sir George, and Mr. Bear), appreciate your patience and hope you found the story well worth the wait.

Grace Burrowes

About the Author

New York Times and USA Today bestselling author Grace Burrowes hit the bestseller lists with her debut, *The Heir*, followed by *The Soldier, Lady Maggie's Secret Scandal, Lady Sophie's Christmas Wish,* and *Lady Eve's Indiscretion*. *The Heir* was a *Publishers Weekly* Best Book of 2010, *The Soldier* was a *Publishers Weekly* Best Spring Romance of 2011, *Lady Sophie's Christmas Wish* won Best Historical Romance of the Year in 2011 from RT Reviewers' Choice Awards, *Lady Louisa's Christmas Knight* was a *Library Journal* Best Book of 2012, and *The Bridegroom Wore Plaid,* the first in her trilogy of Scotland-set Victorian romances, was a *Publishers Weekly* Best Book of 2012. All of her historical romances have received extensive praise, including starred reviews from *Publishers Weekly* and *Booklist*.

Grace is a practicing family law attorney and lives in rural Maryland. She loves to hear from her readers and can be reached through her website at graceburrowes.com.